TENDER TEACHING

"Don't be afraid," he told her, and kissed her. A hard kiss, strong, uncompromising, yet sweet, too, filled with demands and promises her body was eager to explore. His hand, too, had grown bolder, touching a part of her that made her gasp, even beneath the pressure of his lips.

But his fingers were only playing with her, provokingly, intimately, drawing her out of herself until there was a new, overwhelming urgency in her body. And she found herself struggling, hungering, searching for sensations she did not understand. And then she did understand what she had wanted, what her body had been trying to tell her. And she collapsed, quivering in his arms.

"I didn't know," she murmured hoarsely. "I had no idea it was . . . it could be . . . like this."

*But he only smiled. For **this night of love** was just the beginning. . . .*

JOURNEY TO ROMANCE

(0451)

☐ **MIDNIGHT STAR by Catherine Coulter.** British heiress Chauncey FitzHugh had come to San Francisco to ruin Delaney as he had finally ruined her father back in 1850. She had plotted to reject his fiery advances, but even as her mind commanded resistance, her desire exploded. She pulled him to her . . . tenderly whispering the name of this man she had sworn to hate. . . .   (153790—$4.50)

☐ **THE REBEL AND THE ROSE by Joan Wolf.** the handsome Virginian made Lady Barbara Carr shiver with fear and desire. He was her new husband, a stranger, wed to her so his wealth could pay her father's debts. And Alan Maxwell had never wanted any woman the way he wanted this delicate English lady . . .   (153820—$4.50)

☐ **FIRES OF DESTINY by Linda Barlow.** He wanted her desperately—Alexandra could feel it with every sweet, slow, deepening kiss. That was why Roger Trevor, Protestant heir to the Baron of Chilton, had met her at the ancient cottage . . . why she, a Catholic woman on her way to Mary Tudor's court, had stayed after he warned her to run from him, after he told her he could never marry her. . . .   (400011—$3.95)

☐ **FLAME OF DESIRE by Katherine Vickery.** The sheltered daughter of London's richest silk merchant, Heather Bowen had known such fierce desire only in her dreams until she met the dark, handsome Richard Morgan. Through the storms of a land divided by war, Heather burned hungrily for him, and Richard reached out with all his masculine power to claim her. . . .   (400070—$3.95)

☐ **TAME THE WILD WIND by Katherine Vickery.** Beautiful prairie school-marm Cecilia Sinclair knew nothing of the world—until a magnetic Mexican renegade rode roughshod onto her horizon. Locked in Ramon's inescapable embrace, Cecilia rides passion's tempest to the heights of ecstasy until a ruthless rival's plot of betrayal threatens their world of love.   (400682—$3.95)

Prices slightly higher in Canada.

The Silver Swan

SUSANNAH LEIGH

AN ONYX BOOK

NEW AMERICAN LIBRARY

PUBLISHED BY
THE NEW AMERICAN LIBRARY
OF CANADA LIMITED

PUBLISHER'S NOTE

This book is a work of fiction. Names, characters, places, and incidents either are the product of the author's imagination or are used fictitiously, and any resemblance to actual persons, living or dead, events, or locales is entirely coincidental.

NAL BOOKS ARE AVAILABLE AT QUANTITY DISCOUNTS WHEN
USED TO PROMOTE PRODUCTS OR SERVICES. FOR INFOR
MATION PLEASE WRITE TO PREMIUM MARKETING DIVISION,
NEW AMERICAN LIBRARY, 1633 BROADWAY, NEW YORK,
NEW YORK 10019.

 Onyx is a trademark of The New American Library
of Canada Limited.

SIGNET, SIGNET CLASSIC, MENTOR, ONYX, PLUME, MERIDIAN
AND NAL BOOKS are published in Canada by The New American
Library of Canada, Limited, 81 Mack Avenue, Scarborough,
Ontario, Canada M1L 1M8
First Printing, February, 1988

2 3 4 5 6 7 8 9
PRINTED IN CANADA
COVER PRINTED IN U.S.A.

I

AUTUMN DREAMS

1

Australia.

The faintest trace of a smile showed on pretty pink lips as Stacey Alexander spun the globe in Grandfather's old-fashioned wood-paneled study. The fog outside had begun to break, but the windows were stifled in green velvet draperies, and barely enough light filtered through to make out the darkish landmass on the other side of the world. Wide-spaced letters, all in script, spelled out a single word—Australia.

How very like Grandfather!

Stacey giggled as she tossed her head, setting shiny black curls bouncing around an arresting heart-shaped face. She had been born Anastasia, but the name was much too cumbersome, and no one except the servants ever used it. To Grandfather, the world existed exactly the way it had when he was young and came from Russia on a sailing ship to old Fort Ross, up on the northern California coast. Nothing had changed since then. Even the globe on a long library table near the window was an antique, showing none of the skill of current cartographers. The early nineteenth century had been good enough for him as a boy; it was good enough now, even though it was going to be 1885 at the turn of the year.

And Australia, of course, was not Australia at all . . . it was Australasia, an obscure penal colony still waiting for a name.

The thought made her laugh aloud, and she wondered what D'Arcy Cameron would have to say about that. Stepping over to the window, she pulled aside the curtain and looked out. It was a typical November day, and the fog was still heavy in the distance, obscuring the magnificent harbor that had already given San Francisco a reputation as one of the most beautiful cities in the world. But here, on the slopes of the steeply rising hill where old Ivan Alexander had built an estate that rivaled some of the smaller castles in Europe, sunlight had begun to break through, and the garden was ablaze with red and pink and yellow, a riot of late-blooming roses.

Probably D'Arcy wouldn't mind very much. Stacey leaned her head against the curtain for a moment, enjoying the lush feel of velvet against her cheek. D'Arcy had been born and educated in Australia, he had lived there all his life, yet he did not seem to take the place seriously. Certainly he did not leap to its defense the way she would have if someone had showed such abysmal ignorance of America. But then, perhaps D'Arcy had other things on his mind.

Things like . . . her?

Stacey spun away from the window, glancing toward the clock in the center of the massive black-marble fireplace that dominated one side of the room. Ten o'clock. Just time enough for D'Arcy to stop by for a stroll in the garden if he happened to be driving through the neighborhood.

And he had happened to be driving through with increasing frequency this last week or so.

Stacey could not resist a secret half-smile as she caught sight of her reflection in the long, smoky mirror over the mantel. That D'Arcy's visits might have some other purpose—that he might, for instance, be interested in one of her three sisters—was an idea that had not occurred to her. Nor would it be likely to, for she was of an age when she was just beginning to appeal to men, and rejection was still alien to her. At sixteen she was finally emerging from gawky adolescence into quite a captivating prettiness, still so new it was hard not to peek at herself whenever she passed the glass. Her face, which had seemed much too small before, had taken on a unique charm, with its wide brow and strong, pointed chin, touched by the faintest hint of a cleft; and her eyes, though not a deep limpid blue like Olga's, were large and luminously gray, the lashes that set them off black and deliciously curling. As for her mouth . . .

She pouted a little, liking the slightly scandalous hint of sensuality that came into her round, full lips when she did. If only she dared put a touch of rouge on them, just when she was alone, so she could see how it would look. But she knew nothing about makeup—she did not know how long it lasted, or if there would be traces left to show—and Grandfather would lock her in her room for a week if he caught her!

Almost unconsciously her eyes drifted back to the clock. Another three minutes gone and still no sound of carriage wheels on the drive! But then, D'Arcy didn't always use a carriage. Sometimes he came on the bay he had hired from the stables for his exclusive use, and hoofbeats were harder to hear.

She moved over to the window, but the garden was still empty, and the fog had begun to drift farther down the hillside. Even now, though nearly a month had passed, she could still recall every detail of D'Arcy's face the first time she saw him. She had stopped to call at a neighbor's estate, and there he was, totally unexpected, a tall man sitting on the edge of an absurdly small divan with a teacup in his hand. But, oh, his eyes when he had looked up! Clear and blue—devastating against dark skin, dark hair, the dark mustache that gave his mouth a faintly rakish look—and every other man she had ever known had vanished from her thoughts.

She was, she had quickly learned, not the only one intrigued by young D'Arcy Cameron. He had created quite a flurry a few days earlier when he first appeared in San Francisco, very mysteriously, too, with no one, it seems, knowing exactly why he had come. What they did know was that he was from Australia, that he and his brother owned a large sheep ranch there, and that he was very rich . . . and very handsome. There was not a mother within fifty miles who had not begun to make discreet inquiries as to his attitude toward marriage, and not one unattached young lady who had not wheedled her family to invite him at least one time for supper or tea.

But for all their machinations, it was only pretty Stacey Alexander who caught his eye . . . or so it had seemed until today. Stacey frowned faintly as she looked back at the clock to see that it was now ten-fifteen. If he didn't come soon, they would never be alone, at least as alone as one could be in a house full of servants, with three sisters out and about! Grandfather was still upstairs—he had taken to closeting himself in his suite of rooms on the third floor in the morning— but he would be down soon. And when he was . . .

Stacey sighed. When he was, there was no way she and D'Arcy could be together. She wouldn't even dare go down and greet him. Grandfather had very distinct ideas about the qualities he considered suitable in a young man. Handsomeness was not one of them . . . and certainly not charm.

It was not that her grandfather didn't care about her. Stacey glanced over at a portrait on the far wall, showing a stern dark man with hawkish nose and commanding eyebrows, an almost startling contrast to the portrait of the gentle grandmother who had died when Stacey was three. Even when he irritated her most, when she was so angry she couldn't bring herself to speak to him, she was never tempted to deny his feelings for her. He might be a dreadful tyrant sometimes—there were rumors that his vast fortune had been accumulated through less-than-scrupulous dealings, and she had no illusions that they were false— but even his worst enemies conceded him one saving grace, a deep and abiding love for his family, especially the four granddaughters he had raised almost single-handedly.

But love and understanding were not the same thing. Sometimes, Stacey thought, sighing again, she had the feeling Grandfather was planning to rule her life with the same blind rigidity that would not allow him to place a modern globe in his study. A country didn't exist if it wasn't allowed in the house . . . and neither did a potential suitor! If he couldn't bully her into sending someone off on her own, then he would find other ways to do it—like he had with the last man she liked.

Of course, he hadn't been totally wrong about Hugo. Stacey squirmed a little as she recalled how easy it had been for Grandfather to buy him off. A small amount of cash—really humiliatingly small!—and he had been willing to leave town and try his luck elsewhere. Not that that ploy would work with D'Arcy. The Camerons were too wealthy to be fortune hunters. But knowing Grandfather, she was sure he could come up with something else. He would never be satisfied until he had her married off to some dreadfully ugly man twice her age . . . and with not an ounce of humor in his heart!

Well, she was not about to let him get away with that! If D'Arcy *did* show up this morning—although she had to admit it was looking less and less likely—she was going to treat him coolly when they were in sight of the house, just in case Grandfather was in the window of his bedroom looking down. Perhaps she would even pretend to *dislike* him—then maybe Grandfather would try to force him on her!

A slight movement caught her eye, and she turned back to the window just in time to see a subdued flash of brightness in the garden. She could almost hear the rustle of deep blue taffeta as she recognized her sister Tamara out with a watering can, not trusting the gardeners to tend to her precious roses.

Poor Mara. Stacey felt a twinge of guilt as she watched her sister bend down to free her skirt where it had caught on a thorn. She was the only one of the Alexander sisters with no claim to charm. Olga, the oldest, was the real beauty of the family, with jet-black hair framing a perfect oval face, and dazzling sapphire eyes, reminiscent of the grandmother none of them could truly remember. Zee, the youngest, almost fifteen and a half now, was pretty too, in a delicate way, though her fair coloring and light-headed ways had a tendency to give her a faintly vapid look. Only Mara could be called plain.

The clock chimed abruptly, startling Stacey out of her thoughts, and she looked over, surprised, for the

sound mechanism rarely worked nowadays; like everything else in the study, Grandfather had refused to
have it fixed. So it was ten-thirty . . . surely too late
for D'Arcy to show up. She was about to acknowledge
defeat when her ear picked up a faint echo of hoof-
beats, and she threw an eager glance at the path that
led to the gate just as a horse and rider appeared.

She recognized the horse first. The bay was a magnificent animal, too good really for a public stable. As
she watched, he tossed his mane in the sunlight, still
prancing slightly even though it had been a long climb
up the hill. Then her eyes picked out the man on his
back, and every last doubt was gone in a flood of
excitement. D'Arcy Cameron was a hard man to mistake, even with a wide-brimmed hat pulled over his
eyes to shield them from the sun. He was tall, which
was good, for she was tall herself, and very lithe, with
a strange way of sitting a horse—like an Australian,
she supposed—and a manner that might have seemed
affected on anyone less graceful.

So, he had come.

Stacey started to laugh, as much at herself as at the
streams of golden sunlight that had begun to penetrate
even the gloomy study. How foolish she had been to
doubt he would show up. And doubly foolish to think
that his staying away meant he was not interested in
her!

She took a step toward the door, then stopped for
one last quick look at herself in the mirror. She had
chosen one of her prettiest dresses, just in case, a deep
rose-hued lawn that brought out the pink in her cheeks
. . . a summer frock really, with a lace-edged neck a
bit too low for morning, but so flattering she had not
been able to resist wearing it. A wayward wisp of hair
straggled onto her brow—her curls had an annoying
way of tumbling, childishly, out of their pins—and she
had just reached up to tuck it in place when she
became aware of someone standing behind her in the
doorway.

Half-turning her head, she saw Madden, the butler,
hesitating discreetly on the threshold. He had, of course,
caught her peering quite immodestly into the mirror,

but she was just young enough—and irrepressible enough—not to be embarrassed.

"Well, what do you think, Madden?" she asked impishly. "Do you like my new hairdo?"

"Very becoming, I'm sure, Miss Anastasia." Madden held his upper lip straight, though it was hard not to smile. He had been in the family since before the girls were born, and lively Stacey had always been his favorite. Miss Xenia had spirit too—the one they called Zee, a foolish name—but she was too flighty to take seriously.

"I think so too," Stacey agreed as she shot a last glance at the mirror. Grandfather would have kept her with her hair hanging down her back until she was fifty, but Olga, bless her, had interceded in her quiet way. And Grandfather always listened to Olga. "Not that it matters much today. I'm just going out for . . . for a walk in the garden. The roses won't care what I look like, will they?"

Her eyes were twinkling as she looked back, but if Madden noticed, no sign of it showed in those impeccably arranged features.

"I daresay they won't, miss." He stepped aside to let her pass. "I hope you enjoy your walk."

"Oh, I will, Madden." The laughter brimmed over in her voice now. "I will." Somehow she managed to keep her step sedate as she walked past him and out into the hall. But she had started to skip by the time she reached the stairs, and she took them two at a time, like a playful little child. Even if Madden did know what she was up to, it wouldn't matter. He was loyal to Grandfather, but beneath that proper exterior, he was devoted to the girls too. He wouldn't betray her secret.

And after all, she hadn't lied to him. Not really. She *was* going for a walk in the garden. And she was going to enjoy herself.

2

Sunlight was already streaming into the downstairs hall when Stacey reached it. Wide double doors had been flung open to let in the morning air, and bands of pale gold splashed across the floor. On either side, deeper gold patterns showed from rippled yellow-glass panes that had been set into tall, leaded frames.

Sleek Italian marble slid beneath her feet as she crossed the floor, but she barely noticed, except to feel its coldness penetrating the thin soles of her slippers. Nor did she pay more than passing heed to the exquisite green silk wall panels, or the old-fashioned silver sconces with their tapering white candles, the mosaic-topped tables, the priceless antique paintings, darkened with age. Wealth was a part of her birthright. The ostentatious splendor of her grandfather's entry hall, the opulence of the parlors and salons and bedchambers, were things she took for granted, as natural to her as sunlight breaking through the morning mist . . . or that glorious display of gold and red and russet-brown on the trees lining either side of the broad curving drive.

She was just close enough to the outside to catch a tantalizing whiff of roses and autumn leaves mingling with the sea-damp scent of morning when she noticed that the doors to the formal drawing room were open. Pausing, she saw that Mara had come in from the gardens and was arranging a selection of wine-hued roses in a blue-and-white Chinese vase. If it were anyone else, she would have kept on going with a quick smile and careless hello. But her sister was already looking up with a questioning expression, and she sensed that explanations were in order.

Sighing, she went over to the door.

"I see you are doing the servant's work again, Mara," she said teasingly. "Lucky Delia. It saves her an hour every morning, not having to do the flowers. Perhaps more than that—she's so clumsy at it."

There was laughter in her voice, but Mara's back stiffened slightly. "She *is* clumsy—and I do it passably well, I believe. There's no reason why I shouldn't take care of the flowers—don't you think?—since I am good at it and it gives me pleasure."

Stacey felt a little tug of guilt. Mara was right. She did arrange flowers well, and more than just passably. She had a knack for decorating a room, sometimes no more than just moving a chair here or there, and making it look elegant and inviting.

"They are pretty," she conceded, then added with a laugh: "Certainly it's an improvement on anything Delia could have done." The girl was a sweet little thing, timid and eager to please—one of the few who had not been too terrified by Grandfather's fierce eyebrows and well-renowned temper to stay for more than a few weeks—but she had absolutely no sense of style or grace. "I sometimes think Delia's idea of doing the flowers is to see how many she can cram into the vase at one time. They end up so squished together, one can hardly see what they look like."

"They do indeed," Mara agreed, somewhat mollified as her deft fingers adjusted the just-opening buds, matching the lines of their long stems to the graceful curves of the Tang vase, rescued from an obscure corner of Grandfather's study where she suspected it had been used as a spittoon. "But tell me—where are you off to? You seemed in such a hurry, skipping across the hall like a little girl."

"Oh . . . nowhere." Stacey kept her voice vague, trying to sound a little bored. Obviously Mara had not seen D'Arcy Cameron ride up on his rented steed or she would never have been so casual in her questioning. Mara was a bit like Grandfather in that respect: handsome young men set up hackles of distrust on the back of her neck. "It's just such a pretty day, I couldn't bear to stay inside. I saw you before from the window,

out in the garden watering the roses. It's too bad
you're through. I could have offered to help."

Mara gave her a thin smile. "A lot of help you'd
have been. You're about as good with flowers as Delia, poor little thing. You'd start out watering . . . and
end up trampling the tender young branches underfoot."

There was affection beneath her grumbling, and
Stacey knew that her sister loved her. Still, it was hard
sometimes, responding to that awkward affection. It
was not so much that Mara was plain . . . it was that
she always seemed conscious of her plainness, wearing
it like a badge, a shield that set her apart from everyone else.

"Well, then, I shan't offer to take your basket and
gather more buds," she said, laughing. "I daresay it's
all for the best. The fog is just beginning to clear. I
doubt if the dew is dry . . . I'd hate to get my slippers
wet. I shall have to stay on the paths."

She could not keep a teasing twinkle out of her eye,
but Mara said nothing, and she breathed a sigh of
relief as she turned and flitted through the doorway,
pausing for a last quick wave. Mara was hardly the
type to keep her suspicions—or disapproval—to herself.

Outside, the air was cooler than Stacey had expected, and she was half-tempted for an instant to run
back into the house and fetch a warm cashmere shawl.
But she had already wasted too much time talking
with Mara in the drawing room. D'Arcy was nowhere
in sight, having disappeared no doubt down one of the
bridle paths that wound around the side of the house,
and it was going to take precious minutes just to locate
him. If she worried about her delicate, shivering shoulders, she might miss the chance to see him altogether.

She started toward the stable, half-daring to hope
that D'Arcy had left the bay to be curried down and
given an extra handful of oats as a treat after the long
ride up the hill. If he had, it would mean he was
planning on staying a half-hour or so beyond those few
stolen moments they could expect in the garden. It
would be agony, of course, taking morning tea with
him in the parlor under the watchful eyes of her three
sisters . . . and knowing that at any moment Grandfa-

ther might come blustering in. But even if she could only look at him through carefully lowered lashes—even if she had to be unspeakably rude all the time so no one would guess!—at least she would be able to see him and admire the dark masculine beauty that had so caught her eye.

A colorful mantle of dead leaves softened the autumn-cold earth, wet, but rustling as the wind picked them up and drifted them across the path, and Stacey laughed as she lifted her skirt and saw marks where the moisture had begun to stain her slippers. Even if she stayed on the paths—which she had no intention of doing! —her feet would be soaked by the time she got back to the house, and old Eulalia, who had taken care of the girls since they were babies, would be fluttering and scolding and clucking like a barnyard hen. Yes, and bringing out soaking-tubs of warm water, too, and hot mustard poultices . . . and threatening to tell Grandfather when Stacey disdained them. But she was young and strong and she wasn't about to take to her bed with a chill every time her feet got wet, even if it was the fashion!

A soft shuffling sound warned her even before she saw him that D'Arcy had not brought his horse to the stable after all, but had paused somewhere on the side of the house, just inside a ring of foliage that almost completely surrounded the wide, velvety lawn. Leaving the path, she cut ankle-deep through the leaves and rounded a copse of young pine to find that he had already dismounted and was standing with his back to her, staring down like a young god at the city sprawled at his feet.

Just at the moment she spotted him, he turned, and the sun broke through the last high clouds to catch his exotic features in a spate of brightness. As always when she saw him, Stacey was struck by how very different he was from any other man she had ever known. His clothes were suitably fashionable—fawn-colored breeches, a white cambric shirt, open at the neck despite the coolness of the morning, a black velvet-collared jacket, and a wide-brimmed black hat slung across the front of his saddle—but he wore them almost carelessly, with a style and flair all his own.

His face was serious for an instant, almost too dark, too foreign, with his hair and mustache and that swarthy undertone to his complexion. Then all the strangeness flashed away in a sudden grin.

"What a pleasant surprise! Or should I say"—he paused a split second—"it is not a surprise at all?"

Impudence blazed in his dark, handsome eyes, and Stacey turned away, refusing for the moment to pick up the gauntlet. He had chosen a spot perilously close to the house, but a quick glance over her shoulder assured her that the autumn leaves were still thick enough to screen them from sight. Pretending to ignore him, she went over to where the horse was tethered, laughing as she reached out to stroke him, and felt him nuzzle her neck.

"Why, Beauty, what a selfish beast you are!" Officially, the horse was Goldenrod, a silly name—not at all suited to such a splendid mount—but she always called him Beauty. "Here I thought you loved me for myself, and you're only looking for a treat! Foolish thing, there are no pockets in this dress—look for sugar lumps next time, when you see me in my riding habit."

She was still laughing when she turned back to D'Arcy, almost as if she had just remembered he was there.

"I'm surprised you didn't bring Beauty to the stable," she said reproachfully. "There'd be a bag of oats waiting for him there—or one of those apples the stableboy always finds for his favorites."

The disappointment was so transparent on her pretty features, it was all D'Arcy could do to keep a straight face. She was trying so hard to pretend she hadn't been watching from the window, though of course she had. And she had half-convinced herself he was going to sit through that awful farce her sisters put on in the drawing room.

"Spare me another cup of watered-down tea," he protested. "The stuff has no taste, even before you pour in the milk and sugar! Australians know how to make real tea, out of a billy tin over an open fire. As for the conversation . . ." He rolled his eyes heavenward. "It's so polite it's virtually nonexistent—until your grandfather comes in the room. Then it stops altogether!"

In spite of herself, Stacey giggled. "You're incorrigible. What a thing to say!"

"Perhaps, but you know it's true. Surely you can't expect a rugged male to endure that scene more than once."

"Ah . . ." She pursed her lips into what she hoped was a fetching pout. "And here I thought, when you came to see me, that you were willing to endure anything."

"To see . . . you?" D'Arcy raised a faintly mocking brow as he leaned against the back of an elaborate wrought-iron bench that had been placed at the fork where two paths merged into one. "What makes you think I came to see you? It might be one of your sisters—Olga perhaps. She is the prettiest, you know."

Stacey smiled sweetly, her composure not the least shaken. Almost against his will, D'Arcy found himself intrigued by the way she looked, so young, yet so sure of herself. "Oh, I know Olga is more beautiful than I am . . . but that's not why you came. Olga is a beauty, but she's also very devout. And devout ladies are much too proper to sneak out and meet young men in the garden."

"Mara then," he persisted, unable to resist teasing. "Mara is the plain one—your grandfather would settle a tidy sum on the man willing to court her."

"And that appeals to you?" The wind rose, whipping a brown-veined leaf past her face, and she turned to reach out and catch it with one hand. "But you are very rich, they say—you and your brother. What need have you to marry for money?" She had the leaf now and she spun around, her expression curious as she faced him again. "What's he like anyway, your brother? Is he like you?"

"Errol?" D'Arcy stared at her for a moment, caught off guard by the quicksilver twists of her mind. "Good God, no! I beg your pardon—but what on earth prompted you to say that? No, Errol is not the least like me. He is serious and sensible . . . and utterly, boringly decent." He leaned forward, just slightly, that same brow arching again. "I, on the other hand, am a complete scoundrel."

Stacey laughed as she crumpled the leaf, tossing it back to the wind. "But you are a very rich scoundrel," she reminded him. "And that means you didn't come to see Mara."

"Well, then . . . Zee. Little Xenia. She is certainly pretty."

"And flighty." Stacey snapped the words out, bringing a smile to his lips. So she wasn't jealous of Olga, but there *was* rivalry with the younger sister. Well, no wonder—they were so close in age, they had probably torn each other's hair and kicked and rolled in the dirt when they were little. "She hasn't a thought in her head. She couldn't possibly interest a man of the world. Besides, I happen to know . . . she doesn't care a fig about you! She's head over heels in love with that silly Danson boy, and Grandfather is so busy watching me, he hasn't even noticed!"

Her lower lip jutted out, and D'Arcy, watching, felt his pulse quicken. She was a child still, all petulant like that, but she was a woman too, her tall body ripe for the taking, her full young breasts straining against the confines of a tight Victorian corset. Child-women had always appealed to him. Perhaps . . .

"You are are so young," he said suddenly, his voice low and faintly muffled. "I wonder, do you know what you're doing . . . standing here with me alone in the woods?"

"This is hardly a deep, dense forest," she retorted. "It's a bridle path through the gardens of the estate. And I am sixteen. My grandmother had been married a year at my age, as Grandfather never tires of reminding me. She had already borne her only child—my father. So you see, I am quite old enough."

"Old enough to parry words with me anyway." He grinned, breaking the mood he himself had set. He had not come to San Francisco to dally with pretty child-women. "Thank heaven I'm not one of your young swains. I'd hate to be sixteen again and try to match wits with you. You must leave a trail of broken hearts at every ball you go to."

Stacey shook her head, tempted to lie, but knowing it was a lie that was easily caught out. "Actually," she said, keeping her voice flippant, "I've never been to a ball. Grandfather is much too strict. Olga is allowed to attend, of course—she is twenty—and Mara for nearly a year now. But I can't go until I'm eighteen."

"What?" He pretended to be shocked. "You mean a pretty little thing like you doesn't know how to dance?"

"Of course I know how to dance!" Her anger started to flare; then she saw that he was baiting her and relaxed enough to laugh. "I go twice a week to Mrs. Peabody's, where proper young ladies and proper young gentlemen learn all the latest steps. Dancing is a social grace, you see . . . and Grandfather is determined that I learn all the graces, even if he doesn't allow me to use them!"

"I'm surprised he allows you the school then. There must be as much, uh . . . proximity between the young gentlemen and young ladies there as at a ball."

"Heaven forfend!" Now it was Stacey's turn to look shocked, and she did it charmingly. "The young gentlemen dance with the young gentlemen, and the young ladies with the young ladies . . . and not in the same room, mind you! We take turns, leading one dance, following the next, though I am tall so I play the boy more often than not. I can take both parts with equal ease. Let's hope I don't forget who I am supposed to be when I go to my first ball."

Mischief danced in her eyes, and for all his resolve, D'Arcy found his gaze straying back to her bosom, a plump, creamy temptation above the lacy neck of her gown. There was something about her that was not quite innocent, despite the innocence of her words, and he was suddenly tempted to try her, to see how far he could go.

"Perhaps we should practice then. Just to make sure you have it right—before you try it out in public."

"What . . . here?" She threw him a quizzical look.

"Why not?"

"Well, for one thing, there's no dance floor. And for another . . . there's no music."

She looked so sweet in her confusion, D'Arcy was almost tempted to let go. But that subtle glimpse of sensuality had been too intriguing. "All the world is your dance floor, m'lady." He swept her a low, formal bow, indicating the leafy carpet of gold and rich red-brown that stretched out all around them. "And a softer, prettier dance floor you could never hope to find. As for the music . . ."

He began to hum, softly at first, under his breath, then louder, until a clear, true tenor mingled with the rustling sound of the breeze. The melody was so entrancing, the lilting waltz-time rhythm so compelling, Stacey could not keep her toes from tapping on the ground.

And after all, she thought rebelliously, what harm could it do? It might not be proper, but it would be fun—and, oh, what heaven to enjoy her first secret dance in this man's arms!

Bobbing gracefully, she picked up her skirt in one hand, raising it an inch off the ground as she stepped forward.

"I must warn you, sir . . ." She lowered her lashes at the same instant she lifted her eyes. "All this is very new to me. I pray you will be patient."

D'Arcy laid a gloved hand lightly on her waist. "As patient as you need."

The pressure of his hand tightened almost imperceptibly. He waited a moment, picking up the beat of the music; then they began to whirl, round and round, off the path and into the leaves that fluttered around their feet.

Stacey had never danced with anyone taller before—she had not realized it would make such a difference, arching her neck up and gazing into dark, dashing eyes. It was almost as if she were not earthbound at all, she thought giddily . . . as if her satin slippers were floating with the wind-tossed leaves. As if nothing were real but the music and the moment . . . and the feel of D'Arcy Cameron's arms.

Then subtly, so subtly she did not even realize it was happening, the melody slowed and they were dancing slower too, and D'Arcy had begun to draw her nearer, as if to bring her ear toward the waltz that was now so soft it was hardly audible. Then they had stopped, and they were so close Stacey could feel her bosom against the hardness of his chest. His hands began to move, finding her back, sliding upward . . . warm even through his gloves. She knew what he was doing was wrong; she knew she should fight him, but even as the thought crossed her mind, she felt her head tilt back, her lips part instinctively.

All the blood drained from her body as his mouth came down on hers, numbing her all over, except where his lips were touching her. Hard, demanding lips, taking without asking, relinquishing nothing to youth and inexperience.

Quivering from somewhere deep inside, Stacey tried to struggle, resisting the first stirrings of her own sensuality as much as that savage, unexpected assault. Then the sensation was too much, and she felt herself clinging—not moving actually, still standing as she had before, arms down, slightly out from her sides—but with every nerve, every muscle straining toward him. Only the sound of the horse, a sudden nervous whinnying, as if he knew she was in trouble, brought her back to reality, and somehow she managed to push D'Arcy away.

Her head was reeling as she took a step back.

"Sir . . . you are much too bold!"

"Am I?" He barely whispered the words, but he knew she heard, just as he knew she was aware of the way his eyes were caressing every soft contour of her body. "And you are running away now because you don't like it? Is that it?"

'No." She twisted away, just out of his reach—angry or teasing, he couldn't tell which. "No, I am running because . . . I do like it. Much too much."

D'Arcy laughed as she turned and darted into the foliage, cutting across to the lawn where she knew she would be safe. Any other woman would have blushed and turned coy, telling him he was a cad—protesting that she had not enjoyed it at all! But Stacey had a delightful way of turning earthy just when he least expected it. A woman like that was a woman worth having—and it occurred to him at that moment, without really thinking about it, that he had already made up his mind he was going to have her.

Of course, there would be certain . . . difficulties.

He shrugged as he went over to where he had tied the horse and pulled the reins loose. Difficulties, after all, were only difficulties if one didn't know how to handle them. And he had never been a man to let a few qualms stand in his way.

Stacey did not look back as she broke through the fringe of shrubbery onto the lawn, where she did indeed feel safe, perhaps a little safer than she really wanted. Only belatedly did she recall that her grandfather's window overlooked that section of garden, and she slowed her pace abruptly, turning what had been a run into a casual saunter, as if she had just come out for a stroll underneath the trees.

Rather guiltily, her eye flicked toward the third-floor windows, but the smoky panes always turned into mirrors at that hour, and she could not make out even a shadow of movement behind them. For just an instant she wished she had brought Mara's flower basket after all, then caught herself with a laugh. She who had never gathered flowers in her life! Grandfather would be more than a little suspicious of that!

Stooping down, she picked up a twig and tossed it impulsively at a squirrel that had just come scampering across the grass. If Grandfather was watching, he would think she had been playing with it all along. By the time she turned back again, she saw to her surprise that D'Arcy had ridden his horse around one of the paths and was now poised at the edge of the lawn. All she could see beneath the wide brim of his hat was a dark mustache and a white gleam of teeth.

Her first reaction was anger, and she sensed, rightly, that he had come to tease, knowing full well she didn't want Grandfather to see him. But the feeling lasted only a second, receding as quickly as it had come.

How could she stay angry with anyone as handsome—and charming—as D'Arcy Cameron?

Pulling herself slowly to her feet, she kept impish eyes cast downward as she walked deliberately across the lawn, dragging her feet a little, as if performing a chore only out of politeness. When she reached her knavish suitor, she dropped a perfunctory curtsy, barely enough for good manners; then with a shrug—exaggerated a little, in case Grandfather *was* at his window—she turned and began to walk briskly toward the house.

D'Arcy grinned broadly, touching his fingers to the brim of his hat in a mute gesture of admiration as he stole a glance up at the windows. Impossible to see with the sun glinting off them like that, but he'd be willing to bet that the old man was there.

And he'd bet that he hadn't been taken in by the little show his granddaughter had just put on.

3

Ivan Alexander was frowning as he stood at the window, silver-streaked eyebrows coming so close together they formed a single dark line across his face. The panes in front of him were smeared with smoke—the little maids who came and went with predictable regularity were too intimidated to stay long enough in these rooms for more than the most haphazard cleaning—and his eyesight was no longer as sharp as it used to be, but he had not missed that absurd little curtsy of his granddaughter's . . . or the way she pointedly turned her back on young D'Arcy Cameron, as if he were the last person in the world she wanted to see.

And he had been about as convinced as the household mice when Kolya, the old gray cat, stretched out with his back to the holes and crevices in the baseboard and pretended he was not interested in the rustlings behind him!

The little *koketka*! A dull knot tightened in his chest, and he slipped his hand inside his jacket as he watched Stacey flit smugly across the lawn toward the house. Whenever he was agitated, he reverted to Russian in his thoughts, although he never spoke the language aloud and had refused to have his granddaughters tutored in it.

Now his mouth felt dry, and he turned away from the window, going over to a tobacco tin he kept on the large round table in the center of the room. His doctors had been after him for years to give it up. It was too strong, they said—too hard on an old man's failing system—but they might as well have told the fog not to rise out of the bay the next morning. If Natalya had been there, she might have gotten him to listen. But Natalya had been gone these past thirteen years.

The thought annoyed him, as it had often of late, and he felt a kind of peevish anger at the woman who was no longer with him when he needed her. Natalya would have known how to handle this thing with Stacey. Natalya had always known what to do. There were no problems when she was alive, nothing that couldn't be solved with a loving heart and a little common sense. She had known how to handle her Russian bear of a husband; she had let him shout and bluster and rage to his heart's content . . . and then, when it was over, she had spoken a few soft words and everything had been all right again.

He twisted the lid of the tobacco tin loose, then set it aside, his hand wandering over to a miniature of his wife which stood at the edge of the cluttered table. There was a formal portrait of her downstairs, next to his own likeness in the study, but it had been painted much later, and there were days when he barely recognized the stoutish woman with more white than black in her hair and only an echo of luster in once-vivid blue eyes. More and more lately, he had come to think of her the way she was when he had first known her; the past was so easy to recall sometimes—as if it had happened yesterday—while yesterday itself was a blur in his mind.

She had been beautiful, his Natalya, all those years ago. It warmed his heart, even now, to think of it. He had been a young soldier at the old Russian Fort Ross, high on the wave-swept California coast; she had been the commandant's daughter, well beyond his rank and social station. If he had been older—and wiser—he would not have dared raise his eyes to her. But he had been young then, and he had dared . . . and she had looked back.

Ah, the hours spent in a dismal wooden chapel, bitterly cold those winter mornings, pretending to a devoutness he did not feel because she was devout and he longed to be near her. He chuckled out loud as he set the miniature back on the table, a good feeling, easing the tightness in his chest. Eventually they had grown too bold—when were love and youth ever cautious?—and word of their secret passion had reached her father's ears. If it hadn't been for Natalya's quick wit, sending a message that last fateful night, he would have been in irons at dawn, bound for the hold of a Russian ship . . . and prison on some vague charge of "insubordination." As it was, his departure was more hasty than dignified, with only a brief stop at the chapel—to ensure the success of his flight.

He had been certain, that night, that he would never see his beautiful Natalya again, and his heart had been aching as he paused one last time to look back at the onion-shaped domes of the fort, glistening in the moonlight. But he had not counted on her spirit, for there, on that wind-ravished expanse of open land, was Natalya, a long dark cloak flying out behind her as she dared to ride her father's proudest possession, his swift chestnut stallion.

For the first time, perhaps the *only* time in his life, Ivan Alexander had been conscious of a sense of humility as he stood on that sweeping California plain and looked up to see the wildness in her face.

"Get up behind me," she called out as she reined the horse to a stop. "They'll discover you're missing soon—they're certain to come after you. But there's no mount to match the chestnut in the stables. Even riding double, we can get away."

He had stood there for a moment, feeling suddenly foolish, aware of the heavy bundle wrapped in his jacket, wishing he could bury it somewhere in the darkness. But there was no way he could hide it from her. And no way he could keep her from realizing, all too soon, what it was.

"The . . . the candlesticks," he said awkwardly. "I didn't have any money . . . I could hardly ask your father for my back pay. So I took the . . . silver candlesticks . . . from the chapel."

Something flashed, strangely defiant, in the exquisite blue eyes that looked back at him. "I know," she said softly, and he had understood then how deep this woman's love for him was . . . and how much she was willing to give up for his sake.

They had ridden almost completely through the night that followed, stopping to rest only when the first streaks of dawn lightened the sky. It was there, in a field of waving grasses and dry winter wildflowers, that the beautiful Natalya became his wife in everything except the legalities. Those were taken care of three weeks later, in the first town in which they dared to stop for more than an hour, sensing at last that pursuit was behind them. It was a shabby ceremony, performed in a shabby little house by a minister with liquor on his breath, but Natalya hardly seemed to notice, or to mind that the rite of marriage had taken place so belatedly after the consummation. Nor had she reproached her husband when it took him several years to get around to doing the thing again, properly this time, in a Russian church, with a priest of their own faith.

Ivan picked up the tobacco again, his mind drifting in and out of the present, as it was wont to do nowadays. He had given her a good life, he thought; at least it had been good for him, and she had not complained, though Natalya had never been the sort to put her regrets and disappointments into words. They had done well enough those early years, parlaying the candlesticks into a comfortable living; then, unexpectedly, gold had been discovered, and he had dropped everything to hasten to the fields around Sutter's Mill, certain with a thousand other young hopefuls that he was about to make his fortune. And to some extent he had—his claim there gave him more than a modest stake—but it was later, when they had moved to San Francisco and he began a series of shrewd investments, that he had become truly wealthy.

If Natalya had heard the gossip that surrounded those investments—if she knew that he had sometimes been less than scrupulous in his money dealings with others—she had never mentioned the fact to him. Like the silver from the chapel, she simply accepted, not questioning. This was the man she loved, and love, in her pure heart, allowed no room for doubt.

They had had only one child, a boy, born eight months and a week to the day after that first hasty ceremony. If there had been some secret sorrow in Natalya's life, Ivan knew it was that there were no

more, for she had always longed for a houseful of
children. When it didn't happen, however, she took it
as God's will, and with no anger or bitterness he could
see, threw her heart and devotion into that one boy.

Ivan had loved his son too—they had called him
Vassily . . . Wesley, as he was known to the lads at
school—but he had not understood him. And because
he hadn't understood, he had been sterner than he
intended, and they had never been close. God knows,
he had tried, as his son grew, to teach him the ways of
business, but the more he lectured and scolded, the
more the boy rebelled, retreating with quiet stubbornness into a world of his own.

An artist! He had wanted to be an artist! Ivan spat
into a spittoon in the corner, then took out a wad of
tobacco and began to tamp it down in his pipe. It
would not have mattered so much if the boy had been
a good artist. Art had its place, after all. Like many
men with no talent of his own, Ivan Alexander was in
awe of those who had. But his works had been fumbling,
amateurish things, impressing no one, not even himself!

"You must not mind so much, Ivan Alexandrovich,"
Natalya had told him once. "Vassily is different, that
is all. It is not so terrible to be different. What can it
hurt?"

"What can it hurt?" he had blustered. "Even great
artists make no money. Do you want your son to
starve?"

"But you've made enough money for all of us," she
reminded him gently. "You must try to understand."

And he had tried, in his way, though the effort had
not always been visible. But try as he would, he had
never understood, not Vassily, not the woman he had
married—what was her name again? Oh, yes, Mary
Elizabeth. A vain, silly creature, he had not thought
of her for years; he could not even remember now
what she looked like, though they had taken her into
the house with her four daughters after Vassily had
died. Absurd, the way she gave all the girls Russian
names, after one grand duchess or other—Olga, Tamara, Anatasia, Xenia—as if she thought that would
please her rich father-in-law! Hadn't she noticed that

he had anglicized his own patronymic, using it as a surname, Alexander, as if he had been English? And he would have changed the first name too, translating it to John, if Natalya's eyes had not filled with tears at the strangeness of the sound.

Well, no matter now. He lit an old-fashioned flint and held it to the bowl of his pipe as he drew in sharp, audible puffs. Mary Elizabeth was long dead, she and Natalya both, and there was no one either to help or to look over his shoulder as he dealt with the girls.

He took a long, satisfying drag on the pipe, aware as he did so of a sharp, slightly acrid aroma, blending with the stale-smoke smell of the room. His pipe was one of the few things left in him that was truly Russian, except perhaps for the lines of his face and the dark beard he only partially trimmed back. He had long since given up vodka for imported French brandy, which those fool doctors would have denied him too, if they had their way. But he still savored the strong peasant tobacco of his youth, biting against his tongue, stinging his nostrils as he let out a long gray trail of smoke.

The blasted doctors anyway, what did they know? A cigar after dinner, they told him priggishly . . . or perhaps a milder pipe. What the devil would it get him—another month? Three or four at best?

The knot in his chest came back, more than tightness this time, a sharp pain that radiated hotly down his arm and into his hand. In spite of himself, he was alarmed, and he let the pipe drop unnoticed to the ashtray.

"Six months," the last doctor had told him, the young one, with the guts to speak the truth. "Six months at most . . . maybe less." Then his face had grown uncomfortable and he had added a little awkwardly: "If I were you, I'd get my affairs in order."

Get his affairs in order? He pushed the ashtray aside and went back to the window. What did a young *malchik* like that know of "affairs" and getting things "in order"? He wasn't a rich man—with four lively granddaughters to marry off!

Stacey was gone by this time, but D'Arcy Cameron

was still there, hovering at the edge of the lawn, a
modishly graceful figure on a horse that was much too
good for him. It was hard enough for a poor man,
seeing four girls safely settled . . . and young heiresses
had a way of attracting suitors with more than romance in their hearts. If he left his granddaughters
alone and unprotected, they would be easy prey for
the sort of men that made his blood run cold.

Not that he was going to have any trouble with
three of them. The pain was still there, noticeable in
his chest and arm, but it relaxed somewhat as he
reviewed the situation in his mind. Olga, of course,
would be no problem. She was the most beautiful of
the girls, but she was pious and obedient, and he knew
she would abide by his wishes. Nor would Mara cause
him any heartache. Mara was too plain, in looks and
in spirit, to attract a man on her own: she would take
whatever he arranged, gratefully—whether she liked it
or not.

As for Zee, she was a frivolous little thing, much
too much like her mother, but she was wildly infatu-
ated with young Charlie Danson, the son of Henry
Danson, a well-to-do merchant and the only man who
had ever put anything over on Ivan Alexander. The
boy was still young, unfortunately—Ivan would have
liked to wait a few years to see how he turned out—
but at least he came of good stock.

Then there was Stacey . . .

He rested his hand on his chest as he stared through
the window. Young Cameron had disappeared, sometime while he thought he had been watching, and the
garden below was empty in the cool autumn sunlight.
Stacey had always been able to work her way around
him, the little minx, with her laughter and her high
spirits and her willful fits of temper. Olga should have
been his favorite—he saw Natalya every time he looked
at her—but there was so much of himself in Stacey. It
tore his heart apart to think that she might be hurt.

Well, perhaps this infatuation for D'Arcy Cameron
wasn't so bad, after all. Walking back to the table, he
reached for the miniature, then changed his mind,
sensing that Natalya would not approve of what he

had in mind. Stacey was probably in the study now, mooning over the globe again, as she had for the past several days; whenever he went into the room, he always found it turned to Australia.

And if her infatuation for the man had led to an infatuation for the continent, then perhaps . . .

He strode across the room, moving forcefully for the first time that morning as he grabbed the bell cord and gave it several hard, impatient tugs. He was going to have to be clever, that was for sure. If Stacey caught even a glimmer of what he was up to, she would find some way to weasel out of it. But pretty girls in love rarely saw things clearly . . . at least not in time.

He would have to do it publicly, of course. Picking up the pipe, he held it, unsmoked, in his hand, more from nervous habit than anything else. If he could persuade her to agree in front of everyone she knew, then she wouldn't be able to back down. Stacey had always been an independent little creature, making her own rules even as a child, not caring what anyone thought. But she had a fiercely stubborn pride too, and she would die before she let anyone see when she was hurt or confused. That pride would be his ally now.

Where was Madden anyway?

Impatient, he crossed back to the bell and pulled again. He would have to arrange every detail very carefully . . . and in the most public manner possible. And there was one good way to do that—and keep Stacey's mind so occupied at the same time that she wouldn't think of anything else.

He was just giving the cord a last sharp tug when the door opened and the butler appeared on the threshold. Ivan did not even give him time to murmur his usual impeccable "Sir?" but started in at once.

"I want all the rooms cleaned and aired immediately, do you hear me? Have the housekeeper see to it at once. Today. And tell that new little maid—no, tell my granddaughter, she's better at it—to order the finest arrangements of flowers the city has to offer. A week from Saturday, we're going to hold a ball."

"A . . . ball, sir?" Ivan had the satisfaction of seeing

a startled expression cross those usually impassive
features.

"Certainly a ball—why not? We've had none in the
house, I admit, since my wife died—but the girls are
older now. They need a bit of entertainment now and
then. Zee has been begging me to let her go to balls
for months now, and Stacey will enjoy the music and
the laughter, don't you think?"

Madden's lips betrayed him, turning up just slightly
at the corners. "Yes, sir—I think Miss Anastasia will
enjoy it most especially."

"Hmmph, well, so do I. It will give her something
to occupy herself."

"If I may say so, sir . . ." There was a distinct
twinkle in the man's eye now. "I think she will occupy
herself with nothing else."

As do I, Ivan thought, though he kept the words to
himself. "Good, then," he said aloud, "everything's
settled. Go along now. Tell Olga I'll see her this
afternoon about the invitations. Oh . . . and, Madden." He could not resist calling the man back from
the door. "You may inform the staff that there's going
to be an announcement."

"Very good, sir." Madden knew his place; he would
not ask any questions, but Ivan chuckled inwardly as
he realized that everyone was going to assume the
announcement concerned Olga's engagement. It was
no secret that he had already begun negotiations with
a widower of substance, not his sort exactly—piety in
a man always made him uncomfortable—but someone
who would take care of Olga and make her happy.

That he might have something else on his mind
would not occur to any of them . . . least of all Stacey.

"That will be all, Madden."

He waited until the door was closed, then took a
deep pull on his pipe, savoring the searing pungency
of smoke in his mouth and nose.

4

Stacey plopped down on the bed, which one of the maids had just finished making, and picked up a folded red afghan to wrap around her shoulders. The weather had turned brisk a few hours after she and D'Arcy had parted in the garden. Now, three days later, there was a distinctly wintry feel to the air.

Downstairs, everything was in a turmoil. Newly hired day help could be seen in nearly every room, cleaning and replacing old draperies, beating out the carpets, fluffing up pillows, and polishing marble tabletops and inlaid rosewood cabinets, with Mara and the house-keeper sticking their heads through the doors and calling out contradictory orders every few minutes. It was complete chaos, and Stacey, after watching for a while, had escaped upstairs, where at least she would be out from underfoot. With the tradesmen's carriages coming and going all the time, so jammed in the drive there wasn't room to turn around, it was unlikely that D'Arcy would choose to call. And even if he did, there was no place they could be alone.

Who would ever have thought Grandfather would give a ball?

The door eased open, and a furry gray face peeked in. A minute later, the rest of Kolya followed, pranc-ing daintily on white-booted paws, his little pink nose taking tentative sniffs of the air. Stacey laughed and made coaxing noises, but as usual, the cat pretended not to notice, stretching out instead in a patch of sun on the braided oval rug.

"What a funny old thing you are," she teased, but Kolya, true to form, did not open one lazy green eye. He had brazened his way into the house one day when

Stacey was about five or six, a scrawny, half-starved kitten, but even then with a mind of his own. Grandfather had named him Nickolai, after his own father, because he was a feisty little strutter with a taste for a nip of brandy. Four months later, he had presented them with the first of a long series of litters, but by that time he was too firmly "Kolya" in everyone's mind—and too firmly "he"—to be anything else.

Stacey shrugged the afghan away from her shoulders, feeling unexpectedly restless as she went over to the wardrobe and pulled out a light-blue woolen dress with long sleeves and an unflattering high neck. There was no point trying to look pretty this morning. D'Arcy was almost certain not to come, and the yellow dotted swiss she had donned earlier, fetching as it was, left her with a distinct chill. Soon the maids would be laying fires in the morning, and welcome flickers of red and gold would show in the doorways, a sure sign that winter was here to stay.

Really, it *was* funny, she thought as she slipped the dress over her head and readjusted her image in the mirror, the way Grandfather had decided on the ball, and at such short notice, too. She and Zee had been trying for ages to get him to agree to even a modest little soiree, coaxing and wheedling every chance they got, but he had always refused with a gruff: "We had parties enough when your grandmother was alive. She liked all that fuss—I don't." And that had been that.

Now, all of a sudden, with no warning at all, he had changed his mind. It was almost, she thought, pausing to stare at her reflection, as if he had something up his sleeve.

Of course, there *was* that announcement he had been hinting at—Olga's engagement, no doubt. But that hardly seemed enough to prompt such uncharacteristic behavior.

She was frowning slightly as she turned away from the dressing table, but the sight of the cat rolling playfully in the sun made her laugh.

"You're right, Kolya—I am being silly! It's much too pretty a day to worry about anything. I'm just glad Grandfather is finally giving a ball, no matter what his reason!" She tickled the cat playfully on the tummy, pulling back in time to avoid indignant claws, and, still laughing, went out into the hall. There might be chaos downstairs, but it was boring in her room, and besides, she was curious to see what was going on.

She made her way to the back stairway, half-tiptoeing to avoid being caught up in the bustling activities of the ground floor. If she was lucky, she might run into one of the chattier maids, Delia perhaps, and find out if there was any new speculation in the servants' quarters about the extraordinary goings-on of the past three days.

She had just reached the long downstairs hallway and was debating whether to go forward or back when she heard voices coming from Ivan Alexander's study. The sound startled her, and she turned her head, puzzled. It couldn't be ten yet . . . and Grandfather rarely came down much before noon.

But then, she thought, laughing, nothing Grandfather could do would be as surprising as throwing a ball!

For an instant she considered poking her head in to say hello; then, assuming he was busy with some stuffy tradesman or other, changed her mind and headed toward the kitchen. She was halfway down the hall when one of the voices caught her ear.

"I must say, you've taken me by surprise, sir," the smooth tenor was saying. "This is the last thing I expected when you summoned me here this morning."

Could that be D'Arcy Cameron?

Stacey pressed her body against the wall, knowing it was rude to eavesdrop, but sensing somehow that the conversation would cease if they knew she was there. Yes, surely it *was* D'Arcy, and Grandfather was replying:

"Your first offer was totally unacceptable, as I told you at the time. I could not consider it. Even this— well, I must say, I'm none too sure. I'd feel better if I understood why you were really here."

"I thought that was apparent."

"The mission itself, yes, certainly—I don't dispute that. But the reasons behind it? I wonder, have you been telling me the whole truth? It does seem rather unusual."

"Surely not, sir—this kind of thing has been known to happen before. Even in America. Quite frequently, I understand, during the settlement of your western territories."

"True," the older man conceded, though still with some hesitance in his voice. "But there are reasons for what happened in this country. Perhaps it would help if I knew more about the early development of Australia."

The early development of Australia? Stacey started to sigh, then caught herself, just in time. The last thing she wanted now was a history lesson! Why couldn't they get to the point, so she'd know what was going on? Plainly, D'Arcy had come this morning for a reason. And at Grandfather's summons, too, if she had heard that first statement right.

"It's really quite simple," D'Arcy was saying. "Australia was founded shortly after the American Revolution—as a direct result of it, you might say. We were in essence a dumping ground for convicts. The English had been accustomed to getting rid of their undesirables in the colonies. When the upstart Americans rebelled, they had to find someplace else—and we were it."

"Yes, yes, I know all that." Stacey could hear an edge of impatience in Grandfather's voice. He always hated to have someone belabor the obvious. "But I fail to see what—"

"I'm getting to the point, sir. There were, of course, some females among the convicts, though a low percentage, perhaps one in ten, and those were hardly of the highest quality. The officers of the First Fleet, I hear, were appalled at the language—to say nothing of the morals—of the 'ladies' they were transporting. Needless to say, men in those early days often took to, uh, consorting with native women."

Grandfather grunted. "Hmmm . . . yes, well . . . understandable perhaps. Under the circumstances."

"No doubt," D'Arcy retorted dryly. "But we are no longer a nation of convicts, though we are still a nation of men. The ratio of males to females changed little with the immigrants who followed the transportees—only we are more fastidious than our forebears and have no desire to cohabit with blacks. So, you see, it is not a simple matter to choose a wife."

A wife? Stacey leaned closer, intrigued by the unexpected turn the conversation was taking.

"But surely there must be some suitable women," Grandfather was protesting as she strained her ears to listen.

"Oh, there are a few. We aren't all savages and the offspring of convicts. Even in a remote area like ours, there's one young lady of quality and breeding. But she"—he paused, something like laughter coming into his voice—"she is already taken."

Stacey's head began to spin as the implication of those last words sank in, and her mind leapt boldly to the only reasonable conclusion. D'Arcy Cameron had come to San Francisco looking for a wife! That was the mysterious errand that had brought him here. Not secret business dealings or money transactions, but a much more human reason.

And if he was in Grandfather's study discussing the matter with him, then the wife he wanted had to be her!

She almost laughed out loud in her excitement, then stopped abruptly as an unpleasant new thought occurred to her. What was it D'Arcy had said that last morning they were together? *Maybe I didn't come to see you at all. Maybe I came to see one of your sisters.*

What if it wasn't her they were discussing now? Mara was the sensible, undemanding one; she would make a better wife for a rancher. But D'Arcy would never settle for Mara—there was no laughter in her soul!—and Grandfather would hardly part with Olga. He depended on her too much.

Zee?

No . . . Stacey pushed the thought out of her mind, hating the ugly jealous chill that came over her heart just for a second. D'Arcy would not choose lightheaded little Zee. It was she, Stacey, he wanted—and Grandfather was about to give her to him.

The idea was so engrossing, she had almost forgotten where she was. Now she realized with a jolt that the men were still talking, and she had missed much of what they had said.

"I don't question your decision, sir." D'Arcy's voice drifted out to the hallway. "I concur, and whole-heartedly, I might add. But I do question your means of implementing it. It sounds rather . . . risky."

"Why?" Stacey could have sworn she heard Grandfather chuckle. "Because it will take place in such a public manner? But where better for her to agree to what we want than at a ball . . . in front of all those witnesses."

"If she does agree—yes." D'Arcy sounded amused. "But if she doesn't, won't all those witnesses make it a bit embarrassing?"

"Ah, but she will agree. She's the liveliest of my granddaughters—always has been. She could never resist a chance to match wits with me. It's all a game, you see—she never stops to think of the stakes. And she's a proud one, you mark my words. If I trap her in public, she'll never be able to back down."

"You seem sure of yourself."

"Very sure. You can trust me. Now . . . shall we have a drink on it?"

Shuffling sounds came from the room, and Stacey realized, barely in time, that her grandfather had risen and was heading for the bottle of fine French cognac he kept on a table next to the door. Darting away, she half-slid along the wide, polished floorboards, not even minding that she could not stay and listen to the rest of the conversation. She had heard all she needed.

She is the liveliest of my granddaughters, Grandfather had said—*and proud*! Zee was lively too, a sprightly little flibbertigibbet, but she had no pride at all. So Grandfather could only have meant her. And the announcement he had planned for the ball was not Olga's engagement at all. It was hers!

It had worked!

She fairly flew up the steps, not even bothering, with all the flurry in the house, to bypass the ones that squeaked. She had pretended to be indifferent to

D'Arcy Cameron, and it had worked! If Grandfather had thought she cared about him, he would have found reasons to fuss and be suspicious—just because she was sixteen and he thought her judgment couldn't be trusted! But because he was sure she didn't even *like* the man, he was determined to make the match.

And he thought she wasn't sharp enough to match wits with him! She paused for an instant at the top of the stairs, laughing softly to herself. Somehow, at the ball, he was planning on getting the best of her . . . tricking her into an agreement he believed she didn't' want. And he thought it would work because he was too clever for her!

The cat was still curled up on the rug as she threw open the door to her room, and she laughed at the grumpy expression on his face when she picked him up and cuddled him in her arms. Any other time, he would have hissed a sharp protest at this affront to his dignity, but he was too sleepy to do more than rumble a little as she carried him over to the bed.

"Oh, Kolya," she whispered, burying her face in soft, thick fur. "Isn't it wonderful? Grandfather doesn't know it yet, but he's about to make me the happiest girl in the world!"

Her eyes sparkled as she looked up, saying aloud what she had only dared to dream before.

"In a few weeks, I will be Mrs. D'Arcy Cameron."

5

The great hall of the Alexander mansion was shimmering with light and color and sound on the night of the ball. Massive brass-and-crystal chandeliers cast a flickering glow on dark wooden floors so polished they reflected the swirling dancers' gowns, and deep red velvet draperies had been pulled back to show echoes of an even deeper red in the roses in the lamplit winter garden. The weather had turned warm just the night before. The windows were open, and a faint sea breeze mingled with the scent of flowers and perfume in the room.

Stacey paused for a moment at the edge of the dance floor, caught up in the glamour and excitement of the scene before her. No fairy-tale ball could have been lovelier—or more romantic. Flowers seemed to be everywhere. Huge elegant sprays were arranged in stands around the edges of the room, and garlands swung on long, sensuous festoons across the ceiling. A lone table stood at one end, slightly raised, on a platform of its own, draped with a mantle of pure white roses.

Like an altar, Stacey thought, giggling at the inappropriateness of the image. She was a little surprised at Mara for allowing that one unstylish touch in an otherwise superb decor. But no doubt that was where Grandfather was planning on making his mysterious "announcement" at midnight.

Her eyes drifted back to the dance floor, searching for the lithe form she picked out almost at once. D'Arcy was dancing with a neighbor's daughter, a short, not-very-pretty girl who was gazing up at him with obvious adoration in myopic pale-blue eyes. Stacey felt a twinge of annoyance, then shrugged it off with a laugh. It was foolish, being petty on a night like this. Let the girl cling to her hopes while she could. By the end of the evening she, and everyone else, would know who was destined to be D'Arcy Cameron's wife.

The music broke off, and the dancers, laughing and chatting, moved back toward the walls, leaving the center clear for the moment. A young man appeared at Stacey's side, a boy who had never paid the least attention to her until now, when he had apparently discovered that she was all grown up . . . and had turned out to be uncommonly pretty. Any other time, she would have laughed at his gawkiness, but tonight she was inclined to be generous, and she was politer than usual as she declined, saying that she was out of breath—which was partly true, at least—and promising to dance with him later.

Alone again, she took advantage of the respite to look for D'Arcy, but the room was crowded, and she could not find him. Disappointingly, her first dance that evening had not been with him. She had half-expected to see him when the opening strains of music began, but instead she had been claimed by the young widower Grandfather had picked out for Olga, and because the man was kind and she knew he meant well, she could not bring herself to refuse. A business associate of Grandfather's had come next—impossible again to say no—and somehow she had been kept busy until the boys her own age lost their initial shyness and began flocking around her, clamoring for a dance.

Funny, she thought fleetingly—it was almost as if Grandfather were deliberately separating her from D'Arcy. But then, perhaps he was being cautious. After all, he *did* think he was forcing the man on her against her will. He wouldn't want to give her a chance to figure out beforehand what was going on.

She dropped her eyes, smiling a secret half-smile to herself. Midnight, he had told everyone—at midnight, he was going to step onto the raised platform beside that absurd little altar-table—and she was going to find a way to play right into his hands!

She looked up to see Olga standing across the room, staring at her with a curious look. Too late, she realized that her expression might give her away, and she broadened her smile, trying to look like she was just enjoying the excitement of her first ball.

Olga had always been a beauty, but she looked especially beautiful tonight, and Stacey felt a tug at her heart as she realized how much her sister looked like their grandmother in the little miniature Grandfather always kept in his rooms. Even her dress was similar, a true sapphire blue, with a round, old-fashioned neckline.

Grandfather, surprisingly, had taken a hand in their dress that night, choosing colors that left them a rainbow on the cool end of the spectrum. Gowns had been matched with flawless good taste to exquisite selections from the family jewel box, which he had opened for the first time in years. Mara, with a heavy amethyst necklace that none of them had ever seen before, was clad in bluish purple, a subtly draped velvet gown that made her seem almost elegant. Olga, in blue, wore the sapphires that had been painted in the miniature, and Zee, in a lighter shade of the same color, looked sweetly pretty and quite grown-up in aquamarines that had belonged not to Natalya, but to their own mother.

Only Stacey's costume was without color, pure white silk trimmed in yards and yards of imported Belgian lace, with a lace fichu modestly edging what would otherwise have been a daring neckline. She had been a little disappointed when she first saw it; indeed, she might have objected had it not been for the perfectly cut diamonds in that new necklace and matching tiara, which instinct told her would look breathtaking in piles of glossy jet-black hair. The last of her reluctance vanished when she finished dressing and caught sight of herself in the mirror.

"I look like a bride," she protested, laughing at her reflection. But the image was a captivating one, so pretty even she was enchanted, and she could not bring herself to miss the gay colors she had wanted so much before.

The music began again, a rich, swelling sound, only half-muffled by the heavy drapes, and Stacey found herself scanning the spinning dancers, searching for the only one her heart longed to see. At last she caught sight of him, a dashing figure, dark mustache framing white teeth as he smiled down at a bit of pale blue fluff in his arms.

Stacey frowned slightly, hating herself, but unable to resist the pique of jealousy Zee always brought out in her. She knew she was being childish. D'Arcy had to dance with someone, since he was plainly determined not to upset Grandfather by seeking her out. He had probably chosen her younger sister only because Ivan Alexander asked him to. Zee was pretty, but there was no conversation in her and she was not much of a dancer yet—kindness would be required to keep her supplied with partners throughout the evening.

"She's doing very well, don't you think? Not as well as you, of course, but then, I suspect you are going to be the dancer in the family."

Stacey turned to see Richard Halifax standing beside her. He was an older man, forty, perhaps forty-five, and she had heard that Grandfather was considering him for Mara, though she had never paid much attention. Now she found herself studying him—the slightly rounded face, the stocky middle-aged waist, the receding hairline—and noticing what she had missed before, a genuinely warm twinkle in his eye.

"Why, Richard—Mr. Halifax—I do believe you're trying to flatter me."

" 'Richard' will do just fine," he said easily. "I've always hated being called 'Mr.' by pretty young things. And flattery was not my intention, I assure you. I was merely stating the truth. I could not help noticing how fetching you looked out there on the dance floor. Just as I could not help noticing that your sister is doing her best."

"Yes, I do believe she is." Stacey glanced back, feeling a little better about Zee as she saw the effort the girl was making to look good in D'Arcy Cameron's arms. It had to be hard, a year younger, just learning to dance . . . and nowhere near as self-confident as she pretended. "I'm afraid sometimes I tend to be a little harsh on her."

"That's easy to do." Stacey was conscious of the humor in his eyes again. "I may not look it, but I was young once too. I had a little brother myself—and I was merciless with him."

Stacey smiled, finding herself liking Richard Halifax more than she had expected. "Have you ever seen anything so beautiful?" she asked impulsively. "I've never been to a ball before—this is our first dance, mine and Zee's both—but I can't believe any other has ever been as lovely."

"Perhaps you're right. I've been to a great many dances myself—more than I'd care to admit—and I must say, I've never seen a ballroom that looked like this. Whoever arranged it has exquisite taste."

"That was Mara's doing." Stacey eyed him intently, curious to see his reaction. "She did all the flowers— she always does the flowers—and I suspect she had a hand in the other arrangements too. Arranging is what Mara does best."

She was rewarded with a faintly uncomfortable look on those round, good-natured features. "Your sister is very talented," he said, glancing self-consciously toward the place where Mara was standing beside an open doorway. Great trays of food were being arranged on tables in an adjacent room for the feast that would take place after midnight, and she and Olga stopped periodically to check on the servants' progress.

"She looks quite nice tonight, doesn't she? The color of that dress becomes her—Grandfather chose it himself. It makes her hair darker and her skin lighter, don't you think?"

"Your sister always looks nice. She is a very handsome woman."

"Do you think so?" Stacey searched his face for any sign of insincerity, but there was none. It occurred to her that, for a middle-aged man like Richard Halifax, Mara's youth might compensate for her lack of prettiness.

"I do, indeed. She is not a gaudy woman, of course, but gaudiness has never appealed to me. I much prefer subtle good taste."

"You seem very taken with my sister." Stacey's lips turned up at the corner, and she could not resist adding: "They say you have asked for her hand—and Grandfather has given it. Is that true?"

She was amused to see a faint flush come into his cheeks. "I, uh . . . I admire her greatly, of course. But anything else . . . well, anything else you had best discuss with your sister. I would not be much of a gentleman—would I?—if I answered that question."

And I am not much of a lady for having asked it, Stacey thought, but she did not embarrass him by saying the words aloud. "I am sorry—truly I am. I'm afraid I have a tendency to be rather outspoken. It is one of my faults."

"Actually, it is one of your most endearing traits—on some occasions."

"But not this one?" She laughed lightly as she laid an impulsive hand on his arm. "I don't know if the rumor is true or not, Richard—nor do I expect you to tell me—but I hope it is. I would like to have you for a brother."

The remark seemed to please him, more than Stacey had anticipated, and something in the way he did not meet her eyes made her curious. Could it be that Grandfather had more than one surprise up his sleeve tonight? Not only her engagement to D'Arcy Cameron, but Mara's to Richard Halifax as well?

She did not have a chance to tease the truth out of him, for just then the music rose to a low crescendo, almost as if it had been deliberately planned, and Ivan Alexander appeared in the doorway to the entry hall.

He made a dramatic figure. Flickering light accented his nose and sharply chiseled cheekbones, and deepened the shadows in his gray-streaked beard, giving him an almost defiantly Russian look despite the neatly tailored lines of a fashionable evening coat and slim black trousers. He had been gone from the ballroom only a short time, but his reentrance now had the effect of a first appearance, and a slight hush fell over the room as all eyes turned in his direction.

He stood for a moment on the threshold, savoring the effect. Behind him, Stacey could see the servants beginning to gather. Cook, who had been with the family for years . . . the footmen, abandoning their posts at the outside doors . . . the fidgety little upstairs maid . . . old Eulalia, who had raised the girls since they were babies. Plainly midnight was at hand.

Just for an instant, she caught a glimpse of another grizzled beard among the eager crowd of watchers, and she was startled to recognize the stern-faced priest who had been serving the Russian community for years. What is he doing here? she wondered fleetingly, then forgot again as her excitement mounted.

The silence was almost palpable now, and a little thrill of anticipation shivered through the onlookers as Ivan Alexander stepped out of the doorway and into the room. He seemed to be heading for the slightly elevated platform at one end, and Stacey felt her pulse quicken, certain that the dancing was over and the moment she had been waiting for here at last. As he moved, however, he raised one arm, signaling to the band, and the music recommenced abruptly. The guests took a moment to recover, then two by two, began to move, merging into a brilliant kaleidoscope of color.

Stacey's eyes sought out D'Arcy's, across the room, and she thought for an instant he was going to come to her. Then Grandfather passed the place where he was standing, and though not a word was exchanged, he turned away, and she knew he would not look back again. The gesture left her with a strangely empty feeling—a nervousness that was silly, but there it was all the same—and she was glad to accept the first partner who came along, the gawky youth she had refused a few minutes before.

The music was almost heartbreakingly sweet—the same slow, seductive waltz she had danced with D'Arcy in the garden—and she closed her eyes, longing to recapture the poignancy again, to feel as if she were there one more time with the man she adored.

For a moment, it almost worked, and she felt as light as the leaves that rustled beneath her feet . . . felt the warmth of his body, tantalizingly close, that last instant before he pressed his lips on hers. But the boy was nowhere near as skillful a dancer as D'Arcy

Cameron, and the illusion was shattered a second later when he trod roughly on her toe.

"Oops, sorry," he stammered, red-faced.

"That's all right," she replied, but she could not keep from snapping the words out, and he made no further attempt at conversation.

It must have been as much a relief to him as to her when the music finally stopped. With a few barely perfunctory words, she twisted away, only to discover that Grandfather was already standing on the platform. He had just turned with a subtle nod to the musicians, and they were laying aside their instruments and sorting—rather oddly, it seemed to Stacey, for their services would not be needed until later— through the music on their stands. He took a moment to see that his instructions were being obeyed, then turned back, raising his arms, unnecessarily, for silence.

"You must indulge me, my friends." His voice was stronger than it had sounded for years as he pitched it above the last hushed whispers in the hall. "I am an old man who has grown to love the power of holding an audience in the palm of my hand . . . the way an old ham actor clings to the warmth of the spotlight on his face. But this is not my night tonight. This is a night to focus on four beautiful young women. . . . Or should I say, on one in particular?" He paused, an almost boyish light coming into his eyes. "You all know that I called you here to make an important announcement . . . and you think you know what it is. And—in a way—you are right."

In a way? Stacey held absolutely still, not daring to move. Was he talking about her now? Was this to be *her* moment? Then her eyes fell on Olga, standing expectantly a short distance from the stage, and she knew that Grandfather would never be so cruel.

"I am very pleased," he was saying now, as she strained to pay attention, "and very proud, to announce that I have agreed to give the hand of my eldest granddaughter, Olga Vassilyevna—as we would have said in the old country—to Mr. Richard Meredith. I need not acquaint you with his virtues . . . he is a fine man, well known to be intelligent, honest,

hardworking, and . . . devout." He hesitated on the
last word, and Stacey sensed he had included it only as
a courtesy. Then, with a sly grin, he added: "The fact
that he already has considerable means at his disposal,
and can support my granddaughter in a proper and
fitting manner, of course had nothing to do with my
decision."

A sporadic burst of applause mingled with the laughter that greeted his words, and Stacey smiled as she
watched Richard Meredith walk over to stand somewhat awkwardly beside Olga, who looked serene and
beautiful as always. "Richard" again, she thought—
two Richards in the family? That, was going to be
confusing. But then, the confusion would hardly affect
her. She would be off in a new land, with a new
husband of her own.

She glanced over at Richard Halifax, and something
in his face, kind and quietly eager, told her that her
instinct had not been wrong a few minutes before.
Grandfather *did* have more than one surprise in store
that evening. Old Ivan Alexander was going to see
three of his granddaughters safely settled before the
night was over. Or was it four?

Grandfather paused only briefly before going on, as
Stacey suspected, and confirming Mara's engagement
to her solid, generous merchant. When he had finished, he gave her a moment to bask in the attention,
then turned to Zee and asked—with a deliberately
solemn look—if she would consent to be betrothed to
the simpering young man who had been caught un-
awares on the other side of the room with a mouthful
of cake he had stolen from the dining table. The
marriage, he told her, carefully emphasizing each word,
would not take place for two years, when she was
seventeen, but the commitment she made tonight would
be firm and irrevocable.

One look at her sister's face was enough to tell
Stacey that the girl had not known what was going to
happen, though it was obvious both Olga and Mara
had been alerted beforehand. She felt a flash of irrita-
tion, as much at Grandfather as at her baby sister, the
little goose, for that absurdly pleased expression on

her face. Henry Danson might be a shrewd man—the only one who had ever put anything over on Grandfather—but he had a streak of dishonesty as deep as San Francisco Bay, and his son Charlie had inherited only the latter trait. He had always been a sly worm, even as a child, and despite his pretty features, no one except Zee had ever liked him. It looked like Henry had put over one last trick on Ivan Alexander.

Stacey might almost have felt sorry for her sister had not Zee, at just that moment, turned and thrown her a smug look, as if to say: Olga is engaged now, and Mara is engaged—and in two years I will be Charlie Danson's wife. Only you are left standing alone.

Grandfather caught the look too, and ever mindful of the rivalry between the two youngest girls, hastened to go on. "You may have noticed," he said with a pointed glance at Zee, "that there is still one pretty granddaughter whose name has not been mentioned. Perhaps you are saying to yourself: She is so strong-willed, so high-spirited—how will he ever find a husband to tame her? I must confess I have wondered the same thing myself." He held off a moment, waiting for the laughter to die down. "But I have always been a man who admired spirit . . . and I must confess to a soft spot for the feisty little wench, though she has worried more than one of these gray hairs into my beard. But I think at last I have come up with the perfect solution—a man strong enough and bold enough to match wits with my fiery granddaughter.

"Still, I wonder . . . is she strong enough and bold enough to match wits with him?"

It was the perfect gambit, and Stacey could not help admiring him as she took a step forward, conscious of a new burst of laughter in her ears. Even if she hadn't known what he was doing, and wanted it so much, she probably would have walked into the trap.

"I am strong enough—and bold enough—to match wits with any man I ever met, Grandfather. Including you."

Laughter again. This time for her, Stacey thought, pleased with herself. "Bold perhaps," Ivan conceded, pretending to frown. "But are you as strong as you sometimes seem? And adventurous? What I have in mind will require a great spirit of adventure. And more courage than you may as yet have."

Something in his voice, the way he was looking at her, made Stacey falter, and she had the sudden idiotic feeling that she ought to back down, now, while there was still time. But she knew what she had heard that afternoon in his study—she knew what he was really after. All she had to do was play along and she would get everything she wanted.

"I have all the courage I will ever need," she said, tossing her head with a little forced laugh. "Yes, and a sense of adventure too."

"Enough to leave your home and your family? Everyone who is dear to you now?" He gave her a long, steady look. "Enough to venture far away, to a new land . . . and hardships you have never imagined?"

To a land like . . . Australia? Stacey laughed again, with relief this time, though she was careful not to speak the words. She didn't want him to know that she saw what he was getting at. "Enough to go anywhere you say, Grandfather."

"Anywhere?" Ivan Alexander fixed her with piercing eyes again.

"Anywhere."

He did not like the sound of that. Everyone was rapt and curious now, yet somehow he felt dissatisfied, wondering, just at the moment he should have felt the thrill of victory. It was too easy, she was being too docile. If she had looked once toward D'Arcy Cameron, if she even had made a move in that direction . . .

But, no, he had seen to it that the man had not come near her these past several days. Nor had he asked her to dance even once throughout the evening. She was hurt now, and angry . . . and ready to show that she did not care.

"You will do as I tell you then? You will obey without question? Wherever I send you . . . and to whom?"

"I will obey, Grandfather." She dropped her eyes demurely, bobbing an impish curtsy. "As I always do."

Ivan hesitated one last moment. This was his favorite granddaughter. He loved her deeply; it grieved him to think she might be hurt. But she did not look as if he were hurting her . . . and time was running out. He had so few options now.

"You will give me your word?"

"I give my word."

"Very well, then." His voice was soft, as it had been when she was a little girl. "Come, let me have your hand, stand here beside me—and we will see what your word is worth."

He waited until she had mounted the platform. Then he took a step back, raising her arm slightly, as if he wanted to show off the pretty white dress, the elegant jewels he had just given her.

"Ladies and gentlemen, it makes me happier than I can tell you to announce the betrothal of my granddaughter Anastasia to . . ." He took a brief pause, holding back the words: "Mr. Errol Cameron."

6

Stacey stood absolutely still, too stunned for a moment to move or even react. *Errol* Cameron—Grandfather had said Errol. But surely meant D'Arcy. She must have misunderstood him.

Then she turned to look at Ivan Alexander's stern, set features, and she realized with a sinking heart that she had not misheard. He had said Errol Cameron . . . and he had meant it.

Too late the memory of his voice came back, that afternoon in the study when she had eavesdropped on half a conversation. *She can never resist a chance to match wits with me*, he had said—*and she never stops to think of the stakes.* Why hadn't those words sent a shiver of alarm down her spine? Why hadn't she stopped to think that she had heard only a part of what the two men were saying, and that part inconclusive? Why . . . *why* had she been so foolishly sure of herself?

". . . and so I have double cause to celebrate tonight, my friends," Grandfather was saying now. "Not only do I share with you the betrothal of my four charming granddaughters, but the actual vows of one as well. I hope you will forgive an old man's selfishness in being so secretive. But I craved the pleasure of offering a surprise tonight."

Slowly the words penetrated Stacey's consciousness, and she became aware of her grandfather staring at her with something like wariness in his eyes. Below, a sea of faces looked up from the dance floor and doorways, and she sensed dimly that some reply was expected.

"What?" she said mechanically. "I . . . I'm sorry . . . I didn't catch what you were saying."

A low murmur ran through the watchers. Ivan stopped it almost immediately by raising one arm. "I'm afraid the poor child is too giddy for words—a rare occurrence—but how can one blame her? She has had too much excitement for one night. Fortunately, if I recall correctly, she has enough 'spirit of adventure' to recover. As I was telling our friends, my dear"—he angled his head to look at her—"I have arranged for the wedding ceremony to take place tonight."

"The . . . wedding?"

"Certainly. Did you think I would allow it otherwise? Mr. Cameron—Mr. *D'Arcy* Cameron—will be leaving on the *North Star* in three days, and naturally he expects to escort you back to Australia. Eulalia, of course, will go along as chaperone, but still . . . I could hardly permit an unmarried woman to make so long a voyage in the company of a bachelor. Before you set foot on board, you are going to be a bride."

And before she left the ballroom that night, she would be a bride too! With a sudden rush of recognition, Stacey realized how cleverly Grandfather had laid his plans. Once out of sight of all those guests, watching with awed and curious eyes, she would have found some way to squirm out of the commitment he had tricked her into. She would have taken to her bed with a sick headache and not gotten up again until she had thought what to do. But if he forced things to a climax here . . . in front of everyone . . .

She should have known what he was up to. She should have been on her guard! Bitterly her mind ran over the clues she had missed before. The white silk dress with its modest neck and exquisite lace trim . . . hadn't she thought that she looked like a bride? The table decked out as an altar, spread with a mantle of snow-white roses. The priest lurking in the doorway.

"But . . . surely . . ." She caught her breath, trying to force her mind into focus. "Surely even you cannot expect to work miracles. How can there be a wedding . . . when there is no bridegroom?"

"Ah, but there is." His face was harder now than

she had ever seen it, closed to the frantic pleading in her eyes. "D'Arcy Cameron has agreed to stand in for his brother . . . as proxy. It is all legal. My attorneys have assured me of that. And the priest has agreed."

Yes—for a sum, Stacey thought miserably. Ivan Alexander had always been a great contributor to the church in the name of his late wife. A priest might swallow his qualms to keep from losing support like that.

Yet, even between them, what could they do? The faces below her had become a blur now, shimmering in the bright lights of the ballroom, and Stacey sensed that she was standing on a threshold, the last moment when she could still turn back. No matter what Grandfather said, no matter what the priest agreed to, they could not force her. All she had to do was laugh and say she had been joking—and she would be safe.

But was she bold enough for that?

Her eyes lit on her sister Zee, features emblazoned with shock and fascination. Gloating, that was what Zee would look like—positively gloating!—if she made a fool of herself and backed down. She could not bear it if her sister, of all people, laughed at her.

Or D'Arcy . . .

For the first time, she let herself look at the man around whom all her hopes had centered until a few minutes ago. The amusement she had dreaded showed clearly in his dark, sparkling eyes. *He knows*, she thought with a little gasp. He had been watching her all the time, he had known exactly what she was thinking . . . and he was enjoying her reaction!

Well, she was not going to let him laugh! Whatever happened tonight, whatever promises she had to make for tomorrow and the next day—and the rest of her life—D'Arcy Cameron was not going to laugh at her!

"You are right, Grandfather," she said, surprised at how steady her voice sounded. "You are far cleverer than I . . . it would never have occurred to me to use one man for the other—as a proxy, I mean. But I am sure, as you say, it is perfectly legal. And, after all, how could I hope for a more handsome stand-in?"

She punctuated the words with a low, sweeping

curtsy, aware as she did of the irony of the gesture, but knowing it would be pretty enough to fool most of the observers. She did not look at D'Arcy again, nor would she have been reassured if she had. The amusement had deepened in his eyes, mingling with an expression of admiration he made no effort to conceal. It might have weakened her resolve somewhat to realize that he was remembering a promise he had made to himself that last afternoon they were together in the garden. And thinking it might be diverting to keep it.

The stage was set quickly and efficiently for the scene so soon to be acted upon it. Dark-red velvet draperies were drawn back from the wall behind the white-flowered table, revealing an exquisitely ornate antique cross, solid gold set with semiprecious gems, the blue of lapis lazuli and the green of malachite predominating. Servants scurried forward, their faces flushed as they placed tall white candles on either side of the altar, flanking the cross. The lights dimmed slowly—Stacey did not see the footmen slipping along the edges of the room to extinguish the wall lamps, but she knew they were there—and suddenly all that remained were the high chandeliers, casting dark shadows on the floor beneath, and altar candles twinkled like golden stars in the dusk.

The priest stepped forward, accompanied by stately strains of music from the orchestra at the far side of the room. Religious music—one more clue she had missed. Why hadn't she paid more attention when the players rearranged their music at the wrong time on their stands?

The minutes that followed seemed like hours to Stacey, though in reality the ceremony was relatively short. Ivan Alexander, with a good sense of theatrics—and knowing that a standing audience would never tolerate the long, ponderous Russian rite—had persuaded the priest to leave in only the essentials, keeping the mood of the exotic service, but not its cumbersome length, and neither whispers nor shuffles marred the solemn silence. Stacey, struggling to hold her head high, was aware of only a few isolated sensations: the hypnotic glow of the candles, there on the altar, barely

a few feet away . . . the stifling warmth of the room
. . . D'Arcy's body, straight and somehow indolent
beside her . . . the smell of incense floating in the air.

It's all wrong, she thought dully, as the ceremony
drew to a close. All wrong. Even the ring she felt him
slip on her finger was wrong. A massive garnet set in a
heavy band, surrounded by pearls. Rings like that
marked engagements, not marriages. A wedding ring
was a plain circlet of gold.

Then, mercifully, it was over, and she found herself
on the dance floor again, thronged by friends and
family, all crowding around, all talking at the same
time, laughing together, with one voice blending into
the other until they sounded alike. Only then did it
occur to her, suddenly and terrifyingly, what she had
done.

She was Mrs. Errol Cameron now—Mrs. *Errol* Cameron. Only she did not know who Errol Cameron was.

She looked down to see that her youngest sister,
fully three inches shorter, had pushed past the others
and was gaping up at her, eyes wide and unexpectedly
frightened.

"Are you really married?" The words were scarcely
a whisper, yet somehow they carried over the general
din. "Are you *really* married. To him? But I thought—I
was sure—it was D'Arcy you wanted."

"Well, that shows how much *you* know, little sister." Stacey fought to keep a quiver out of her voice.
Only Zee would be tactless enough to blurt out something like that. "I married the better man . . . by far.
Grandfather had him checked out, of course—he
wouldn't let any of us wed without looking into back-
ground and character and all that—and Errol Cameron is a wonderful catch. They say that he is even
handsomer than D'Arcy. . . . And richer."

"Then it's all right?" The look that flooded the girl's
face was, surprisingly, one of relief. "This is really
what you want . . . and you are happy?"

Stacey stared down at her sister with mixed emotions, realizing for the first time that she might have
misjudged her. Zee was a frivolous little thing, but she
was not cruel . . . perhaps not even envious. She would

have teased if Stacey had backed down before—but she would not have gloated.

"Of course I am happy," she said softly. "Don't you worry about me—*never* worry about me. I am clever enough to know what I am doing—haven't you figured that out yet? I would never let anyone make me unhappy."

She managed a wan smile, but it faded the instant she turned and caught sight of D'Arcy Cameron, standing a short distance away, watching with that same sardonic amusement in eyes that suddenly seemed dark and hooded. Her blood ran cold, and all she wanted, childishly, was to hoist up her skirts and race out of the room.

Only he would laugh for sure if she did. And she had sacrificed too much to let that happen.

Excusing herself from the group, she walked over to him, head still high, though only with an act of will. Obviously he had heard what she said to Zee, and obviously he did not believe it.

"Are you scoffing at me, Mr. Cameron?" She forced a brightness she did not feel into her voice. "I think you are. But surely you don't believe I would lie to my own sister?"

If she had caught him off guard, he did not show it. "Far be it from me to call any lady a liar. And after all, what reason would you have for not telling the truth?"

"What reason, indeed!" Stacey bristled at the ego that showed in his face and manner. "Unless perhaps you think I had my eye on . . . the other brother."

"Perhaps . . . You did give me cause to hope, you know."

"Did I? What a curious thing to say. All I recall is a little flirting . . . and I flirt with everyone. I'm well known for that. Surely Grandfather must have mentioned it to you." His expression told her that Ivan had more than mentioned it, but she could see that he wasn't convinced. "He told you a great many things, didn't he—that morning in his study? Ah . . . you thought I didn't know about that."

A faintly wary look had come into his eyes, and she

realized she had surprised him. "I was listening at the
door. Not very ladylike, I admit, but then, you were
hardly gentlemanly, you or Grandfather, discussing
me behind my back like that. I heard you tell him all
about how hard it was for an Australian to find a
wife." She cast about in her mind, looking for something that would prove she had been there. "You said
there was only one suitable young lady in the neighborhood . . . and she was already taken. Does that
sound familiar? Yes, I knew all along what Grandfather had planned for tonight. I knew he was setting a
trap, and I knew it would be my choice, whether I
walked into it or not."

"And you chose to do so?" He was frankly incredu-
lous.

"In a way, yes. But then, it really wasn't much of a
choice. Grandfather was determined to marry us off in
short order. If I had turned down your brother, he
would have settled on someone else who might have
been sixty years old and ugly as sin!" She started to
walk away, then glanced back over her shoulder, almost as an afterthought. "So, you see, I really *was*
flirting with you. As I said, I love to flirt."

She did not turn back again; she did not have to.
She knew he was staring after her with somewhat less
smugness than before, and she felt a small surge of
victory. At least she had salvaged a shred of her pride.

But for what? she thought, feeling strangely empty as
she walked over to the long row of French windows
that led onto the terrace. For a life she did not want?
For marriage to a man she did not even know?

The windows were still open, and she slipped through
them, unable to bear the stifling air and well-wishers
in the ballroom a second longer. Now, when it was too
late, she kept asking herself: Why, why, *why* did I let
this happen to me? But there was no answer . . . and
it wouldn't matter if there were. What had been done
was done; she could not go back and change things
now.

The breeze had picked up, swirling cold sea air from
the base of the hill, but she was not even tempted to
leave the terrace and go back inside. In a strange way,

the biting chill was almost welcome. At least it cut into
the terrible numbness that had enveloped her before.

"Stacey . . . ?"

She glanced around apprehensively, then relaxed as
she saw Olga standing in the doorway. The light came
from behind, giving her face a Madonna-like softness
and making her blue eyes almost black.

"I saw you come out here, and I was worried. Are
you all right?"

No, Stacey longed to cry out, no, I am not all right!
I'm alone and frightened, and I don't know what to
do! But the time for pleas was over and even Olga,
who had been a surrogate mother, wiping away the
tears and healing the scrapes and scratches, could do
nothing now. It would not be fair to burden her gentle
sister with the pain she had brought on herself.

"I'm fine. I . . . I just wanted to be by myself for a
while, that's all."

"Well, if you're sure . . ." Olga sounded doubtful.

"Of course I'm sure. It's just that it's so . . . crowded
in there. And noisy. I can't hear myself think. I need a
little space—and time—to begin making plans . . . to
dream . . ."

Olga smiled, seemingly satisfied. "Very well then.
I'll leave you—for now. But call me if you need anything. Or if you want to talk."

The garden terrace seemed even colder after her
sister had gone. Stacey was shivering as she moved out
of the light, not really wanting to be alone, but not
wanting anyone else to come out and ask for explanations she was too tired to make up. Time to dream?
An odd choice of words . . . they had just slipped out.
How ironic to speak of dreams at the moment when
all her dreams were dying. But it seemed to satisfy
Olga, so perhaps it was for the best.

Funny, how easy it had been to fool everyone. Zee,
Olga . . . even D'Arcy to some extent. Everyone except herself.

Torches had been lighted on both sides of the wide
drive that curved up to the house, and a faintly shimmering golden glow spilled across the garden, giving
the sky above a warm, hazy look. Farther away, the

night was moonless and black, an inky expanse of
nothing, though the setting was so familiar, she could
almost make out details in the darkness. The gate to
the main road, massive, ornately curling, open to receive their guests. The stretch of greenery beyond.
The harbor in the distance, piers and ferry-steamers
and tall-masted ocean vessels, all nestled together in a
crystalline blue-green sea.

And somewhere among them, safely at anchor, the
ship that would carry her—where?

The name Australia meant so little now. It had
seemed such a romantic place before. She had thought
she knew all about it, where it was and what it was
like; but all she had known was a picture on the globe.
She had no idea what she was going to find when she
got there, what the land would look like . . . the
houses . . . the people . . .

Or the man she had married.

She peered into the darkness, trying to form a picture of him, but her imagination, usually so fertile,
balked at the task. What was it D'Arcy had said, that
one time she had asked about him? That he was sensible and serious . . . and decent. But "sensible" and
serious" were matters of opinion—and dear heaven,
what did "decent" mean to a man like D'Arcy Cameron?

Was he handsome? her heart longed to cry out. He
was D'Arcy's brother, after all, and looks tended to
run in families—and, oh, she was still young enough to
long for a handsome, dashing escort to take her out on
his arm. Was he fun? Did he know how to laugh and
tease the way D'Arcy did, and was he as good a
dancer? Was he warm, generous, amusing, gentle . . .
kind?

She shivered again, aware of the cold more than
ever. Kind. How strange that sounded. Kindness had
never mattered to her before; gentleness and consideration were not qualities she had looked for in a man.
But she was going so far away now. Away from the
influence of family and friends. Away even from Grandfather's domineering hand. She would belong completely, exclusively, to a man she had never met.

And she would be totally in his power.

"Oh, please," she whispered, staring out into the blackness, longing to pray but unable to, confusing somehow the God of her childhood with the gray-bearded priest who had been bought by her grandfather. . . . "Please, be gentle with me . . . and understand that I am far from home."

7

The windows of the small private salon were misted with spray, diffusing the light that filtered through until the room seemed to glow, an eerie gray-green. Stacey readjusted her weight on a hard, inadequately cushioned bench, bolted to the wall so it would be impervious to the capricious rolling of the sea, and frowned at the sketchbook propped on the table in front of her. This was the fourth pencil drawing she had started in half as many hours, and not one of them satisfied her.

She had been on board the *North Star* for eleven days now, and each day seemed longer than the last. Indeed, the minutes and hours blended so tediously, the only way she could be sure how long it had been was to look into the small leather-bound journal where she recorded the date each morning. Little else appeared on those pristine pages, for from the beginning, she had kept strictly to herself, even taking her meals in her cabin, and there was nothing to write about beyond the progress of her sketches, which would hardly have been noteworthy even if they were going well.

With a sigh, she forced her eyes back to the unpromising sketch. She must have been seven or eight that morning she had explored the attic and stumbled across the room that had been her father's studio. A wonderful clutter had been strewn all around, brushes and charcoal and drying tubes of paint, and she had been fascinated, as much by a sense of the man himself—the father she had never known—as by the implements of his craft. Excited, she had raced down the steps to her grandfather's study, pestering and pleading until he agreed, reluctantly, to let her try them for herself. She had clever hands, not truly talented, but capable, and she had quickly proved a better artist than her father, though she had been too undisciplined to follow up that initial interest with practice and so had never advanced beyond pretty sketches and watercolors.

She reached mechanically for an eraser, then changed her mind and tossed it back on the table. Drawing had never occupied her interest for more than a few hours at a time; eleven solid days of it was almost intolerable. She had made still lives of every object in the room, until she was thoroughly sick of them all, and the dogs and horses of her childhood no longer appealed. Now she was trying her hand at fantasy likenesses, conjured up from her imagination since she had no one to model for her. Only every woman she created came out hopelessly bland. And every man—like the head she was working on now—looked like D'Arcy Cameron.

Disgusted, she picked up the book and hurled it into the corner. Her body was cramped from sitting too long on the same hard bench, and she got up and paced over to the window. It was because of D'Arcy, originally, that she had decided to remain in her cabin. She was still furious with him, and she had sworn not to see him, or utter a single word to him, for the entire voyage. But the first time she stuck her head out and saw the other passengers promenading on deck—looking remarkably friendly and ready to chat—she realized he wasn't the only reason for staying inside.

How could she possibly face all those people? What is your name? one of them was sure to say, not prying, just casual conversation. Where are you from, where are you headed in Australia . . . what are you going to do when you get there?

And what was she supposed to say? I am Stacey Alexander . . . clinging stubbornly to the only name that felt like hers? And I am going to Australia to join my husband—whom I have never seen!

Oh, sweet heaven! Color flooded her cheeks at the

mere thought. She could almost see the look on those friendly faces, the curiosity and the pity . . . and hear the gossip that would go on behind her back! No, better to stay in her cabin, no matter how boring, than subject herself to humiliation on deck.

Turning away from the window, she glanced back at the sparsely appointed room. This was the owner's suite, rarely allotted to passengers—plainly the Cameron name carried some weight on vessels bound for Sydney—and it was comfortable enough, as ships' cabins went. The salon, or main room, was compact, with no movable furnishings, only benches along the walls that could be made into narrow beds if the occasion arose, and a longish table on the side adjacent to the corridor. The sleeping chamber, partially visible through a half-open door, had a double bed built into one wall, a small stand containing a basin and pitcher, and a chest of drawers, all of mahogany with polished brass trim.

It was, in fact, an attractive, if somewhat gloomy suite, and the dark, well-oiled wood provided a pleasing foil for deep-red cushions and curtains that pulled back from the windows. But she had been in it so long it seemed stifling, and she was beginning to loathe everything about it. Even Eulalia's presence, such a burden before, would have been a welcome break from the monotony.

She sat back on the bench, drawing her knees up to her chin. Poor Lalie, she had not wanted to come; even the promise that she did not have to stay in Sydney but could come back straightaway on the same boat had not comforted her. Stacey could still see her, hefting her bulk up the gangplank and down the narrow stairs, along the hallway, muttering under her breath all the time that some unspeakable fate was waiting for her in that dank, ill-lighted cabin.

In a way, she had not been wrong. The ship had barely glided out of San Francisco Bay when she became deathly seasick. The first two days, she had lain on one of the hard benches in the outer room, moaning with every breath she took, terrified she was about

to die. By the third day, she had begun to pray for it
. . . anything to put her out of her misery.

Stacey had done what she could, but she had neither
the knowledge nor the patience to deal with illness.
After a while, she had had the ailing Eulalia moved
into the small bedchamber, which had at least provided some respite. The bench-bed in the salon might
not have been comfortable, but it had given her a little
space to herself, though moaning sounds still came
through the doorway, even when it was closed, and
the smell of vomit and disinfectant never completely
left the room.

The situation had lasted almost a week when the
cabin boy—a peculiar misnomer, Stacey thought, for
the "boy," Armand, was easily fifty—came up with
the perfect solution. There was, he told Stacey, an
empty room amidships, well above the level of the
water, where the suffering woman could be made comfortable . . . and he had located a trained nurse among
the passengers to look after her. Of course, that would
leave Stacey without a chaperone, but then, she was a
married woman, and a chaperone was not technically
required.

Stacey had leapt at the opportunity, barely waiting
until Eulalia was gone to air the stale smell out of the
room and freshen it with perfume. Now, however,
alone in the suite she had thought she wanted to
herself, she half-wished the woman were back. Even
an ill, moaning companion was better than no companion at all.

The light had changed subtly, turning gold for the
few brief moments the sun was aimed directly through
the windows. The worst thing about being alone was
the time it gave her to think. At least, those last three
days before she left home had been a flurry of activity,
with rounds of lunches and teas, and fittings with the
dressmakers who were working day and night to make
up her trousseau. She had been too angry with Grandfather even to speak to him, but she had spent as
much time with her sisters as she could, sensing that
she might not see them again. She had even felt an
impulsive urge to give all the dresses she was not

taking with her to Zee, who had thanked her by promptly bursting into tears.

"I don't want you to go," she had wailed. "I *hate* your going. I want you to stay here—with us!"

"Why, Zee," Stacey had retorted, trying to laugh, "you should have been delighted to get rid of me. Just think! There'll be no one to boss you around anymore . . . or make fun of you when you're foolish."

"You could make fun of me all you want! I wouldn't care—not really. I feel . . . oh, now you're going to laugh again, but I can't help it . . . I feel like I'm losing my only sister."

"You have two other sisters," Stacey reminded her gently, "and they love you very much." But all the same, she knew what the girl meant. Mara and Olga were so much older. They would be married soon and leading lives of their own. It was going to be lonely for Zee, with only Grandfather and the servants to keep her company.

Just as it was going to be lonely for her in Australia, without her sister to badger and tease and fight with all the time.

The carriages had come a few minutes later, four of them, and they had all piled in, Stacey and her luggage and her three sisters, and even the servants, who had been given the morning off to wave good-bye at the dock. It was a bustling scene, with shouting and laughter, joined at the last minute by a fifth carriage containing the two Richards, Halifax and Meredith, come with the others to wish her well, and there had been no time, thankfully, for tears and private farewells.

Grandfather had not come with them. He had remained behind, standing alone, a strangely solitary figure at the top of the stone steps leading to the front entrance. Stacey, still stinging from the trick he had played, kept her head averted, but she had seen him out of the corner of her eye. She had not noticed then, but she did now in memory, how thin he looked, how uncharacteristically frail, with all the color drained from his face, and despite her anger, she could not help feeling sad. Could it be that he had hurt himself as much as her?

Dinner was unfashionably early on the *North Star*, and it was still light when Armand brought a tray from the kitchen. He gave her a curious look, but said nothing as he set about placing the dishes on the table. Stacey sensed he wanted to chat—there was an almost fatherly kindness in his manner toward her—but the same hesitance that kept her from speaking to the other passengers made her reticent with him, and she offered only a cool thank-you as she stood at the side of the room and waited for him to finish.

The food on board was surprisingly good, for the cook was skilled, and the owners, who charged premium rates, made every effort to keep their first-class passengers happy. Stacey had spotted a chicken coop near one of the promenades on deck, which supplied fresh eggs every day and an occasional fricassee; and plainly there were pigpens somewhere, for dinner tonight was fresh ham, prepared with a sweetened mustard glaze and quite tasty mustard potatoes. Any other time, she would have fallen on them with relish, but her mind had begun to wander again, and she had lost her appetite.

Only the coffee tasted good to her, strong, sweet coffee with a rich aroma, the kind Grandfather always insisted on at home, and she lingered over it, passing up the ginger pudding she would ordinarily have savored down to a last lick of the bowl. Armand came for the dishes and went away again, leaving a fresh pot of coffee, and she sat for a long time with her hands around the cup, feeling the warmth ooze into her fingers. They were nearing the equator now, and night fell quickly; one minute there was light in the windows; the next, it was dark, with only the glow of a single lamp illuminating the room.

She got up impulsively, wrapping a fringed China-silk shawl around her shoulders. It was just after dinner, and everyone would be inside. She could hear the sound of music coming from the passenger lounge as she threw open the door and made her way to the stairs—someone playing with more enthusiasm than skill on an old piano, slightly out of tune. It was the perfect time for a stroll without worrying about running into anyone. She was still alone, as she had been in her cabin, but at least here she did not feel confined, and the thoughts that had been closing in on her all day were not quite so oppressive.

A brilliant half-moon shimmered in a cloudless sky, and the deck was bathed in soft blue light, seeming almost brighter than the shadowy cabin. She had no trouble making her way between jumbled coils of smelly, oil-stained rope to a relatively uncluttered area where she had noticed that the passengers tended to congregate in the daytime. Now it was deserted, and silent except for an occasional soft clucking from the chicken coops, built into a low platform that doubled as a bench. Stacey wandered over to the railing and leaned against it, staring out at the sea. The night was relatively calm, with only a faint breeze stirring, and sharp-edged ripples glittered like dark glass.

If only she could stay here forever, she thought helplessly. If only time and the ship would stop and not go on to Australia. If only she did not have to meet Errol Cameron . . . and find out what kind of man he was.

Something vague and yellowish glinted on the rail, and Stacey glanced down dully, too caught up in her thoughts to be more than faintly puzzled. By the time she recognized it as lantern light and realized someone was there, it was too late to retreat.

Turning reluctantly, she found herself eye to eye with D'Arcy Cameron.

"You!" she started to say, then caught herself abruptly. She could not hope to get away from him—he had looped the lantern on the rail and his hands were free now as he leaned back, almost insolently—but she could at least preserve her dignity. Shrugging casually, as if it did not matter, she turned back to the sea . . . but not before she had caught a glimpse of his face and seen, with a tug at her heart, that he looked even handsomer than usual.

"What a delightful coincidence." His voice was light in her ear. "This is the last thing I expected tonight. I don't suppose you've been lingering here on purpose . . . on the off chance that I would wander out and join you? No—well, at least you didn't run away when you saw me. It has occurred to me, these past few days, that you might just possibly be avoiding me."

"*Avoiding* you?" Stacey looked back with exasperation. "Why, whatever gave you that idea, *Mister* Cameron? The fact that I have been cooped up in a stuffy cabin for eleven days, without coming out more than five minutes at a time? Or the fact that I have more than sufficient cause?"

"My, my . . . do I note a hint of sarcasm in those dulcet tones? And here I thought we had gotten to be such friends."

"Did you, indeed? Well, so did I. Friends and more—until you played that despicable trick on me!" She was so furious, she had forgotten to be cautious. "You knew all along that I thought you were courting me. You encouraged me to think it! And all the time, you were scheming with Grandfather—behind my back!"

"Ah." A curious look came into his eyes. "But I thought you knew all about that. Didn't you tell me you overheard us talking the morning your grandfather summoned me to his study?"

"Well . . . yes . . . of course!" She snapped the words out, a little too quickly. "I did know, but . . . that doesn't excuse the way you behaved! You are an . . . an opportunist. And a cad! You came to see me when no one else was there, you strolled with me in the garden, you coaxed me to dance—which was absolutely scandalous. You even kissed me! And all the time, you wanted me for your brother."

"You?" He had begun to laugh softly. "I forgot what an egotistical little creature you are. No, my child, I had nothing of the sort in mind. It was not *you* I wanted for my brother at all, but Mara."

"Mara?" She stared at him, stunned.

"Certainly Mara. Why does that surprise you? Mara is older, and considerably less spoiled. She was a much more suitable choice."

"Then . . . then why . . . ?"

"Your grandfather, I'm afraid, would not hear of it. Mara has always been, uh . . . malleable. It was easy to marry her off. As a matter of fact, he already had a suitor lined up. He didn't have to send her halfway around the world to a man he had never met. You, on the other hand—"

"I, on the other hand, have never been anything but trouble." Stacey was unable to keep the bitterness out of her voice. She had always thought she was her grandfather's favorite, she had taken it for granted— now she was not so sure. "He wouldn't take chances like that with Mara. But he was willing to take a chance with me."

"Not that much of a chance, really," D'Arcy said, somewhat more gently. "You weren't wrong, what you said to your sister the night of the ball. Your grandfather did check into my brother's character, very thoroughly, and he found it, I guarantee you, to be absolutely sterling. Errol has friends all over the world to vouch for him. And, incidentally—or perhaps not so incidentally—he has enough money so that neither you nor I will ever beg for alms. Nor, I might add, will you have to worry about the weight of your jewel box."

As if the weight of a jewel box mattered now, Stacey thought, resting her hands wearily on the rail. She would trade even her grandmother's diamonds to be free again. "So," she said softly, "you switched your suit to me when you couldn't get Mara. Why did you do that, I wonder."

"Actually . . ." He leaned forward; she did not look at him, but she could feel him almost against her shoulder. "It was your grandfather's idea. The thought never entered my head. I was stunned when he told me that my first offer had been unacceptable—but he was willing to entertain another." He broke off, studying her quizzically. "But surely you know all this? If, as you say, you were listening at the door—"

"I came later." She brushed aside the question, barely hearing it. "You must have finished discussing Mara by that time. But all this doesn't make you any less of a cad! If you really cared about me, if you weren't just playing games, you would have told Grandfather the truth when he brought up my name. You would have confessed your feelings and suggested yourself as a husband instead of your brother."

"Suggested *myself*?" To her consternation, he burst out laughing. "Dear girl, my character is not at all 'sterling'—and there are as many men to swear to that as there are to vouch for Errol! I assure you, Ivan Alexander would not for one minute have considered me a suitor for you."

"Then . . ." Stacey looked away, puzzled. This was not the way she had expected the conversation to go. "Then you really didn't know, when you kissed me, that I was to be your brother's wife. But still . . . *you* never planned to court me . . . you never really wanted . . ."

"Pretty Stacey . . ." His hand came to rest on hers. In spite of herself, she had to turn back. "You wrong me, you know—and yourself. I did not flirt with you to win you for my brother. I was not even thinking of him then. I flirted with you because you are charming and I wanted to. And I kissed you because I . . . wanted to."

He tightened his hold on her hand, pulling it slowly away from the rail, drawing it upward, tempting her toward him as he did.

"There is something between us, Stacey . . . I felt it the first time I saw you. You felt it too . . . you know you did. All the marriage vows in the world can't change that."

There was a low urgency in his voice, as compelling as the pressure of his hand, and Stacey felt something deep inside her respond, felt the will ebb out of her as their bodies moved closer. He was right, heaven help her: there *was* something between them, and she did not know if she was strong enough to resist.

A burst of laughter came from somewhere behind. D'Arcy turned his head, just for a second, but it was enough to break the spell. A couple was emerging from the shadows near the main lounge, so engrossed in their conversation they had not noticed anyone was there. With a stifled cry, Stacey pulled back, and clutching her skirt in both hands, the way she had wanted to at the ball, she fled as fast as she could into the darkness. She did not even care that the sound she heard was his laughter ringing in her hears.

She did not stop until she had reached the door to her room and slammed it shut behind her, leaning weakly against the solid wood as her breath came in short, painful gasps. What was she doing? What was she thinking, letting herself be drawn toward a man who had already used her so callously? If that couple had not come along when they did . . .

Shame flooded through her. She closed her eyes, trying not to think about it, but unable to forget. If that couple had not come along, she would have let him kiss her again.

And D'Arcy Cameron was not a man to stop with a kiss.

She started away from the door, then hesitated, feeling a little funny as she went back and secured the bolt. She had never locked the door before—she had never felt the need—but tonight, somehow, she did not feel safe alone.

Perhaps, after all, Grandfather had known what he was doing when he insisted on sending a chaperone. Only he should have picked one with a stronger stomach.

Grandfather . . .

She moved over to the bench under the window, feeling suddenly very tired. What, she wondered with a wry twist to her lips, would Grandfather have to say about this? She saw him again, just for an instant, the way he looked that last morning on the steps . . . a haunting picture, unsettling somehow. Had he guessed then—had he even the faintest inkling—that he was putting her in the very position he wanted to avoid?

The bench felt hard as she sank onto the thin cushion. It was not the morality of what she was doing that disturbed her. She was too young yet to have developed a rigid sense of values, and the husband to whom society told her she must be faithful was a vague figure, shadowy and unreal in her mind.

What did disturb her was this sudden unexpected reaction to a man she thought she had forgotten.

She had been so sure when she boarded the *North*

Star—it was the one thing she had not even stopped to think about—that nothing would ever make her look at D'Arcy Cameron again! But one encounter, one touch, and it was there all over again, the same smoldering physical sensation that had attracted her to him in the first place. Was this to be her fate then? Not the terrible emptiness she had feared in her life, but worse?

Was she destined to be married to one man . . . and desire his brother?

8

Stacey had more than enough time in the days that followed to brood over her feelings, for that one encounter with D'Arcy had warned her it would be foolhardy to venture out on deck, even for a few minutes in the quiet evening hours. She left her room only twice, both times at noon, when she was sure the passengers would be at lunch, and then only to check on Eulalia, who, as it turned out, was being well-cared-for by the nurse Armand had found. So well, in fact, that there was nothing for Stacey to do, and feeling unneeded and strangely restive, she left after five minutes and drifted back to her own quarters.

It was not, after all, she decided a few days later, as she sat alone in her private salon and watched the midday sun glint off hazy windows, all those conflicting emotions that were the most tormenting—or even her fears of the future. It was the terrible, monotonous boredom that made her so frustrated sometimes she wanted to scream. She could hardly believe that only a short time earlier she had longed for the journey to go on forever. Now all she wanted was to reach the port of Sydney and get off the ship, no matter what happened when she did . . . or what Errol Cameron turned out to be like.

She was still feeling restless a short time later when Armand came to collect the dishes from lunch, which had been served earlier than usual. He was dressed in a clean new outfit, not the typical sailor garb he usually wore, but white duck pants and a sporty checkered shirt.

"We'll be crossing the equator anytime now," he

told her, breaking through the reserve that usually kept them aloof. "There's a special ceremony. A 'ritual,' they all it, but in faith, it's more like a party—or a brawl! Everyone has a good time, men and passengers alike."

"It sounds like fun," Stacey said wistfully. It was bad enough, being stuck alone in that gloomy suite on an ordinary day. But to know there was a party on deck . . . !

"Well, then, why don't you come?" Armand gathered the dishes, balancing the tray on his arm. Ordinarily he would never have been so bold, but he had pretty nieces of his own, and he knew how they would have hated to miss the excitement. "Everyone is going to be there—including King Neptune."

"King Neptune?"

"You haven't heard? He lives on a nearby island with his lady. Every ship that passes, they come on board to see their children." He caught her expression and laughed. "Those who have crossed the equator before. For the others, there's an initiation into the 'family.' You must have noticed—we picked them up last night. Late in the evening, as we passed their island."

Stacey, who had seen no islands since the voyage began, and who was sure the ship had not stopped during the night, was puzzled. Then she saw the look on his face and realized it was part of the game.

"You said there was an initiation?" she asked curiously. "What kind?"

"The best kind—wild and bawdy!" He laughed again, winking this time. "But don't worry, the law forbids harassing passengers, and the captain wouldn't allow it anyway. Only the crewmen are involved—those who have never crossed the equator before, though this year . . ." He broke off, grinning. "Well, never mind. Come and see for yourself. I can promise you a rousing good hornpipe . . . and a glass or two of champagne."

It was a tempting invitation, and Stacey, who had never tasted champagne before, could not help thinking about it, even after Armand was gone. It *had* been

dull, these last days alone in the cabin, with only her
own unwelcome thoughts for company. And, oh, she
did long for the sound of laughter again, and music.

And really, what would she be risking? Armand had
said everyone was going to be there. It would be much
too crowded for more than the most superfluous chatter. And even if he wanted to, D'Arcy could hardly
get her alone in some dark, secluded corner.

She opened the door a tentative crack, listening as
the first sounds drifted down, music, or something that
passed as music, raucous and comically off-key, and
she felt the last of her resistance fade away. She had
dressed for a day alone in her cabin, in a pearl-gray
muslin skirt that fit her slender waist without a corset
and a white blouse of slightly lighter fabric, with a soft
round neck and sleeves that flowed to her wrist. Hardly
the gown for a party, but then, if she took time to
change, the festivities would be half over before she
got there. Besides, judging from the "music," it was
an occasion that was more festive than formal.

As she reached the top of the stairs, she saw that
Armand had been right. Everyone *was* there, all the
classes mingling for the first time since the *North Star*
had set sail, laughing and waving and calling out greet-
ings to each other. She felt a funny little twinge as she
stood on the sidelines, realizing for the first time how
completely her isolation had cut her off; then, forcing
the thought from her mind, she took a step forward
and began to look around. This was her one moment
of fun, and she was not going to let anything get in the
way!

Farther along the deck, amidships, she spotted an
odd assortment of men, an impromptu band which
looked as if it had been thrown together at the last
minute. Primarily sailors, she guessed, though one or
two might have been passengers joining in the fun.
Fiddles predominated—surprisingly, there were three—
and a horn of some sort, a pair of mouth organs, two
flutes, and a makeshift drum carved out of a cedar log.

The sound was loud rather than musical, but there
was a certain rhythm to it, and Stacey found her toes
tapping on the deck. Armand, who had changed from

his role as cabin boy to one of waiter, appeared at her side, smiling as he offered champagne in crystal glasses from a rough-hewn wooden tray.

Stacey hesitated. There had been champagne at her wedding, of course—and Grandfather had unbent enough to allow the girls to try it—but she had been too upset even to take a taste. Now she reached for the glass, thinking only to be sociable as she lifted it to her lips and took a cautious sip.

It was better than she had expected, sweet and wonderfully fizzy, with little bubbles teasing her nostrils, and she decided that a second sip wouldn't hurt.

She was just lowering her glass, which somehow seemed to be half-empty after only a few swallows, when a passing man paused to smile.

"Ah, our mysterious lady. We had feared you were seasick. We saw you the first day or so, then you never appeared again. . . . But you must forgive me, I'm being rude. There's so little to do on board—it's hard to keep from speculating about our fellow passengers."

In spite of herself, Stacey could not keep from smiling back. Speculation was exactly what she had feared, but it was much too nice a day to fret about anything. "I've seen you before too," she said, steering the conversation to safer ground. "On deck with your sketchbook. At least that's what it looked like. I draw myself, but I'd never dare do it so openly, where everyone could stop and look. You must be very good."

"On the contrary," he said good-humoredly, "I am very bad. That's the one nice thing about getting older— you no longer have to worry what people think."

Stacey laughed. "My father was an artist, and he was bad too. But he enjoyed it all the same. I seem to take after him—in both respects."

The man started to reply, but Stacey missed what he said, for a commotion had broken out in the stern. As she turned, she saw that King Neptune and his court had arrived.

They made a startling picture. The man was tall and angular, with long flowing robes which must once have been white, and a dark beard, lightened with some powdery stuff—flour or cornstarch, she suspected. Beside him, his "lady" was equally tall, though not nearly as slender. Her face was gaudily painted, so thick it looked like a mask, and a crown of artificial flowers circled the raven-hued wig that flowed to her waist. A pair of coconut shells had been artfully arranged at the front of her gown, pointing out, if anyone needed the clue, that "she" was not a she at all, but one of the sailors acting a part.

Laughter greeted their arrival. The "lady," a better sport than her rather stiff Neptune, acknowledged it with little mincing steps which brought forth a burst of applause.

Their entourage was equally outlandish. A dozen or so men were dressed in preposterous outfits, with badges on their breasts proclaiming them as the law, and two others carried buckets and long, wicked-looking razors. The policemen set to work at once, rooting out sailors who were encountering the equator for the first time and dragging them back, amidst protests and uproarious howls of laughter, to where the barber and his assistant had set up shop on deck.

Here, heads were smeared with a foul-smelling lather, composed—according to proclamation—of tar and grease and refuse from the pigsties, which Stacey's nose told her was very likely true! Faces were also covered, but with whitish stuff, looking suspiciously like shaving soap, and she guessed that the captain had altered the ritual slightly for the welfare of his crew. Beards were whisked off in minutes, sharp blades spilled swatches of tar-clotted hair on the deck, and the entire ritual was climaxed by buckets of cold salt water, sloshed with great energy by the rest of the crew on the screaming initiates.

Stacey was laughing so hard by this time, she had spilled the rest of her champagne, and when Armand came by with a fresh tray, she helped herself to another glass. It was colder than the last, much more refreshing, and she took a long gulp, telling herself it was better to empty it a little so it would not spill again.

"By rights they are supposed to toss all hands overboard after they are shorn," explained the man, who was still standing beside her. "So the sea can wash them off. Not a bad idea—considering that some of them smelled none too sweet *before* the ceremony. But sailors are notoriously poor swimmers. I daresay the captain didn't want to be left shorthanded."

Most of the men were wonderfully good-natured, Stacey noticed—their cries of protest were more in fun than anger. Only one seemed to take the thing badly, kicking and cursing . . . and shouting that he had crossed the equator a dozen times already and they had no business treating him like this. The captain was called to arbitrate, and he threw himself into the spirit of the game, pretending to search through the records and announcing in solemn tones that the man was new this voyage. If he had been across the equator before, there was no proof of it.

Like the others, Stacey half-believed him. Only when she caught the twinkle in his eyes did she realize that the hapless sailor was telling the truth. No doubt he was unpopular with the rest of the crew—he seemed a blustering, bullying sort—and they were taking advantage of the occasion to teach him a lesson. And plainly the captain, who ran a tight ship every other day, was not about to spoil the fun.

"A rather barbaric ceremony," a male voice said in her ear. "But with a certain raw charm, wouldn't you say?"

Stacey glanced around, thinking at first that the same man had spoken, but recognizing those familiar tones a second before she saw D'Arcy Cameron standing next to her. The man had gone—he must have slipped away while she was sipping champagne and laughing at the antics of the crew—and they were alone.

"It is amusing," she replied coolly, "if that's what you mean." She started to move away, but he stopped her.

"What are you doing?" he asked, his voice pitched just high enough to be embarrassing. "Are you planning on running away again . . . like a little child?"

Stacey forced herself to look back. "No, I am not

going to run—but I'm not going to stand here and talk with you either."

"Why not?" He reached out before she could stop him and took the glass from her hand. Signaling one of the waiters, he put the empty glass on the tray and handed her a fresh one.

A faint flush showed in her cheeks, and D'Arcy noticed that she steadied her hand as she took a sip of the bubbly liquid. So . . . she had had more than a drop or two already. It was cheap champagne, sweet and overcarbonated—the kind his brother, Errol, with his breeding and English education, always disdained— but it would appeal to a young girl.

"You don't like me then?" he said softly. "You don't find my conversation diverting?"

"It's not a question of liking . . . or not liking," she replied, taking another sip of champagne to cover her confusion. She was beginning to feel funny, light-headed, and it was hard to concentrate on what she was saying.

"What is it a question of then?" It seemed to her his eyes were flashing, dark and impudent. "Are you afraid of me?"

No, she longed to cry out—no, I am not afraid of *you*. I am afraid of myself . . . and the way I feel when you are near me. But that was the last thing she wanted him to know.

"You have no morals at all, D'Arcy Cameron," she said evenly. "And no qualms. You have played games with me more than once—and you would play them again if I let you. Yes, of course, I am afraid of you."

She did not run, as she had said she would not; she turned, very calmly and deliberately, and walked over to the rail, a little away from the rest of the revelers, yet close enough so they were still in sight. The light-headed sensation had gotten stronger now—she felt almost giddy—and she took another sip of champagne to steady herself.

She was a little surprised, as she looked down, to see that the glass was empty, and she stooped to set it on the deck. But the action made her dizzy, and she changed her mind, clutching it instead in her hand. A loud splash erupted below . . . the sailor who had crossed a dozen times before had been initiated for real this time and was thrashing in the water while a group of laughing crewmen lowered a boat to rescue him.

By the time she turned around again, D'Arcy was nowhere in sight, and she started to giggle, feeling pleased with herself as she headed for the stairs. She had handled the situation quite neatly, she thought . . . though there was no point tempting fate by staying on deck. Things might not work out as well a second time.

She felt strangely weightless, almost as if she were floating down the stairs, and the dimly lighted hallway seemed to shimmer in her eyes as she found her room and laid the champagne glass carefully on the table. Then, remembering, she went back and locked the door, double-checking to make sure the bolt had caught.

A funny sound came from the bedroom, odd and stifled, like someone muffling a laugh. More curious than alarmed, she went over to the door and peeked in.

D'Arcy Cameron was sitting on the bed.

The curtains of the small sleeping chamber had been pulled across the windows, and a subtle half-light left the room almost twilight dim. D'Arcy remained where he was for a second, then rose slowly and stepped toward her, smiling as he saw her hesitate on the threshold.

"You seem startled to find me here," he said, a teasing lightness in his tone. "Surely you didn't think I was going to be satisfied with that little exchange on deck? You wrong me, my dear, if you believe I can be so easily put off."

"But . . ." Stacey faltered, feeling suddenly awkward. What do you want of me? she had started to say—only that sounded foolish, and she wasn't sure she wanted the answer. "I mean, why—why are you here?"

His teeth flashed white as he took another step. If

she were going to run, she would have done so when she first caught sight of him.

"I told you before, there is something between us. You didn't deny it then—you could not . . . and you cannot deny it now. I am here because it is time to come to terms with the things we feel for each other."

"No . . ." Stacey caught her breath, feeling so giddy the whole room seemed to be turning around. "No, there isn't any . . . anything between us. Not like that." Why was she so light-headed? It was impossible to think when everything was whirling and he kept looking at her that way. "It was just . . . just a flirtation—that was all."

"No, that was *not* all . . . and you know it." He had moved closer, when she had not been paying attention; now his hand was on her waist, and he guided her gently toward the side of the room . . . toward the bed where he had been sitting before. He must have felt her stiffen because he stopped, but he did not take his hand away. "It was not just a flirtation. Not for me . . . or for you."

His hand had begun to move, slowly, easing up her back, fingers spreading until his thumb was resting just at the edge of her breast, much too exposed in those loose, uncorseted garments. She trembled in response, a faint rise of nipple showing beneath the soft fabric of her blouse and thin chemise.

"It was much more than flirtation," he whispered huskily. "Much . . . much more. Don't you know, minx, the effect you have on me? I wanted you the first time I saw you."

"Not enough to fight for me," Stacey reminded him, all the humiliation of that night in the ballroom flooding back. "Not enough to defy my grandfather and ask for my hand. Or refuse the very generous offer he made . . . to marry me to your own brother!"

"Ah . . ." His lips turned up, a half-smile. "And what would you have had me do?" She was weakening, and he knew it. There was longing beneath all that anger and hurt pride. "Did you want me to say no to your grandfather? To say I would not bring you back for Errol? But that wouldn't have done any good—he still wouldn't have given you to me. I would have gone off with another bride for my brother . . . and never laid eyes on you again. Is that really what you wanted? For me to sail off and never see you again?"

His voice had risen, ringing with a passion that was only half-contrived, for desire had grown more urgent now, hardening and throbbing in his groin. Taking hold of her chin, he tilted it up until she was forced to look in his eyes.

"Is that really what you wanted?"

"No-o-o . . ." Stacey tried to focus her mind, but it was too much, the champagne, the nearness of him, the way he was touching, as no man had ever touched her before—and everything seemed muddled and unclear. *Was* that why he had agreed to bring her back for his brother? Not because he was callous at all, but because he could not bear to lose her? "But even if that's true—even if you really wanted me for yourself—it's too late now. There's nothing we can do . . . no way we can be together. Have you forgotten? I am married to your brother."

"Yes," he said softly, ". . . by proxy."

"But . . . that's still binding. You heard Grandfather—he said his lawyers told him it was legal."

D'Arcy could feel her pulling back, and he tightened his hold, his arm rigid as he held her taut against him. "In America, perhaps, but laws are not always the same in a British colony. Besides, Errol didn't agree to anything in writing. He can hardly be bound by the words I spoke—if he chooses to repudiate them. He is a sensible man, as I believe I mentioned once before. If you were to go to him . . . if you pleaded with him . . ." He felt her begin to relax, and he eased his hand down her neck, taking advantage of her confusion to unfasten the little pearl buttons on the front of her blouse before she realized what he was doing. "Well . . . he might release you from your vows."

Stacey's knees felt weak, and she sank back on the bed, aware every second that D'Arcy was still beside her, his fingers teasing as he slipped the blouse slightly

off one shoulder. What was he saying then? That he
truly cared for her? That he loved her, though he had
never felt free to declare the words? That he would
marry her if he could? "Then . . . what you wanted
. . . all the time . . ."

"What I wanted all the time—what I want now—is
you."

He lowered his head, tracing a line of kisses down
her neck, along the soft bare skin of her shoulder.
Stacey could feel his hand searching for her breast,
tugging away the protective layer of muslin, cupping
slender, rounded flesh through the thin silk of her
chemise. Too bold, she thought helplessly, much too
bold—yet so tender and tantalizing, it was hard to
resist.

"We . . . we can't do this," she murmured, knowing
she should pull away, but powerless to move. "We
mustn't."

"We have to do it—now." The last word was muffled, for he had lowered his mouth to her breasts,
half-kissing, half-devouring as he freed them from their
gauzy veil. Stacey heard a tearing sound, and she
knew it was her blouse, the last buttons at her waist
resisting his assault. "I want you too much—we have
gone too far to turn back. I won't let you deny me
now."

He pulled away, not a retreat but a challenge, his
eyes heavy and hooded as he rose and stared down at
her, enjoying what he saw. Her breasts were still small,
almost childlike, but they were nicely shaped, the nipples dark and temptingly engorged. He held back for a
minute, then reached out with both hands and brushed
them lightly.

A slow shiver ran through her. Stacey felt the warmth
in her breast radiating outward, making even her toes
tingle. Her head was hopelessly fuzzy now, she could
not think—she did not even want to. All she could
feel was the longing that made her weak all over. All
she wanted was to have him draw her into his arms
again . . . kiss her the way he had kissed her once
before.

But tenderness was no longer part of his mood. Passion had advanced too far for that. There was an almost frenzied abandon in the hands that tore at his shirt, pulling it off to expose a tanned, slightly sallow chest, as naked of hair as a girl's, but hard and faintly contoured with muscle. Stacey stared, fascinated in spite of herself, as those same hands continued downward, fumbling at his belt, removing his trousers with a quick, almost angry motion.

There was no subtlety in the gesture, no consideration for innocence and lack of experience, and even before he had finished undressing, she felt her body turn cold with alarm. One minute she had been so wrapped up in new, compelling passions that she had forgotten everything else; the next, she was conscious of nothing so much as her own nakedness as she sat on the bed and looked up at this man who had suddenly become a stranger, taking off the last of his clothes.

"Oh . . . no . . ." she whispered, horrified. "No, I can't. I'm sorry, but . . . I can't. We can't. It would be wrong . . ."

Her voice trailed off as she caught sight of his eyes, dark, piercing, colder than she had ever seen.

"So . . . this is just a game. And you accused me of playing games with you. It amuses you, does it, to tease a man into declaring his feelings? To stir his passions until he no longer has any control over them, and then say 'no'—'we can't'—'it's wrong'—'I mustn't!' "

His voice had turned shrill, a deliberately cruel imitation of girlish tones. "Oh, no . . . no . . ." she whispered hoarsely. It hurt so much when he looked at her like that. She could not bear to think he might hate her. "I didn't mean it that way. I wasn't playing games. I swear. I didn't know . . . I didn't understand . . ."

"Didn't you?" His hands had begun to move again; the last of his undergarments was off now. Stacey tried not to look, but she could not keep from gaping at that part of him she knew only vaguely, from gossip in the servants' quarters. "I wonder—it seems to me young ladies know more than they like to let on. At any rate, it's all perfectly clear. If you love me, the way you say, you're going to have to prove it. You can't lead a man on, torment him with desire, and then *try* to say no."

"Try?" Stacey drew back, feeling strangely numb as he started toward her again. He was right in a way, she *had* led him on . . . though she hadn't meant to. But she had let him take scandalous liberties—she had hardly done a thing to push him back. And, oh, she would die if she lost him now!

"You heard me." He was beside her on the bed, not tender and coaxing as he had been before, but rough, demanding. "There is no way out—for you. I am going to have you this afternoon, whether you say yes or no. Only . . . it will be much pleasanter if you say yes."

He was pushing her back on the bed then, not giving her time to think or react. Her skirt was off in seconds, her petticoats with it, and he was tossing them in a heap on the floor. Stacey wanted to say something, wanted to cry out, but suddenly she was afraid. Afraid of losing him . . . afraid of the terrible violence she sensed in his manner.

"Oh, please," she whispered, "Please." But even then, she didn't know what she was pleading for. *Please don't do this to me . . .* or *please be gentle and woo me as you did before.*

He missed the yearning in her voice. "So that's how it is." He rolled on top of her and thrust a hand abruptly between her legs. "All right then. You've made your bed—let's see you lie on it." His other hand found her mouth, clenching down, half-stifling until she felt so giddy she was sure she would faint. "You didn't think I'd bring a little tease like you home to my brother, did you? You're going to learn to deliver on your promises first."

He released her mouth briefly, leaving her a second to scream, to try to get away. But it was hard to struggle when she loved him so much she would do anything to keep him. Then his mouth was where his hand had been, savage, hungry, and she knew he was going to have his way.

A wave of dizziness swept over her, worse than before, and suddenly everything seemed to be spinning . . . and a soft veil of blackness dropped over the room.

When she finally opened her eyes, the room seemed strangely dark, and she lay there for a moment, still only half-conscious, thinking dazedly that she must have slept through till evening. Then she caught sight of a ray of light spilling through the half-open doorway, and she realized the salon was bathed in afternoon brightness.

D'Arcy?

She sat up abruptly, too groggy to recall details clearly, but half-remembering he had been there with her. Only everything was quiet now—the room was empty in a way that seemed faintly ominous, though she could not figure out why. Every part of her body seemed to ache, sore and bruised, especially there between her legs, and she looked down to see that the sheets were smeared with blood.

Her blood. Shame flooded through her as memories came rushing back. D'Arcy, sitting on the edge of the bed when she got to the room . . . D'Arcy, slipping her blouse from her shoulders, touching her naked breasts with his hands and his lips . . . D'Arcy, tearing the clothes from his own body like a man possessed. She knew little about the goings-on of the marital bed— only tidbits whispered by serving girls, more to tease than inform—but even she knew enough to realize that a bride's first blood was greatly prized.

And she had just spilled hers for a man who was not her husband.

Her eyelids flickered, half-closing for a moment, as words came back, disjointed, hard to make out. Hadn't he promised to marry her . . . if she could get out of her vows to Errol? Hadn't he said he loved her? She was sure he had . . . or at least that he cared . . .

She threw back the tangled covers and tried, half-heartedly, to get up. But her head was beginning to throb and her stomach felt so queasy, she let herself drop back on the bed. Where *was* D'Arcy? If he really cared, wouldn't he be there? Wouldn't he want to

hold her in his arms and kiss her and tease her—and
tell her he loved her now more than ever?

She was just beginning to feel apprehensive when a
faint shadow blotted out the light from the doorway,
and looking up, she saw that he was there after all,
standing in the other room.

He was facing the side of the small salon, staring at
the windows, it seemed, and she had a moment to
study his face in the hazy golden light. He had dressed
and tidied his hair, probably with the brush from her
stand, for she noticed it was gone, and he looked as
neat and well-appointed as if nothing had happened.
In profile, his face lost some of its arrogance, and he
looked comfortingly weak, almost as if he were as
vulnerable as she.

This was the man she would belong to for the rest of
her life, she thought with a sudden burst of affection.
She would love him . . . and cater to him . . . and be
the best wife in the world. No more flirting with other
men, no more scheming and planning and dreams of
wild romance. The commitment was made, firm and
irrevocable—and she was his forever. There could be
no turning back.

She made a slight noise, no more than a sigh, but he
heard it, and turning, saw that she was awake, sitting
up in bed and staring out at him. His lips tightened
slightly, not altogether with pleasure, for he had hoped
to be dressed and gone before she roused herself and
the inevitable recriminations set in. Still . . .

He stepped over to the doorway and paused to look
in. She *was* a pretty little thing . . . and she did seem
to have lost some of her fight now that he had taught
her who was in charge.

His eyes drifted down to the bedsheets, and he
could not resist a faint smile. So, she had been a
virgin, after all. One could never tell, the way her
grandfather was in such a hurry to marry her off, and
he had been too preoccupied before to notice. Errol
would have liked that. He set great store by little
things like honor and purity in a woman.

"Not bad for the first time," he said lightly. "You
have a responsive body. It moves instinctively. Quite

nicely, too . . . even when you fall into a ladylike swoon. Of course, you still have a few things to learn." He let his gaze slide slowly down her body, past her breasts, her belly, resting on the dark curl of hair between her thighs. "Maybe next time . . ."

"Next time. . . ?" Stacey shuddered under the lewdness of his eyes. Only a moment before, she had been telling herself she would love him forever. Now suddenly she needed more time. "You . . . you mean . . ."

He gave a dry laugh. "Right now? Hardly." What was there about women that made them expect a man to be Hercules, performing all twelve labors in a single night. There were men who boasted of such exploits, of course, but he had always suspected it was mostly bravado. At any rate, once was enough for him. Satisfaction—and a quick good-bye. "You are quite safe . . . for now. But later, maybe tomorrow—"

"No . . ." Her voice was soft, but surprisingly steady. "No. I love you very much—if you need proof of that, you have just had it. But we cannot be together again— this way—until after we have been married."

"Married?" His brow knitted unconsciously. "What are you talking about? You are married already, or has that little fact slipped your mind? To my brother."

Stacey felt all the color drain out of her face. "But you said that . . . that he would be . . . sensible about it. You said he would release me from my vows."

"As no doubt he will . . . if you ask him." D'Arcy leaned irritably against the doorframe. Why the devil had he pulled that stupid trick? Hinting at marriage because he knew that was what her girlish ears wanted to hear. It hadn't worked anyway—he had had to force her in the end. "I suspect, however, when you think it over, you will not be quite so rash. You are hardly in a position to bargain for a new husband— now. In any case, whatever you decide, you cannot count on me to escort you to the altar again."

Stacey stared at him, stunned. There was so much finality in his words, his voice. "But you said . . . you let me believe that you cared."

"And I do care, very much. You are an adorable

little creature. But be reasonable, my dear. A man
cannot marry every adorable little creature he meets.
Anyway . . ." He eyed her coolly, hesitating for a
second. He was going to want her again before the
journey was over, but would it really be worth all the
trouble those pretty illusions were going to cause?
"Anyway, I am already spoken for. Do you recall,
that day in the study, I told your grandfather there
was one young lady of quality in our part of the
country? Her name is Maude Quinn, and she is mine."

"Y-yours?" Stacey faltered, feeling sick inside. The
one possibility that had not occurred to her. "You
mean she is your wife?"

"My fiancée," he corrected. "We have been engaged as long as I can remember. The marriage was
arranged at birth. Her birth, actually—she is four years
younger than I. The Camerons and Quinns are the
largest landowners in the area. It seemed only natural
that the families be joined . . . and desirable."

Stacey sank back into the pillows, too weak for a
moment to speak. She had loved him so much, she
had risked so much to be with him—and all the time
he was engaged to someone else.

"Then it was a lie," she said at last. "Everything
you told me. Even now . . . when you said you
cared . . ."

"No." D'Arcy stood in the doorway, his coldness
melting as he looked in at her. She was so young, after
all, sixteen, just turning seventeen. What did she know
of the ways of the world? And she *had* given him quite
unexpected pleasure that afternoon. "No, it was not a
lie. I do care, more than you want to believe right
now. But I cannot marry you because . . . because I
cannot. Someday, perhaps, you will understand."

He came over to the bed and kissed her lightly on
the forehead, then turned and moved swiftly out of
the room. The shadows seemed almost stifling as Stacey
listened to the sound of the bolt sliding back. Then the
door closed, and she was alone.

She lay back on the bed, eyes open, staring, unseeing, for a long time at the ceiling. He *had* been lying—
every bit of reason in her brain told her that. He had

only wanted to seduce her, and he had accomplished that all too well! But, oh, his eyes had been so soft, that last moment he had stood there and looked down at her. Almost as if he felt as much pain as she. As if . . .

As if he loved her.

The thought was startling, jolting the tears out of her eyes even before she could shed them. Perhaps he *did* love her. She curled her knees up, almost up to her shoulders, hugging the pillow unconsciously against her breast. What was it he had said? *I cannot marry you because*—and then there had been that funny catch in his voice—*because I cannot.*

Because a marriage had already been arranged for him? Because the Camerons and the Quinns had to be united, no matter what? *Someday you will understand*, he had said. But she understood now! He had not chosen this girl, this Maude Quinn. She had been chosen for him—when he was four years old and had no say in the matter! He was going along with it because he felt a sense of duty.

Maude Quinn. An absurd name, she thought, taking comfort in the plainness of those short, blunt syllables. Old-fashioned and downright frumpy. No doubt Maude herself was as drab as her name, thick of waist, with a round pink-cheeked face and a frizzy fringe, last year's fashion, across her forehead. The sort of girl D'Arcy Cameron would never look at twice.

Well, D'Arcy wasn't the only Cameron man to live up to the family obligations.

Stacey hugged the pillow tighter as her mind, young and resilient, dared to pick up the thread of her dreams again. Maude was closer to D'Arcy's age, true; the pairing had ben a logical choice. But she was three years older than Stacey—which made her more appropriate for Errol as well! Plainly D'Arcy's brother was not particular about whom he married, since he had allowed his brother to make the selection. And prettiness could hardly be a factor if Mara was considered first.

Let Errol marry the Quinn girl then! Family interests would be served just as well, and she and D'Arcy could follow their hearts.

It might work, she thought, pulling the covers up to hide the patch of crimson on the bed. It was a good solution, the perfect solution—if only D'Arcy could be persuaded to agree. Her head sank deeper into the pillows. She was tired now, so tired it was hard to stay awake. It *would* work . . . if she wanted to enough. If she believed in it enough.

It had to work—because there was nothing else left for her.

9

The entrance to Sydney harbor made a striking sight, viewed in the brilliant clarity of the hot Australian sun. On either side, steep sandstone cliffs rose dramatically out of the sea, tall sentinels guarding the city beyond. Stacey leaned against the railing, fascinated as the ship glided between them. To the north, she could see only barren rock, stark and awesome; on the South Head, a solitary lighthouse stood out against yellowish stone, sparkling a greeting in the shimmering light.

She turned away to steal a look at D'Arcy, tall and silent beside her. If he saw, however—if he even remembered she was there—no clue showed in his face. His eyes were fastened on the shore ahead, as if somehow he could see past the hills and water to the streets of Sydney itself.

Sighing, she rested her hands on the railing again. She had not seen D'Arcy Cameron since that afternoon in her cabin . . . the afternoon she had tried to say no and found it too late. A faint flush colored her cheeks as she recalled the shame she had felt after he was gone. It was not that she loved him any the less for what had happened, nor could she bring herself to believe he did not love her, for love was all she had to cling to. But there was something about lying there all by herself, conscious of the drying blood on the bedsheets around her, that was so humiliating she could not think about it even now.

She had fallen asleep a while after he left, but restlessly, more from the effects of the champagne than true tiredness, and when she woke again, it was dark and everything was still. Dinner was on the table in the salon, cold by that time, but with all the dishes neatly in place, and she realized that Armand had come and gone hours before. Mercifully, D'Arcy had left the inner door barely ajar, and the steward had not been able to see inside and guess the truth.

It had taken her half the night to scrub the stains out of the sheets, using water from the jug and basin on the washstand. The stewards were all male—she could hardly pull one of them aside and whisper something about "that time of month" and "a little accident" —and the mere thought that they might gossip behind her back was too embarrassing to contemplate. Only the mattress could not be cleansed, and that she managed to turn over, hoping no one would discover the traces until she was long gone and they had forgotten who she was.

In the days that followed, she did not leave her cabin even once. She dared not trust her feelings for D'Arcy—hadn't they led her astray already?—and she knew she could not chance being alone with him. The door to the suite was locked all the time, and she avoided Armand's eyes as she told him offhandedly that she thought it was a good idea—she could not imagine why it had not occurred to her before. Twice it seemed to her she heard a soft knocking sound, and once or twice she thought a hand was trying the knob, but she could not be sure.

Better not to respond, she decided as she sat alone in the small salon, trying not to think of the days that lay ahead . . . trying not to be afraid. Better to let him brood about her silence, to wonder if she was so angry she would never want to see him again. A little time away from her, a little time to remember what had gone between them, and surely he would miss her to distraction.

Not, she thought now, glancing back at his profile in the sunlight, that he looked like a man driven to distraction. All she could see in those dark, almost black eyes was a glow of barely concealed excitement. But then, he was going home after an absence of several months, and didn't a man on his way home have a right to be excited when the shores of his native land came into view?

It was not until the day before—when Armand had told her that they were due to land the next afternoon, two days ahead of schedule—that she had finally worked up the courage to try to see him. She had had so many dreams floating around in her head, so many ideas and schemes to enable them to be together, and yet she had not said a word to him! Of course, they were arriving early; it was possible there would be no one to meet them, but she could not count on that. They needed time to work things out before being engulfed by friends and well-wishers . . . before her introduction as Mrs. *Errol* Cameron was too public to retreat.

Feeling as much apprehension as excitement, she had gone to the main salon in the middle of the morning, expecting to see him with the other passengers, and not at all sure what she was going to say, though she had been rehearsing it for hours in her cabin.

To her surprise, D'Arcy was nowhere to be seen. She searched the public rooms and deck thoroughly, she even asked some of the crew, but no one knew where he was. She panicked for a moment—could it be he was deliberately avoiding her?—then realized that she knew nothing about his patterns all those long days at sea. Perhaps he, as she had done, kept to his cabin even for meals.

That seemed to be the case, for he did not appear at dinner or at any time throughout the long evening, and she was beginning to feel anxious as she went back to her suite. She had slightly better luck the next morning, for D'Arcy was already at the rail when the Sydney Heads came into view. But he had stopped at Eulalia's cabin on his way out, and the old nursemaid was beside him, effectively inhibiting conversation.

Stacey felt a little guilty as she caught sight of the faithful servant who had cared for her all her life. In the turmoil of the last few days, she had completely forgotten about Eulalia. She seemed somewhat better now, having recovered from her bouts of seasickness, and she was eating normally again, she said. But there was no trace of color in her formerly ruddy cheeks, and she had lost so much weight her clothes hung on her.

If anyone ought to have been eager to get off the ship, even for the few days it would be moored in Sydney, it should have been Eulalia. But to Stacey's surprise, she refused to set foot onshore.

"But Lalie, it would do you a world of good," Stacey protested. "Imagine, feeling the ground under your feet again—and knowing for sure your dinner will stay down!"

But the old woman remained unmoved as she turned toward the shore, a strange, dark look coming into those usually unsuperstitious features. "You won't catch the likes of me in that country. There's something evil about it, you mark my words—a hellish place. I'll have no part of it."

"Why, Lalie!" Stacey made no effort to conceal her astonishment. "Hellish? What a thing to say! It's a little hot, I'll admit, even at sea, but they say the seasons are reversed here, so it's the middle of summer even though it's barely January. And it looks quite nice. See how clear the sky is. And the sun's so bright."

"Sun or no," the woman replied stubbornly, "I'll not get off the boat. No, and I wouldn't leave you either if your grandfather hadn't insisted. It's a bad place to be—there's trouble ahead, I feel it in my bones. What he can have been thinking, sending a child like you to live among heathens, I don't know. Heaven help us, he's a strange one when the mood strikes him."

Stacey refrained from pointing out that Australia was primarily Catholic and Anglican—to Lalie that would seem as "heathen" as Russian Orthodox! She tried to tease her out of her gloomy premonitions, but the woman's mind was made up, and she left a few minutes later, refusing even to remain on deck when the ship pulled into port. By that time, it was too late for all the things Stacey had planned to say to D'Arcy, for people had begun to gather, crowding the rail, and it was impossible to be alone.

Just as well? she asked herself, wondering what on earth had made something like that pop into her head. She had to talk to D'Arcy . . . she had to tell him about the plans she was making . . . had to convince him, if necessary, that it was the right, the *only* thing to do. And yet . . .

Yet something in the way he was looking at the shore, something in his manner now, the smoldering fire in his eyes made her strangely nervous. It was as if he really *had* forgotten she was there. As if she did not matter to him at all.

Was Eulalia right? The thought sent a faint shiver down her spine. Was Australia a bad place for her to be? Was there trouble ahead?

She forced herself to laugh as she turned back to the shore, surprised to find that they were completely into the sheltered part of the harbor. What a foolish thing to think! D'Arcy did love her. He had said as much that last afternoon, if not exactly in those words. The arrangements for his marriage, which he had had to confess to her—what gentleman could do otherwise? —had been made years ago, when he was barely a baby. Once she had explained her plans to him, once she had shown him how easy it would be if only Errol could be convinced to take poor, plain Maude instead, he would be delighted and everything would be all right.

The harbor was even more spectacular now that they were past the Heads. The sun glinted off countless bays and coves, exquisitely dotted with emerald-green islets, and here and there Stacey caught tantalizing glimpses of rivers or deep arms that pushed back into hills. It was a quiet day and the hustle and bustle she had half-expected was lacking, or perhaps it was just that it was lost in the vastness of the waterway, and only a few steam ferries chugged past, belching little black puffs of smoke into a cloudless blue sky.

The city showed itself slowly, coming into focus bit by bit as the ship moved closer. Looking at it, Stacey found it even harder to take Eulalia's dire predictions seriously. It was a little like San Francisco, she thought—not quite so developed, but picturesque in

the way it huddled along the shore. The water was
dark, the pollution of too many people living too
close, and a mistlike smoke covered certain areas, but
the hills that climbed out of it were dazzling in the
sunlight. Near the harbor, everything was relatively
flat, but behind, in all directions, the earth seemed to
soar, dotted with white villas as it undulated into a
range of the most vivid blue mountains she had ever
seen. A pretty place, exotic in many ways, yet serene
somehow . . . almost welcoming.

It was midafternoon by the time they finally pulled
up to the wharf in Sydney Cove. Everyone was on deck
now, and Stacey had to cling to the railing to hold her
place as she leaned forward with the others, curious
for her first glimpse of city streets. She was a little
dismayed to see the crowd that had gathered on the
shore—obviously their early arrival had been widely
broadcast—and she found herself scanning anony-
mous faces for the one that might be Errol Cameron,
though common sense warned her he would not be
there. He had not gone to San Francisco himself,
D'Arcy had informed her, because he was too busy
tending to the affairs of the station, and he was not
planning on meeting his bride at the ship but at Cameron's Creek, nearly three days' journey out of Sydney. Even if he changed his mind and decided to
come, he would hardly have set aside the extra time to
show up two days early.

A sound of excitement ran through the crowd, a
spontaneous cheer as the deckhands eased the gangplank into place, and Stacey could hear a band playing
somewhere onshore. Handkerchiefs were out now, little flashes of white on the dock, and thousands of
hands seemed to be waving wildly back and forth.
Everything was indistinct at first, a blur of color and
motion; then slowly, individuals came into focus.

One in particular, a woman, fascinated Stacey, and
she forgot everything else for a moment as she watched.
She looked quite young, anywhere from sixteen to
twenty-five, and dark golden hair gleamed reddish in
the sun as it half-tumbled out of her coiffure onto her
shoulders. She was a tiny thing—she could have been

no more than five feet in fashionable little heels—and she was dressed in a modest gray suit, but even in that milling crowd, she stood out. There was something almost untamed about her, an aura of wildness that went with the profusion of flaming hair and keen eyes that seemed a pure cornflower blue.

She was, Stacey thought, intrigued, the most beautiful creature she had ever seen. Not beautiful in a conventional way, but with a uniqueness and spirit all her own.

She seemed to sense Stacey's gaze, for she turned that way, and just for an instant their eyes seemed to meet. Stacey raised her hand, tempted to wave, when she realized that the woman was not looking at her at all. She was looking at the tall, slim figure beside her.

Maude Quinn?

Even before she glanced over at D'Arcy, she knew he had already picked the girl out of the crowd and was watching her as if nothing else existed. So this was Maude. Not the plain, homely Maude she had imagined, but a beautiful, dazzling, utterly captivating seductress.

And judging from the look in D'Arcy's eyes, he had long since fallen under her spell.

She had lost him. Stacey knew that, suddenly and irrefutably. She had lost the treasure she had wanted so much . . . and which had never truly been within her grasp. All the time D'Arcy Cameron had been flirting with her, all the time he had pretended to care—the time he had been in her bed—he had been in love with another woman.

The next few minutes would be forever hazy in her memory. Somehow—later she would not even remember how—she managed to push through the crowd on deck to the gangplank, D'Arcy preceding to break the way. Somehow she got to the bottom, stumbling as her feet touched the ground. But it was not D'Arcy who reached out to prevent her from falling; it was one of the ship's officers stationed on the pier. D'Arcy had already gone ahead to clasp Maude Quinn in his arms.

Their reunion was so intense that Stacy felt as if she

were intruding. She could not see D'Arcy's face—he was turned away—but every naked emotion showed on Maude's pretty features. Now that she was nearer, Stacey could see that her eyes were not blue, as they seemed from a distance, but greenish, a clear sort of aquamarine, like the water in paintings of exotic tropical islands.

And what was it she saw in their depths? Not joy exactly, not excitement that her man had come home, but . . . What? Triumph? A strange emotion for a moment like that.

Stacey had no chance to ponder it, for just then Maude saw her standing there and, pulling away from D'Arcy, thrust out an impulsive hand. Her eyes had changed again, sparkling now with something that looked like mischief.

"Is *this* Errol's fiancée?" Her voice was soft but rough-edged, with much the same accent as D'Arcy. "But how unfair. You should have written, D'Arcy, to tell us she was so pretty. Errol isn't expecting such a beauty."

D'Arcy grinned. They had pulled a little away from the crowd and were headed for a long row of carriages lining the edge of the quay. "Surely you wouldn't deny me a little surprise or two. And actually, Stacey is not Errol's *fiancée*—she is his wife. They were married by proxy in San Francisco."

"His . . . wife?" Maude stopped abruptly, staring at Stacey for a long moment, guardedly, it seemed. "Well . . . you were right about one thing. You *are* full of little surprises today."

Then, before he could reply, she recovered, and her smile seemed genuine as she extended her hands.

"Welcome to the family, Stacey. I am a Cameron too, you know, or I will be soon, so I can say that. I hope that you will like Australia—I *know* you will like it—and that you will be happy here."

The words were correct, the tone just right, yet somehow Stacey sensed restraint in that greeting, and it was all she could do to murmur an awkward thank-you as she climbed into the carriage, with Maude sitting beside her and D'Arcy opposite. She felt a little pang as she looked at the handsome man she now recognized as shallow and self-absorbed, but the feeling was less a sense of lost love than a very real and unpleasant awareness of her situation. She had trusted him so much—she had gambled everything on a future with him—and he had betrayed her. Now what future did she have?

She barely sensed her surroundings as the hired carriage rattled through the unpaved streets of Sydney. All she noticed was the dust. It seemed to settle like a yellow film over everything, the buildings on the sides of the wide boulevards, the boardwalks, the horses, the sparsely planted lawns, the open carriages, even the pale lavender of her skirt, dulled within minutes to a gritty brownish-purple.

Plainly the people of Sydney were not overconcerned with sanitation, she decided, wrinkling her nose as they bounced up a steepening incline. The houses on the hillside were too close together—no provision had been made for refuse—and sewage drained into lower dwellings from those that had been built above. It must have been unbearable when the weather was not so dry and rain streamed down in torrents.

The ride was bumpy, and Stacey was aware of a dull, cramping sensation as they jolted over the unevenly rutted roads. Her period must be starting, she thought, too naive to be relieved at having been spared the worst consequences of her foolishness with D'Arcy. All she felt was a kind of vague annoyance. She had always been so regular before—she suffered so little discomfort. Now she was half a week early, and it looked like she was in for a difficult time.

She glanced only vaguely at the exterior of the hotel as the carriage turned into a wide drive bordered on both sides by well-tended gardens. Petty's Hotel, though she was unaware of it at the time, had a reputation as the finest in Sydney, the choice of French and English noblemen when they visited the city. Inside, the public rooms were tastefully appointed, with just the right amount of dark wood and brass showing that no expense had been spared. Suites had been ordered, one for D'Arcy and one that Maude and Stacey would have shared, but an apologetic clerk had to inform them that they were still occupied—the Cameron party was, after all, two days early. The best he could offer were adjoining rooms for the ladies, a separate room on another floor for the gentleman.

D'Arcy was plainly annoyed, but all his blustering accomplished nothing—apparently the Cameron name was not enough to have people evicted from suites in the best hotel in Sydney—and in the end, he had to accept what was available. Stacey was too tired, and much too discouraged, to care where she slept, and Maude, surprisingly, did not seem to mind as they were shown to rooms which turned out to be quite pleasant, if a bit small and cluttered with too many furnishings. The ladies' were on the second floor, with balconies opening onto the front and offering splendid views of the city.

Maude and D'Arcy made plans to dine in one of the most elegant restaurants in town, and though they tried to persuade Stacey to come with them, or at least Maude did, she begged off, claiming with some truth that she didn't feel well. Her cramps were worse now, and the thought of going out did not appeal to her. Besides, how could she bear to sit at a table with D'Arcy and remember how much she had once cared for him—and watch him stare into Maude Quinn's limpid turquoise eyes?

Dinner arrived shortly after seven, brought up to her room by an impeccably dressed waiter. On a tray again, she thought, staring down moodily after he had gone. Like all those lonely meals at sea.

A single pink rose in a cut-crystal vase adorned the tray, accompanied by a little note in slightly spidery handwriting saying they hoped she was feeling better. Maude's idea, no doubt—she couldn't imagine D'Arcy giving a second thought to her now, except perhaps to hope that she wasn't going to cause trouble. Probably just casual courtesy. She didn't like to think that Maude might be kind as well as beautiful. The last thing she wanted now was to be tempted to like her.

She forced herself to try a little of the dinner. There were several quite excellent slices of leg of lamb, garnished with fresh mint sauce, and a little iced cake for dessert, but she was not hungry and barely nibbled at it. Not wanting to be disturbed again, she took the tray, flower, crystal vase and all, and placed it on the floor in the hall outside her room.

It had grown quite dark by the time she finished, and all the lamps were lit. The waiter had seen to it when he left the tray, though she had protested then that she did not want so much light. Now she extinguished them, all except one; even that she turned down until there was only a faint glow of warmth in one corner.

The shadows seemed to deepen, intensifying into odd shapes and swirls, and for a moment she almost thought she could see her grandfather staring out at her from the darkness. The way he looked that last morning, she thought, when she rode off in the carriage. As if there were something he wanted to say.

"What were you trying to tell me, Grandfather?" she half-whispered into the shadows. "What are you trying to tell me now? And why, *why* did you put me in a position like this?"

Questions, she thought, suddenly feeling tired. So many questions—and no answers. She pulled off her dress and laid it, together with her corset, on one of the chairs, but she did not bother unpacking her luggage to get at her nightgown. Instead she lay on top of the covers clad only in a thin chemise. It was almost unbearably close. The night had cooled somewhat, but even with the windows open there was little relief inside, and the room felt hot and stifling.

After a while, she drifted off, but sleep came fitfully, haunted by dreams that seemed to slip away before she could grasp what they were. Only her grandfather's face kept recurring, again and again, looking strangely pinched, as if he were in pain. She could see him so clearly sometimes, she almost believed she was awake and he was there in the room beside her. She could see his beard, grown so gray in recent months . . . see his skin, gray too, deeply lined with wrinkles she had not noticed before . . . his eyes, dark and burning as he fixed them on her face.

Always, always, trying to tell her something. Only she didn't understand what it was.

It was still dark when she woke. She had no idea what time it was; she knew only that it must be late, for there was no clatter of carriage wheels on the drive or the streets outside. At first she thought it was the cramps that had awakened her. They were sharper now—it would be a relief when her period finally started—and she curled up instinctively, seeking to ease the pain. Then she heard soft noises coming from somewhere nearby, and she knew that that was what had disturbed her.

It was a moment before she realized what they were. The walls were thin, and they were coming from Maude's room, next door. The soft sound of laughter, barely held back—that was hers. . . . And the answering moan was D'Arcy's, enjoying whatever she was doing to him.

Sick at heart, Stacey lay alone in the darkness, listening. And every soft laugh, every deep moan was like the twist of a knife in her heart, destroying the last of her feelings for D'Arcy Cameron . . . forcing her to face the truth.

D'Arcy did not love her, he did not even *care*—he only wanted to use her, and like a fool she had let him. She had not come to Australia because her grandfather tricked her into it. She saw that now, all too clearly. She had not come because she was too proud to back down in front of her friends. She had come because she wanted D'Arcy. Because she hoped, against all logic, that somehow, if only she stayed with him, things would work out and they could be together.

Only they had not worked out—and they never would. She and D'Arcy would never be together.

Nor could she go home again.

She got up and walked to the window, pulling the curtain aside, standing in the moonlight in her chemise. At least it was cooler there, and no one was below to look up and see. Errol Cameron might be willing to release her from her marriage vows, as his brother had implied, but it would make no difference if he did. At last, she understood what Grandfather had been telling her with his eyes that last morning as he stood on the steps in front of the house. What he was saying tonight in her dreams.

He was ill.

It was so simple, she wondered why she had not figured it out before. He was going to die, and he knew it—and he had wanted to make sure she was settled first. She *was* his favorite; he feared for her more than any of the others. And because he feared, he had forged ahead and done the one thing that was most disastrous of all the choices he could have made.

But right or wrong, he had made it—and he would stand by it. He would not accept her at home even if Errol Cameron allowed her to go.

Her breath came in a soft sigh as she turned back to the room. Not that it would do her any good if he did. What was it D'Arcy had said, that afternoon when he left her? *You are hardly in a position to bargain for a new husband.* Better to stick to the husband she already had—one who might be inclined to keep her, even after he discovered the truth, if only to avoid the public embarrassment of disavowing his bride and sending her home.

But perhaps he didn't need to know the truth.

The lamp was still on and she went over and blew it out. There was enough moonlight to fill all but the darkest corners of the room. Her period was just beginning, the blood would be flowing in the morning. If they left Sydney tomorrow . . . if it took the better part of three days to get to the station . . . if Errol Cameron was as impetuous as his brother when it came to consummating the marriage—then she might be able to deceive him.

She wished now she knew more about the things that went on between a man and woman in the privacy of their bed. Being raised without a mother put her at a disadvantage. She did not even have knowledge of the sanitized rudiments of sex that Victorian women confessed to their daughters—and all those hints thrown out by various serving girls were far from adequate. Was there something besides blood on the sheets a bridegroom looked for on the night of his wedding?

Other clues that would tell him she was not a virgin? Something she might be able to fake if only she knew?

He was not the man she loved, of course—but love might never come to her again after the way she had been betrayed. At least he was her husband, and she would have a secure life with him. And if he was kind, perhaps it would not be so bad.

Yes . . . she just might get away with it. She went over to the bed and curled up again, clinging to her cramps now, trying to prolong them. She just might fool him into thinking she had come to him all youth and pretty innocence. If she could, things might still work out. If not . . .

She shivered, lying alone in the darkness. If not, if Errol Cameron guessed the truth—and if he hated her for it—he had the power to make her life a living hell.

II

FIRST IMPRESSIONS

10

The sun blazed down, reflecting off parched earth until the air all around felt like a furnace. Stacey reached up and brushed back a wisp of hair plastered damply on her forehead.

She had never seen anyplace so dry in her life, or totally devoid of color. The earth had been baked to a hard, cracked crust, and waving knee-high grasses were so brittle and silver-gray in places they were almost blinding. Rolling hills merged into one another until it was hard to tell where one left off and the other began, and heat rose in visible ripples, making the distant mountains shimmer like a desert mirage.

The carriage seat was narrow, much too cramped for three, and Stacey, in the middle, felt perspiration running in trickles down her neck, soaking the high collar of her rose poplin traveling dress. She stole a glance at Maude, who had been uncharacteristically silent for the last hour or so, as they approached Cameron's Creek. Pink spots showed in her cheeks, but the rest of her face was almost alarmingly pale, and Stacey wondered if the vibrancy she had sensed that first afternoon on the dock wasn't an illusion after all. Could it be, for all the vivid red-gold hair and dynamic bursts of energy, Maude Quinn was not as strong as she pretended?

It had been a long, uncomfortable journey from Sydney. Much to Stacey's relief, for she had been afraid she would have to find excuses not to linger in town, they had left most of the luggage at Petty's—it would be sent on later—and gone to the railway station shortly after breakfast. A private compartment had been found somehow for the two women, but

D'Arcy had had to share his accommodations with
three other men, and it had put him in such a foul
mood that he had been unfit company for a good part
of the two-day journey.

Not that she had minded his long, moody absences.
Stacey grimaced as she recalled the way she had felt
those few times he dropped by to chat with Maude.
She had no more illusions about him; the love she
once felt had died forever that night in Sydney as she
lay alone in her bed and listened to the sounds coming
from the next door. But the hurt was still new, and she
had curled up in a corner of the compartment, pretending to be too tired to talk as her eyes drifted shut,
or stared out the window at a landscape that grew
bleaker and bleaker with each passing mile.

The carriage from Cameron's Creek was not there
when they reached what D'Arcy and Maude called a
"town," though to Stacey's eye it was no more than a
few ramshackle buildings plopped down in no order at
all. One seemed to be a store of some kind; another,
an inn, was a low one-story building with room for
little more than the pub, which apparently was well
patronized, even in that desolate area. The sign on the
railway platform identified it as "WOMBA," a half-
name at best, for several of the letters had been oblit-
erated and never painted back in.

It was still early in the morning, barely past dawn,
and Stacey had been afraid at first that they would
have to stay the entire day, perhaps even spend the
night in a flea-infested room in the inn, for D'Arcy
had told her it was a full day's ride to the station. But
somehow a "buggy" had been produced, the word as
much as misnomer as "town," for it was little more
than a wagonette, with a single seat in front of a boxy
body and no cover to protect them from the glare.
Stacey had climbed up reluctantly, grateful for the
small ivory-handled parasol Maude had produced for
the two of them to share. Perhaps its meager shade
would compensate for the small brim on the one bonnet she had brought with her from Sydney, a pale
cream straw with violet ribbons and white birds' wings,

decidedly chic, but impractical in the merciless Australian sun.

It had not helped much. Sighing, Stacey handed the parasol back to Maude as she reached up and tried for the hundredth time to touch her hair back into place. A slight wind had picked up, gusting occasionally, but it brought no coolness, only a fine spray of sand. Her hair had begun to stiffen, even under the bonnet, and her teeth felt gritty when she ran her tongue across them.

They had reached the bed of a dry river, and D'Arcy slowed the buggy to ease it over the bank. He drove well, though recklessly, with an abandon that showed as much arrogance as skill, and Stacey watched with grudging admiration as he worked the reins, coaxing the hired horses down the steep incline.

They had passed several creeks on the way, all without a trace of water, though they must at one time have run deep, for the sides were sheer, almost perpendicular—as high as fifteen or twenty feet in places—and they had had to detour several times to find shallow crossings. This was not a stream, however; it had been a river once, so wide she had to shield her eyes with her hand to see across.

"Imagine what it looks like after a rain," Maude said, gripping the side of the buggy as they jolted over the edge. There was a little water left—stagnant pools that Maude called "billabongs," dark brown with a brown film on top—but for the most part the river bottom showed only sand dunes, loose and powdery, misting into dust at the faintest breeze. Stacey could feel the banks crumbling under the carriage wheels as they half-rolled, half-skidded to the bottom.

"I can see it must be . . . impressive," she said skeptically.

"It's so magnificent, you can hardly believe it," Maude went on. "The water flows from this bank all the way over to . . . there! See that line of willows—it marks the far shore." Her voice had taken on a new eagerness, and her face did not look so tired anymore. "You picked a terrible time to come. Summer is always too hot for newcomers, and this year has been drier than most."

Stacey, who had not picked the time at all, was hardly inclined to like the place any better for that. "You mean it isn't always like this?"

Maude laughed good-naturedly. "Sometimes it seems that way. We've been suffering from a bad drought, the worst in several years. That's why Errol couldn't go to San Francisco himself, or even meet us in Sydney. Managing a sheep station is a responsibility in the best of times. And he not only looks after Cameron's Creek, but our Mirandola as well—Father has been ill for years. Now, with the drought, he's been working day and night for months."

"But . . . how long has it been going on?" Stacey stared at brittle grasses peeking out of sandy crevices near the billabongs.

"Too long. It's a year since we've seen rain."

"A . . . year?" To Stacey, accustomed to the moisture and fog of the northern California coast, it sounded incredible. "How can anything survive for a year without water? And . . . how much longer can it continue?"

"A great deal longer," D'Arcy said gloomily, "if we're unlucky. There are places in Australia where droughts have lasted five years. When the first rains come, people go crazy, running outside in their clothes and wallowing in the mud like animals. All except the littlest children—they scream in terror because they've never seen water falling from the sky before. If Errol had any sense—"

"Those are other areas you're talking about," Maude put in firmly. "Not here. I've never known a drought to last that long. In fact, we're expecting it to break soon. I stopped by to talk to Errol before I left—I borrowed the new American buggy to go to the station—and Billy Two told me it's going to rain any day now. He's been watching the animals, he says—they're coming back, which means that rain is on the way. He's part black aborigine, you know, and aborigines know these things. It was their land before it was ours."

"He's all black, as far as I can see—and that's never given him any sense."

"Not about some things," Maude admitted. "But Fitz Blackburn said so too. There are more birds every day in the grove around his house—sometimes the cockatoos are so thick, the trees are white with them, like great flowering gums. He thinks it's a good sign."

'Fitz has been living like the blacks for so long, he's almost one himself," D'Arcy grumbled.

"Then he must know what he's talking about," Maude replied, unruffled. "Any way, you're scaring this poor child with stories about five-year droughts and babies who've never seen rain. She's going to think Australia is all gray and brown—and she'll never see anything pretty again." She turned toward Stacey, eyes alight. "The grass is going to be green, I promise—right after the next rain. And the hills will be scarlet and gold with wildflowers. Then you'll see how beautiful this country is . . . and you'll love it as much as I do."

Stacey did not reply, but doubt showed on her face as they worked their way up the far bank and emerged onto a broad landscape every bit as gray and brown as the one they had left behind. The cracks in the soil were wider here, scars gouged out of the earth, and the wind spun clouds of dust like tumbleweeds across the road.

An oddly shaped animal appeared at the edge of a nearby field, pausing and rearing on enormous haunches to stare at them. Then, turning timid, it bounded away, a grotesque creature, yet graceful too, despite the distortion of oversize rear legs. A second later, others followed—or had they been there all the time, so far away she could make out nothing but that gawky loping gait?

Kangaroos? she wondered, turning to watch their flight. They sounded so intriguing when she read about them in books. So romantic. Now all they did was remind her how strange this country could be—and how far away from home she was.

A flash of black and white showed in the sky, a bird Stacey had never seen before, dazzlingly clear for an

instant, almost pretty despite the heaviness in her heart.
Then it, too, was gone, and nothing was left but the
vast, overwhelming stillness of the bush.

Like a nightmare, she thought as she stared at the
sere, bleached land. Like a surrealistic nightmare from
which there could be no awakening.

What if the drought did not end soon, as Maude had
promised? What if it went on for five years . . . or
longer? Was this what her life was to be like? Drab
and dry, with no sparkle or color—and only an occasional glimpse of beauty, like the bird that had flickered tantalizingly for a moment, then disappeared
forever?

She closed her eyes and leaned back, trying not to
think as they found the rutted track that passed as a
road and moved on toward Cameron's Creek.

A man stood on the crest of a nearby hill, barely
visible in the heavy shadows of a small grove of euca-
lyptus as he stared down at the cart working its way
across the valley floor.

He was tall, but not straight, his broad shoulders
stooped as if it were too much bother to hold them up.
Muted shafts of light flickered through the trees, catching on hair that must once have been red-brown, but
was now liberally splashed with gray. His beard, bushy
and slightly darker, had also begun to grizzle, not
evenly like his hair, but with streaks of white that gave
him a dramatic, slightly sinister air.

He had just come out of a weathered wooden house
and was holding a mariner's spyglass in his hand, but
he made no effort to raise it, watching instead almost
idly as the party drew nearer. Behind, in a patch of
sunlight, a sturdy easel stood beside a rough-hewn
table, and a brown bottle and half-eaten sandwich
could be glimpsed amidst a jumble of artist's supplies.

The painting on the easel was still in the rough
stage, but even then striking enough to catch the eye.
It was an almost uncanny likeness of the scene below,
yet softened, tinged with a vaguely pinkish hue, as if
caught in the first light of dawn, though the sky on the
canvas was hazy blue and the sun showed clearly.

Only the subtlest incongruities stood out: a tree at one side, small, but stark, a naked gum that had been ringbarked years before and stubbornly refused to fall; a magpie in the branches, enlarged and darkened until it looked like a vulture.

A real magpie fluttered its wings, a flash of black and white as it lit on the ground in front of the easel. The motion caught the man's eye and he turned, laughing when he saw it cock its head, as if wondering at that distorted reflection of itself.

Breaking off a piece of bread, he tossed it in the air. The bird squawked greedily, catching it almost before it touched the ground, and the man turned back to the scene below. The wagon was closer now and he could make out three people on the front seat.

The woman Cameron had sent for from America? They were at least two days early, but then it was possible the ship had arrived ahead of schedule, and there was no mistaking the slant of young D'Arcy's back, or the arrogant tilt to his head, even with a slouch hat pulled forward to hide his eyes. He raised the glass and focused it curiously on the slim figure in the center.

She was pretty; he could see that even though the glass was not strong. More than pretty; there was a kind of languid elegance about her as she lifted her hands to remove that absurd little bonnet, revealing an abundance of jet-black hair. Young, too. What would Cameron have to say about that? he wondered. He would have wagered Errol was looking for someone more mature, a companion rather than a playmate. A woman to share his thoughts and worries and dreams, not the sort of decorative creature a chap liked to put on the shelf and take down every now and then when he wanted something pretty to look at.

It would be amusing to be there when he saw her for the first time. The man lowered the spyglass and took a swig from the bottle on the table. Ordinarily he didn't touch alcohol while he was working, but with this damn drought he didn't have a choice. Everyone drank beer when the rain disappeared. It wasn't as precious as fresh water, and it tasted a hell of a lot better than the swill from the billabongs in the creek.

The party had already moved past, and the man set the glass on the table. A thousand to one he'd done it on purpose, the younger one, choosing a bride he knew wouldn't suit his brother. If a man had a taste for vengeance—and if he wanted to get even with that clan—he wouldn't have to do a thing. He could just stand on his hillside and watch while they tore each other apart.

He turned back to the painting, squinting as he studied it in the changing light. Did she have spirit, he wondered, the pretty child with the black-black hair? He hoped so. He liked women with spirit, especially young ones with extraordinary, paintable faces. God knows, she was going to need it where she was going.

Perhaps, after all, it was just as well he wasn't going to be there. He hated seeing pretty things hurt.

The gate was closed when they reached it. Maude leapt down, laughing with a new lightness, as if all the exhaustion had gone out of her, and swung it open. The barest outline of a house, gray against gray fields and gray hills, showed ahead, and Stacey felt her heart beat faster. She had been so involved in the landscape around her, the bleakness that seemed to stretch on without end, she had almost forgotten what she was doing there. And that she was about to come face-to-face with the man who was her husband.

What was he like? she wondered, trying to swallow back the lump that kept rising to her throat. What did he look like, act like . . . *think* like? Always, in her fantasies, he had taken on a shadowy form, vague and featureless. He was still without features, but the shadow was larger now, and she knew the moment she had been dreading was at hand.

The road rose slightly, enough to provide a view, and Stacey felt an irrational sense of relief as she saw that the building ahead was a rough shack, large, but rambling and unpainted. Not the main residence then, but an overseer's house, perhaps a caretaker's, and they were stopping only to run some errand D'Arcy hadn't seen fit to mention. It was idiotic, feeling like this—she was only postponing the inevitable—but she couldn't help being grateful that she would not have to meet Errol Cameron for a short time anyway.

She barely looked at the house as they pulled up and D'Arcy jumped out, tossing the reins to a slim black man who came running around the corner. Her impressions were vague: high stilts raising the structure four feet or so off the ground, wide steps leading to a veranda which seemed to run around three sides, walls that were not weathered wood at all, but paint, pocked and grayed by gusting sand. The roof was generously sloping, long sheets of galvanized iron, heavily whitewashed. For protection from the sun?

Stacey frowned distractedly. Better, she thought, glancing around, to plant a few trees for shade. Come to think of it, she hadn't seen any trees since they had entered the large paddock that surrounded the house. It seemed an odd way to live, even for a caretaker.

She glanced up to see D'Arcy standing at the base of the steps, staring at her with a distinctly amused look that sent a faint shiver down her spine. He seemed to be expecting something—waiting for something—though she could not figure out what it was.

Then, suddenly, she realized, and she looked up at the house with a growing sense of horror.

Was *this* Cameron's Creek? This ungainly building, with not a trace of grace or style? Not a caretaker's shack at all, but the owner's residence? The place she was expected to live?

She felt slightly nauseated as she climbed down, but she forced herself to move normally, determined not to give D'Arcy the satisfaction of seeing how badly she had been shaken. Her expression must not have been as cool as she thought, for Maude took one look at her and said gently:

"There is another house—Glenellen. You'll see it in time . . . and like it, I think. It was built years ago for Ellen Cameron, but never finished. Not on the inside anyway."

"Unfortunately, my mother died before the decor

could be completed," D'Arcy remarked dryly. "I was six at the time, but I remember it clearly—we were very close. She used to take me on her lap and rock me on the porch on hot nights, and tell me how beautiful the new house was going to be and how happy we would be there. Even then, I knew she only lived for the hope. It was insufferable, a woman of her breeding in a place like this. I sometimes think . . ."

His voice trailed off, and Maude took over. "John Cameron never had the heart to live there after she was gone. He didn't even put covers on the furnishings. He just walked away and let the dust take over. Errol had hoped to have it refurbished for his bride, but the drought came and . . . well, there wasn't time. This is the old homestead." She glanced up at the house. "Part of it is anyhow, the central room. Everything else was added piecemeal, with no regard, I'm afraid, for architecture or order. Still, it's quite comfortable. You'll be surprised by the inside."

Stacey doubted it, but she could think of no appropriate comment as she started up the steps, struggling to keep her head high. At least D'Arcy had stepped back, making no attempt to accompany her. Once before, she had let her pride keep her from revealing her true feelings, that time with disastrous results. Now it was all she had, and she clung to it, knowing if she let go, she was going to break down and weep.

The place did look better, she had to admit as she stepped onto the polished flooring of the veranda. The sun was low in the sky, and the distant hills had taken on a warm glow, dust radiating in a halo effect around them. The porch was wider than she had expected, ten or twelve feet, and what looked like flowering vines twisted around the posts, though they had no blossoms now, only thin, dusty leaves. The roof was sloping here too, boarded on the underside and painted a glossy cream, and sofas and chairs had been scattered around, rough bent-pole creations with faded chintz cushions sagging in the center, as if much of the life of the house took place here.

"Y're back early."

The voice was sharp enough to startle Stacey, and she spun around as a middle-aged woman emerged from a door at the side of the veranda. She was squat and square-faced, with dark eyes and almost mulatto-dark skin, but her hair was light, a pale chocolate frizzed red from the sun. There was not a trace of welcome in her face or voice.

"Sorry, Mrs. Sweeney," D'Arcy said with a shrug. "The ship was early, and I couldn't persuade my pretty traveling companion to stay in Sydney another minute. No doubt she was eager to see her new home. But come, is that any way to greet the lady of the house?"

The woman ignored him, stepping out of the doorway to give Stacey a closer look. There was something incongruous in the way she moved, an animal grace that did not go with the harshness of her features.

"She's a youn'un, ain't she?" Her eyes took in Stacey without blinking. "Not what the master ordered, heh? Well, she's pretty enough—maybe he won't mind—but I wouldn't want t' be her when he gets back." She made an unpleasant sound, like a chuckle deep in her throat, and headed back to the door, not bothering to turn as she reached it. "Don't mean nothin' to me, one way or th' other," she grumbled. "S'pose I'll have to feed 'er."

Stacey could only stand and stare, dismayed, as the door swung shut and the woman was gone. Wasn't there *anything* pleasant about this place? Not even a servant willing to offer a smile of welcome?

Maude broke the uncomfortable silence with a laugh. "You'll have to excuse Mrs. Sweeney. There's no *Mr.* Sweeney incidentally—or rather there have been several in the last two years. We've learned to look the other way. She's a good housekeeper and a tolerable cook. I guess that's all one can expect nowadays. Servants are in short supply in the bush. We put up with a great deal to keep them from running out on us."

"Which they do anyway," D'Arcy said. "Usually in the middle of the night—with a piece or two of the family plate."

"Her bark is worse than her bite," Maude went on.

"Especially with strangers. Don't worry. She'll get used to you soon."

"If she stays that long."

"Oh, D'Arcy, hush!" Maude protested, but Stacey could hear laughter in her voice, and she knew she was amused.

They went in through an oversize door in the center of the veranda, Maude leading the way. Stacey followed reluctantly, not really wanting to see the inside, but not wanting to stay there and chat either. Fortunately, Errol Cameron didn't appear to be home.

There was no entry hall, and Stacey found herself immediately in a long, rather narrow room that must have served as both family parlor and formal salon. It was hard to see, for the only windows led out to the veranda, which was already dark with shadow. It took a minute, but her eyes began to adjust and details came into focus.

She was not impressed with what she saw.

The room was an awkward shape, not impossible, but one that demanded an effort in decoration, and plainly no effort had been expended. The furniture, sparse to begin with, had been lined up along the walls, with no variety or cozy conversational groupings. There was a door at the left, leading to a hall, she supposed; two others on the right, flanking a large stone fireplace. Shades had been drawn across something at the far end of the room—another window perhaps, opening onto an interior court?—and she spotted alcoves on either side, or perhaps more hallways, leading to service areas at the rear.

The floor was bare, much like the veranda, and a thin film of sand crunched under her feet as she moved. Clearly Mrs. Sweeney was not the housekeeper Maude claimed—or perhaps she didn't believe in working when there were no women around to supervise her. A straw mat must have been spread out at one time, but it was rolled up now in the corner.

"We were planning to have the carpet down when you arrived," Maude apologized. "We don't usually put it out in weather like this—the dust is impossible—

but we wanted the place to look nice the first time you saw it. Ordinarily, we use the mat over there."

"Not always the tidiest choice," D'Arcy volunteered. "Those nasty little crevices in the straw are a breeding ground for vermin."

Stacey shuddered, and Maude shot her fiancé a sharp look. "Hush!" she said again. This time there was no amusement in her voice, and surprisingly, D'Arcy obeyed, moving sulkily to the side of the room. "I'm afraid everything isn't quite as we had hoped, but at least your room is ready. It's the, uh . . . the main bedroom. Errol moved into his dressing room so I could see to it myself before I left for Sydney. It needed a woman's touch, he thought. You reach it through either of the doors there, beside the fireplace. The hall on the other side leads to the guestroom and D'Arcy's bachelor quarters"—she paused, flushing faintly—"which he won't be needing long."

Stacey nodded vaguely, only half-hearing as she looked around. The fireplace surprised her, though she knew it shouldn't. Seasons had a way of changing, even here, she supposed, and there must be nights when the warmth of a fire would be welcome. Then her eyes drifted up, catching sight of a painting that had been centered above the massive stone mantel, and for just a moment everything else vanished from her mind.

She could not imagine why she hadn't noticed it before—the shadows must have hidden it—but once seen, it dominated the room. The setting was magnificent, a sweeping silvery expanse of moon-drenched water, a lake perhaps, or the riverbed that had seemed so unnaturally dry a short time ago as they crossed. It was not the setting, however, that caught her imagination, not the ethereal glow of the water, but the single figure floating on it, a swan so shadowy it almost looked black. Serene, Stacey thought as she stared at it in fascination. Hauntingly serene, yet wild too, as if the exquisite creature were about to stretch its huge wings and soar into the air.

"Beautiful, isn't it?" Maude had stepped up from behind to look over her shoulder.

Stacey could only nod mutely. The artist, whoever he was, had created a compelling mood, breathing life into the land that had seemed so dead before. Yet there was something personal about it too . . . something that touched a deep core of wildness in her that she had not even sensed before.

"He calls it *The Silver Swan*," Maude said. "Though it's the water that's silver really—the swan, of course, is black." She stopped, laughing. "Not 'of course' at all to you. Your swans are white, I understand. Here, they're black, with white showing under their wings when they fly, and beautiful red beaks."

Stacey barely heard her chatter. "But who," she asked, absorbed, "painted it?"

"Fitzhugh Blackburn. He's a local artist. Always has been—at least since he was a young man. He must be in his fifties now. But he's much too brilliant to keep to ourselves. He's going to be very famous one day, Errol says."

Stacey nodded again, unable to tear her eyes from the painting. It *was* brilliant. Brilliant in ways she had not expected to find in that stark country . . . far beyond anything she had seen outside a museum. So brilliant, in fact, there wasn't even a trace of the envy she might have felt for a lesser work, not so far out of her grasp.

She was still caught up in the painting, studying every deft stroke, every graceful, perfectly balanced line, when she became aware of the silence behind her. Much too heavy, she realized with a sinking feeling in the pit of her stomach. Too awkward. Even before she looked around, she realized there were no longer three of them in the room.

Errol Cameron had returned.

Her first impression was one of rugged, almost crude masculinity. He seemed to fill the entire doorway. Or perhaps, she thought helplessly, it was just that the sun was coming from behind, throwing him into exaggerated silhouette.

He was the same size as his brother, equally tall, though with slightly broader shoulders, and his color-

ing looked swarthy in the shadows. But there the
resemblance ended. She could see nothing of D'Arcy's
smoothness in the man who faced her now, nothing of
the style and chic and charm that had so captivated
and stolen her heart. If anything, he looked like a
farm worker—or a common laborer! His pants fitted
nicely enough, clinging to rippling calves and muscular, well-shaped thighs, but they were hardly tailored
at all, as if he disdained the style his money entitled
him to, and his shirt, a dusty, sweat-stained homespun, was carelessly open at the neck to expose a
tangle of dark curly hair. A broad-brimmed hat dipped
low, shadowing much of his face, but she was uncomfortably aware of a broad, almost defiantly square
jaw.

He remained in the doorway for a moment, staring
at her, in no hurry it seemed. Then he took a long
stride into the room.

"What the devil is this?"

Stacey recoiled as if he had slapped her. His voice,
like everything about him, was rugged and intensely,
almost threateningly masculine. Now that she could
see him better, she was surprised to find he was quite
good-looking, not polished perhaps, but strong, with a
blatant, almost feral sensuality that was appealing in a
purely physical way. His jaw seemed even firmer than
it had at first glance, but now she noted that his lips
were wide and generously curving, as if he were used
to laughing—whether with delight or scorn, she could
not guess. His eyes seemed to draw her against her
will. Large, dark, hypnotic eyes framed by unreason-
ably long lashes. Eyes that would have seemed melting
at any other time, in any other face.

D'Arcy had taken the place the other man vacated
in the doorway. " 'This,' " he said pointedly, "is Stacey.
Or 'Anastasia,' if you prefer—though I think she pre-
fers 'Stacey.' "

Errol let his eyes linger on her for a moment, running them expertly up and down her body, taking in
every detail of her figure and dress, then cast them
back to his brother.

"I do not prefer either. What is this, D'Arcy—your idea of a joke? I believe, when I sent you to San Francisco, I gave you a list of what I was looking for."

"Quite an exact list," D'Arcy agreed sarcastically. "Like a shopping list for hardware and supplies. So many nuts and so many bolts and so many ha'penny nails. Did you really think I was going to plunk it down on a counter somewhere, get the order filled, and come home again?"

"What I thought"—there was a faintly menacing look about him now, as if he were barely holding his temper in leash—"was that, given the circumstances, you might use your judgment. I couldn't trust you to manage the station while I went there myself, as the thing should have been handled. But I thought I could trust you to follow a relatively simple set of instructions."

Stacey stared helplessly from one man to the other, sensing for the first time the friction between them. She should have realized before, from the way D'Arcy had talked—or more accurately, the way he had refrained from talking—about his brother. Now it showed clearly in the anger in both men's faces.

"Be that as it may," D'Arcy replied petulantly, "I did my best, all considered. This is the girl I found, and this is the one I brought back. So I'm afraid, dear brother, you are simply going to have to take it—or leave it."

Errol Cameron did not reply. His eyes returned to Stacey, and suddenly she felt cold inside. It was so unfair, the power this man had over her! But power it was, and all she could do was stand there and take it.

"How old are you?" he asked abruptly.

The question threw her off guard. "Sevente . . ." she started to say, then caught the look on his face. "All right, seventeen in six weeks! But I'm not a child, if that's what you're insinuating. I'm old enough to know what I'm doing."

"Are you?" His eyes took in her figure again, openly insolent this time, reminding her unpleasantly that she did *not* know what she was doing. She was on very shaky ground. "That dress, madam." He eyed her gown, such a becoming color, a deep rich rose when she had started—now it was stained with dust. "Did you think you were going to a garden party? If you really knew what you were doing, you wouldn't have chosen such a heavy fabric . . . or long sleeves with frilly trim. And that hat . . . ? Good God!"

Stacey followed his eyes to the chair where she had tossed her hat. It *was* a silly thing, wispy straw with ribbons and lace, and pathetic birds' wings sweeping out on either side. It hadn't occurred to her before that a living thing had been destroyed to adorn it, but she knew it had to him, and she sensed he despised her for it.

"I'm sorry," she said softly. And truly she was. He might be hard, he might be coarse, but fate had handed her over to him, and her life was going to be miserable if they couldn't come to some kind of terms. "I'm sorry you don't like my hat or my dress—or anything about me. But I've never been here before . . . and no one bothered to tell me what it was like. I had no idea how I was expected to dress."

"No, I suppose you didn't." His voice had softened somewhat, though not with kindness, she sensed—more like indifference. "At any rate, it hardly matters. Obviously this is a mistake . . . one that, fortunately, can be easily rectified. You may stay here tonight, of course—we will do everything we can to make you comfortable. But tomorrow my brother will find you a chaperone in town and arrange your passage home."

"Home?" Stacey stared at him numbly. Of all the dreads and anxieties, this was the one thing she had not considered—that he might ship her off even before the marriage was consummated and he discovered she was not all he had bargained for. She had counted on pride to make him keep her—foolishly, she realized now. Errol Cameron *was* proud, intensely so—she sensed that in every pore of his being—but it was a pride that was directed inward. A man like that wouldn't give a fig what other people thought! And he wouldn't hesitate to send her home if she displeased him—before or after he had bedded her!

Only home was the one place she could not go. Not after what had happened that afternoon on the ship.

Ironically, it was D'Arcy who rescued her. "I'm afraid that won't be possible. 'Rectification,' in this case, is not quite so simple. You see, you and the girl are already married. I stood in for you myself at the ceremony . . . as a proxy."

"You *what?*" Every muscle in Errol's body was tense as he whirled to face his brother. Not just anger, Stacey thought—more like shock. As if he hadn't known.

"You heard me. You were married by proxy, three days before the *North Star* left port. Old Alexander, the grandfather, wouldn't have it any other way. What the hell did you expect? That he was going to ship the girl off for your inspection, like a packet of wool on consignment?"

Errol did not make a sound. Stacey, watching, was reminded suddenly of the ring D'Arcy had slipped on her finger. The garnet that had seemed more a token of engagement than marriage.

"He is right," she said quietly, avoiding his eyes. Errol Cameron hadn't sent his brother to San Francisco to find him a wife at all. He had sent him to bring back a woman he could court! "We are married."

"So!" The word came out of his lips, an expulsion of breath. "It's all over, is that it? A *fait accompli?* You are my wife now—and like it or not, I'm stuck with you?"

Stuck with her? Stacey felt something snap inside. She was tired and frightened—she knew she had to make peace with this man—but docility had never been part of her nature, and she wasn't about to take it up now. He might have her in his power, but no one had ever treated her like that, and no one ever would!

"You may not be pleased with me, Mr. Cameron," she said tartly, "but if you think I'm any more pleased with you, you've got another think coming! I've had a long hard trip today, to say nothing of yesterday and the day before, and the whole tedious sea voyage before that! I didn't expect to come to a . . . a hovel in the middle of the ugliest country I've ever seen in my life. No, and I didn't expect to be greeted by a man who looked—and behaved—like a peasant! Why, you're . . . you're positively filthy! You look like you've been digging in the fields." She knew she was being irrational—he probably *had* been working in the fields—but she was so angry she was beyond caring. "You don't even have the manners to take off your hat in the house!"

Whatever reaction she was expecting, she did not get it. Errol raised his hand, but not to take off the hat, only to push it farther back on his forehead.

"Well," he said softly, "it has spirit after all."

"It?" Stacey glowered at him, furious, the last of her control gone with that maddening way he was looking at her. She had been wrong before. It was not defiance she sensed in his jaw. It was arrogance! " 'It' is not 'it' at all—it is either 'you' or 'she,' depending. And 'it' has much too much spirit to stand here and be looked over, as your brother so aptly put it, like a consignment of wool from a bunch of smelly sheep."

She held her head high as she spun around and went over to the door beside the fireplace, turning back just in time to forestall an answer. He looked, she was pleased to note, mildly surprised.

"As I mentioned before," she said, "I am very tired. So if you don't mind"—she spat the words out—"I'd like to go and rest."

She was shaking when she found the hall, and she had to stop, leaning against the wall for a moment before she dared look for the room Maude had mentioned before. Her knees were so weak she was sure she'd collapse if she tried to go on.

Dear heaven, it was even worse than she had imagined! Errol Cameron was not ugly, as she had feared. He was even handsome, in a crude, physical way. But he was arrogant and unfeeling—and totally self-centered! There was not a bone of kindness in his body. Or sensitivity! It had not once occurred to him to ask how *she* felt, whether she was lonely or exhausted . . . or terrified out of her mind. All his thoughts were for himself. His own needs. His own blasted *inconvenience*!

And this was the man she was married to.

She swayed weakly, pressing her hand against the wall to steady herself. This was the man with whom, "like it or not," she was going to have to spend the rest of her life.

And if there was any hope of smoothing over the rough beginning they had made—any slim prayer that he might accept her with some good grace—this was the man she was going to have to take to her bed tonight.

Stacey reached up, using the long silver handle of the hairbrush to prod a reluctant curl back into place as she stared at her reflection in the mirror. Nightfall came late in the bush, and there was still a hint of sun filtering through the window to mingle with the glow of lamplight in the room. Now that she had had time to freshen up—though the water in the large copper bathing tub had been far from "fresh": she had had to douse it with perfume before she could climb in—she was beginning to feel more like herself, and she couldn't help wondering, somewhat guiltily, if she hadn't been as unfair to Errol Cameron as he was to her.

Not that he hadn't been a boor. She laid the brush back on the dressing table with a sigh. Heaven knows, he had! But he had obviously been expecting someone older, more staid in appearance—and D'Arcy's revelation must have come as a double shock. She had had her own shock earlier, that night at the ball when her grandfather had tricked her in front of all those people, and it had left her head reeling. Mightn't Errol Cameron's head be reeling just as much now?

She stood up, taking stock of her reflection in the glass. The dress she had chosen was almost childishly simple, white book muslin with a rounded neck and dusky pink sash at the waist, hardly suited to the occasion—she had brought it from Sydney only at the last minute because it could be tucked into a corner of her valise. But the mauve silk she had planned was an elaborate affair, shirred and bustled, and recalling his reaction that afternoon, she had decided not to take any chances. At least her hair looked pretty. She had not had time to wash it, but vigorous brushing had restored the natural sheen, and she had managed to twist it into a fashionable upsweep, leaving loose ends to flow down her neck. Her only jewel was her grandmother's cameo, looking sweet and demure on a black ribbon at her throat.

If only she could have a little more time to get to know him.

She held back for a moment, knowing she should go out to the parlor, but worrying suddenly about the cramping sensations that were no longer there. In fact, she had hardly felt any bleeding since their arrival. She had contemplated, briefly, trying to delay the inevitable, pleading youth and the strangeness of the situation so he would not come to her bedroom tonight. But a delay now meant delaying for a full month. And the man she had seen that afternoon did not seem the sort who could be put off for a month.

She smiled wanly at her reflection in the mirror. Book muslin? He had thought she was too young before—now she looked like a schoolgirl off to her first party! Well, young or not, she had no choice. There was nothing more appropriate in her wardrobe, so she was going to have to settle for what she had.

And she was going to have to go out and face him.

The parlor looked slightly more inviting as she entered. There was still no carpet, but rugs were scattered here and there, adding a touch of color, and the floor had been freshly swept, though a thin layer of dust was already beginning to blow in from outside. She felt a flicker of relief as the golden lamplight revealed an empty room. But it lasted only a second, for a faint noise came from somewhere at the back and she looked up to see him coming toward her.

He seemed to see her at the same instant, for he stopped abruptly, caught in the glow of the lamp he was carrying. Stacey hesitated on the far side of the room, feeling as if her heart had ceased beating as she stood and stared at him.

He hardly seemed the same man she had seen earlier. He had washed and changed into slightly more formal attire, black trousers again, but silk worsted this time, and superbly cut; and a loose white shirt with a pearl-gray ascot tucked into the collar accented skin that seemed more tanned than swarthy. He was even better-looking now, but still unconventional; black hair, curling too much for fashion, fell loosely to the nape of his neck, and she could not help noticing that that strong, defiant chin had a softening cleft in the center. The same magnetism was there, the potent physical appeal she had sensed before, as disconcerting as ever, though somehow not quite so objectionable now.

He seemed to sense her thoughts, for his lips twitched, just slightly at the corners as he stepped forward and set the lamp on a polished cedar side table. His eyes were playing with her again, running all the way down her figure with slow deliberation, then all the way up again, but this time there was no disapproval in them.

"Very lovely," he said softly. "And quite unexpected. I must say, I didn't know you were going to look like this."

Stacey tried to stay cool, but it was hard not to enjoy the flattery in his eyes. "Actually, I was about to say the same thing about you."

"What? No more filthy, common peasant?"

"Oh . . ." She could feel the color rising to her cheeks. "I . . . I'm sorry about that. It was a terrible thing to say. It's just that . . . well, I was angry and hurt, and it slipped out. I do, truly, apologize."

"Don't." His voice was gentler than she remembered, but still deep and distinctly masculine. "You had every right to be angry. If anyone ought to apologize, it's I. But I've always said that apologies are a waste of breath . . . and usually much too late. We got off to a very bad start—you and I. Shall we begin again?" He took a step backward, bowing slightly as he held out his hand. "How do you do? I am Errol Cameron, and I am delighted to meet you."

There was something disarming, almost boyish, about him, and she could not keep from smiling. "How do you do? I am Stacey Alex— " She broke off, giggling. "I am Stacey *Cameron*—and I think we have something in common." She laid her hand in his, expecting him to shake it firmly, like an American. Instead, he bent over, holding it for just an instant, lightly against his lips.

The gesture sent a quiver through her, as unexpected as it was involuntary, and Stacey realized once again the sheer physical force that this man exerted. The feeling confused and alarmed her. Legally, he was her husband, morally as well, she supposed, but she had just met him, and it seemed wanton somehow, responding with such fervor to the lightest brush of his lips on her hand. She had been so sure she would never fall in love, would never *care* for anyone again, and now with one smile, one touch, he had made her feel more like a woman than D'Arcy ever had with all his charm and easy compliments.

She went over to the hearth, staring at the painting to cover her confusion. It was funny, art usually changed in different light, but with this painting, color and mood remained the same. By the time she composed herself enough to turn, he was standing with his back to her, and a little popping sound told her he had opened a bottle of champagne.

"A small token to take away the bad taste of that very rude greeting—and offer a belated welcome." He poured the frothy liquid into a pair of glasses, then extended one to her. "I should have inquired, perhaps, if you drink?"

"To be honest," she said, laughing as she accepted it, "I've only held a champagne glass in my hands once—with disastrous results. No, that's not quite true. I did *hold* one before, but I didn't take a sip. It was at my . . . our wedding."

She expected a sharp response, but he only grinned. "Was it a good wedding?" he asked easily. "Would I have enjoyed it?"

"I don't know," she confessed. "I was in a daze the whole time. Grandfather had sprung it on me unexpectedly—I hadn't been aware of a thing beforehand—and I was so bewildered, I hardly knew what was happening." She took a taste of the champagne. It was quite tart, not at all like last time, and though she sensed it was better, she did not like it as much. "So you see, I'm hardly the person to ask."

"Perhaps—but you're the only one I *can* ask."

Except for your brother, she thought bitterly. But

the last thing she wanted now was to bring D'Arcy's name into the conversation. It had been so pleasant, these past minutes with Errol, she had almost forgotten there were other, darker things between them. She took another slow sip from the glass and tried to look casual as she wandered over to the painting again.

"That's quite a nice work. I was admiring it before."

If Errol noticed the abrupt way she had changed the subject, he was tactful enough not to mention it. "Yes, I saw you looking at it this afternoon." He sauntered over to join her. "Though I had too much on my mind to mention it at the time. It is unique, isn't it?"

"Yes. I've never seen anything like it before. Maybe a little Corot in the natural way the artist handles the trees on the bank . . . but even that's pushing. The treatment of color and light is exceptional."

"You know art." Stacey could almost see him revising his opinion of her, deciding she wasn't the bubblehead he had thought. "You must visit some of our galleries, in Sydney perhaps. I think you would enjoy John Glover's landscapes—he has a way of making even our harsh countryside idyllic—or Conrad Martens, particularly the harbor scenes. There isn't a great body of Australian art as yet, but much of what we do have is quite fine."

"So I see—if this is an example."

"Fitzhugh Blackburn is one of the best," Errol agreed. "He has done some extraordinary work, though this, I must confess, is my favorite."

"I think I might have guessed." Stacey smiled. "You do have it hanging in the most predominant spot in your home."

Errol laughed. "Purely by coincidence. The only reason I have this particular painting is that Fitz allowed me to take it, and the only reason it's hanging over the mantle is that that's where he decided it should be. He has his own very emphatic feelings about which of his works should go where—and when. That's why you won't see them hanging in any of the museums. He doesn't want them there. The world is simply going to have to wait to admire him posthumously."

Stacey stared at the painting, her curiosity piqued. "What is he like? This Fitz Blackburn?"

"As a man, you mean?" Errol gave her a sharp look, then seemed to shrug as he turned back to the painting. "It's hard to say—and really, does it matter? With someone like that, in a way, the art *is* the man. Certainly it will be remembered after the petty details of his life are forgotten."

"Perhaps." Stacey did not try to argue. She had sensed something closed and hard in his voice just now, though clearly he admired the artist's work. It occurred to her that there were depths to this man she could only guess at, and it would be wiser not to press him until she had had time to figure them out. "I don't think I've ever seen anything more graceful on canvas, or quite so haunting. I can see now why he calls it *The 'Silver' Swan*—the color dominates, echoing out of the water until it seems to be absorbed into the black. I'd love to see the model someday, if there is one."

"Oh, there is." He smiled. "We even call her the Silver Swan now, after the painting, though she used to be the Wild Swan. She comes back season after season to the stream at the base of the hill . . . when times are good, that is. She's been gone almost a year now, since the drought began. But she'll be back. She always is. Soon, I hope."

Stacey could not help echoing the feeling as her eyes lingered on the graceful creature on the moonlit waters. If there was any truth in the painting, and she sensed there was, then there had to be more to Australia than the barren ugliness she had glimpsed that morning, and she found herself longing to see it.

"You know . . ." Errol's voice was thoughtful as he broke into the silence, "she reminds me a little of you."

"Me?" Stacey looked up to see that he was studying her with an unsettling intentness.

"There's a kind of elegance about you—I noticed it this afternoon even in that silly dress with the high neck and puffy sleeves that made your arms look like watermelons." He raised his hand, warding off her protests. "I see it even more tonight. That's a very becoming dress, you know—ladies with long, graceful necks should never wear high collars. And with your dark hair and those stunning silver eyes—yes, you are very much like the swan."

Stacey recalled suddenly the way she had felt before, that affinity for the wildness in the painting, and she wondered if he wasn't right in ways he had not even guessed at. . . . Or perhaps he had.

"I believe you're teasing me," she said softly. "And that's not fair. I don't know yet how to take it."

He smiled as he took the glass from her hand and set it on the table. "I think a sip or two is sufficient. I have a bottle of wine picked out for dinner. A pleasant little Riesling. It's much sweeter—I suspect you will like it better."

Stacey sensed he was teasing again, but this time she did not protest. His hand was still light as he placed it on her arm, leading her toward what she assumed was the dining room, but once again, tremors of response were running through her body, and she felt a kind of wariness she had not expected. Before, she had been so afraid she was not going to like him, not going to be able to bear the thought of his touching her. Now she was terrified she was going to like his touch too much. She had left herself vulnerable once, and she had paid for it dearly. She did not want to open herself to that kind of hurt again.

She caught a glimpse of the dining room as they passed, looking large and rather uncomfortably formal. But Errol was already guiding her toward the place where a table had been set on the side veranda. It was dark now, and candles cast a flickering circle, highlighting creamy damask and ornate silver flatware and delicate, translucent china edged in gold.

Stacey was so surprised, all she could do was stare while Errol pulled her chair out.

"I didn't expect this," she said, finding her voice at last. There was even a centerpiece, a black japanned tray with glasses of some sort forming a backdrop for the subtle hues of artfully arranged dried flowers. She couldn't imagine that Mrs. Sweeney's talents ran to floral displays, but it hardly seemed likely Errol had done it himself.

"We are not totally crude." He grinned. "It only seems like it at times. As a matter of fact, that's one of the more whimsical aspects of life in the bush. We lead, of necessity, a rather basic existence, but we like to pretend we're back 'home' in jolly old England—with all the refinement of tea on the terrace and Milford the butler serving."

Stacey giggled. "Madden."

"What?"

"Madden—he's the butler back home. Only we had tea in the parlor. And believe me, it's just as silly—and pretentious—in San Francisco."

Laughter broke whatever awkwardness was still between them, and to Stacey's surprise, dinner was a comfortable meal. A buffet had been set up along the wall, and they helped themselves to vegetable broth from an elaborate tureen, and coarse wheat bread made more appetizing by a generous portion of rich, smoky Devonshire cream. Errol proved a considerate host, regaling her with stories about the countryside and giving her a lesson in history as well, which proved not dry at all, as she might have expected, but quite fascinating. His family, it seemed, were among the first settlers, for his great-grandfather, Harry Cameron, had come over with the First Fleet in 1789.

"There are two kinds of people in Australia," he explained. "The 'legitimates' and the 'illegitimates.' My ancestors are definitely among the legitimates, which means they had legal reasons for being here."

Stacey wrinkled her brow. That seemed an odd way to put it. "You mean they entered the country legally? As immigrants?"

"Emigrants," he corrected. " 'Immigrant' is an American word. And no, that's not quite what I had in mind. Legality has nothing to do with emigration. It's not restricted here—for whites. The Chinese, poor devils, don't stand a chance. Old Harry had a much more basic 'legal' reason, he came at the request of a judge. The First Fleet was a convict transport. He had been sent up on charges of pickpocketing and murder—

and was guilty on both counts, no doubt! He was lucky to escape the hangman."

He was watching her as he spoke, and Stacey had the feeling he half-expected her to be shocked. "Lucky for you, too," she said dryly. "Or had your next ancestor down the line already been born?"

"No. Old Harry settled down late. He married— and I use the term loosely—an Irish aborigine servant girl. My grandfather was their only surviving child. He was known as Black Mick, and not just for his charac- ter either—the aborigine blood showed quite clearly then. He wasn't so lucky, incidentally. He tried to strike it rich in the Gold Rush. When that didn't work out, he found a quicker way to come up with his ore—bushranging." Seeing her puzzled look, he added, "Our term for highway robbery. Quite literally, he put on a mask and robbed coaches on the highway . . . only he had the misfortune to pick a high government official with a taste for vengeance. So it was he and not Old Harry who kept the Cameron date with the hangman."

Stacey found herself laughing. Now she knew he was trying to shock her. "He sounds a little like my grandfather."

"Who? Harry or Black Mick?"

"Both," she conceded. "There's a little of the 'bush- ranger' in my grandfather, that's for sure. He ran away with my grandmother when he was a soldier and she was the commandant's daughter, and he financed their elopement with the candlesticks from the church! But I was thinking more of Old Harry. Grandfather is too shrewd to get caught."

Errol pushed back his chair, refusing to let her help as he cleared the dishes and brought back a plate of rabbit stew deliciously scented with herbs. With it came a salad of some green she did not recognize.

"It sounds like they would have been a match for each other," he said. "Old Harry and your grandfather."

Stacey had to smile. "Yes, I think they would."

The conversation dwindled as they attacked the stew, Stacey finding that she was much hungrier than she had realized. She was none too sure about the salad—it had a strange tang, slightly hot, as she took an experimental taste of it—but the rabbit was superb, cooked to succulent perfection and seasoned just right.

"This is really excellent," she said as she swallowed another tasty morsel. She was feeling comfortable enough now to lap up the liquid with a crust of bread. Maude seemed to have been wrong about the housekeeper on both counts. "I thought Mrs. Sweeney was just a passable cook."

Errol looked amused. "She is—and that's a generous way of putting it. But I thank you for the compliment. I prepared the meal myself."

Stacey was so startled she dropped her fork onto her plate. "You prepared it? Yourself?"

He laughed aloud at the expression on her face. "Men learn to cook in the bush. Especially simple stews that can be prepared over a campfire when it comes time to move a mob of sheep. Or perhaps you think only women can master a pot and a stove."

"No, it's not that . . . exactly." Stacey faltered, trying to explain. "It's just that you seem such a . . . a contradiction. You've been so thoughtful tonight, seeing to it that I got a good meal, on damask and real china—and I have a feeling you *did* arrange the flowers too. It's hard to reconcile the man who did all that with the man I met this afternoon."

"I thought," he said ruefully, "that I had made up for that."

"You have. It's just that . . . well, it's hard to figure you out. Who are you really? The sophisticated man sitting across from me now, or"—she paused, daring to smile—"the common filthy peasant?"

To her relief, he did not seem offended. "Neither," he said easily. "And both. I do have a veneer of sophistication. My mother was an Englishwoman, and I was educated at 'home.' I polished my manners at Oxford. But I'm still a farmer. I run a sheep station, I work with my hands and my body, and I've been known to come in a good deal filthier than this afternoon. And I do have a short fuse when it comes to patience."

"But . . . ." Stacey leaned back in her chair, studying

him in light that made strong features even stronger, more masculine. "Whichever you are, gentleman or farmer, I can't understand why you felt the need to send all the way to America for a wife. Surely you could have found one here. Unless of course it's because . . ."

"Because of my rather dubious pedigree?" He filled in the words she had been reluctant to say. "Criminals and serving girls and a taint of bastardy—yes, and mixed blood to boot! Anywhere else I daresay you'd be right. But here . . . ? Shake an Australian family tree, and it'd be rare if a convict or two didn't tumble out. As for black blood—well, we don't talk about it, but that's not unusual either, given the circumstances of our founding. Aristocracy *is* important here—breeding and lineage count. But there is a new aristocracy, too, based on money. And I have enough of that to buy my way into the most snobbish family in the colony."

"Then . . ." Stacey hesitated again, more confused than ever. "Why *did* you send for me? Or someone like me?"

Errol did not answer at once, but cleared the table, offering a platter of fruit and tinned biscuits, which Stacey refused. She had already had more than enough, and she was curious to hear what he was going to say.

"That's not an easy question." He sat down again, playing with his wineglass, but not, she noticed, helping himself to fruit. "There are, of course, no suitable young ladies in the vicinity—except Maude." He seemed to hesitate, just slightly, as he uttered her name. "But she was promised to D'Arcy the day she was born. I must have been thirteen or fourteen then; I remember it distinctly. He has always grown up with the assumption that one day they were going to be married. I wouldn't take that away from him . . . even if I could."

"Yes, but there must have been suitable young ladies in Sydney."

"A few," he conceded. "But not ladies I wanted. The daughters of wealthy men are too pampered to live in the bush. And pretty little servants tend to get married about sixteen"—a flicker of irony crossed his face—"which is much too young for me. Besides, if I'm going to be honest, I don't particularly enjoy going to Sydney. The social scene there holds little appeal for me. Or in San Francisco, for that matter. I think I was a little relieved when the drought lingered and it was impossible to go myself."

"So you sent your brother instead."

She was totally unprepared for his reaction. He shoved his chair back and went over to the rail, tensing one hand into a fist, as if he wanted to smash it against the post. "Yes, I sent my brother, and by God . . . !" He turned, controlling his anger with effort. "I mean no offense by this, but D'Arcy was given specific directions. A shopping list, as he so crudely put it, but that was not far from the mark. He knew precisely what I wanted—and you were not it."

No, and he hadn't expected the commitment to be made before he had a chance to meet her, Stacey recalled uncomfortably. D'Arcy *had* behaved badly. And yet . . .

"You aren't being quite fair, you know," she said quietly. "To your brother."

His face darkened, and he gave her a long, searching look. Almost, she thought, puzzled, the way he had looked when she asked what Fitzhugh Blackburn was like as a man.

"What do you mean?" he said guardedly.

Stacey swallowed. "Just that you set him an impossible task. There aren't many families in San Francisco that would allow a young lady of quality to journey halfway around the world to marry a man they had never laid eyes on. If my grandfather hadn't been so headstrong, I wouldn't be here myself."

His hand unclenched, and she could see him relax as he leaned back against the rail. "Ah, but you see, I wasn't looking for a lady of 'quality.' I would have been happy with a shopkeeper's daughter. Or a capable little seamstress."

Stacey stared down at her hands, pale and perfectly manicured. He had said the daughters of wealthy men in Sydney were too pampered. Could a young lady of quality from San Francisco be any better? "I can cook," she said awkwardly. "A little. I spent time in the kitchen when I was growing up, and I saw what was going on. I even helped until I got too old for it to be proper. I am not quite as useless as I look."

"I don't need a cook." His eyes seemed even darker as he came over to the table and looked down at her. "Or a laundress or a house cleaner or a seamstress. What I need is a wife."

Stacey felt almost naked under the scrutiny of those intense eyes. "I don't suppose your list to your brother included piano playing or passable French."

"Not exactly. The requirements I had in mind were more basic. Like character. And maturity."

"Not . . . looks?"

"No." He was still staring down at her, studying her in ways that made her blood run warm. "No, beauty was the last thing I had in mind . . . then."

They seemed to bore through her, those dark, dark eyes. Stacey had never been so aware of anyone in her life as she was of this intensely physical man. For a minute she was sure he was going to lean over and kiss her—and she did not know if the thought excited or frightened her. But then he broke the mood, reaching for a bottle of sherry on the sideboard and casually offering a glass.

Stacey refused. She had consumed almost a whole glass of wine, and remembering her last encounter with alcohol, she decided to abstain. Her head was already spinning, and she had the feeling she was going to need all her faculties tonight. Errol did not press, but poured a glass of brandy for himself and went back to stand at the rail, staring out into darkness that had begun to look deep and very mysterious.

After a moment, Stacey went over to join him. A faint breeze had picked up—she could barely feel it, a whisper against her skin—and the pungent aroma of tobacco drifted in from somewhere nearby, mixing with the smell of dried grasses and farm animals and dust. Horse bells jangled faintly in the paddocks. Frogs were croaking in mudholes in the creek that ran behind the house, and far away, wild dogs had begun to howl, an eerie, dismal sound like children wailing in the night.

Errol took her arm and eased her around until she was facing him. "We have talked of everything," he said gently, "except the one thing that matters. Don't you think it's time?"

"It's . . . time?" Stacey was aware that she was parroting the words, but suddenly she felt afraid. As afraid of the way her heart had begun to flutter as anything he could say.

"I realize you came here in good faith, and I respect you for that. But I didn't know when I sent D'Arcy to San Francisco that he was going to make an irreversible contract in my name. And you admitted yourself you were in too much of a daze the day of the wedding to understand what was going on. It's not too late to back down."

Stacey felt a tightness in her throat. She was still afraid, but she did not know of what. "I . . . I'm not sure what you mean."

"What I am trying to say is that I will not hold you to vows you were coerced to make. If you are sorry . . . if Australia is not what you expected . . . if *I* am not what you expected, I will send you home, with no shame to you. You do not have to be trapped in this marriage if you do not want to stay."

Stacey drew in a deep breath. The words she had prayed for on that terrible night in Sydney when she lay awake and longed for home. Only she knew now that she could not go back. And standing there in the sultry night, feeling the nearness of him beside her, the new and conflicting emotions, she was not certain she wanted to.

"You are very generous," she said. "But you don't know my grandfather. Once he has made up his mind, that's all there is to it. If you send me home, he's perfectly capable of putting me on the next ship and bundling me back again. But I don't feel trapped in this marriage, and I do want to stay."

"You are sure?"

She hesitated, willing the words to come out. "Yes, I am sure. I told you before, I know what I am doing."

"Well, then . . ." He raised his hand slowly, running his fingers down her cheek, a subtle touch again—why did it feel as if her skin were on fire? "I will make you one more offer. I know this must all seem strange to you—I am still strange. We have had so little time with each other, and you are very young. I will not come to your bed tonight if you are hesitant . . . or frightened."

Oh, if only she could accept. Stacey clung to the thought longingly. She *was* frightened, though not for any of the reasons she had expected. She was not physically averse to him; quite the contrary, she was attracted—much too attracted. He had already gotten a terrifying hold over her, and in only a few short hours. She trembled to think what was going to happen when she lay in his arms. Perhaps . . .

"You would be willing to . . . to do that for me?"

"I would be willing." His hand was still on her cheek, not demanding in any way she could recognize, but so compelling she could not think of anything else. "You are a beautiful woman, and I won't pretend I don't desire you. I am a man—I have a man's wants and a man's needs—and, God help me, if I had my way I'd take you right here on the ground, like the common peasant you thought I was. But if it would be better, if it would make things easier for you, I can wait . . . for a few more nights."

Stacey did not fail to catch the subtle inflection of his voice. He would wait a *few* nights. But not a month . . . never a month.

"No," she said, so softly she could barely hear her own voice. "No, it would not be better that way . . . and I am not afraid. I am ready to be your wife . . . tonight."

12

Stacey resisted the temptation to get up and look in the mirror one last time. Errol had not come with her to her room, as she had half-assumed he would, but left her on the veranda, promising with faintly veiled sensuality that he would join her as soon as she was ready.

She had been grateful at the time, sensing the embarrassment she would feel if she had to undress in front of him—or worse yet, stand there while strong, capable hands did the job for her! But now, lounging self-consciously on the bed, with pillows propped up behind her and freshly brushed hair spilling jet black over her shoulders, she almost wished he had been more impetuous. Nothing could have been more awkward than waiting for a knock to sound on the door . . . and not knowing how she was going to react when it did.

But the knock never came.

All Stacey heard was a faint noise as the knob turned; then the door slid inward and Errol was there, standing on the threshold. He had changed out of his clothes and was wearing a dark blue dressing gown of some soft fabric that molded itself over his strong, lean body, giving the distinctly unsettling impression that he had nothing on underneath. The sheer sense of him, the dark hair tumbling onto his forehead, the sun-bronzed skin, the way he was looking at her, made her heart stop for a moment, and she realized suddenly that what she had taken for fear a second before, when the door swung open, was in reality anticipation.

She had expected to feel only hesitancy at that moment, expected the welcoming half-smile on her lips to be forced and stilted, more duty than anything else. Instead she knew, as she had never known anything in her life that this was right, this was what she wanted, what she needed, what she had been looking for all along though she had not known what it was.

"I'm glad," she said softly, "that you came to me tonight."

"So am I."

He took a step forward, then stopped. Only a single lamp was burning, turned low, but a shimmering glow filled the room, and Stacey sensed that her gown was more revealing than she had thought. She had chosen, instinctively, the simplest of her nightdresses, not the elaborate affair that had been planned, all creamy satin and bows and lace, but plain white, with a single ruffle at the low, dipping neck and a row of tiny buttons down the front. Now, seeing his expression, she sensed she had made a mistake. The gown was too simple . . . too innocent. And innocence was the one thing she could not give.

Should I tell him the truth? she thought fleetingly. Now, while I still have the chance? Will he discover it later if I don't . . . and hate me for it?

But he had already closed the door and was coming over to her—now he was sitting on the edge of the bed—and whatever little courage she had had was gone. She could not tell him. She *dared* not tell him. She might not be coming to him innocent of body, but she was innocent in her heart and in her soul, and she longed for this, the first time she would ever truly, wholly, be with a man, to be a night of perfect sweetness.

Errol did not miss that faint flicker of hesitation, and misunderstanding, took it for a natural youthful fear of that act to come. His face softened, longing muted by new and unexpected feelings of tenderness. He had intended, when he came to her bed, to draw her into his arms cautiously but firmly. Now he changed his mind, and taking both her hands, lifted them to his lips.

"Don't be afraid," he said hoarsely. "I know you're very young, and this is all new to you . . . and threat-

ening. But I'm not some sort of animal to cater to my
own instincts and force you before you're ready. I'll
take the time to make it beautiful for you, too, I
promise. . . . And I will be gentle."

"I . . . I am not afraid," she said softly. The words
were half a lie. She knew so little about lovemaking—
that one time with D'Arcy had been a haze of semi-
consciousness; she had only the vaguest memories of
pain and humiliation, but every instinct told her it
would not be that way with Errol. Only she *was* afraid,
afraid of her own reactions, the way her body began to
quiver every time he touched her . . . afraid of what
would happen if she let herself care too much.

"No?" He was laughing, but kindly, with no trace of
mockery. "Then why do I detect little tremors in your
voice? Do you have any idea how lovely you are . . .
how soft?" He stretched out his hand, fingers playing
with the neck of her gown, tracing the pattern of the
fabric, just where it met her flesh. "Do you know how
much I want to touch you, caress you . . . hold you in
my arms?"

So gentle. Waves of helplessness washed over her.
His hands were so gentle she could hardly feel them
. . . yet she could think of nothing else. What was
there about this man that drove away all sense of
thought and reason?

She tried to laugh, tried to enlighten the mood, just
for a second. "I told you twice already, though you
don't seem to listen: I know what I'm doing. Why is it
you refuse to believe me?"

"Perhaps," he said slowly, "because I hear more
pride than conviction in your tone. Or perhaps because I want to be sure." His eyes seemed to darken,
watching her intently. "You're my wife now, Stacey.
Coming here tonight, offering myself to you, is an
acknowledgment of the vows spoken by my brother.
Accepting me is a promise on your part. I do want
you . . . very much . . . but I want it to be right. What
happens between us tonight will form the foundation
for a relationship that's going to last the rest of our
lives. I want that foundation to be solid, based on
affection . . . and mutual trust."

Sincerity mingled with the longing in his tone, and Stacey felt her uneasiness return. Tell him, a little voice nagged at the back of her mind. Tell him *now*. If he finds out by himself, he's going to know you for a liar too.

Only she couldn't. Not while his fingers were there lightly at the edge of her gown, not while the memory of his lips on her hands was still so potent . . . not while she longed to know what those same lips would feel like, hard and urgent against her own. If she told him the truth, he would be angry. She could not bear it if he took her in anger, roughly, crudely, with none of the tender wooing his manner had promised.

Or worse yet, if he got up with a terrible, cold look in his eyes and walked out of the room.

"Well, you're right," she said, managing a smile at last. A sweet half-smile, more seductive than she realized. "Partly right, anyway. I was lying before, I admit it—I *don't* know what I am doing. But you're wrong if you think I'm afraid. I know you will be gentle . . . as you promised."

"Oh, God . . ." The words came out in a low, hoarse moan. "You would hold me to that. It's going to be hard, keeping my promise . . . when you look at me that way." His hands had slipped down, playing with the small pearl buttons on her nightdress, evoking tremors that embarrassed her, but could not be controlled. "You inflame my senses, you make me want to forget everything—and blast it, minx, you know it." He lowered his head, lips buried in the soft curve of her shoulders, finding the throbbing pulse at the base of her neck while his hands continued to undo, one by one, the tiny buttons.

Stacey stiffened as the last button popped out of its dainty stitched hole, and Errol, sensing her response, drew his hands back. A slow motion, barely skimming the sheer fabric that peaked over taut nipples.

"I make you one last reluctant offer . . ." He was leaning over her now, looking down with something dark and hungry in his eyes. "I seem to be doing a great deal of that this evening. Would you like it . . . would it be easier for you . . . if I turned out the light?"

Stacey shook her head. "No, I . . . I don't like the dark. I never have." She had always been afraid at night; she could remember as a little girl waking up and screaming, and Ivan, indulgent, instructing the servants to keep a lamp burning.

The response seemed to amuse him. A crooked half-smile touched his lips. "Very well—I have made the offer, and I must say, I'm not unhappy to be refused. Now you're going to have to endure the lustful impertinence of my eyes devouring every tantalizing curve of your body. And I warn you, I intend to do just that . . . and I intend to enjoy it enormously."

He opened the gown, slowly, not hurrying, savoring every inch that came into view as he slid it from her shoulders, her breast, the slender line of her waist, flinging it away at last to leave her exposed and utterly vulnerable. For one brief moment he did not move, did not speak, then his breath came out in a deep sigh.

"You are very beautiful," he said at last. "Just what I imagined, slim . . . and sensual. I knew you were going to look like this when I first saw you."

'You *imagined* me? Like this?" Stacey struggled to quell the conflicting, very confusing emotions sweeping over her. "What were you doing? Undressing me with your eyes?"

"Of course." His grin turned roguish. "Did you expect anything else?"

"But . . . when you first saw me? Even then? When you came into the parlor and found me there?"

"Yes. I thought you were a foolish, pampered, frivolous little creature—which impression, incidentally, I'm not at all sure was wrong. I also thought you were much too young . . . and I know I was right about that. But I couldn't help seeing that you were beautiful. And very desirable."

His voice had dropped deep in his throat, and Stacey was aware that he was looking at her with that same compelling hunger. He had not touched her again, but his eyes did not leave her, and she could almost feel them, a physical presence, lingering on her breasts, caressing them slowly, thoroughly, sending strange and warming sensations through her.

Suddenly self-conscious, she spread out her hands, half-covering her breasts. "I . . . I always thought I was . . . too slim," she confessed.

Errol took her hands, drawing them gently back. "Don't hide your body, Stacey. Not from me. You've no need . . . and it gives me such pleasure. Surely you can tell how it pleases me to look at you."

"But I . . . I . . ." She stammered slightly. "I always thought men liked women who were, well . . . bigger . . . there."

His laughter touched her, warm and throaty. "Men' are not a fixed entity, one mind, one body, always liking this and that and never the other thing. We have our own tastes, you know, just like women. Some of us are actually unique. And some of us—don't get shocked now—have been known to be disappointed when a pretty woman removed her corset and her breasts flopped down to her waist."

Stacey tried not to giggle, but she couldn't help it. It seemed so inappropriate, laughter at a time like this, but it made her feel better somehow, closer to him. "You're sure?" she said softly.

"Very sure." His eyes turned serious, glowing with a warmth that made her feel self-conscious again, though the sensation was not altogether unpleasant. "Don't ever be ashamed of your body . . . or anything about it. You have beautiful breasts—look, love, they're made to be touched." He began to trace the contours, emphasizing every word with sweet, subtle motions that set her blood on fire. "Firm and high . . . with large . . . very kissable . . . nipples."

He bent down, teasing with his lips, and Stacey sighed as she felt him suck those hard little peaks into his mouth. But gently, so gently it was impossible to be afraid, impossible to feel anything but the heat coursing through her veins . . . the heat and the closeness of him and the longing that took everything else away.

"And a beautiful belly," he went on. He was lying beside her now, still clad in the dressing gown as he drew her into his arms, one hand resting for a moment on the rounded flesh just beneath her waist. "Nice and soft . . ." He had begun to move again. "And beautiful hips . . . and thighs . . . and . . ."

He let his hand linger, one tantalizing instant, then moved slowly inward, not quite touching her, there, between her legs . . . not yet. Stacey tilted her face up, compelled by some instinct she did not recognize. Then she saw his lips, parted, inches from hers, and she knew what she was looking for, and her mouth opened to receive him.

A hard kiss, strong, uncompromising, yet sweet, too, filled with demands and promises her body was eager to explore. His hand had grown bolder, slipping between her thighs with an impertinence that made her gasp, even beneath the pressure of his lips, and she tensed for a moment, embarrassed, unsure.

But his fingers were playing with her, his thumb had found that secret little spot where all her desires centered, and resistance ebbed as he began to manipulate, provokingly, intimately, drawing her out of herself until there was nothing left but the new, overwhelming urgency in her body, and she was struggling, hungering, searching for sensations she could neither define nor understand. And then they were there, and at last she did understand—what she had wanted, what her body had been trying to tell her since he came in the room—and she collapsed, quivering and spent in his arms.

"I didn't know," she murmured hoarsely. Her head was on his chest; she was aware of the texture of his robe against her cheek. "I had no idea it was . . . it could be . . . like this."

He was laughing again, a soft male sound, tantalizing in her ear. "That was just the beginning—I wanted to keep half my promise at least. I wanted you to know the excitement and joy of love before you felt the pain." Slowly, tenderly, he shifted her weight in arms that now seemed so familiar, though she had been shy of them before. "Look at me, love . . . let me see those pretty silver eyes. There are many things you don't know. *Many* things . . . and I am going to teach them all to you."

His voice had a roguish sound now, only half-teasing,

and Stacey could feel him slipping off his robe, could feel the surprising hardness of strong male flesh, the texture of his body hair, coarse against her cheek, her fingers. She had not expected anything more for herself, she had thought that brief moment of intense sensation was all there was, but as he began to caress her, hands deft as before, sure, she felt warmth returning to a body that was suddenly alive again, and quivering with anticipation.

"Yes," she whispered, surprised at her own boldness. "Oh, yes, my darling—my love. I want you to teach me. I want to learn everything . . . from you."

His response was a sudden, almost convulsive shudder. His arms grew hard, tightening around her, like a vise. "Damn," he muttered hoarsely. "I'm sorry, sweet—so much for good intentions. I don't think I can wait any longer." He held off for a fraction of a second—she could feel the tension in his body, like a jungle animal coiled to strike—then he was on top of her, hard and demanding. "I will be gentler next time, I promise. But I need you too much now. I want you too much."

And then, suddenly, with no more coaxing, no preliminaries, he was inside her, and Stacey felt her whole body respond; a new, totally unexpected, uncontrollable force had hold of her, and her hips surged up to meet that swift downward thrust. He seemed to stop for a second, startled, almost surprised, as if the sudden savageness had caught him as much off guard as her, but Stacey was too absorbed in new needs, new compulsions, to notice. Then he had begun again, sharp, rhythmic, stabbing motions, hard but not hurtful, and instinct had taken over, surging her rapidly, inexorably, abruptly toward the surrender she shared with him.

She was trembling when he finally released her. He had pulled away, retreating to his own side of the bed, she supposed, and she curled up contentedly, clinging to the residue of passion as it drained slowly from her body. The nudity that had embarrassed her before seemed natural now, welcome in the stifling heat of the room, with not a breath of air seeping through the open windows.

It was a minute before she realized Errol was no longer there, and she stretched out her legs, too satiated to more than wonder idly why he had left her. New feelings held her now, new sensations—not passion, but tenderness . . . not excitement, but gratitude and quiet pleasure . . . and love. She had not understood until that moment that there might be an exact, definable point at which a girl crossed the threshold into maturity. She had been a child when Errol opened the door and came into her room; she had not known it, but she was, as pampered and frivolous as he had intimated before. She had been a child when he came to the bed and took her in his arms. But she was a woman when he left . . . a woman who somehow in that short space of time had fallen completely, passionately in love with her own husband.

All those silly crushes, she thought, smiling to herself as she sank deeper into the pillows. All the handsome youths she flirted with and schemed over and thought she wanted so much. Now she recognized her feelings for what they were, not love at all, but the yearnings of a young girl who was eager to love and did not yet know how. She had not realized, had not guessed, until she met Errol Cameron, how deep the passions between a man and woman could run, or how wonderfully enveloping they could be.

She stirred restlessly, more aware than ever of Errol's absence. Opening her eyes, she looked around the room, half-expecting to find that he had left her to attend to some male needs she knew nothing about. Instead, she saw him standing against the far wall, near the window, staring down at her with an expression that made her blood run cold.

"What . . . ?"

The word died on her lips. Too late, she recalled the little voice that had tried to warn her before. And the way he seemed to hesitate, just for a second, when he entered her body, though she had been too wrapped up in her own feelings to pay attention. Shivering with dread, she shifted her eyes down, seeing what she had feared.

The sheets were immaculately white—with not a trace of blood.

Betrayed. A surge of anger and hurt ran through her. Betrayed by her own body. She had always been so regular before—her period came and went like clockwork. Now, the one time she had needed it, it had ended, fully a day early, with not the slightest blood to offer a shred of doubt.

She looked up, hoping, praying that she was wrong, that that was not what he was thinking. But the eyes that looked back at her were cold as ice.

"You have done this before, haven't you?"

It was phrased as a question, but there was no question in his tone, and Stacey could only stare at him helplessly, cursing the Victorian prudery that had left her so ignorant. If only she had known why he had hesitated before, whether there could be any other explanation for whatever he had sensed . . . for the lack of blood on the sheets. If only she knew if it would do any good to lie.

"Yes," she said at last, averting her eyes. "Yes . . . I'm sorry, but . . . yes, I have."

The words seemed to echo in the silence of the room. Stacey sat up, wrapping the sheet unhappily around her. For a minute she thought he was not going to speak again, that he was just going to stand there and stare at her forever. Then his voice came, hard and ironic.

"When were you planning on discussing this little detail with me? Or did you think it was going to slip by and you'd never be called to terms? By God, that's it, isn't it? You really expected to get away with it. Come now, I'm curious. Did you think I was too naive to figure it out—or too hot-blooded to notice in the heat of passion?"

His contempt tore at her heart, all the more because Stacey knew it was true. She *had* hoped to get away with it, not because he was naive, but because she was. Only how could she tell him that? "No, I . . . I didn't think that . . . not really . . ."

"What did you think then? That I wouldn't be able to do anything about it? That it was going to be too late . . . once I took you to bed? Did you really think I was the sort of man who would simply shrug it off and accept the inevitable?"

"No," Stacey replied, thoroughly miserable now. That was the one thing she had not thought, not since she came to Cameron's Creek and met him face-to-face. "I knew better than that, but . . . Oh, please, try to understand. It was all so hard, and I . . . well, I guess I . . . I just didn't think at all."

"I daresay you didn't." He swung away, facing the window for a moment, his body lean and deceptively casual in the lamplight, though Stacey could almost see the tension snapping in the air around him. When he turned back, his lips were twisted in a mirthless smile.

"You made a point this evening of asking why *I* would consider such an unconventional liaison. Apparently I should have made the same inquiries of you. No wonder your grandfather was so eager to marry you off."

"Oh . . . no!" Stacey gasped, surprised. "Grandfather didn't—" She caught herself just in time. If she told him she was a virgin when her grandfather contracted the marriage, then he would know she had been a virgin when she boarded ship—and he'd guess the rest. There was enough bad blood between Errol and his brother as it was. "I mean, Grandfather *wouldn't*—he'd never do anything like that."

"Of course not. Your grandfather is much too honorable for such underhanded tricks. You mentioned his honor before, I believe, when you told me how much he had in common with Old Harry."

"I . . . I know, but . . ." Stacey hesitated. More lies, and foolish ones, too. She hated lying to him, especially when she kept getting caught. "Grandfather isn't the most honorable man in the world—I don't suppose there's a trick invented he isn't capable of. But . . . well, he may not be honest all the time, but he's hardly stupid. He would have known he couldn't get away with something like this."

"Unless he thought he was sending you so far away it wasn't going to matter. I am hardly in a position, am I, to call him to account?" Errol paused, raising one brow, a deliberately ironic gesture. "But I know one thing he apparently didn't. I never authorized my brother to stand in for me at a proxy marriage, and I cannot be bound by it legally. Tomorrow morning, madam, I expect you to have your things packed. One of the hands will drive you into town. There's no train until Thursday, but you'll be reasonably comfortable at the inn until then. I don't think, under the circumstances, a chaperone is necessary, but someone will contact you in Sydney and arrange for your passage to California."

"But . . . tomorrow!" Stacey gaped at him in horror. She had expected the anger, she had expected the blustering and the threats, but she had been so sure she'd have time to try to talk him out of it. "You . . . you can't do that."

"Can't I? I think if you ponder on it, you'll realize that I can hardly do anything else. I have a high regard for virtuous women—chastity and honor are traits I have always considered essential in a wife. You have shown neither." He paused, studying her so coldly she could feel herself shiver. "I might have understood your attachment to another man. I'm not saying I would have been able to forgive you, but . . . I might have. What I cannot forgive—or understand—is the fact that you lied."

"But I . . . I didn't," she protested. "Not really."

"You knew I thought you were innocent and inexperienced. I as much as told you so, and you let me go right on believing it. That is the same as a deliberate lie, and you know it."

Stacey blinked back her tears. He was right, she had lied, consciously and deliberately, and he had every right to be furious. But to send her away? Never to see her again—or let her see him? Even if she weren't afraid of what Grandfather was going to do when she came back with no explanations, she would have been desolate now. The things she had learned tonight, about her body and her heart—the feelings he had stirred in her—were too intense to fade with time, and she sensed her life would be forever empty without him.

"Please," she said softly. "I know I was wrong, and I said I am sorry. I don't blame you for being angry

. . . or hating me. But even if you can't forgive me now, couldn't you wait just a little? Give me another chance?"

"The time for chances is over." There was a cold finality in his voice, and Stacey felt her heart sink. "I expect your bags to be ready in the morning." He started toward the door.

"But . . ." Stacey cast about in her mind, searching for something, anything, to hold him back. If he got away now, she might not be able to speak to him again. "What if . . . what if I'm pregnant?"

He turned slowly, a flicker of something showing just for a second in his eyes. "It's hardly likely that you've been impregnated by this one encounter."

"Maybe not . . ." Stacey felt her heart beat faster. She knew precious little about such things—no one had ever told her exactly what was required for pregnancy and whether once was enough—but it must not be impossible or he'd be laughing at her now. "But I could be, couldn't I?"

"I think," he replied, pausing for a moment, "that that's a risk I can live with."

"You're forgetting my grandfather," she said desperately. "He's going to be wild when he finds out. You don't know what he's like when his Russian temper is roused. It'll be bad enough if I have to send word from the docks for a carriage to come and fetch me. And if I show up pregnant . . . ? There'll be no limit to his rage."

Errol gave a short laugh. "Forgive me if that Russian temper doesn't make me quake. I wouldn't be afraid of your grandfather if he owned the next station. As it is, with an ocean between us, I hardly need fear reprisals."

"But this would be your child," Stacey persisted. She had seen something in his eyes, she was sure she had. If only she could discover what it was. "Your son, perhaps . . . and Grandfather would never forgive you. If you changed your mind later, if you wanted some share in the life you had started, he would make sure you never saw the boy or had any contact with him."

He wavered slightly. "I am not so arrogant that I require an image of myself to dote on. Do you think a son would be more important to me than a daughter?"

"Well, then," she said softly, "a daughter." She had him, and she knew it. She had seen the hesitation in his eyes just now. "A little girl to love . . . and need you. Are you really willing to give up all claim to your child, Errol? Because that's what you'll be doing if you send me away tomorrow."

One corner of his lips twitched, and she sensed he was laughing, not at her but at himself. "It is very unlikely, as I said before, that you are already pregnant. But you're quite right, my dear—and very clever of you, too—I am not willing to take the chance. You may stay until we know if you are pregnant."

"And if I am . . . ?" She barely dared to speak the words.

"If you are—God help me, I want my child."

It was as much of a concession as he could give, and her heart ached as she stared at him in the doorway. He had not bothered to take up the robe where it lay beside her bed, and she was conscious of every sinewy line of his tall, bronzed body. She loved him so much— she knew that with a terrible certainty, now that it was too late—and she would die if she lost him.

"And if I am not . . ."

"If you are not, there is a train twice a week. I think we can manage to find a place on one for you." He started out, then turned, all the dark irony she had sensed before clear on his features now.

"Good night, madam. Sleep well."

13

The room seemed strangely silent after Errol had gone. Stacey sat up for a long time, in a straight chair by the tall windows that looked out onto the veranda. She had found her nightdress where it had fallen to the floor and slipped it on, but the front was open, unbuttoned for coolness as she stared out into the night.

She could stay, he had said, until he was sure she wasn't carrying his child. But what did that give her? A few weeks' grace, five at most—six?—and then her excuses would begin to wear thin. Then, if she wasn't pregnant—and every instinct in her body told her she was not—he was going to send her away.

What was it she had heard the serving maids whispering once? She drew the gown shut, holding it tight over slender young breasts. Something about the time of month when men never came to a woman. She could not have been more than eleven or twelve; it had seemed so titillating then, every stolen word about deliciously forbidden subjects, and she had savored the atmosphere more than the facts, which had gone in one ear and out the other. Now she wished she had listened more closely. If it was true, if men really didn't come to women then—even men who wanted to father a child—could it be that that was not a time for conception? That even that one slim hope was gone and there wasn't a prayer she was pregnant?

Faint hints of gray had begun to show in the sky by the time she finally gave up and went back to bed, though she knew sleep was beyond her. Why had she been such a fool before? Why hadn't she listened to the instincts that had urged her to tell the truth? If she had, he might have understood, might have forgiven—hadn't he said so himself?

She closed her eyes, listening to the last sounds of night as they faded into dawn. She had made so many mistakes, bitter mistakes, but she was not going to make them again. He had seen the worst of her tonight, the naively transparent lies that fear had forced her into; from now on, she would show him only the best. If there was any chance she could win him back—any chance she could make him want her again before he discovered she wasn't pregnant—she was going to have to stop pretending and learn to be brutally honest about herself.

And she *was* going to win him back, she vowed, youthful resilience coming to her rescue in the dim half-light. She had to win him back. The aching loneliness in her heart could not accept the possibility that she had lost him forever.

Morning brought no respite, only a renewal of the searing heat that seemed ever drier and dustier than it had the day before. Stacey got up groggily and dug through her luggage until she found a cerise-and-cream-colored basque, not her favorite among the new dresses that had been made up for her trousseau, but light and loose-fitting enough to be worn without a corset and bulky, concealing petticoats. She had a feeling she was going to be sick to death of it before the next few weeks were up; that and the white book muslin were the only outfits she had brought from Sydney suitable for the bush. She could hardly expect Errol to order up a seamstress for her, even assuming one was available in this godforsaken spot.

She had no idea what arrangements had been made for breakfast, but she decided to try the dining room she had glimpsed the night before, thinking it likely that a buffet had been set up so they could help themselves. Her nose told her, even before she reached it, that she had been right—and that she was not going to particularly like what she found. The odor of grease was sticky in the air, thick and faintly rancid, and she could almost feel it coating the inside of her nostrils.

Not that it mattered, she thought wryly, clinging to

what was left of her humor. After last night, she hardly had an appetite.

A tall, lanky figure showed through the doorway, seated at a polished red-gum table, and for just a second Stacey's heart leapt up and she dared to think Errol was there. Then the man turned, setting down the newspaper he had been glancing through, and she realized she had been foolish to hope.

D'Arcy. With all that had happened, she had completely forgotten he was there. Now, as she gazed in at him, this man she had once thought she loved, all she could see was how pretty and shallow he looked, with his thin little mustache, neatly trimmed, and crisp white cambric shirt.

"I didn't expect to find you here," she said, making her voice as icy as she could. "May I assume you're not in the habit of getting out early to tend to your chores?"

If she thought to shame him, she was disappointed. "Early or late," he said easily. "Chores are Errol's prerogative. He likes managing the station—his ego thrives on being 'boss man'—and I like staying out of his way. I must say, though, I hadn't expected him to be quite so conscientious this morning. I thought he might, uh . . . tarry in bed until noon." He paused, letting his tongue run dryly over his lips. "Or did he play the gentleman last night, deferring to maidenly modesty and abstain from coming to your bed?"

Color rose to her cheeks. Stacey hated the feeling, hot and betraying, but there was no way she could keep him from seeing. "What happens between my husband and me is none of your business," she said angrily.

"Ah? He did bed you then?" D'Arcy pushed back his plate, empty of everything except grease and a half-slice of jam-smeared bread, and watched her with frank curiosity. "I thought somehow he might. And he didn't stay till morning? Was he a bit piqued, I wonder, when he found that his precious young wife was somewhat less than the sweet vestal he had been pining for?"

Stacey drew in a sharp breath. Had he always been

this despicable and she was just too foolish to notice? She turned away, trying not to let him see that her hands were shaking as she approached the sideboard, where a number of dishes had been laid out. Even had she been hungry, the soggy scrambled eggs and grease-glistening portions of something that smelled like mutton would not have appealed to her, but she took a plate anyway and scooped a portion onto it.

"I told you before," she said coldly, "my relationship with my husband is none of your business."

"Ah, but I think it is." He had risen so silently she had not noticed, and was standing next to her, coaxing her with his voice to turn. "I have a distinctly proprietary interest in you, as you will recall. You know, I rather suspected it might work out this way. For a man of the world, Errol can be distinctly prudish, especially on the subject of feminine frailty."

Stacey stared at him, sickened. "You sound as if you're enjoying this."

"Yes, well . . . why not? There's no love lost between my brother and me. Admiration maybe—on my part. I do admire Errol, quite sincerely. The estate was nearly bankrupt when he took over. Now we can afford the finest tailors in Sydney and the wolf has been driven from the door. He, I'm afraid, has only contempt for me. So you see . . ." He reached out, catching her wrist as she started toward the table, an intimate gesture that sent a shiver of revulsion through her.

"I'll thank you to let go of me."

"So you see," he went on, ignoring the demand, "there's nothing to stand in our way." His eyelids were drooping, dark and deliberately sensuous over mocking black eyes. "My brother kicked you out of his bed, but not out of his house. I find that little fact most intriguing. Does it mean you're going to be around for a while? A delightful possibility, I must say. It could prove, uh . . . pleasant for both of us."

His meaning was blatantly clear. Stacey jerked her hand back, picking up the plate and going over to the table. It was almost laughable, the way he thought she was going to rush into his arms again, though in a way she supposed she had asked for it. To him, a fallen woman would be a fallen woman. What matter that the fall had come about as the result of a few glasses of champagne and his own brute force?

"I would think you'd have enough to keep you occupied with Maude," she snapped tartly. "I heard what was going on between the two of you that night in Sydney in her room."

To her surprise, he stiffened somewhat. "Maude is my fiancée. There's no reason why we shouldn't enjoy a little . . . prenuptial pleasure. A taste of the fruit while it's still forbidden, so to speak. But . . . ." He had moved across the table from her and was fixing her with a dark, unpleasant stare. "Maude has a way of dallying only when she wants to, and she tends to be a bit more cautious at home, where her 'reputation' is at stake. I'm going to be very lonely these next few months before the wedding. And so are you, I think, with Errol obviously determined not to partake of the joys of your bed. We might . . . comfort each other."

Stacey dropped her plate with a clatter on the table. Even for D'Arcy, that was going too far. She *would* be lonely if Errol stuck to his resolve and stayed away from her—her body would be aching in the long, empty nights—but even if she lost him forever, the last person in the world she would seek "comfort" from was the one who had caused her pain in the first place.

"I think you are disgusting!" All she wanted was to get out of that room, away from him.

His laughter followed her to the door. "What about your breakfast?" he called out.

It was the last straw. Stacey spun around. "I would rather starve to death than stay in the same room with you!"

Anger carried her through the door and down the steps into the yard at the side of the house. She was still shaking, but more in control than before, and after one quick look over her shoulder to make sure he was not following, she stopped to catch her breath. Really, the arrogance of the man! The supreme and rather stupid arrogance. That she had found him fascinating once, when he had gone out of his way to be charming and debonair, was one thing. But how could he think she would have anything to do with him now?

The air was brutally hot—Stacey could feel it after only a few seconds outside—and she looked up, surprised to see that the sun was already high in the sky. It must be nearing noon. If the men came in from the fields for their midday meal, they would be back soon. Did he really believe he was so irresistible she would fall for him again? Or was he just baiting her, amused at the flashes of temper she could not control?

She brushed her arm across her forehead, wiping away the sweat and the dust. If the men came back, would Errol be with them? She swallowed nervously, glancing back at the house, realizing for the first time how close she had come to being caught in that revealing conversation. Errol had not come in while she was talking to D'Arcy, but he might have. And if he had . . .

She shuddered, imagining the scene as vividly as if it had taken place. Errol standing in the doorway, Errol listening to every word that passed between them . . . Errol guessing the truth. . . .

And even if he didn't guess, D'Arcy was capable of telling him out of spite.

An exquisitely colored bird, so scarlet it was almost gaudy, lighted on a branch nearby, but Stacey barely saw it. She was going to have to be careful from now on, very careful in her dealings with D'Arcy Cameron. Errol had been angry enough when he found that she had been with another man before she came to him. What was going to happen if he discovered that that man was his own brother?

The brother for whom he had nothing but contempt.

D'Arcy stood behind the table for some minutes, staring out at the shadows on the veranda, then eased himself slowly into his chair. He reached out automatically, toying with the half-piece of bread on his plate, but it was dry and unappetizing, and he flicked it away with an impatient gesture.

It was amazing, the effect Errol had on pretty women.

The sweetly girlish blush that rose to Stacey's cheeks had told him more than the mere fact that his brother had gone to her bed last night. It told him that she had liked it, unexpectedly . . . and very thoroughly.

Blast him, the bastard! He got up and went over to the doorway, jamming his hands into his pockets as he rested his shoulder against the frame. Everything was always so easy for Errol. The English education, the subtly English accent, the combination of suave self-assurance and rugged masculinity that was so damned attractive to women. Even a bit of froth like Stacey, who had been so completely *his* until they came to Cameron's Creek, had fallen captive to Errol's charm, and that after only one quick tumble in the hay.

Everything he wanted—and he got it just like that!

The smell of mutton fat and oversweet marmalade mixed cloyingly with the stale scent of dust from outside. He remembered a girl he had met once, on vacation from one of those dreary boarding schools outside of Sydney. He must have been fifteen; it was the first time Errol had taken him into town and treated him like a man, bringing him to his club for a drink, then dinner afterward in an expensive restaurant. He could see her now, all candy pink and white, with silk roses in her hair and flaxen curls and enticingly round eyes. He had been frankly captivated, and though she was a year older, he was sure she had been amused by his clever repartée—until Errol barged into the conversation. From that point on, it was as if he hadn't existed.

It was, in a way, the story of his life. He pushed away from the door and moved out onto the veranda, searching the landscape with his eyes to see if he could tell where Stacey had gone. He was Errol Cameron's little brother, interesting enough, even charming to a degree. But he didn't exist when his brother was there.

He let his eyes run across the barren paddock and down the hillside, smiling as they lit on a small grove of willows beside the last of the half-dry mudholes in the creek. She had not gone back inside, he was sure of that, but he doubted that she could stand the glar-

ing sun either. There was only one place to find shade
and privacy within a mile of the homestead.

It might be amusing to seek her out again, now that
she had had a little time to think things through. The
heat was oppressive—it seemed worse with each passing hour—and he snapped open the collar of his shirt,
disliking the untidy way it looked, but welcoming that
hint of coolness on his neck. She might have been
satisfied in bed last night, but he had a feeling she had
been humiliated too, when Errol found out that she
was not as pure as she looked. And then, she was a
hot-blooded little wench—he had sensed that the one
time he had been with her, though she had been so
nearly unconscious that she had reacted more with
instinct than emotion. It was hard to imagine someone
like that pining all by herself in the sweltering heat of
sultry summer nights.

Yes, it would definitely be amusing to seek her out
and see if she hadn't begun to regret those hasty
words.

He found her, as he had expected, in the willow
grove. In gentler times, it formed a pretty glade, green
and cool, with a hint of music in the breezes that
whispered through the trees. Now the leaves were dry
and brown with dust, and sun glared through thin
branches, half-blinding him as he picked her out in a
mottled patch of shade.

"Did you really believe I was going to let you escape so easily?" He laughed as she jumped and whirled
to face him. "You do have the silliest way of running
all the time. I would think by now you'd have figured
out it wasn't any use—but, no, you persist. Foolish,
foolish girl."

"Is that what you think?" Her eyes were still wide,
but she had pulled herself together and he sensed a
new and rather surprising maturity in her bearing.
"That I was running away from you?"

"Of course you were, and—"

"No, I wasn't. You're wrong. I may have run before, but all that is in the past. I'm not going to run

anymore—and I wasn't running now. I left because I find your company distasteful. That's all."

There was a quiet emphasis in her voice that grated on his nerves. He had planned to speak teasingly, to court her with smooth charm, the way he had—and so successfully—before. Now all he felt was a surge of anger.

"You think you're immune to me, is that it? After one night in *his* bed?" She started to move away, but he caught her wrists in both hands, jerking her back until he could almost feel her body against his. "Let me tell you something, sweetheart: brother Errol doesn't want you anymore. He may be stuck with you, but he doesn't want you, and he's never going to. You're not quite pure enough to be the wife he's always imagined, and he hardly needs another mistress. I may be second choice, but I'm the only choice you're going to have. So why don't we drop this chaste little act and get down to what we both want."

His grip tightened, and Stacey sensed the anger vibrating through him, sensed something else too, though she did not know what it was, and suddenly she was afraid.

"What kind of man are you?" she whispered hoarsely. The shadows seemed to darken, and she realized for the first time how isolated the grove was, how far from the house. "You said there's no love lost between you and your brother, but do you hate him so much? I am his wife . . . I belong to him, whether he wants me or not. Have you forgotten?"

"Forgotten?" He laughed harshly. "No, I have not forgotten—and no, to answer the question I see in your eyes, I'm not going to feel the least bit guilty, possessing my brother's wife . . . just as I didn't feel guilty that first time in your cabin at sea. As a matter of fact, I found it rather amusing. A kind of ironic justice, as it were." He was laughing again, but there was no warmth in the sound, no humor. "It seemed appropriate that I should be the first man to have his wife . . . since he was the first to have mine."

"What . . . ?" Stacey felt something cold run down her spine as she stared at him. "What are you saying?

What do you mean?" Then, slowly, the truth began to close in. "You don't, you *can't* mean . . . Maude?"

"Precisely." He lowered his head until she could feel his breath on her cheek, threatening now, as she knew he intended. "My charming little fiancée, so lively—and agreeable. She was betrothed to me, but that didn't stop her . . . or him. She's always wanted him, you see, from the time she was a little girl—though I was too much of a fool to see it! Everyone wants virile, exciting, very rich Errol Cameron. Only, unlike some of the others, she got him."

"But surely he wouldn't . . ." Stacey's head was spinning, trying to take in everything at once. "Oh, D'Arcy, he's your brother . . . he couldn't . . ."

"Don't be dense. Of course he could—and he has. Many times. Oh, he can't take her away from me, not technically at least. She was left to me—literally—in my father's will. It was all very clearly spelled out. Errol gets control of everything material . . . the land, the animals, the finances . . . and I get Maude. If he does anything to interfere, he loses it all. And Errol is not the sort of man to lose something that is his."

"But . . . that's incredible!" Even ignorant as she was in matters of law, Stacey found it hard to follow. "Your own father! How could he put something like that in his will?"

"He knew his son very well. Both of them actually. I am a total incompetent—nine years old when my father died, and already I was incompetent!—and Errol is totally immoral. A neat little arrangement, you see: we are protected from each other." His voice had risen and his hands were trembling as he forced her closer, eyes burning into hers. "Dammit, Stacey, I'm not made of stone. I loved her so much—don't you understand that? I truly *loved* her. The first time she let me come to her, I was so young, so naive, I didn't know the difference. I thought she loved me too . . . and all the time she was just sharing her favors. God, he probably sent her himself! Do you have any idea what that did to me? To find out that the woman I worshiped was a whore? And my brother's whore at that?"

"Oh, dear heaven . . ." Stacey barely dared whisper the words. The rage in his eyes was frightening now, still directed at Errol and Maude, but any minute she knew he was going to turn it on her.

"Where do you think he is now?" he went on. "Your precious husband whom you have such qualms about betraying? Off tending to his sheep? Well, no doubt he is—Errol is conscientious to the point of boredom. But he tends the sheep at Mirandola too, and the men say he rode in that direction this morning. They'll have the house all to themselves—Maude's never kept much of a staff. And that father of hers is nearly blind . . . and so senile he doesn't know what's going on half the time."

"No . . ." Stacey felt as if she were going to faint. She hated the ugly seeds he was planting in her mind, but she couldn't keep them from taking hold. "Why are you saying these things? They're all lies—they have to be! You know they're not true!"

"Would to God they weren't!" His voice came out in a strangled moan. "Believe me, Stacey—*believe me*—before it's too late and he destroys you too. Believe . . . **and** take solace where you can." He had worked both wrists to one hand, still holding so tight she couldn't get away. Suddenly his other hand was on her back and he was pressing her against his hips. Her body went rigid as she felt the proof of his desire, hard, unmistakable, telling her beyond a doubt what he had in mind.

"Let me go!" She managed to tug her hands free. Wedging them against his chest, she shoved him roughly back. "You're not going to get away with it, do you hear me? Not this time! Try anything you want—but it's not going to work!"

"Oh?" To her surprise, he made no attempt to clutch at her again. As if, she thought with a shudder, he didn't think he had to! "How do you propose to stop me?"

"I . . . I . . ." A wave of helplessness flooded over her. He was a good five inches taller, and he had easily fifty pounds on her. But he was going to have to kill her before she'd let him defile her again! "I'll scream if you make a move! I swear I will."

"Yes?" He looked amused. "The way you did before?"

"I didn't scream then," she admitted. "And I was a fool. But this time I will—and nothing can stop me!"

"Well, then . . . scream your head off if you want. There's only Mrs. Sweeney and the kitchen boy. Even if they hear, they'll think it's another domestic quarrel in the black quarters. It happens all the time. As for the men . . . I don't suppose they're within earshot."

"Maybe not." Stacey eyed him warily. The look of anger was gone now, but the cold calculation that had replaced it was even more terrifying. "You might be right . . . but can you afford to take the chance?"

He stepped back, looping his thumbs through his belt, eyes openly insolent now. Not anxious, not hurried . . . as if her fear added savor to the victory. "It seems to me you're the one who'd be taking a chance. It's hardly in your best interests to have my brother find out about us."

"Or yours." Stacey was surprised at how calm her voice sounded, though inside she was shaking. "Your father's will gave Errol control over everything—he could make things difficult for you if he wanted. How would you like it, I wonder, if he cut you off from those expensive tailors in Sydney? Or, heaven forfend, made you work for your keep?"

It was a desperate gamble, but it worked. Stacey knew it almost at once. His expression changed, turning thoughtful for an instant, assessing; then, to her relief, he unhooked his thumbs and stepped aside to let her pass.

"Such a pretty little thing to be so smart. I don't think any of the men *are* within earshot, but you're right—I'm not going to take the chance. Anyhow . . ." She had started up the path toward the house, but something in his voice drew her around. To her surprise, he was still standing where she had left him, not angry at all, but smiling, as if the whole thing were a jest. "I don't think I am going to have to force you. Sooner or later, you're going to be furious and hurt enough—and lonely enough—to need someone to turn to, and I'm the only someone around. Sooner or later you're going to be mine again . . . of your own free will."

Sooner or later . . . The words echoed in Stacey's ears as she made her way up the hill to the dry, open pastureland that stretched between the homestead and the nearest outbuilding, the stables. There was something almost hypnotic in those cool, easy tones, a faintly sinister quality that drew and fascinated her in spite of herself. It was as if he were two totally different people, dark and ominous one minute, bright and laughing the next. And he could change from one to the other without the slightest warning.

She paused at the top of the hill, staring idly at the distant horizon. There seemed to be something there, gray and elusive, like storm clouds massing, but when she tried to focus on them, they disappeared. More than ever, she knew that D'Arcy Cameron was dangerous and she had to avoid him. She wasn't afraid he was going to come after her, or try anything quite so overt again. She hadn't been bluffing when she had said she would scream, and he knew it.

But what was going to happen if someone angered him? Errol or herself . . . or Maude? That raging temper could come flashing out at any time, and with it the whole sordid truth—and her world would collapse if it did.

Had he been right?

She tried to catch her breath, but it kept sticking in her throat and she couldn't swallow it back. Did Errol love Maude? Was that why he had hardened his heart so resolutely against her? Had he been looking for an excuse not to accept her as his wife?

She turned away from the dry creek bed, sensing watching eyes in the shadows, even though she couldn't see them. *D'Arcy has always grown up with the assumption that he and Maude were going to be married,* Errol had told her that one evening they had talked. *I would not take that away from him—even if I could.*

And he wouldn't. Stacey knew that as surely as she had ever known anything in her life. Errol had too much honor, too much pride, to steal his brother's fiancée, and it had nothing to do with his father's will. He would never have set out to love Maude, she was sure of that—he would have done everything in his power to stay away from her if he felt an attachment forming. But, oh, it was hard to forget how beautiful she had looked, standing on the dock in the sunlight, her hair a glorious red-gold fire around her face. Beautiful and wild somehow, untamed . . . like the land that was so much a part of Errol Cameron.

He would never have set out to love her—but could he have kept it from happening anyway? And could a man that strong and virile deny the physical side to his passions?

Her eyes were stinging, and she blinked angrily, trying to pretend it was dust and not tears. What about Maude? Beautiful, wild, unconventional Maude. Was she in love with him too?

Impossible to stop the memories now. Maude's face, that same day, when D'Arcy raced down the gangplank and clasped her in his arms. No sweet surrender in those dazzling turquoise eyes, no gentle, yielding love . . . only a kind of wild excitement that had seemed puzzling even then. What if she didn't care about D'Arcy at all? What if it was only triumph she felt because her beauty had brought him back to her?

A woman like that . . .

Stacey shivered, realizing for the first time that her position with Errol was even more precarious than she had thought. What a fool she had been, assuming all she needed was his forgiveness. A woman like that enjoyed her power over men . . . and she wasn't likely to give it up.

And really, in the end, did it matter what Maude's motives were? She could be a calculating schemer who only played with men, or a woman genuinely, tragically in love with her fiancée's brother—or her heart could belong to D'Arcy as she had pretended all along. What mattered was how Errol felt about her.

And if he loved her, could any other woman ever win his heart?

The stable door opened, and she looked up as a slim

youth came out and started across the fields, heading
her way. She turned automatically, then thought better of it, and shaking the dust in a little cloud out of
her skirt, forced herself to walk forward. D'Arcy had
done his best to poison her thoughts that morning, and
if she stood around and felt sorry for herself, he was
going to succeed.

"Hello," she yelled out, trying to sound bright and
carefree. "Wait a minute—please."

He stopped, turning his head slightly, and Stacey
saw it was not a boy at all, but a man, perhaps Errol's
contemporary, with skin much darker than the sun
could make it, and deep lines around his eyes. His lips
moved, as if he wanted to smile, but he seemed too
shy.

"I am Mrs. Cameron," she said, then laughed as she
realized how ridiculous that had to sound. Of course
she was Mrs. Cameron. Everyone on the station would
have known within minutes of her arrival; they had
probably talked of little else the night before. "I
wonder—would it be all right for me to go in the
stables for a few minutes? I don't want to get in the
way, but I do love horses. I had one of my own at
home."

"Sure, missus." The mouth opened now, a broad
grin that showed a missing tooth, and dark eyes looked
up with flattering admiration. "You bin go anytime.
Now? Well, sure, missus. Mine bin show you. Sure,
sure, sure."

14

His name, as he was to tell her at least a dozen times in the next hour, was Billy Two, and once over his initial shyness, words tumbled out of his mouth in a stream as bewildering as it was fascinating, for the Pidgin he spoke bore little resemblance to any English Stacey had ever heard. Still, his enthusiasm was contagious, and she could not keep from smiling as he showed her through the stables, pointing out the stalls, which were empty now in the midday heat, but cleanly kept, and the large room at the end, where saddles, blankets, and bridles had been set out in an array so tidy it would have done even her tyrannical grandfather proud.

It was the corral outside, however, that fascinated her most. Like the stable, it was well-maintained, with a sturdy rail fence and small unwalled structures here and there to provide shade and stands for feed. A little bird could be seen at one of them, pink and gray and parrotlike as it bobbed for seeds in the grain, but otherwise the only movement was the lazy flicking of the horses' tails. Some of them were stockmen's mounts, solid of leg and chest, but others were truly magnificent, thoroughbreds by the look of them, blacks and grays and a chestnut with an exquisite white blaze, and Stacey leaned hungrily over the fence, longing for a ride. One in particular caught her eye, a lively little bay, creamy with a mane that looked like a cloud of dust when it tossed its head, and a spirit that could be seen even from a distance.

"Oh, look," she cried, excited. "Isn't it beautiful?"

"Sure, missus," Billy Two agreed, repeating what appeared to be his favorite word. "That fellow, 'e bin

pick out good horses. Real good. 'E bin, smart, that
fellow."

"That fellow," it seemed, was Errol, though with
Billy Two it was hard to tell. He was, he informed her
with pride, a cowboy, or as he put it, "Mine bin
cowboy," though he bore no resemblance to the thirsty,
hard-faced men Stacey had sometimes seen riding into
San Francisco after a trail drive to Stockton. A cowboy in Australia, apparently, was just that, a boy—of
whatever age—who looked after the cows. In between,
he did odd jobs, like chopping wood or running er-
rands or helping out when Rudi, the kitchen boy, got
behind in his chores.

Billy Two proved a godsend in the days to come. It
was he who introduced her to the home paddock, the
large enclosure that contained not only the house and
barn, but the blacksmith shop as well, and the wool
sheds, the store, which supplied the entire station, and
the squat weathered outbuildings where the feed was
kept. And it was he who read the aching in her eyes
when she looked at the horses, and arranged for her to
have a mount of her own.

She did not know what to expect when he came
running out of the stables with a "Quick, missus, you
come—mine bin give you horse," but she followed
gamely, finding to her amazement, not a plodding
stockhorse, but that same leggy bay she had noticed
the first day in the paddock. Golden Girl, she was
called, and the name was wonderfully appropriate, for
Stacey could almost see sunlight in that thick, rippling
mane, and distinct flashes of gold showed in eyes that
sparkled with mischief, as if to say: Come on, silly girl!
You *said* you could ride. Let's see what you can do!

Had Errol picked her out? Stacey ran her hand over
that long sleek neck, laughing as the pretty filly tossed
her head with obvious impatience. It hardly seemed
likely. He had been so busy since that first night, she
rarely saw him—she got the feeling sometimes he was
avoiding her on purpose. She couldn't imagine his
taking time out of his precious schedule to worry about
her needs. Yet surely Billy Two wouldn't offer anything so valuable without the "boss man's" okay.

Having the horse gave her a whole new perspective, and almost in spite of herself, Stacey began to see the station with new eyes. Sheep ranching was not quite the careless pastoral occupation she had imagined. Nearly every morning, boundary riders set off for far paddocks with a week's provisions in their saddlebags, and men with tired faces seemed to be endlessly repairing fences or hauling metal tubs of water for cooking and bathing from billabongs in the river, over a mile away. Sometimes, in the late afternoon, she would follow, at a distance so she wouldn't get in the way, while supplementary feed was doled out to the flocks, or mobs, as they were called.

It never failed to intrigue her, the way the sheep all seemed to sense the feed wagon at the same time, raising their heads in a single motion and surging forward, a rolling sea of merino gray. One of the men would take the reins, guiding the cart in a wide circle while others leapt into the back, splitting open the bags and tumbling grain out in a stream behind. The sheep would follow greedily, baaing and bleating until a woolly gray arc was stretched across the barren ocher of the field.

Even with the restrictions imposed on her—Stacey had strict orders to ride only in the home paddock, and then only along the fence, or on the well-marked path that led to the river—there was a wonderful sense of freedom, just in being in the open again, and she felt as light as the wind that whipped through her hair. And sometimes, just sometimes, when she gave the horse its head and they cantered together across an open stretch of sand, spewing dust in feathery trails behind them, she almost forgot she had a care in the world.

Other times, it was harder to forget, times that came most often with dusk, when the sun was fading but the gold of the lamps had not yet taken hold. She was especially aware of it one evening as she sat in front of the mirror and stared at her reflection, all dressed up for dinner—a pretty fashion plate that no one was going to see.

At least I don't have to worry about wearing the

same outfit every day, she thought wryly. She had
been surprised that first afternoon, after Billy Two
had given her a tour of the stables, to come into the
parlor and find a gnomelike woman waiting for her.
Once, when she was younger, she had been the housekeeper—surely an improvement over Mrs. Sweeney!
Now she earned her keep mending and making dresses
for the servants. Stacey had not expected much, but
four days later she had a wardrobe of as many new
dresses, simple but serviceable, three everyday frocks
and one slightly more elegant gown for evening wear—
all in shades that would look stunning with Maude
Quinn's eyes, telling Stacey where the fabric had come
from.

Maude . . .

Her lips puckered slightly as she looked at the glass.
Maude had been nothing but kind these past two
weeks, riding over at least every other day to see if
things were all right or there was anything she could
do. But try as she would, Stacey could never feel
comfortable with her.

It was not that she saw her as a rival . . . not really.
She had been frightened when D'Arcy spit out those
ugly accusations—she had spent a sleepless night thrashing with the jealousy that churned in her stomach,
making her physically sick—but in the morning, she
had seen things more clearly, and she had to admit she
was being foolish. Nothing in Maude's manner, nothing she had said or done, gave the least indication that
she was, or had ever been, in love with Errol Cameron. A dalliance perhaps. Stacey could believe that
. . . there was something distinctly unconventional about
Maude, a defiantly fey quality that might make that
sort of risk appealing. But dalliances in the past could
not hurt her now.

She fidgeted restlessly, picking up her brush, then
putting it down again. Nor did she truly believe that
Errol, no matter how he felt, was carrying on a sordid
affair with his brother's fiancée. He had a strong code
of honor—as little as she knew him, she was sure of
that—and while she was still under his roof, still tenta-

tively his wife, he would keep a rein on any masculine impulses he might have.

Only how was he going to feel later if he learned that she and D'Arcy had been lying? How was Maude going to feel? What would happen then to dalliances of the past?

Stacey dined alone that night, as she had every night since her arrival. D'Arcy either ate by himself in his bachelor quarters on the other side of the house or rode off to Mirandola, where he spent the night, in the guestroom theoretically . . . with Maude's senile, half-blind father as chaperone, for all that she was supposed to be concerned about her "reputation"! In a way, it was a relief, for Stacey had been more than a little nervous at the thought of having to sit across the table from him and make small talk, though she had to admit, since that one incident at the creek, he had treated her in an almost gentlemanly manner. No more advances, no lewd insinuations—nothing but a hint of amusement in his eyes sometimes to let her know he had not given up and she would be a fool to drop her guard.

As for Errol, she almost never saw him now. The drought had continued, despite those few dark clouds she saw more than once on the horizon, and the land was so brittle she could almost hear it cracking as she sat on the veranda steps and stared out at the paddock. It seemed to her he was busy all the time, full days spent in the fields, sometimes even nights. And on the rare occasions when he got back at a decent hour, one of the men always seemed to appear a few minutes later, dragging him off on some emergency or other.

"It's getting worse, isn't it?" she said one night. He had just come back and was brushing the dust off a wide-brimmed slouch hat before entering the parlor. "The drought, I mean."

"You might put it that way," he replied, tossing the hat on a chair as he headed toward the kitchen, where Mrs. Sweeney kept salt beef and a loaf of bread for sandwiches. Then, catching her expression, he turned and added: "It's not so much that it's worse as that it hasn't gotten better. We've been expecting it to break anytime now. I could have sworn the other morning when I woke up it was going to rain. I could feel it in my bones, like an old hatter with rheumatism. But all we got was more dust."

"I know . . . it's frightening to look outside and see how dry it is. D'Arcy said the day I got here that droughts can go on for five years—or more."

Errol's brow tightened into a frown. The mention of D'Arcy's name, Stacey wondered—or what he said? One of the kelpies had followed him and was lying just outside, its nose and paws on the threshold. She had tried to make friends with it once, but like the others, it was a working dog and would have nothing to do with anyone but its master.

"In the outback maybe," he conceded. "But not here. My brother has a tendency to overdramatize. Charming in the drawing room, I'm sure, but hardly appropriate on a sheep station. Several months is considered a drought for us. A year without rain—which is what we've had—can be a disaster."

A note of tension had crept into his voice. "If it goes on then," Stacey said uncertainly, "if it lasts longer . . ." Her eyes widened, making her look more frightened than she realized. "Could it ruin you? Would you lose everything?"

"Not likely." He smiled, dark eyes first, then his lips. "I'm afraid I'm guilty of overdramatizing too . . . though not, fortunately, of poor business sense. I've made a few investments in Sydney—all the profits haven't gone into the land. The Cameron family fortune is never going to rise or fall on the fate of one sheep station. Even if we lost every head on the place and had to restock completely, we'd survive. Which, by the way, isn't going to happen. Cameron's Creek isn't overgrazed like most stations in the area."

"And that makes a difference?" Stacey was not just asking questions to keep him talking. The complexities of sheep ranching were proving surprisingly intriguing.

"All the difference in the world." He seemed to respond to her interest. "There are too many damned fools milking their land for all it's worth. They run a sheep every three, four acres, risky enough in good years—then they wonder why they're wiped out in a drought. I allow ten acres a sheep, and only with irrigated land to provide oats and lucerne. I've cut the stock at Mirandola too, so we'll all get through. But I don't mind telling you, I'll be glad to hear that first clap of real thunder and see raindrops pelting down."

"So will I," Stacey said feelingly. She knew she ought to worry about the station, the way he did, but all she could think of was the terrible heat and how cooling rain would be. "I keep imagining I see clouds on the horizon, but every time I let myself hope, they disappear."

"I've seen the same thing," he admitted. "Dust clouds, most likely—we'll be getting the first flash of heat lightning any day now. And for God's sake, don't get your hopes up then." He refrained from mentioning the thought that was uppermost in his mind, the danger of bush fires, every station owner's dread. There was no point alarming her unnecessarily. "You've never seen one of our dust storms—Aussie showers, my grandmother called them. I think she liked the grim humor. There was always a touch of the macabre about 'Crazy Kate.' Fortunately they give plenty of warning. The sky turns a tawny color and darkens until it almost looks like night. Then the winds come, and God help anyone caught in the open! Make that Rule Number One when you're riding—"

"I thought," Stacey interrupted, grinning, "that Rule Number One was " 'Never go off the road or out of sight of the fence.' "

"So it is. Sensible, too—mind you remember it. Rule Number Two then: If the sky darkens, you turn around and come home. No questions, no stopping, no nothing. Agreed?"

Stacey shivered a little, his voice sounded so harsh. "Are they really that dangerous? Dust storms?"

"Everything in this country is dangerous if you don't know how to handle it. A shepherd can ride out a dust storm in his hut; even the sheep know enough to lie down and huddle together—and if they're lucky, they won't be suffocated in a mound of dust by the time it's

over. But a woman alone, no shelter, no way to get
her bearings in the blinding swirls of dust—yes, it
could be *very* dangerous. There's something strangely
compelling about an Aussie shower, a kind of magnificent fury. Fascinating in a way, but utterly uncontrollable . . . wildness with a will of its own."

He was surprised to see her laugh. "I think that's
what you should have named the filly I've been riding
. . . Aussie Shower. She's a willful creature—sometimes
I think I have hold of a whirlwind when I try to pull
back on the reins. Spirit I call it when I'm enjoying the
ride . . . though I suspect stubbornness is nearer the
mark."

"You like her then?" He caught the excitement in
her voice, and it seemed to please him. "I thought
when I chose her, you'd be a match for each other. It
seems I was right."

So he *had* picked the filly out for her. A generous
gesture . . . yet he'd said nothing about it. "Yes, I like
her very much. And you're right. I think she's even
feistier than I am."

He did not answer, only smiled again, rather wearily
it seemed to Stacey, and made his way back to the
kitchen, leaving her to stare after him.

Would she ever figure him out? she wondered. Would
she even have the chance to try? He could be so
thoughtful sometimes, giving her the horse, arranging
a wardrobe to replace the clothes she had left in Sydney, but he never let himself get close, never for an
instant dropped that maddening aloofness he had
wrapped around himself like a protective cloak. She
had been so sure at first she would have time to get to
know him, time to persuade him she was not as shallow and deceitful as she had seemed. But how was she
going to do that if they never talked about anything
but weather and dust and how she liked her horse?

She tried to keep herself occupied in the long hot
days that followed, knowing it was the only way to
keep from brooding. Still, it wasn't easy when there
was so little to do. Running the household was plainly
out of the question. She had no experience, and Mrs.
Sweeney was hardly one to accept even capable super-

vision. Maude had been right about the housekeeper, after all. She was not nearly as untidy as she seemed; in fact, she made quite a show of cleaning, though it was a losing battle. Every morning she would go through the house from one end to the other, armed with a mop and a quarter-pail of precious water. But no sooner had she finished than the dust would seep in again, and by noon the floor was gritty underfoot.

The kitchen offered no better possibilities, though cooking was much more in Stacey's line. She had never prepared an entire meal by herself, nor was she particularly eager to try, but she had a real talent for sweets, which she naively assumed would be welcome since it would take some of the burden off Mrs. Sweeney. Her blancmange had always been tasty—better than Cook's at home—and while she had been allowed to bake a cake only once, it had come out light and perfectly textured.

Mrs. Sweeney, however, had other ideas about the appropriateness of another woman in her kitchen. She did not exactly tell Stacey to get out the one time she ventured along the covered passageway to the self-contained structure at the rear of the main house—out-and-out rudeness to the owner's wife was apparently not tolerated on Errol Cameron's station—but she might as well have.

"Mind the corner," she said sharply as she bent over to stoke the ancient black iron cookstove that had already turned the small room into a furnace. They had killed a bullock in the morning, unusual for that hot weather, and the choicest cut had been sent to the homestead, where it was now roasting in the oven. The rest had gone to the cookhouse, to be prepared for the men and their families or corned for later use. Unlike some of the smaller stations, Mrs. Sweeney was expected to tend only to the house and its occupants.

"The corner?" Stacey echoed, puzzled.

Mrs. Sweeney took a mound of dough from under a damp cloth and slapped it down on the long wooden counter. "Behind you."

Stacey turned. She could make out nothing in the

dark shadows but a bit of moisture where something must have spilled. "I don't see anything."

"Snakes." Mrs. Sweeney dug her hands up to the wrists in dough, kneading it back and forth with grim efficiency. "They like th' corners where it's dark. Nice 'n wet, too. Y' stand round the kitchen, ye're askin' t' git bit."

Stacey got the message. From that point on the kitchen was Mrs. Sweeney's, and she put up with soggy cakes with depressions in the middle and a variety of puddings that all had different names when they came to the table, but looked and tasted the same to her.

Perhaps if there had been neighbors nearby, girls her own age she could laugh and gossip with, other young matrons, she would not have been so restless. But the only women on the station were the wives of the few married men, and even had class structure been less distinct, they looked so busy and harried, with crying children tugging at their skirts and loads of laundry in their arms, she would have felt uncomfortable intruding on their time. And the only other station in the area—the only building, as far as she knew—was Mirandola, where she very definitely did not want to go.

Thus it came as a complete surprise one afternoon when she ventured a short distance off the road—not so far she couldn't see it over her shoulder; she had not forgotten the sternness in Errol's voice when he reemphasized "Rule Number One"—and came across a house on a shallow hill in the midst of a grove of tall trees with peeling bark that she now recognized as gums, or eucalypti.

It was little more than a shed, she saw as she approached, though sturdily, if curiously constructed. A long open room ran across the front, rather like a porch with posts as a roof, and walls that came up two or three feet, to the place where windows would have been if there were any. There was an unexpectedly pleasant look about it, casual but airy, and generous splashes of light spilled on a rough-hewn table and rustic chairs made of barked wood, like the chairs on the veranda at Cameron's Creek.

She had just dismounted and was about to call out when a man appeared in the doorway. At first glance, he seemed as eccentric as his house. Darkish hair, about as gray as auburn, tumbled untidily over bushy eyebrows, and his beard was a startling black with streaks of white. He was wearing a smock of some sort, from which the sleeves had been ripped out, a splotched, muddy brown, with loose burgundy trousers and shoes that might have been any color before the dust attacked them.

He stared at her curiously. Then his eyes narrowed in what might have been the beginnings of a smile.

"Mrs. Cameron, what a pleasure."

"You know me?" Stacey looked up, surprised, as she looped the reins over a post that seemed to have been placed there for that purpose.

"We have a small community here." The smile had come out now, incongruous somehow with the unkempt beard and rather satanic eyebrows. "Very small . . . as I suspect you've found out by now. Naturally I know who you are."

"Of course." Stacey laughed in spite of herself. She was the newcomer here. Her presence could hardly be a secret. "If you came to San Francisco and mingled in my circles, I'd know everything about you in two days flat. I daresay you discovered me in ten minutes."

"Make that a minute and a half." He started toward the shade of the open front room, gesturing for her to follow. "I saw you ride by in a rented wagon with the younger Cameron and his bride-to-be. I'm afraid all I have to offer is a bit of tepid tea, but it was brewed a short time ago . . . unless, of course, you prefer beer."

"Tea would be fine." She reached up, removing the broad-brimmed hat she was sure was hopelessly unbecoming, and let a faint breeze blow through her hair. The cream-colored bonnet with its sad little birds' wings was hardly suitable for riding in the searing Australian sun, and the hat had been appropriated from one of the younger station hands. "I hadn't realized I was so thirsty. I thought it was late enough in

the afternoon for a ride, but the heat is as intense at
four-thirty as it was at noon."

"It doesn't cool off until well after dark," the man
agreed. He picked up a china pot and poured pale-
looking liquid into a cup he had taken from a cup-
board by the door. "Thirst is a way of life here . . .
and the dust doesn't help. It coats the inside of your
mouth until you think nothing will ever wash it away."

"Thank you." Stacey accepted the cup and took a
welcome sip. The flavor was subtle, but distinct, like
green tea she had had once in a shop Grandfather had
taken her to in Chinatown. "I don't think I've ever
seen a room like this before—do you call it a porch? I
love the way the air and light come in. It must be very
practical. In summer, at least."

"In the winter too." A bottle of beer lay open on
the table, but he made no move to pick it up, pouring
a second cup of tea instead. "I don't mind the cold,
never have, but I can't abide a gloomy place. Light is
essential . . . for my soul and my work."

"Your work?" For the first time Stacey noticed an
easel in a shaded corner, just out of the direct rays of
the sun. "You're an artist then?" Without waiting for
an answer, she went over for a closer look.

The painting on the easel was the same one he had
been working on the day she arrived. Finished now, it
awaited only the last whim of the artist to be taken
down and set with the others in the storeroom. The
colors were softer than they had been earlier, blending
into each other with a subtlety that almost made the
scene look hazy, though every detail was sharp and
well-defined. The tree no longer dominated, as it had
before, or the magpie, oddly predatory in its branches,
but they were still there, disturbing somehow, waiting
for the eye to pick them out.

"Why . . ." She turned to look at him, startled.
"You're Fitzhugh Blackburn."

The announcement seemed to amuse him. "You
see, this *is* a small community. A pretty woman newly
arrived can be none other than Mrs. Errol Cameron.
And a man with a painting on an easel must be Fitz
Blackburn, the mad artist."

"Are you really mad?" Stacey laughed as she cocked her head to one side, studying the painting. She had an almost uncanny sense that she was looking at the real Australia, hidden somewhere behind that vast, arid wasteland. "I should say you were anything but mad . . . though there is a touch of madness in that bird on the branches. Actually, no one said a word to me about where you lived, or that you were within riding distance of the homestead. I knew you by the mood and brushstrokes on the canvas. Only the man who created *The Silver Swan* could have painted this."

"You recognized my style?" He made no effort to conceal his surprise. Like Errol, apparently, he had not expected anything resembling brains beneath that pretty face and rather dusty hairdo. "Most unexpectedly, I must say—I thought your husband was the only one who had a passing acquaintance with art in this godforsaken spot. Next you're going to tell me you're a painter yourself and I'm in for some serious competition."

"Not exactly." Stacey tried not to giggle, but it was hard playing the sophisticated lady when she was still some days short of seventeen. "I dabble in it, that's all . . . mainly pencil drawings and watercolors. I've tried a few sketches since I've been here, but it's no use. I think you have to work in oils to do justice to the colors, and I've never had the nerve to try."

She glanced around as she spoke, finding the place strangely Spartan, devoid even of artist's supplies except for the tubes and brushes crowded on a single small table, as if openness and lack of clutter were as essential as air and light to his work. It was a minute before she realized that there was a second easel, standing even deeper in the shadows, draped with a white cloth which gave it a mysterious appearance.

She had just opened her mouth to ask about it, when he stepped in front, carelessly, but deliberately, as if he didn't want her to see it.

"I have some other paintings in the back," he said. "Perhaps you'd like to see them. And"—he had already started toward the door when he turned with a disarming grin—"I tell you now you ought to feel honored. I don't allow everyone to see my paintings."

Stacey spent the next half-hour in a large dark room in the rear of the house, standing next to the only window, absolutely fascinated as Fitz Blackburn sorted through dozens of paintings stacked against the walls and selected a few to bring over to the light where she could see them better. They were all landscapes, or predominately landscapes, though some had figures in them, workers for the most part, weary-eyed shepherds or shearers with stooped backs and elongated arms, men who had spent too long in the dust and lost whatever it was that made them unique and individual.

The real Australia, she thought again, sure now that her first instinct had been right and she was seeing something deep and undeniable. The real Australia. Beautiful and desolate, wild and serene, a challenge and a passion and a hardship to splinter men in pieces . . . and she sensed she would never see the land around her with quite the same eyes again.

"I am almost speechless," she said, pausing impishly as they ventured out again. "Almost . . . but not quite. I'm never at a total loss for words, I'm afraid—as my sisters used to point out at home." Her eye landed on the mystery painting again, still hidden beneath its dusty shroud. "Aren't you going to show me that one?" she asked, feeling relaxed enough to tease a little.

He shook his head, not annoyed, but definite. "I show only the paintings I choose—I always have and I always will. And that is not one I have chosen."

"Oh?" Stacey stared at him curiously. "It isn't finished yet?" Artists were often sensitive about works in progress, she knew. But to her surprise, he shook his head again.

"Quite the contrary, it's been finished for many years—but it's private. No one has ever seen it but me."

There was enough firmness in his tone to warn her not to press, and for all her unsatisfied curiosity, Stacey could only smile and accept the biscuits he offered out of a rather battered tin. He was a funny man, but likable enough, and she supposed it was an artist's prerogative to be eccentric. After all, Errol had told her he even refused to have his paintings displayed in a museum.

A rustling sound came from somewhere behind her. Looking around, she saw a flicker of movement in the shadows under the table, and two yellow-green eyes peered out. A moment later a small body slithered into sight, a scrawny cat that might have been an indistinct brownish color—or might just have been rolling too much in the dust.

"Well . . . hello." Stacey crouched down, holding out her hand, half-expecting the cat to skitter away, but delighted when it didn't. She had not realized until that moment how much she missed having a pet to play with, and she was so interested in the cat, she barely registered the sound of hoofbeats coming up the hill. "Who is your friend?" she asked Fitz, laughing. "Does he have a name?"

"Blasted if I know," the artist replied. "I didn't invite the thing here, that's for sure. I toss a crumb to the magpies now and then, pretty creatures—much more pleasing to an artist's eye—and what comes prowling around but that little scrounger. Have to feed it, too, or there wouldn't be a bird left on the hill."

Stacey, who had noticed a plate and a water bowl under the table, suspected he was fonder of the cat than he was willing to admit. She broke off a piece of the biscuit and held out her hand again, not even noticing as she did that the hoofbeats had come closer, stopping somewhere just around the corner of the house. The cat hesitated a second, eyeing the food warily, then snatched it out of her hand and retreated under the table again.

The movement startled her. She jumped up, stumbling as her heel caught in the hem of her gown. Fitz Blackburn's hand came out, steadying her arm, and she looked up, laughing, to see that he was laughing too.

It was a comfortable moment, the first she had had since she arrived in Australia, and she felt almost as if they had been friends for years. It didn't occur to her even to think about proprieties—to wonder if his hand had lingered a second too long on her arm—until she saw his expression change, as if something behind her had startled him. Too late, she recalled the hoofbeats she had heard before, and she turned apprehensively.

There, a few yards away, with the darkest, angriest expression she had ever seen, was her husband.

Crimson flooded her cheeks as she realized how she must look, standing so close, her face turned up to a virtual stranger . . . his hand resting on her arm. Yet it had all been so innocent.

"Errol—" she began, but he didn't let her get another word out.

"I would ask what's going on, but I don't want to know. Get on your horse, madam—we're going back to the homestead. *Now*. As for you . . ." Fury flashed, barely controlled in his eyes as he looked back at the other man. "You can do anything you want . . . with any woman you want . . it's none of my business. But this woman is off limits!"

"Dammit man!" The artist's face was darkening to match his. "Get your mind out of the gutter. She stumbled, and I caught her. That's all there is to it. What would you have me do? Let her fall?"

"What I would have you do," Errol replied, jaw tautly clenched, "is stay away from my wife. Have you got that?"

Fitz Blackburn did not answer, but he didn't back down either, and it seemed to Stacey, watching, that the two men were going to stand there facing each other forever. When the tension finally broke, it was Errol who turned away. Without another word, he strode over to where he had left his mount, a magnificent chestnut stallion, and swung with savage grace into the saddle.

Numb and heartsick, Stacey could only follow as he touched his heel to the horse's flank and started, much too fast, down the hill. She had almost thought—she had dared to hope for an instant!—that he was jealous. Only it wasn't his passions that had been touched when he rode into the yard and saw her with Fitz Blackburn's hand on her arm. It was his pride! The same possessive pride that made him reject her out of hand when he discovered she had belonged to another man first!

"You're being unfair," she protested when they reached level ground and he had slowed to an easier gait. "He was telling the truth. I *did* stumble. He just reached out to catch me."

"I daresay he did—this time." He had cooled somewhat, but the grim irony in his tone was no more comforting than that flash of hot temper a short time before. "Fitz Blackburn has never cultivated a reputation as a gentleman. His cottage is hardly an appropriate place for naive little girls to linger over tea. When one of the men told me he had seen you ride up—" He broke off, not finishing, but Stacey could imagine what was going through his mind.

"How was I supposed to know?" she cried out helplessly. "You never said anything about him. You never told me—"

"I did tell you I wanted you to stay on the road," he reminded her dryly. "I believe I was most emphatic about it. Rule Number One—or had you already forgotten?"

"No, of course I hadn't forgotten. And I did stay on the road . . . almost. I never got out of sight of it, not for a minute. And it didn't occur to me you wouldn't want me to talk to Fitz Blackburn. I . . . I thought you admired him."

"Did you?" He flicked the reins, pushing ahead, and Stacey had to prod Golden Girl to keep up. "Admiring his talent, which I do—very much—is not the same thing as admiring the man. He is a brilliant artist. I am perfectly ready to support him. House, food, paints . . . whatever he needs. But that doesn't mean I have to like him. Or that he has to like me, for that matter."

"You're . . . his patron?"

"Certainly. How did you think he survived if he wouldn't sell his paintings or show them . . . or hang them in a gallery?"

"But . . ." Stacey gasped as a new, unpleasant thought came to her. "Surely you wouldn't cut him off

because of . . . of this misunderstanding. He really *is*
brilliant. His work is as fine as I've ever seen. It would
be a shame if—"

"Don't worry, my dear." Errol stopped his horse,
thrusting out a hand to take hold of her reins and look
for a long moment into her eyes. "I'm not likely to
jeopardize the career of a man we both agree is brilliant, am I—for a wife who isn't going to be here more
than a few weeks at most?"

It was the closest they had come to speaking of the
thing that was on both their minds, and Stacey gulped
back the hot retorts that rose to her lips. Why am I
quarreling with him like this? she thought miserably as
they started forward again. Why do I keep answering
back when everything I say makes him angrier? They
had so little time together—all she wanted these few
precious minutes was to get closer to him, to make
him want to get closer to her. He looked so handsome
when she turned her head, glancing up through lowered lashes. He could be so gentle and kind when he
chose; yet he seemed more and more distant with each
passing day, and she didn't know how she was ever
going to reach him.

Errol left her when they arrived at the station and
rode across the yard to speak with some of the men
who had just come in from the fields. The dogs were
milling around, yelping and fighting among themselves,
and she could see Mrs. Sweeney headed toward the
house with a heavy metal bucket in each hand. Ordinarily she would have tended to Golden Girl herself,
but she was so tired and so discouraged, it was easier
to hand the reins over to the stableboy.

D'Arcy had just come in and was standing by the
rail, close enough to hear the men's conversation as he
waited to turn over his own mount. He looked up
slowly, half-smiling when he caught sight of Stacey—an
unpleasant expression that sent a shudder of revulsion
through her. He knows, she thought, disgusted. He
knows what happened between Errol and me, and he
thinks it's funny! She wanted nothing more than to get
away, but it was too late, for he was already coming
toward her.

"Trouble in paradise?" His voice was low and insinuating, and Stacey bristled at the laughter in its depths. "Such a brief, brief honeymoon—and now I hear your handsome husband, to whom you insist on being true, found you at Fitz Blackburn's place. Leapt to the wrong conclusion, too, I'll wager. Errol's very good at that."

Stacey gave him her iciest look. "News travels fast around here—especially if you're good at eavesdropping."

"Ah?" The barb slid off his back. "He *did* leap to the wrong conclusions then. You wouldn't be so testy if he hadn't." His voice changed, growing almost thoughtful, as if he wanted to drop the waspish mask but didn't know how. "You can't blame him, you know. You didn't exactly come to him pure as the driven snow."

Didn't I? Stacey thought bitterly. And whose fault was that? But she didn't say anything as she turned and walked around the corner, toward the steps that led to the veranda. D'Arcy was a troublemaker. She hated herself for listening to him, but he did have a way of hitting on the truth. She *hadn't* come to Errol pure, and it looked like he wasn't going to forget it.

Why, *why* had she been so foolish? She started up the steps, pausing at the top. It was bad enough, getting herself into a compromising position, albeit unknowingly—but to argue with him too! Why couldn't she have been demure just once in her life? Why couldn't she have looked up with big repentant eyes and sweetly said, "I'm sorry," even if she hadn't done anything wrong?

He had a temper, that was clear . . . and she had a temper too, heaven help her. Discouraged, she sat down on one of the chairs and stared out at the mountains, already turning purple in the early haze of dusk. If neither of them could back down—if they both clung to their stubbornness and their anger—how were they ever going to work things out?

It was not until later, when she was getting ready for bed, that it occurred to her to wonder what it was that made Errol dislike Fitz Blackburn so much. She had just tucked the mosquito netting around the four-poster on the sleeping veranda where she now spent her nights, and she sat for a moment there watching the play of moonlight on gauzy white.

It was not because of her—his words had made that clear. Nor was is some kind of prudish reaction to that rather unsavory lack of a "gentleman's" reputation. He had said it was none of his business what the artist did, and he had meant it.

But plainly there was something there, something beneath the surface . . . something that went back a long way . . . and she drifted off to sleep wondering what it was.

15

Stacey woke up the next morning feeling utterly drained, as if she hadn't slept at all. The heat seemed to have gotten worse—or perhaps it was just the constant, day-after-day soaring temperatures that was so depleting—and it was much later than usual by the time she dressed and forced herself out.

She had expected to find the yard nearly empty, and in fact it was, though Errol was still there, repairing one of the gates, a routine task she would have thought he'd leave for the men. To her surprise, all the hot anger of the day before seemed to have disappeared, and he was relaxed, almost jovial as he waved her over, chatting casually for a few minutes, which he rarely did in the middle of the day. Apparently there were a few things she still didn't know about him. Yesterday she had discovered how fast his temper flared up. Today she was learning that it ebbed away just as easily, and he didn't seem to hold a grudge.

"I didn't mean to be so hard on you, Stacey," he said, letting up for long enough to lean against the rail, a large iron hammer in his hand. "But the rules are there for your protection. Going off the road, even for a few minutes, even if you *think* you have it in sight, can be disastrous. Paddocks here aren't small, orderly pastures. They can be five, ten, twenty miles square—not twenty square miles—and even if you know where the nearest water is, a difference of half a degree in orientation can throw you off. We had an old hatter just last year who thought he'd save some time, taking a shortcut across one of the paddocks. We found his bones several months later . . . a couple of hundred yards from the water hole he'd been trying to reach."

Stacey caught the point, shivering. She noticed he had made no mention of Fitz Blackburn, and she didn't either. "What's a 'hatter'?" she asked curiously.

"An old shepherd—so called because they tend to go quite mad. It's a lonely life out in the far paddocks with no one but the dogs and sheep to talk to. Be a good girl now—stay on the road. Even if the wind grabs your hat and blows it across the fields, don't go after it. Agreed?"

Stacey couldn't imagine it made any more sense, riding in the sun without a hat, but she wasn't about to repeat the same mistake she had made yesterday. "Agreed," she said sweetly, grinning to herself when she saw that the answer pleased him.

Not exactly an apology, she thought later as she strolled behind the kitchen shed, where the last of the morning shade was quickly disappearing. But then, she hadn't exactly apologized either. Perhaps that was as close as two stubborn people like Errol Cameron and her were ever going to come.

Budgie, the little black washerwoman, was bent over a rusted iron tub scrubbing soiled table linen up and down a corrugated metal board. Stacey paused for a minute to watch. Poor girl, her name was almost whimsically appropriate, like a combination of "bulge" and "pudgy," which aptly described the thick waistline that made her look like a muffin with legs. They had had a regular laundress before, an excellent Irish girl, but she had left a few days after Stacey got there, whether to get married or seek employment in town, no one seemed to know. Probably the former, Stacey thought, for men outnumbered women in Australia and a girl who was even passably pretty with a willingness to work had her choice of husbands, no questions asked.

Even from a distance, she could smell the soap, great yellow bars boiled from fat and caustic, and the hard mineral-laden water had a scum on top which left everything that was washed in it stiff and sulfury. The odor was nauseating, and Stacey turned away, braving

the sun to walk across the yard. Someone had set out
a bowl for the dogs, and a gray-and-pink bird was
splashing futilely in the last dregs of moisture at the
bottom. The air was as dry as ever, the clouds still
elusive, but it seemed to Stacey there were more birds
now than she had seen when she arrived. Just the
other morning, she had gone for a ride, and one of the
gums on a hillside not far from the river had been so
massed with magpies, it looked like it had sprouted
black-and-white blossoms. Entranced, she had stopped,
hearing for the first time the sweet, liquid sound of
their voices.

From Billy Two she was learning about the birds of
the bush. She could pick some of them out now and
call them by name. The magpies were the first she had
seen, and she still privately thought them the prettiest,
the vivid contrast of their plumage managing somehow
to look sparkling and clean even in the dust. The pink
parrotlike birds, disguised with plainer color on top,
so they looked like a sheet of gray all dappled in the
dust, were galahs, with the emphasis on the last
syllable—ga-*lah*—and the large white bird with the
brilliant feathered crown that strutted into the yard
like he owned the place was a sulphur-crested cockatoo.

Her favorites were the drabbest of them all, the
brownish-gray kookaburras, with their bright eyes and
somber little faces and the strange shrill cry that had
earned them the nickname "laughing jackasses" from
the early settlers. Billy Two had taught her how to
coax them up on the rail with bits of meat, which they
would take right out of her hand, testing tentatively in
long delicate-looking beaks. Fresh beef and mutton
they adored, and she would have a whole line of them
sometimes, all along the veranda. But try to pass off
something spicy, like sausage or salt beef, and they
would spit it out with contempt. Nothing went to
waste, though, for the magpies, bold as brass, swept in
and snatched it up.

Talking to Billy Two was an adventure. Now that
she was used to the Pidgin he spoke, she could understand him fairly well, but he had a way of mixing
pronouns that was as exasperating as it was amusing.

Everything was " 'e" or "that fellow," with an occasional "she" thrown in for good measure, no matter what the gender of the object being discussed! Thus, "that fellow, 'e bin come," might mean that Errol was on the way or that Rudi the kitchen boy was there—or there was an especially pushy cockatoo in the yard. Or that Maude had just been and left. And "she" might be one of the rams who had been brought in with a bad case of foot rot!

"Why do they call him Billy Two?" she asked Errol later that same day when they met for a few minutes in the horse paddock where she had stopped to curry Golden Girl, not trusting the stableboys to do it properly. "Is there a Billy One?"

"Don't be so logical." He looked tired, but his eyes were twinkling and Stacey sensed he enjoyed the question. "Aborigines are given names when they're babies, but they only use them, the males at least, while they're children. Once they come of age, they're known by the class they belong to. A boy who has gone through the ceremony where his front teeth are knocked out, for instance, is known as 'Kogomoolga,' and an old man might be called 'Thowmunga' by the tribe. They don't seem to mind not having names of their own until they come into contact with us and see that it's part of the white culture. Then they tend to ask the squatters—the station owners—for names . . . as Billy Two asked me."

"But why—?"

"I didn't." He laughed, forestalling the obvious question. "I find the names most people give offensively 'cute.' Gooseberry comes to mind, and Billy Chops and Ricketty Dick, though the natives don't seem to be insulted. I tried 'Dan,' a good name, I thought, but apparently too plain, for he looked around and found another."

"Yes, but where on earth did he pick up something like 'Billy Two'?"

"At Mirandola. Al Quinn gives his men classical names—Apollo and Copernicus, things like that. One was Plato, which somehow got corrupted to Billy Tool, easier on the aborigine tongue. I guess—and which our boy corrupted further when he took it as his own. *Voilà*, Billy Two! And not a Billy One in sight!"

It was the last time Stacey was to see Errol for the next several days, and she was glad, thinking it over later—and wondering if he had planned it that way—that the moment had been one of shared laughter, and not of anger. She had not realized it then, but lambing was just beginning, one of the busiest seasons of the sheep calendar, and it was a rare man, including D'Arcy, for they were shorthanded, who had any time to himself . . . or got more than three or four hours of sleep. Even Rudi was pressed into service, leaving only Billy Two at home to help a disgruntled Mrs. Sweeney in the kitchen and tend to all the chores in the barn and stables.

Lambing was always a critical time, even more so this year when every eye was turned anxiously toward the sky, searching for the rain that never materialized despite the clouds that seemed to be getting darker and thicker every day. Without rain, there could be no green shoots in the barren earth, and without the green, ewes would be too weak to suckle and scraggly little lambs would follow after them with pathetic jerking motions, little puppets pulled on strings. In a good year, a station like Cameron's Creek, with its large herd of purebred merinos, the aristocrats of the sheep world, would mark many thousands of lambs. If the drought continued, the count might be in the hundreds.

The men rotated their busy schedules, sleeping in short shifts as they went out into the paddocks to make sure everything was going smoothly—"lambing down," it was called. Each ewe was carefully watched and placed shortly before or after it had lambed in a separate hurdle pen, where it would be kept until sometime the next day. That was only the beginning, however, for a lamb's first days of life were precarious: dingoes prowled around the paddock fences, coming dangerously close to the shepherds' fires at night; crows hovered on branches and fenceposts, looking for a chance to peck out a newborn's eyes; and the vultures, the only living things that profited from the drought, formed great soaring circles in the sky. The lambs in the home paddock were kept out during the day and brought back each night, those that had been well mothered being put in pens of their own. The others went in separate pens with their mothers.

Stacey turned seventeen a week later, a hot day marked by winds that sent flurries of dust across the yard. Lambing was still at its height, and she had not expected the day to be any different from all the others. But when she went to dinner, alone as usual, there was a small package at her place, wrapped in silver lace with an elegant black velvet ribbon.

From Errol? It had to be, for no one else would give her a gift, but, characteristically, he had left no note, allowing her to draw her own conclusions. She had not even thought he knew when her birthday was, though she supposed Grandfather must have sent her birth certificate along with other important papers when he had packed her off to her new husband.

She turned the package over in her hands, enjoying the anticipation almost too much to open it. It was funny, every other birthday had been just a day for presents and attention; this time she truly felt different. Perhaps seventeen really *was* older, or perhaps she had just matured so much she no longer recognized the frivolous, flirtatious girl who had lived only to twist her grandfather around her little finger and get exactly what she wanted. Just a few months ago she would have torn the little parcel open without stopping to think, eager only to see what was inside. Now, what mattered was that Errol had given it to her, not the gift itself, and she slipped the wrappings off slowly, taking care not to crush the pretty bow.

As she lifted the lid, a small but perfect diamond caught the light, every tiny facet flashing with fire.

Stacey gasped as she slipped it out of the box, holding it on the palm of her hand, only dimly aware of the tears that made it sparkle even more. Everything about it was exquisite, the stone itself, the yellow-gold setting, the slender gold chain to wear around her neck, and she knew without needing to be told that

Errol had spent considerable time and th ght picking it out for his bride. She was touched th he wanted her to have it . . . touched, but saddened too, in ways that tugged at her heart. If she had been the woman he expected, the *wife* he expected, this would have been hers on their wedding night—he would have slipped it around her neck with an achingly tender kiss—and she would not be sitting there alone wondering if he was going to send her back.

And he was planning on it. She could see that now with a new objectivity she had not allowed herself before. The days of pretending and hoping and hinting at pregnancies that did not exist were over, and she had to face the truth. When lambing was done, when he had time to himself again, he was going to sit her down, gently perhaps, but firmly, and tell her he was arranging to have the marriage annulled. And it was going to tear her apart when he did.

She slept badly that night. The air was as stifling as ever, hot and dusty, but she had chosen to remain inside. It was more comfortable on the sleeping veranda, but the moon was full, and she longed for the privacy of her room, with only a single lamp turned low in the corner. The little diamond was on its chain around her neck, just long enough to touch the first swell of her breasts as she finally fell asleep.

Dreams haunted her, nagging, restless dreams, with sounds that kept coming out of nowhere. The ocean at home, the coolness, the smell of salt. Was that a foghorn she heard in the distance? But, no, it had changed, and it wasn't a horn—it was something else— and she was out in the paddocks with the men, and lambs were bleating all around . . . sad, lonely cries for mothers who were not there.

The sound came again, louder this time. Stacey sat up groggily, brushing her hair back from her eyes and wishing she had had the sense to twist it in thick braids on top of her head. She has just reached for a handkerchief to wipe her brow when she heard it again. Real now . . . not a dream at all. There *was* a lamb, and it sounded like it was right in the house.

Curious, she slipped a lightweight negligee over her

chemise, simple white jaconet with a modest trimming
of lace, and went out into the hall. If anything, the
sound was more muffled there. She followed it into
the parlor, where several of the lamps had been left
burning, then through the long hallway that led to the
kitchen passage. She had just reached the end when
the door opened and Errol came in from the opposite
direction.

The light in the hall was dim, and for a moment all
she could make out was a shadowy form, which she
recognized more by instinct than sight. The diamond
was still around her neck, and she had just started to
say something about it when he stepped forward and
she saw a baby lamb in his arms.

"Oh!" Stacey reached out, all other thoughts, even
the generous gift, flying from her mind. "What a darling. Have you ever seen anything so sweet?" The
lamb gave a low, piteous "maa-a-a-a" as she rubbed
her fingers across the woolly topknot, and she drew
back, realizing she had frightened it. "Poor little thing.
How old it is anyway? And what on earth is it doing
here? Where did it come from?"

Errol laughed at the questions spilling out of her
mouth. "I expect it came from the same place lambs
have come from since the beginning of time. It was
probably born this morning, though it might be two
days old. Rudi found it in the fields. He was coming
back from Emu Paddock with nothing but the moonlight to see by, and he noticed something white beside
the fence. It was just lying there, he said, with its head
up, looking straight ahead, as if waiting for someone
to come and rescue it."

"Or waiting for its mama to come back," Stacey
said. Errol had set the lamb on the floor, and it looked
like it was trying to figure out where it wanted to go,
moving tentatively on long legs that seemed to wobble
in all directions at once. It was shaking, but it did not
pull back when Stacey held out her hand again, and
she could feel it beginning to relax. "Maybe she left it
there for a reason. Won't she be worried when she
returns and finds it gone?"

Errol shook his head. He had gone into the parlor

and was back now with a lamp which he set on a small side table. "I'm afraid she abandoned it—that happens sometimes. If Rudi hadn't brought it in, it would have died before morning. It still may. They aren't always strong, these little orphan lambs. They don't all make it through the night."

Stacey sensed he was warning her not to form any attachments, in case something happened to the "little orphan." But it was impossible not to be attached, and anyway, it was such a spunky thing, she couldn't believe it was going to die. The trembling had stopped now, and it had begun to check out the passage, curiosity getting the best of coltish legs as they slid and skidded on the stone floor.

"How could its mother have abandoned it like that? Unless . . . Oh!" She stopped as an unpleasant thought hit her. "You don't suppose she . . . died."

"I doubt it," he replied, "though it's possible, of course. My guess is that it was a twin. Or maybe this is her first lamb. Ewes don't always make the best mothers on the first time around—they're better at it when they've had more experience." He pulled the lamb toward him, and Stacey noticed for the first time that he was holding a wine bottle. Something had been inserted in the cork—a quill, it looked like on closer examination—forming a narrow drinking tube.

"Wine for its first meal? Isn't that a little . . . debauched?"

"Very," he agreed, grinning. "But the debauchery was all mine. I drank the wine myself. This little chap's getting milk, with an egg mixed in for nourishment. It's the nearest thing to mother's milk, good and wholesome—if we can get enough of it into him." As if to emphasize his words, the lamb balked, setting its teeth and bleating stubbornly as Errol pried its jaw open with one hand and shoved the bottle in with the other. The first few drops had to be poured down its throat; then it seemed to get the idea, and clamping down on the makeship nipple, began to suckle in earnest. "There . . . look at him go. If he keeps this up, the greedy little beggar, he's going to do just fine."

They were laughing together by the time the lamb
had finished half the bottle—enough for now, Errol
said—and Stacey could see that he was pleased when
he had to fight to get the nipple back. The baby was
showing its spirit, and Stacey had all she could do to
confine its curiosity to the hallway as Errol went outside looking for a box and some rags to make a bed.
He was back a minute later with a stout wooden crate
from the henhouse and a surprisingly large pile of old
sheeting. Some of it they used to line the box; the rest
Errol tossed aside, saying with a broad wink that it
would come in handy soon enough. He seemed to
know what he was talking about, for it was only a
second later when the lamb slid its feet a little farther
apart and a sudden deluge flooded over the floor.

"Oh!" Stacey gave a little squeal, laughing as she
tugged at her hem, barely managing to rescue the lacy
jaconet. Errol threw the rags in the center of the
puddle, spreading them around with his boot, and
Stacey, who had taken care of baby animals since she
was a little girl and was not squeamish about such
things, picked them up, gingerly but efficiently, and
dropped them outside the door where Budgie would
find them and take care of them in the morning.

When she reentered the hallway, she saw that Errol
was watching her with a strange, almost speculative
look on his face, searching, it seemed, for something
he wanted . . . or expected. It was a moment before
she realized that she was wearing only a thin chemise,
and the barely adequate negligee that covered it had
come open in the front. She reached up awkwardly
and tugged it shut, trying not to let him see that her
hands were quivering as she fastened the tie.

She was not worried that the sight would bring out
his baser urges. Their closeness this evening had reminded her all too vividly of the one time they had
been together, and she would not have uttered a breath
of protest had he swept her up in his arms and carried
her off to bed. But she couldn't forget the anger in his
eyes, the disgust that afternoon he had found her in
Fitz Blackburn's cottage, and she wasn't about to give

him another excuse to think of her as wanton or immoral.

"Have you decided what you're going to name it?" she asked, blurting out the first thing that came to mind. "Or am I being oversentimental? I don't suppose it gets a name if you're just going to throw it out in the paddock in the morning with the others."

"Like the heartless fiend I am?" The expression on his face had changed subtly, but he was still watching her, and Stacey was finding it hard to concentrate. "No, it's not going in the paddock—unless we can find a mother for it, which is doubtful. It'll have to be hand-fed for months, I'm afraid, after which it's going to be so used to hanging around the house, it'll only be fit for a pet." He glanced down at the lamb, which was looking a little uncertain, trying first its front legs, then its back, as it tried to figure out how to lie down. "Shall we name it after you—since you helped take care of it the first night? How about Alexander? Or since it's a royal name, Alexander I?"

"Much too pompous," Stacey said, giggling. "Anyhow, it ought to be named after Rudi. He's the one who found it. What's his full name? Rudolf?"

"If it isn't it'll do. Rudolf." Errol pulled the lamb up, peering under its back legs, then grinned as he set it down again. "Or in this case, perhaps Rudolfina? It seems to be a little ewe."

"Rudolfina, then." Stacey smiled as she watched him put it in the box. That same feisty spirit was showing again, and it kicked at the sides, baaing indignantly because they were too high to get out. And just as well, too! She couldn't imagine, recalling the size of that puddle a few moments before, that Mrs. Sweeney would appreciate what little Rudolfina would do to the straw matting in the parlor. Errol had gone over to the open doorway and was standing there looking out into the darkness. Inside, the lamb quieted, and everything was so still Stacey could hear the sound of the lamp sputtering on the table.

She leaned over the box, surprised as she did so to catch a flash of something glittering at her breast. The delicate pendant he had given her earlier.

"I want to thank you," she said, "for the beautiful present. I meant to say something before, but . . . well, I saw the lamb and I forgot everything else. But I don't want you to think I'm not appreciative . . . or that I take it lightly. A girl doesn't get diamonds every day."

He had turned, and she saw that he was smiling. "I'm a sheep rancher, Stacey. These woolly little newborns are my lifeblood. Do you think it displeases me, finding you more excited by a lamb than a mere diamond?"

"I'm not sure I'd go that far." Stacey had not missed the teasing in his tone, and she couldn't help responding. "I do love little animals—I always have. But if you were to put me to the test, I'm not at all sure I'd chose a sheep over a 'mere diamond.'"

"Well, then, I'll remember not to put you to the test."

His voice had changed, deepening somehow, subtly seductive, and Stacey felt her confusion return. Averting her eyes, she saw that the lamb had finally given up struggling and learned to lie down, long legs tucked underneath it. When she looked up again, Errol was watching her with the same expression she had seen on his face before.

"Did you love him very much?" he asked quietly.

For an instant she stared at him, puzzled. Then suddenly she understood, and all the pleasure went out of the evening.

"No," she said reluctantly. She had known this was coming—she had known one day she would be called to account for what she had done—but she had not wanted it to be now, not when they were getting along so well. "No . . . I thought I did, but I didn't. And he didn't love me. I was so young then—I didn't understand what I was doing . . . or what love was."

"But you went to him anyway?" He stared down at her, aware of something hard and cutting inside, but unable to stop the words. She looked so beautiful, black hair tumbling onto her shoulders, silver-gray eyes brimming with tears that begged to be kissed away. "You gave yourself to him . . . of your own free will?"

"In a way, yes." She had caught that faint hint of a question, and she sensed, illogically, that he was asking for the one thing she could not say. "I didn't go to him, he came to me . . . but I didn't reject him. That's the same thing, isn't it?"

"Yes." He turned away again, back to the doorway, but Stacey could still see his face in profile. "Yes, it's the same thing."

"It was only that one time, and I . . . I didn't really mean it to happen." She knew how feeble that sounded, but she had to explain anyway, to try to make him understand. "I was playing games, I think—he accused me of it, and he was probably right. I thought I could flirt with fire, be wonderfully, scandalously daring, and get away with it. But things had gone too far for that. When I tried to say no—and I did, truly I did—he . . . he wouldn't let me."

"You mean he *forced* you."

Horror vibrated in his body as he spun around. Stacey could see the anger, the disgust that the very thought brought out of him, and for just a second, foolishly, she let herself hope. If she lied to him now—if she cried rape and made him believe it—would he be able to forget?

Only there had been too many lies already. Too many mistakes she couldn't call back. If he caught her out in this, he would never, never forgive her.

"He was stronger than I was," she murmured unhappily. "And I did try to struggle . . . when it was too late. But we were in— " She broke off, realizing almost too late that she had nearly given herself away. "We were in a place that was not far from other people, and I didn't cry out. I could have screamed for help—I would have been heard. If I'd even tried, I think he would have been frightened and stopped. Only, you see . . . Oh, I wish I could make you understand. I was afraid he'd be angry, and he'd hate me and never want to see me again. It was foolish, I know, but I thought . . . I really believed . . . he loved me. . . ."

"And so"—he was still staring at her, his face inscrutable again—"you let him have what he wanted."

This time there was no question. "Yes," she said miserably. Yes, I let him have what he wanted."

If he had turned and walked out of the room, she would not have been surprised. But he only regarded her for a moment in silence; then, unexpectedly, he touched his hand to her cheek. Light, gentle, no promises at all . . . but warmth went flooding through her, and she ached for the virile pressure of his arms.

"Thank you," he said at last, "for telling the truth. Honesty is important."

But not important enough, she thought miserably. Everything in his eyes, the way he had touched her, the softness of his hand on her cheek, told her that. If she had been honest with him before, perhaps . . . But the past was over, and there was no way to go back and change it now.

"I know it doesn't help," she said, "but I never, for a single second, felt with him what I felt with you. I didn't know anything about love, about lovemaking, until you . . . came to my bed . . ." She faltered, embarrassed at the words she had never spoken out loud. "I . . . I didn't know it could be like that . . . between a man and a woman."

"But you did respond to him?" His face twisted wryly. He hated himself for asking, but he had to, even when he knew what the answer was going to be. Dammit, of course she had responded! "You are a very beautiful . . . very responsive woman. Pleasure is a part of your nature. You may not have set out to . . . I believe you really did try to say no . . . but you couldn't keep from surrendering in the end."

The accusation in his eyes hurt, even more than the bitter words she knew she deserved, but Stacey forced herself to meet his gaze.

"To be frank, I don't really know."

"You don't . . . know?" His dark eyes narrowed, and she sensed she had caught him off guard. "Oh, you mean, looking back . . . viewing it in retrospect . . ."

"I mean at the time. You see, I . . . I fainted . . . and everything that happened is a blank. Ironic, isn't it?" She tried to smile, but her lips were trembling. "The one taste of forbidden pleasure that ruined me forever—and I don't remember a thing about it."

It was he who finally managed the smile. The corners of his mouth went up, just slightly, a tribute to the humor she had not quite lost. She saw it clearly, saw, too, that it made no difference, and she was certain in that moment that it was over. She might win back his friendship, she might even win his respect, but she would never, never have his love . . . and love was all she wanted.

Two days later she learned that Grandfather was dead.

The letter had arrived that morning, with the mail that came every three weeks to the station. Stacey sat alone on the paddock rail, the wind blowing faintly through her hair as her fingers ran back and forth over the jagged edges of the envelope in her lap. She did not take the letter out again; she did not have to. She had opened and closed it so often, folded and refolded it, read it so many times, every sentence was etched on her heart.

She had been so excited when it came—tidings from all her sisters, even a page from Cook and the maids— and she had raced to her room where she could be alone, hoarding in privacy all the gossip and good wishes and affection her heart craved. She had not expected much in the way of news. It took so long for anything to go all that distance, she knew it would have been posted shortly after she left. But it felt like home, just holding it in her hands, and she had settled in the middle of the bed, sprawling out to enjoy every word.

Olga's letter had fallen out first. Not the long chatty one she had written originally, but the short note tucked in on top. The minute Stacey opened it, the words had leapt out at her.

Grandfather is gone.

She slid down from the fence rail, tucking the letter in one of the pockets the seamstress had provided in her skirt. The lamb was playing in the paddock. Little

Rudolfina had not only survived her first night, she was so lively she was already getting into mischief. Now she was kicking her heels as she gamboled across the yard, not running exactly, more like prancing, as if she had been born only to send up puffs of dust in the air.

It was hard to believe he was really dead. She stared unseeing at the distant mountains, dusty blue with a frustrating backdrop of black clouds. He had died in his sleep, Olga said. "Peacefully" was the word she used, but Stacey had a feeling that was her gentle sister's way of cushioning the blow. Nothing Grandfather had ever done was peaceful. He had blustered and struggled and fought through his life, and she could not imagine his dying any other way. Still, he *had* looked tired that last time she saw him . . . as if he might have been weakened by illness. . . .

She squirmed at little, recalling her anger, the way she had refused to look in his eyes. He had hurt her badly—she had been right to be furious!—but she had not known then that that would be her last chance to set things straight with him. She had tried to write since her arrival, tried at least to reassure him she was all right, but it was hard to know what to say, considering the precariousness of her relationship with her husband, and she kept putting it off. Now it was too late.

Regrets. She patted her pocket to make sure the letter was still safely tucked away and started slowly across the yard. A funny word "regrets." She had never thought it applied to her. To old people maybe, with a lifetime of things undone, but not an impetuous young woman, sure of herself and what she wanted. Now it seemed all she was doing was looking back . . . and regretting. That afternoon with D'Arcy on board ship when she had not had the sense to call out, the night she could have been honest with Errol . . . how many times had she wished she could go back and live those moments again? And the last time she saw Grandfather, old and lonely on the steps of the house. What wouldn't she give to swallow her pride—and her anger—and throw her arms around him one more time?

One of the dogs had come closer, a scruffy Queensland blue, and he and Rudolfina were eyeing each other from a wary distance of several feet. The dog moved in, sniffing curiously, as if trying to figure out what it was, this funny little thing that smelled like a sheep but didn't look like a sheep at all. The lamb backed off a step or two in alarm, then turned and bolted over to where Stacey was standing.

Well, one thing at least was certain. She started back toward the homestead, the little lamb bleating as it clung to her heels. Even if Errol sent her away—an imminent possibility now that her slender waistline was growing more and more glaring—she couldn't go home. Things would be changing already. There would be a new head of the family, one of her brothers-in-law perhaps; though, knowing Henry Danson, she suspected he was already maneuvering to get as much control as he could over the Alexander heiresses. Olga and Mara would be safe enough, but Zee's wedding was sure to be pushed up, and he wasn't above trying to get Stacey under his thumb if she came back. And if he couldn't find her a malleable husband . . .

Stacey shuddered, startling the little lamb, who looked up, puzzled at this odd demonstration of human behavior. If Henry Danson couldn't find her a husband, it wouldn't bother him—her ruin would suit him just fine! She would live out her days with the title of spinster, her fortune neatly "managed" by a benevolent brother-in-law's benevolent father, and she would never know another minute's freedom in her life!

The mountains beckoned, and she paused to look over her shoulder, seeing the awesome splendor she was just beginning to recognize. Even with the drought, there was something compelling in the vastness of the land, a desolate beauty, so stark and haunting it felt sometimes as if it were becoming a part of her. She didn't know what it was—perhaps Fitz Blackburn's paintings made everything look different, perhaps it was Errol and the love she bore him, perhaps just time and the force of the place itself—but it was getting under her skin, and she felt an urge to stay.

And, after all, why shouldn't she?

She turned back toward the barn, where Billy Two was struggling with a heavy door that didn't sit right on its hinges, but no one had had time to fix it. Australia was a land of men and few women, and even serving girls with plain faces and no dowries at all found husbands. Errol would be generous, she knew— he might not want her himself, but he would not use his control over her inheritance to stand in the way of what she decided to do. If she asked, he would help her find a good man among the many good, strong men in this strong new country, and she could begin again.

It would not be a bad life.

She looked around at the land again, feeling more than ever that she belonged; even the dust seemed to seep into her blood. It was hard, giving up, but giving up was all that was left . . . and going on. It would not be a bad life. It would be a life of color and interest and purpose, and perhaps, if she was lucky, even honest affection. But it would not be a life with a man she had learned to love, the man who could make her pulse quicken with the lightest touch of his fingers on her cheek. It would be a life of regrets and second choices, and a part of her would weep forever for what she had lost.

16

"There is is—Glenellen!" Maude's azure eyes sparkled with suppressed laughter as she drew the light American buggy to a halt beneath the dusty willows of the dry creek. "Didn't I tell you it was beautiful? It looks like a storybook castle, doesn't it—up on the hill all by itself, with only the sky and mountains behind it?"

Stacey shaded her eyes with her hand, wishing she had worn her hat instead of the cream straw bonnet, birds' wings removed now and a pale saffron scarf wrapped around the crown. The house Errol Cameron had hoped to have ready for his bride did indeed make a spectacular sight in the shimmering sunbeams that had broken out of a thick cloud cover, though the effect was more graceful than princely. Storybook castles to her were all towers and turrets, with angles and flourishes and fluttery Victorian gingerbread. Glenellen was almost Georgian in its simplicity, soft lines and rounded dome giving the illusion that it was a natural extension of the hill itself.

"It is beautiful," she agreed breathlessly. "I've never seen anything like it before."

Maude laughed out loud as she flicked the reins, guiding a lively pair of grays expertly into the rutted path that ran through silvery grasses to the base of the hill. The excursion today, surprisingly, had been Errol's idea. When Maude had stopped by Cameron's Creek earlier in the morning, he had paused to chat, not in itself unusual, for they always enjoyed each other's company. But this time his mind had seemed to be more on Stacey than the new lambs, and he had

muttered something vague about "homesickness" and
letters received the day before.

"Wait till you see the inside," Maude called over
her shoulder. "You can't imagine what it's like. I used
to believe it was haunted. Now I think it's just sad and
lonely, waiting for someone to live in it at last." The
horses seemed to sense they were getting closer for
they had grown so frisky it was all she could do to hold
them to a trot. She loved driving, but she had never
been strong, and it was tiring after a while, clinging to
the reins, especially with a pair like this who had
enough spirit for four at least.

The ride was rough, and Stacey gripped the side of
the narrow seat, hanging on for dear life as they reached
the edge of the plain and started up the twisting trail
to the top. Maude drove like D'Arcy—recklessness
seemed to be an Australian trait—and the American
buggy teetered so badly a couple of times, it drew a
gasp from her lips. Still, it was surprisingly strong, its
four wheels and light frame skimming over rocks and
ruts and gullies that would have broken a heavier
vehicle.

She had been a little reluctant when Maude suggested the trek to Glenellen. But thoughts and feelings
had been closing in so much these past few days, she
was ready to grab at almost any diversion. She was
still unsure of the other woman's feelings about Errol,
but she had to admit, throwing a glance at her profile
in the dust-hazed sunlight, that Maude had given her
no reason for suspicion. If she was the least bit uncomfortable with Stacey, if there was any jealousy at all—
and surely there would be if she loved him!—it did not
show, and Stacey thought again, as she had before,
that anything between them had to be on Errol's side,
not hers.

It took the better part of an hour to get up the hill,
for distances were deceptive on the vast Australian
plain, and things that seemed just ahead often turned
out, in reality, to be miles away. The house had been
constructed on high ground, not merely for conve-
nience, but to take advantage of the view, and as they
came to a stop, Stacey sat for a moment in the car-

riage, overwhelmed by sweeping vistas that stretched out on every side. Rolling hills and parched grasslands, gums so dusty they seemed to have lost their color, creek beds meandering like curling ribbons into the lavender mist of mountains on the horizon. Out of all that natural ruggedness, Glenellen rose like a citadel, massive blocks of yellowed sandstone impervious even to the worst of the heat. Symmetrical wings extended from either side of a central portico, and tall Ionic columns carried the eye to the dramatic grace of the dome on top.

It was a minute before she realized that Maude had climbed down and disappeared into the shadows of the portico. By the time she followed, one of the large double doors was already open and she stepped into the most breathtaking entry hall she had ever seen in her life.

Nothing could have prepared her for the elegance that met her eyes. "Splendor" was the only word for it, yet it was a splendor tempered by such perfect proportions and exquisite taste, even the extravagant use of space did not seem ostentatious. The floor was not marble, as she had thought at first, but stone of some sort, so smooth and expertly fitted she could not feel the seams beneath the thin soles of her slippers. Floor-to-ceiling French windows ran across the back, leading to what appeared to be a porch or veranda, and in the center, an imported crystal chandelier dangled over a circular staircase that curved up to open galleries on the second and third floors.

Above it all, capping and defining the area, was the same magnificent dome, even more compelling now that she was inside. The sheer size of it, the vaulted curves, caught and held her eye so completely she barely noticed the faded, half-completed cherubs swimming in an eighteenth-century fantasy across the cracked plaster surface. What she did notice, as she sensed the architect had intended, was the circle of columns that held it up, Ionic again, but slim and unutterably graceful. Behind, glassed windows let in a spill of sunshine, and everything below seemed to be flooded with gold, the crystal chandelier, the arcing stairway, the agate-smooth stones, even the dust that lay like a velvet mantle over it all.

"Oh!" Stacey caught her breath, barely able to believe what she was seeing. "You're right—I couldn't have imagined it. Not in a million years. It's absolutely . . . stunning!"

Maude laughed softly, enjoying the sight through Stacey's eyes. She had always loved Glenellen, but it was a love more of the intellect than the heart, a recognition of balance and grace and airiness. For herself, she preferred the sprawling homestead, rooms tacked on with no rhyme or reason over the years—there was a sense of life and living in those walls—or the more conventional Mirandola, with its generous sloping roof and wide verandas. But she could see someone like Stacey reveling in the beauty of Glenellen, standing at the base of the stately staircase, darkly handsome husband at her side, greeting guests who had come from hundreds of miles, and for just an instant a little part of her ached for the things that would never be hers.

" 'Stunning' " is exactly the word for it," she agreed, shrugging off her melancholy. "There's never been anything like Glenellen in this part of the country. Perhaps anywhere. I don't suppose there ever will be."

Stacey was not inclined to disagree. "The architect must have been an extraordinary man. What amazing vision—there's genius in the way he uses lines and light. His design is simple, almost common in ways, yet he dares to deviate when it suits his purpose."

"Well, you're half-right." Maude had swung the door shut, but it hardly diminished the effect of brightness in the hall. "The architect, in fact, was quite ordinary . . . though he was skilled enough in technical matters. And he did have the gift of setting his own ego aside when it came to drawing up another man's ideas. It was John Cameron who created the design. And yes, John Cameron was extraordinary."

"*John* Cameron? You mean Errol's father?" The description surprised Stacey. She had heard about Old Harry, and Black Mick the renegade son. But Errol had never spoken of his father. "I got the impression somehow that he was an unexceptional man."

"Hardly that." Maude removed her hat, shaking off the dust before hanging it by its ribbon on the door handle, though the rooms had not been cleaned in half a generation. "John Cameron was a poet. A very good one, too. I only heard bits and snatches Father recited years ago, and even those I've mostly forgotten, but there was a publisher in London waiting for a manuscript to put out a printed volume. I've always thought he ought to have been a rich man's son . . . in a grand house on the banks of the Murray. You know, lounging on the terrace and sipping iced champagne while he penned beautiful love poems in a crimson leather journal."

"He sounds like a dreamer," Stacey said, smiling. It was hard to imagine Errol's father mooning his life away on pretty poems. Or D'Arcy's either, for that matter.

"He was," Maude agreed. "And the greatest dream of his life was the beautiful Ellen D'Arcy. They say he courted her for years before she finally agreed to be his. It was for her he built this house—heaven knows, he couldn't afford it. Most of the family assets were taken by the government when Mick Cameron was hanged as a bushranger. John spent everything he had left, and every cent he could borrow, too—it took nearly ten years—to build a castle for his fragile fairy-tale princess. Ellen, you see, couldn't bear living in a place like the homestead . . . fairy-tale princesses wither and fade in crude surroundings. And Ellen had to have her heart's desire, no matter what the cost."

She broke off, silvery laughter echoing through the empty hall.

"I make her sound shallow, don't I? Well, perhaps she was, though I suspect I see her from my own perspective. D'Arcy was always her favorite. He remembers her holding him on her lap and crooning pretty lullabies, though I wonder if she loved him quite as much as he thought. Wait till you see where the nursery is. As far from the adult living quarters as possible! I sometimes think she's as much a figment of

D'Arcy's imagination as she was of John Cameron's. But come, you want to see the rest of the house."

She led the way through a recessed door, slightly ajar on the wall to the left, and Stacey found herself in a room that was obviously intended as a formal parlor. Like the entry, the design was superb, spacious yet comfortable, with tall windows set deep in thick walls, but the furnishings were surprisingly conventional. Heavy silk draperies which must once have been a deep pinkish bronze—absolutely the wrong color for the room—had been streaked and faded to salmon-peach; the carpet had common, rather ugly flowers splashed all over it; and spindly Victorian chairs were clumped in an awkward grouping in front of the fireplace at the far end. Except for the beautifully burnished wainscoting and teak floor that held its polish despite years of disuse, the decor was almost painfully ordinary.

"How odd," Stacey said, thinking out loud. "It's so mismatched . . . it doesn't go together at all. It's almost as if whoever decorated this room didn't like the house and was trying to change it."

"I believe you may be right." Maude gave her a curious look. "John wanted only the best for his wife— heaven knows, he spared no expense—and Ellen was probably grateful in her way. But what was best in his eyes and best in hers might not have been the same thing. They *were* oddly mismatched, as you say . . . yet I think there was love on both sides. If he had been able to give all this to her sooner, he might have made her happy. That's her portrait over there."

She pointed toward the far wall, where a pair of portraits hung amid a clutter of ornaments over the painted carved-wood mantel. The one on the right caught her attention first, not because of the subject so much as the bright colors that seemed to radiate out of the canvas. It was a woman, handsome at first glance, sumptuously clad in emerald velvet, with dark blond hair piled on her head and deep hazel eyes that might have had buried hints of green. Her face was almost too oval, her features too perfectly shaped to be truly interesting, and Stacey got the impression she was pretty enough, but rather conventional, like the room she had decorated.

"She's not what I expected," she confessed. "I thought she'd be . . . well . . . a great beauty!"

Maude's laughter came from somewhere behind. "The portrait doesn't do her justice. She did have a reputation as a beauty. Men from miles around were madly in love with her, Father says—all except him, of course. I was barely three when she died, but whenever I think of her, I have an impression of absolutely dazzling loveliness. I don't know if that's memory exactly, or something I got from John Cameron's poems. That's his likeness next to her."

Stacey shifted her gaze to the other portrait. She would not have needed Maude's words to tell her who it was. There was a strong resemblance to his sons, Errol especially; it showed in the shape of his brow, the narrow, aristocratic nose, the cheekbones that somehow did not look quite as strong on him. His hair was dark, his eyes jet black, but his skin was almost pallid, and she detected none of the force, none of the will and power and vitality she sensed even in D'Arcy.

"He looks like a poet," she said thoughtfully.

"He was a very gentle man, in the truest sense of the word . . . and talented, but he lived only for his dreams. When those dreams were gone, when he had lost his beautiful Ellen—'with the secrets of the night in her eyes and the moonmist in her hair'—a part of him died with her. The part that was the poet. Like the house, which he never set foot in again, he turned his back on his life's work. On the day they buried her, he put everything he had ever written in the fireplace and set a match to it."

"He *burned* it?" Stacey stared at the portrait, stunned. It seemed such a strange, sad thing to do. "All of it? Even the manuscript that was to go to the publisher?"

"Every last scrap and scribble. There was nothing left of him after that, they say. I remember myself the way he looked, sitting on the porch at the homestead, just staring at the mountains, hour after hour after hour. It was hardest on D'Arcy, you know—he was only nine at the end. He had lost his beloved mother, and his father withdrew into a world of his own. It must have seemed as if no one had ever loved him . . . and perhaps in a way they hadn't."

Yes, Stacey thought as she retreated back through the door, it would have been hard on D'Arcy. The golden bath of sunlight was gone now, and only gray filtered down from the dome, giving a moody feel to the spacious hall. But it must have been hard on Errol too. How old would he have been then? Nineteen? Twenty? What an agonizing responsibility, being called back from an education in England to try to salvage a sheep station that was only land and debts. There would have been no time left for a baby brother and his needs. Was that when it started? The friction between the two of them?

The doorway across the hall was half-open, and Stacey pushed it the rest of the way to reveal a large, airy ballroom, not quite finished but with enough curlicues and gilt to give a sense of the opulence that had been intended. It should have been filled with people—it cried out for laughter and movement and the sound of carriage wheels rolling up the drive—but like everything else, it was covered with silence and a thick layer of dust. A musty smell hung in the air, and Stacey could not help recalling Maude's description. A sad, lonely place . . . waiting for someone to move in and bring it to life.

With Maude as guide, she covered the rest of the ground floor, a tour as confusing as it was fascinating, for Glenellen had even more rooms than her grandfather's mansion at home. An elegantly appointed music room, containing a grand piano that must have been the latest thing when it was purchased, though it looked as if it had never been touched, opened onto a small sitting room, cozy for winter, with a fireplace screen to shield the ladies' complexions; and the door from the dark, traditionally paneled library led to a small chamber that might have been planned either as a poet's hideaway or the office from which station business could be transacted. There were three drawing rooms at least, as near as she could count, and another formal parlor, and a dining room with a long mahogany table at one end and a small round one at the other, by the windows, for breakfasts and light suppers. The kitchen was separate, as it was at the homestead, but here it was attached to the main building by a butler's pantry that even Madden would have envied, with huge copper sinks for washing the china and a press to put creases back in the linen.

Stacey's head was spinning by the time she got back to the hall, and she had the feeling, if she lived in that house for years, she still wouldn't be able to figure out where everything was. The sky had continued to darken, and shadows were as thick as dust in the corners as she began to climb the wide circular stairs to the upper stories. Maude had disappeared, going off somewhere by herself, but Stacey did not mind. It was much more comfortable—and more fun—exploring on her own.

The second floor was orderly, and she got her bearings easily as she went from room to room, throwing open windows to air away the staleness. Even the dusty breezes smelled different now. She almost thought she could detect a scent of moisture in them, though perhaps that was because she had been in the house so long.

Both wings were identical. Airy galleries came first, extensions of the large, domed hall; then long passageways, with bedrooms on both sides, and baths with large enameled tubs, leading to suites at either end. One was obviously the room John Cameron had never shared with his wife, and Stacey stood for a moment in the doorway, feeling like an intruder as she stared at elegant silver brushes and mirrors on the dressing table, and dainty crystal bottles from which the perfume had evaporated, leaving only a brownish stain. Then she shut the door and slipped back into the hall.

She spent only a few minutes on the third floor, which turned out to be considerably smaller than the bedroom wings below. It contained little of interest, except perhaps the nursery, which Stacey could not help noticing was at the opposite end of the building from the master suite. Perhaps, after all, Maude had been right. It looked like Ellen Cameron hadn't wanted to be disturbed by children crying in the night.

The area under the great dome had grown even darker in the short time she had been on the third floor, almost like dusk, and the air felt strangely heavy as she started down the stairs, no longer quite so eager to be alone. She was just passing the second floor when her eye lit on a painting, half-hidden in a narrow niche, difficult to see from any other angle.

It was a rather indifferent portrait, she noted as she drew closer, a girl in an old-fashioned gown with pale blond curls around her face. The artist, whoever he was, had painted by formula—style and personality had eluded him—but the face itself was arresting. The features were Ellen's, and for an instant Stacey thought it might be another portrait of her, at a younger age. But there was something different about this girl, a kind of haunting prettiness that even clumsy technique could not conceal, and she found herself wondering who it could be. She had just turned back to the stairs, planning to find Maude and ask her, when a sudden shimmer of glare-white flashed through the hall, followed by an almost deafening crash of thunder.

The dust storms Errol had warned her about? Alarmed, Stacey looked up, but the windows around the dome showed none of the tawny coloring he had described. The sky was dark, but it was more gray-black than hazy, and she could not believe that was heat lightning she had just seen. Then, before she could think anymore, the hall was filled with sound, a loud, rhythmic tattoo echoing from the roof, and she realized suddenly what was happening.

Rain. The drought had broken, and it was raining at last.

The front door was open. Stacey noticed it even before she reached the bottom of the stairs, and she ran out onto the portico where the sound and feel and smell of rain were even more intense. Maude had gotten there before her—no doubt that was where she had gone, she must have scented the same moisture Stacey had—and she was standing on the drive, head tilted up, oblivious of the ruin of dress and hairdo as water poured in a deluge down her face.

Stacey did not know whether the other woman was

laughing or crying. Then she realized it was both, and she was laughing too, and tears were running down her cheeks as she held out her hands and felt the coolness spilling over her arms and spattering up on her skirt. She had not known before what it was to be an Australian, to suffer drought for months and years on end, to live and hunger for rain. But she knew now. She knew and, like Maude, rejoiced. The drought was over, the station was saved for Errol—and the newborn lambs would live.

Maude turned suddenly, grinning as she saw her standing there. A moment of unity, Stacey thought. Shared exhilaration, and they would never feel quite the same about each other again. Then she was running up the steps and back into the house, shaking her dress in puddles on the floor as Stacey followed.

"You must think I'm mad." Her laughter was audible, even with the great pounding of raindrops from outside. "Perhaps I am—heavens, yes, I know I am! What am I thinking, standing around like a little girl playing in the rain? Thank goodness there was no stable to unharness the horses! We have to get back to the homestead as fast as we can. Before it gets too dangerous."

Excitement had turned to alarm so quickly Stacey could not follow. "Dangerous?" She cast a skeptical eye at the storm. It was raining heavily, but it was still possible to see, and it wouldn't be dark for some time yet. "Surely it can't be as bad as all that. We must have hours to get back."

Maude tossed her head, sending hair in a wet cascade down her back. "You don't know this country like I do. The ground is dry—it can't absorb this water all at once. Storms always cause flooding. Rivers turn into torrents in front of your eyes—and even the creek runs too high to ford. We have to get past before that happens."

"But . . ." Stacey had heard of flash flooding in the California deserts, too, but recalling that narrow little creek bed, she found it hard to believe. "Surely it will be days before that happens. If at all. And besides . . . Oh!" She broke off abruptly. "The windows! I left them open in all the upstairs rooms! If we don't close them, everything will be ruined."

Maude cast an anxious glance at the door, and Stacey thought she was going to resist. But she only hitched up her skirt, which clung, rain-wet, to her ankles, and headed for the stairs. "You're right," she called out as she hurried up. "Things *will* be ruined if it keeps raining like this. And a few minutes can't make that much difference."

It was fully half an hour before they finished, for windows that have not been opened in years tend to stick, and the sudden moisture made them swell so badly Stacey had to tug and pound to get them shut. The rain seemed even heavier when she came down again, almost a solid sheet of water, and she hesitated a second in the doorway while Maude scurried to unhitch the horses. Could it be that the other woman's fears were not as foolish as they had seemed? Certainly Stacey had never seen so much rain. It might well be unpleasant, if not dangerous, getting across the creek.

They had a moment's panic when they reached the gap in the fence where a gate had been planned but never erected and felt the wheels mire in the mud. But Maude, proving her skill as a driver, snapped the reins deftly, and the horses lurched forward in unison, jerking the buggy free.

Maude was driving with a frenzy now, eyes bright as she pressed the bolting horses on. Why, she likes this, Stacey thought. She likes the excitement and the challenge—and the risk! But she only held on harder, not daring to complain, even when the buggy slid so badly it nearly skidded sideways. More and more she was realizing that Maude's concern had not been unfounded. Water seemed to be everywhere, building up more quickly than she had dreamed—there were pools all around that must have been halfway to her knees— and she sensed that those minutes lost for the windows could cost them dearly.

She knew the instant they reached the creek that they were in trouble. This was not the gentle, gurgling stream she had imagined, but a wildly flowing river, still only a foot or two deep, but easily ten yards wide, and growing wider with each passing minute. And worst of all, it was not still, but moving . . . white water that swirled and rippled over the rocks, foaming so badly it was impossible to see beneath.

Maude pulled the horses to a stop a few feet from the bank. Her face was pinched as she glanced over her shoulder, and Stacey knew what she was thinking.

"Maybe we ought to go back," she ventured.

Maude shook her head grimly. "The flooding could go on for weeks, and there are no provisions in the house. Besides, if we don't show up at the homestead, someone's going to come looking for us. And if you think it's bad now, imagine what it'll be like in a few hours."

Stacey felt her heart sink. Maude was right. Proud, strong-willed Errol was sure to come after them, and it would be risking his life to cross that stream if it got any higher. "Let's go then," she said, more bravely than she felt. "Now!"

The words were not necessary, for Maude had already started forward, urging the horses with a strong hand over the bank. They balked for a second, then, plucky little Australians, plunged into the raging current of the creek.

The ground was treacherous. Stacey could feel the wheels catching on unseen stones and ruts, and the buggy swayed so badly she was terrified it was going to tip over. She eyed the far bank warily, assessing her chances of jumping out and wading the rest of the way. But the water was rising at an alarming rate—it was more than halfway up the wheels, nearly level with the horses' bellies—and the current was too strong to risk.

They almost made it. The bank was tantalizingly close—another two paces, no more—and Stacey was about to breathe a sigh of relief when she turned and saw a rush of water hurtling toward them. It seemed to come all at once, not a gradual rising, but a solid wall, churning and roaring as it bore down on them.

Maude responded instantly. Throwing the reins forward, she leapt into the stream. For a split second

Stacey thought she was trying for the bank, which was well within reach. But she whirled instead, catching one of the horses by the bridle, and with an almost superhuman effort, tugged and prodded, giving a brisk slap on the flank when she finally forced him to pass. Stacey let out a sharp cry as she felt hooves catch at the earth, and she knew she was safe. The buggy followed, scraping up the bank, and she jumped down and turned to stretch out her hand.

As she did, she saw Maude stumble.

All she could do was stand there and gape at her in horror. One minute she had been thigh-deep in the stream, strong and seemingly sure of herself. The next, water was swirling all around and she was down, and Stacey could see nothing but the pale aqua of her dress and a startlingly vivid red-gold spill of hair.

17

Stacey stood absolutely still for a second. Then, reacting more by instinct than reason, she kicked off her thin kid slippers and plunged into the water.

"It's all right, Maude," she cried as she felt the current swirl around her legs. "It's all right. I'm coming."

The stream had grown deeper, even in that brief stretch of time. The sheer wall that had frightened her before was gone—it had crashed and broken on a dramatic outcropping of stone—but the water was rising at a terrifying rate. Well above her waist now, halfway to her shoulders, and she thrashed wildly, half-wading, half-swimming as she tried desperately to get to Maude.

She had nearly reached her when the eddying currents caught her up again, carrying her like a poor broken bird just out of reach down the stream. Stacey could have wept with despair. Only inches away—then suddenly she was gone. All she could do was watch helplessly as the churning water hurled her against the branchless skeleton of a dead tree, jutting three or four feet out of the water. That she was alive and conscious, Stacey saw with relief, for a delicate hand fluttered out and caught at the trunk. But she was plainly weak, and her grip could not last for long.

Stacey hesitated one last second. She was not far from shore. If she pushed back now, she was sure she could make it—and she didn't know what would happen if she went on. But Maude had been close to shore too, and she had not tried to save herself.

Letting go of the ground, Stacey flailed out with both arms, trying frantically to beat her way against the current. It was no use. She realized that almost at once. She was a strong swimmer, but that angry swell of water was even stronger, and no matter how she kicked and fought and struggled, she could not keep from being washed downstream.

There was nothing she could do now, no way to help herself . . . or Maude. Only instinct was left, and it was all she could do to keep her head above water as logs and debris rushed past with savage force. There must have been some pattern to the current, for when she felt something ram against her side and reached out to clutch at it, it was to be the same jagged trunk that had saved Maude. She managed to get an arm around it, securing herself just at the moment Maude let go.

She would never know how she did it—afterward she would wonder how all her instincts worked together so quickly—but somehow she tightened her grip on the tree at the same time that she caught hold of Maude, dragging her back, though it fairly wrenched her arm out of its socket.

One glance was enough to tell her that the other girl was no longer conscious. Her face was pale, her lips already beginning to turn faintly bluish, and Stacey was even more frightened for her now than she had been before. She struggled to pull her closer, working that inert body between herself and the tree, where at least it was slightly easier to hold on.

There was time to think now, and with thought came the fear that had only been a flash of instinct before. There was nothing she could do to save the two of them, no clever plan she could make all by herself out in the middle of the stream. She saw that as clearly as she saw how foolish it had been to rush into the water with no idea of what she was going to do. If it were just herself, it might not have seemed so hopeless. But trying to hold on for Maude too, trying to survive for both of them, was excruciating, and her arms were already beginning to ache so badly she did not know how long she could go on.

Oh, please, someone, come, she thought desperately. Please, please *come*, though she had no idea what anyone who came along could do. He would be on the bank and she and Maude were all the way out in the water! She wished she knew more about floods, wished she knew if the creek had a way of receding as quickly as it rose. Then it occurred to her it was just as well she didn't know, and she concentrated on holding on, willing herself to think of nothing but the tree trunk and the strength that remained in her arms and the need to keep on trying as long as there was a breath left in her body.

She had no way of knowing how long she clung to the rotting wood with Maude's body in her arms. It felt like hours, though it must have been less, for the water was coming up rapidly and it was still only a few inches higher on the trunk. All she could feel was the exhaustion in her arms and her body, and she sensed that she was at the end of her endurance when something brushed her shoulder.

She shuddered convulsively. Visions of reptiles came to her, slithering through the water. Were there alligators in Australia, or crocodiles? Then whatever it was tightened, an uncanny sensation, as if a hand were on her shoulder, and suddenly there was another hand, strong and visible, gripping the trunk next to hers. A large masculine hand with big square fingers and red-brown hair matted on the back.

Looking up, she found herself staring at bushy brows and a black beard streaked with white. Fitz Blackburn was no longer a young man—certainly he was not conventionally handsome—but she thought she had never seen anyone so beautiful in her life.

He wasted no time assessing the situation. His eyes passed over Stacey to Maude, lingering for a moment on the unnatural pallor of her cheeks, then snapped back to Stacey again.

"I'll get you out of this," he said brusquely. "Though I'm blasted if I know how you got into it. The buggy's safe on land."

"It was Maude who got it to shore," Stacey managed to gasp. "We were caught in a rush of water and she jumped out and . . . and . . ." Just the thought made her shudder. "She got the buggy on the bank,

but the current caught her up and she went under! I
thought I was strong enough to get her, I thought I
could swim if I had to—"

"You jumped in after her?" His voice was incredu-
lous. "With the water rising like that? What a damn
fool thing to do!"

"I had to," Stacey protested. "I couldn't just stand
there and watch her die."

"No, I suppose you couldn't." His eyes were working constantly, checking the current and the distance
to the bank. "Well, never mind, all's well that ends
well—or so they say. Though how the devil I'm going
to manage with both of you at once—"

"Don't worry about me," Stacey cut in hastily. She
had no idea how he was going to get even one of them
to shore, much less two at a time. "I can hang on
longer if I have to. It won't be so hard without Maude.
Anyway, she's in worse shape than I am. Get her out
first."

He gave her a quick look, then nodded. "You're a
brave girl. I hope he appreciates you, that hot-tempered
husband of yours." He eased Maude's weight out of
her arms, and Stacey felt deliriously light for a second.
"I'll be back before you know it. Just hang on for all
you're worth. Try to think of the wonderful adventure
you're having . . . and what fun it'll be, telling your
grandchildren all about it."

Stacey doubted it would ever be fun, recalling that
afternoon, but she sensed he was trying to lighten her
mood, and she made an effort to smile as she watched
him move away with Maude. She had been so sure it
would be easier, holding on only for herself, but her
arms were so tired they were almost numb, and she
was afraid suddenly he was not going to get back in
time. He had brought a rope with him, one end knot-
ted around his waist, the other lashed to a sturdy
willow on the bank. She could almost hear him grunting with exertion as he looped the cord again and
again around his arm, inching his way painfully toward
shore. Once there, he stayed only long enough to set
Maude's frail body well beyond the bank, then pushed
back into the creek.

She was crying when he reached her, though she was not aware of it, the rain was so wet on her cheeks. She didn't know if her strength gave out because she no longer needed it, or if he reached her at the last possible second. She knew only that she saw him there, saw his hand reach out, and suddenly her own hand gave up, releasing its grip.

He caught her instantly, drawing her toward him, strong and reassuring, and every instinct in her body told her she was going to be all right.

"Can you put your arms around my neck?" he was saying. "If you hold on, I'll have both hands free. Or am I going to have to throw you over my shoulder like Maude?"

Stacey, who noticed that he had not thrown the other girl over his shoulder at all, but carried her as tenderly as possible under the circumstances, replied: "I can manage quite well, thank you. You're not going to make a sack of old grain out of me."

It had seemed forever, the time it took him to get Maude to shore; it seemed even longer now. She was not frightened, she was just so tired she could barely hold on, and her eyes kept closing against her will. She sensed rather than felt the moment his feet got a hold on the bank, and she forced herself to turn, stumbling as the land came up to meet her. Then she was scrambling up the muddy incline, reaching out to try to find the rope so she could help herself.

But it was not the rope that met her groping hands. It was other hands, warm and hard, and she was being pulled up, high on the bank. Arms were around her then, a strong masculine chest found her trembling cheek, and she knew even before she looked up that Errol was there.

"My God, what happened?" he cried out. But it was Fitz's voice that answered.

"They're all right. I got them out in time, I think. That one's fine—she's a spunky little wench. But I'm worried about the other."

They went on talking, fretting about Maude, discussing both of them, but Stacey barely heard their voices or felt anything but the strength of Errol's arms around her. Her knees were so weak suddenly, she could hardly stand. Now that it was over, she realized for the first time how close she had come to dying in those cold waters, and she began to tremble violently. But Errol was there to steady her, Errol, the only man she would truly love. The only man whose comfort she wanted now.

Only, if Fitz Blackburn hadn't come along when he did, she wouldn't be there for Errol to comfort! She looked up to see if she could detect any of the anger and jealousy he had displayed before. But only concern showed in that hard, set jaw.

Everything happened quickly after that. A wagon seemed to come from nowhere, driven by a slender figure in an oversize raincape—Billy Two, his face so ashen he almost looked white. Errol gave a sharp cry, "Get the blankets," which sounded absurd in all that rain, but suddenly there they were, and waterproof oilcloths, and they were being wrapped up in tight little cocoons. Maude had begun to stir, just slightly, and soft whimpering sounds were coming out of her throat.

Another tarp had been slung over the back of the wagon, and the men stretched it taut to form a makeshift shelter. Crude, but it worked, at least passably well, and before Stacey knew it, she and Maude were lying on more blankets on the floor and Errol was climbing in beside them. She didn't know where Fitz was. Driving the buggy, she supposed, for he was nowhere to be seen, and a horse, presumably his, was tied up behind. She could hear the faint *clop-clop, clop-clop, clop-clop* of hooves in the mud as they started forward.

Errol put his arms around her again, gently now, as if he were afraid of hurting her, and Stacey saw that he was studying her with anxious eyes.

"You don't have to look at me like that." She managed a weak smile. "If I didn't dissolve in the water, I'm not going to turn into a melting sugarplum now. Wasn't it lucky, though, that Fitz happened along when he did?"

"He didn't just *happen* along," Errol told her. "He had seen you ride by earlier—he has a view of everything from that hilltop of his. After the rain started, he was in and out, trying to get things stashed away, but he kept one eye peeled for you. When you didn't show up, he got worried and came looking . . . just as I did. Only his house is closer, and he got there first."

"Well, thank heaven for that," Stacey replied with feeling. "I don't think I could have held on a minute longer. I know you don't like him, and I'm sorry, but I'll always be grateful. He saved my life . . . and Maude's."

She saw his eyes slip away, a response to her words, she supposed, and she realized sadly that his thoughts were no longer on her. Raising her head slightly, she followed his gaze to the place where Maude lay, quiet now on the heap of blankets. Much too quiet, she thought guiltily—with no warm, protective arms to care for her. Her skin was almost transparent; small blue veins stood out at the temples, and her breathing was so light it was barely perceptible.

"I'll be all right," Stacey said. It tore her apart, but she knew she had to do it. It had been an even exchange, her life risked for Maude, Maude's for her, but she sensed the debt had not yet been paid. "You had better go to her. I think . . . I'm afraid she needs help."

He gave her a long, penetrating look. "Are you sure?" he asked, and her heart ached, though she noticed he did not leave until she had answered.

"I am sure," she said quietly. He slipped his arms from around her and went over to kneel beside Maude. For a moment he looked strangely helpless, as if he didn't know what to do. Then he took her in his arms and cradled her tenderly against the warmth of his chest.

His face was clear, even in the greenish light that came faintly through the tarp, and Stacey lay there watching as he looked down at the woman in his arms. Any last doubts she had had about his feelings were gone now. He cared for Maude, cared deeply . . . whether it was love or not, she could not say, but it was more than the casual feeling of neighbor for neighbor.

Strangely enough, the realization brought no jealousy. Maybe after what she had been through, there wasn't room in her heart for petty feelings . . . or maybe she and Maude had come so close, it was impossible to hate her anymore. Or maybe it was just good having an end to the doubts and questions at last.

She sank back into the blankets, feeling a kind of contentment she had not expected. The truth was not what she had hoped for, but it was not what she feared either. Errol cared for Maude, loved her perhaps . . . but he could not have her, and he knew it.

And it was to Stacey he had come first that afternoon. It was Stacey he held in his arms while Maude was lying unconscious on the ground. Perhaps, after all, his heart was not completely closed to her.

The hours that followed would be forever a haze in her memory. Only isolated impressions stood out. The wagon pulling up to the door of the homestead; people running out, a blur of voices speaking all at once. D'Arcy's face, frantic with fear, hair plastered black and wet on his forehead as he stared at Maude's inert body in the wagon. Errol's arms around her again, lifting her up, carrying her through the rain to the bedroom. Errol gently removing the wet garments from her body; Errol heaping blanket after blanket on the bed as if the room were not already stifling hot; Errol coaxing her to take a few sips of tea, though she was so tired she could barely open her lips; Errol holding her hand as she drifted off to sleep.

It was night when Stacey woke, or at least it felt like night, for the lamp was turned up on the dressing table and no light came through the windows. At first she thought she was alone. Then she saw Errol standing in the doorway, looking in at her.

When he saw that her eyes were open, he came and sat beside her on the bed. "Fitz told me what happened," he said. "The way you jumped into the stream after Maude. That was a courageous thing to do."

The sincerity in his voice was flattering, and Stacey longed to respond. But something in his words was vaguely discomforting.

"Is it so important to you?" she asked sleepily. "That I saved Maude's life?"

"What is important," he said, his voice soft and even, "is that you were very brave . . . and very unselfish. And I am very proud of you."

He leaned down, brushing damp curls away as her eyes closed again, and it felt to Stacey, just for a second, as if his lips touched her brow. Then she was groggy again, and she couldn't think anymore, couldn't feel anything but the strong sense of him beside her, and she slipped back into sleep.

She could remember waking only one other time. It was considerably later, or so it seemed, though it was hard to get her bearings in the darkness. The storm had intensified. Rain was battering on the roof and thrashing against the side of the house, and she could hear the sound of voices coming through the half-open veranda window. Male voices, raised over the howl of the wind.

"I owe you an apology." Errol. She would know his voice anywhere, even straining against the wind and rain.

"For what?" Was that Fitz Blackburn? Certainly it sounded like him. "It seems to me you've been remarkably civil all afternoon. Complimentary, even."

"I'm not talking about this afternoon, dammit, and you know it. I'm talking about the other day when I bit your head off like an overgrown adolescent. I'm afraid I made some pretty unjustified assumptions."

"Unjustified?" Laughter rang through the darkness. She was sure now it was Fitz. Who else would roar like that? "Unfounded maybe—but unjustified? Hell, any man who finds his pretty wife with Fitz Blackburn damn well better be suspicious! I have an unsavory reputation when it comes to women . . . which I've gone to great lengths to protect. And don't tell me I haven't succeeded. It would be the grossest ingratitude, after what I've done, hurting my feelings like that."

"God forbid. Your reputation is safe with me. Only, Fitz . . ." His tone changed, making Stacey faintly uncomfortable. "I did think perhaps, because of . . .

other things, you might want to hurt me through my wife. It seems I was wrong."

"You were," came the quiet reply. "I have no desire to hurt you . . . or your beautiful wife. I make a distinction, incidentally, between women and ladies, and I treat them as such. Mrs. Cameron may be high-spirited, but she is every inch a lady."

If Errol had any response to that last comment, Stacey could not tell. "You accept my apology then?" he said.

"Why not?" Fitz laughed again, the sound lost in a burst of thunder. "I've taken everything else from you—money, a house, food. If you accept a man's money, you ought to be able to accept his apology too."

The voices faded then—they seemed to be moving to the other end of the veranda—and Stacey was left alone with nothing but the pelting of the rain on the tin roof above.

I thought because of . . . other things, you might want to hurt me. The words came back, turning over in her mind as she tried drowsily to sort them out. She had been right before, there *was* something between Fitz Blackburn and her husband, something vaguely unpleasant that seemed to have its roots in the past. But whatever it was, it hadn't gotten in Errol's way when it came to supporting the man whose talent he admired. And he had found it easy enough to apologize tonight.

He was grateful, he had said. She tossed sleepily. It was hard to focus, but hard, too, to let go of her thoughts. He was grateful. But was he grateful to Fitz for saving her . . . or Maude?

18

The rain continued for two weeks, almost without letup. Mud slicks were knee-deep in the yard, well over the tops of Errol's boots, and the few times he managed to get home, he had to change on the veranda before coming into the parlor, or even the small dressing room where he kept a narrow bed.

Stacey had expected to see more of him now that the drought was over, but she soon found she had been naive about the responsibilities of a squatter, as the large landowners called themselves. Rain nourished the earth and provided feed for nursing ewes, but it created problems too. The ground was so boggy in places, supplies had to be carried to boundary riders on foot, and rumors of disaster abounded. Whole herds of cattle had been washed away, it was said, farther north—though Billy Two scoffed at the exaggeration—and the wreckage of buildings could sometimes be seen with crops and carcasses on the swollen, rushing river.

As the water rose, hilltops turned into islands, and kangaroos and paddymelons were trapped and bleating mobs of sheep who didn't have the sense to get to safety. Hawks seemed to be circling all the time, waiting for something that had been cut off to die, and the men were kept busy day and night, rescuing as many as they could. Even D'Arcy had been pressed into service, overseeing operations at Mirandola. Surprisingly, he had not seemed to object, almost as if the responsibility pleased—or perhaps flattered—him.

Unfortunately, the only serious problem occurred there, for D'Arcy, being inexperienced, neglected to send men to one of the more vulnerable paddocks and

several hundred head were lost. Stacey, by chance, was
in the back hallway when he returned to face a livid
Errol, and seeing the look of anger and hurt pride on
his face when he was berated like a small child, she
almost felt sorry for him.

The rain stopped a few days later, as abruptly as it
had begun. The silence was startling after the battering on the metal roof, and Stacey went out onto the
veranda to see that the clouds were receding. In the
distance, the mountains were etched with incredible
clarity, dazzlingly and deep vivid blue, against the
horizon. Bright sun was already intensifying the heat,
which had never completely gone away, and the earth
had begun to steam.

Now moisture was the problem, as dryness had been
before. Merinos, imported in the early years of the
colony, had proved an inspired choice for Australia.
Their wool was highly prized and they tolerated the
arid climate remarkably well, but they were suscepti-
ble to foot rot, which created whole new sets of time-
consuming cares.

Not that the men had all the problems, Stacey thought
wryly. Laundry took days to dry, if it dried at all, and
mold seemed to have taken over the house. Bread that
was baked fresh in the morning sprouted thin green
fuzz by night, and the soles of her favorite shoes were
beginning to look as if she had foot rot herself! Frogs
seemed to be everywhere—great green frogs the size
of a teapot, and small cream-colored frogs, and fat brown
frogs that had a way of settling in the bathwater and
looking up with a startling *chug-a-rum* when she dipped
in her toe—and she had the feeling Mrs. Sweeney's snakes
were coiled up contentedly on the slimy kitchen floor.

All that hardly mattered, however, for the world
outside had changed dramatically, and even Stacey,
who had a horror of snakes, could not bring herself to
mind. The river receded slowly; the creek flowing
behind the house eased back to its banks; and the
earth, which had seemed parched and dead, sprang
suddenly to life. She had never seen anything like it
before. Within a day, sprigs of green were everywhere; another day and the muddy paddock was cov-

ered with a soft velvet carpet. Flowering gums, washed by the rain, glittered until they looked as if they had been carved out of white agate and jade, and a honeysuckle-like fragrance filled the air. Even the kitchen garden was showing young sprouts, though Stacey doubted they would ever make it to the table, for the fowls nipped off their heads the instant they peeked out of the ground.

It was the birds that delighted her most, satisfying her craving for color, and creating pictures she knew would be engraved forever on her heart. Galahs fanning across the paddock, a mass of palest gray, bursting into coral-pink as they suddenly took flight. A twittering bouquet of mountain larries filling the branches of a wild lemon, almost shockingly bright in scarlet and blue. Dozens of cunning little budgerigars, all azure and lemon and sapphire and lime. White cockatoos, great strutting bullies with bright yellow combs, and blue-black crows lined up on weathered fences, looking less like carrion birds now that the land was alive. And magpies and shimmering blue warblers, and firetails fluttering on feathery convolvulus by the creek, and willie wagtails riding the backs of dairy cows, impudent little tails waving hello.

Even the swans had come back, and Stacey watched, fascinated by ebony-black plumage and bright red beaks, as they glided proudly on the lake formed by waters of the creek in a hollow not far from the house. She could hear them overhead sometimes at dusk, their long melancholy cry luring her out to marvel at the distinctive white markings that showed on the underside of their wings.

Only one did not come back—the wild one they called the Silver Swan—and it made Stacey sad sometimes to think it might never return. Errol had said, that first night, that the swan reminded him of her, and she could not help wondering if its absence was an omen. No more swan, no more Stacey . . . no more chance to get to know this strange and beautiful land and the man who had already become more important than anything else in her life.

There was little time to dwell on sadness, however,

for as the water went down, Stacey found herself busier than she had expected. She had thought, with everyone wrapped up in chores, except D'Arcy, who had taken to skulking around the house, that the days were going to pass slowly. But Errol had caught her one morning after breakfast—a time at which he was usually long gone—and asked if she would like to take a hand in the renovations at Glenellen.

She had been surprised, to say the least, but not too surprised to accept with alacrity. She knew nothing beyond the basic principles of decoration—she had no idea, practically speaking, how to go about it, especially in a country where she couldn't name a single draper or furniture dealer—but she was not about to rebuff any overture, however tentative. Besides, the time it took her to finish was a time in which her position at Cameron's Creek would be at least slightly more secure.

She felt a little foolish that first day, after she had the stableboy hitch up the American buggy, which had required amazingly little in the way of repair, and started off to Glenellen. It was a pleasant enough ride—the creek was still high, but a short detour brought her to an easy ford, and the path up the hill was almost completely dry—but she was feeling dismayingly helpless by the time she arrived. She had half-expected Maude to offer to come, but the other woman had not been feeling well—Stacey had not seen her since her dunking in the creek—and she realized she was going to have to face the task alone.

It was not that it wouldn't be fun, she thought as she opened the front door and went inside. It would. Decorating had always appealed to her. It was just that she didn't know where to start, and she spent the first hour wandering around the house looking at room after room on the lower two stories, getting vague ideas in her mind of what she wanted to do if only she could figure out how to go about it.

She had just returned to the staircase and was coming down from the second floor when she heard hoof-beats approaching the front of the house. She made it to the door just in time to see Fitzhugh Blackburn dismounting from a powerful-looking bay with a sleek black mane and tail.

Her first instinct was to call out a greeting. She liked the artist, with his gruff, mocking sense of humor,.and it was already becoming tedious by herself in the house. Then she remembered Errol's reaction that one time she had been alone with Fitz Blackburn, and the smile chilled on her face.

"It's not that I'm not glad to see you," she said somewhat stiffly as he tethered his horse and started up the shallow steps to the portico. 'I haven't forgotten what you did for me—I owe you my life, but . . . well, I can't think what my husband would say if he found you here."

"Fear not, fair lady." Fitz swept off his dusty slouch hat as if it had a curling white plume and offered an exaggerated bow. "It is m'lord himself who sent me here."

Errol? Stacey found that hard to believe, even after the apology she had unintentionally overheard. But when she said as much, he laughed.

"Your husband is hotheaded, madam, but he's not a fool. I have assured him I'll play the perfect gentleman with you, and he knows I mean it. I'm only a churl when I'm drunk . . . and I am stone sober. See—I'll blow in your face so you can test my breath." He grinned as he saw the smile return to her lips. It intrigued him, the way she looked, very pretty, almost sweet, but with an underlying spice that challenged the artist in him. "Besides, for all that you're a mere girl—and rather ingenuous in appearance—I get the feeling you have a tongue that could slice me in two if I tried anything."

Fitz proved as good as his word. Not only was he a gentleman—or as close to a gentleman as he was ever going to come—but his help was invaluable, and Stacey did not know how she would have managed without him. It was he who suggested sending riders with letters to the Sidney train twice a week, and shortly afterward, samples began arriving: swatches of fabric for curtains and upholstery, large sheets of wallpaper that would do nicely in the bedrooms, paint colors

splashed on lengths of board, even surprisingly good
sketches of every piece of furniture she could possibly
need—some of which, judging by the furtive looks Fitz
cast at them, actually met with his approval.

He did not approve of much else. He was wonderfully helpful when it came to moving tables and heavy
dressers back and forth, and taking down draperies
and measuring walls and windows and floors never
seemed to try his patience. But he had little liking for
her sense of style, and no tact at all when it came to
saying so.

"Good God, woman," he blustered one afternoon
when he came into the parlor and found her sorting
through sketches of the furnishings she had chosen.
"You have the taste of a Victorian dowager. Look at
that . . . and that . . . and that!" He ripped the
papers out of her hand, throwing them one by one
contemptuously around the room.

"Well, what's wrong with them?" Stacey seethed
inwardly, but she did not move as sheets of white
fluttered around her. She was not going to give him
the satisfaction of stooping to retrieve them!

"What's *wrong*? You're like every female of your
era. You persist in choosing twice as much furniture as
a place can possibly hold, then you double it for good
measure! Every couch has to have antimacassars—every
table and mantel is covered with *bric-a-brac*." His lips
pursed around the word as if he had unexpectedly
sucked on a lemon. "This room is spacious—it's designed for grace and proportion—and you fill it up
with little clusters of chairs . . . and lamps with fringed
shades!"

In spite of herself, Stacey had to laugh. He was
being a perfect beast, but she had to admit he was
right. She had thought herself, the day she first saw the
room, that the furnishings were wrong. She had chosen more elegantly, of course—there was not a single
fringed lamp in all the sketches he had scattered around
the floor!—but she had not altogether avoided Ellen
Cameron's mistakes. The room *was* graceful and airy,
and constraint, not clutter, was what it called for.

He was equally opinionated, she was soon to discover, when it came to her choice of colors. But here she was surer of herself, and when the swatch of fabric she had planned for the curtains, blue-violet silk, to be thickly lined of course so it wouldn't fade, brought forth the next explosion—"Whoever heard of purple in a parlor?"—she held her ground. Hadn't he just berated her for being too conventional? Besides, she had always had a good eye for color—the swatch was more blue than purple—and she was amused later, when the first draperies arrived, to catch him holding them up to the windows with a curious look on his face.

"They might," he conceded on careful consideration, "turn out to be right after all. The windows are deeply recessed—the color brings out the coolness in the light." His eyes drifted toward the end of the room, and Stacey could almost hear the wheels clicking in his head. "If things go as well with the rest of the decor, I might permit you to hang *The Silver Swan* over the mantel."

"Oh, surely not there." Stacey followed his gaze, dismayed. The parlor was a lovely room, but hardly important enough for the painting, which she had secretly decided was going to be the focal point of the house. "I thought we'd put it in one of the open galleries—on the second floor. Maybe where that painting of the girl is, if the niche can be enlarged so it will show from all directions."

She had not counted on Fitz and his stubborn insistence that everything he created belonged to him forever. "*If* I allow you to hang the painting," he said rather loftily, "I will pick the place. Over the mantel perhaps, or in one of the other rooms—wherever *I* choose. Certainly not in a niche at the top of the stairs."

He had, it turned out, other plans for the galleries, indeed for the entire area under the dome. Stacey, who had learned to trust his instincts by that time, listened as he talked of sunlight spilling through open space . . . white walls and polished stone floors with not a rug or marble-topped side table or painting, however exquisite, to mar the elegant, sweeping lines.

The half-finished cherubs on the ceiling, which she
had noticed that first day only as a minor distraction,
had to go, of course.

"Only a damn fool would have put them there in
the first place," he grumbled, somewhat less gruffly
now that he sensed she was not going to defy him.
"What the devil do cherubs have to do with Australia?
Leave hypocrisy like that to the Europeans and their
gilded rococo. A nation of convicts with angelic pre-
tensions would be absurd!"

Stacey agreed, smiling, though not for quite the
reasons he had expressed. It was not the people and
their origins, but the land itself, the rugged mountains
and dusty sprawling savannas, that seemed ill-at-ease
with overpainted cherubs floating on a pastel ceiling.
She had half-expected Fitz to insist on whitewashing
the whole thing, leaving it plain to match the graceful
Ionic columns, but to her surprise, he suggested re-
painting. Not a string of individual pictures, like the
cherubs, but a bold diorama, typical of the countryside
that showed in glimpses through the deep-set windows.

This was Australia, he reminded her, passion ringing unexpectedly in his voice. The outside curve of the
dome had been created to echo the roll of Australian
hills. The inside should be as natural and as unique as
the land itself. A forest glade perhaps . . . a grove of
tall eucalypti soaring overhead.

As he painted the picture—he was as potent with
words as a brush—Stacey could almost feel herself in
the deep woods that had covered much of the plains
before the settlers arrived. Looking up, she saw
branches of tall gums arching overhead, flowering with
blossoms that shimmered white in the muted midday
light. Life seemed to be everywhere: fluttering budgerigars, adding a fantasy of color; arrogant sulphur-
crested cockatoos; kookaburras with large heads and
long scissor beaks; and there on the notch where two
branches joined, a funny little koala with its sweet, shy
face. Then a bellbird added its clear, musical tones, not
imagined but real, for the windows were open, and
she knew suddenly that he had won her over. His

vision was hers, and she longed to see the domed hall decorated as he had described.

She was not quite so sure, however, later that evening, when she tried to convey the picture to Errol. He had given her *carte blanche* with the house—"Decorate it any way you want," he had said—but surely he hadn't expected anything that drastic?

"It really would be pretty," she concluded rather lamely. What an insipid description, *pretty*, for something that would be truly spectacular. "Fitz said he would do the work himself. I daresay it's a great honor—he seems to think it is."

Errol frowned slightly, and Stacey thought for a minute he was going to refuse. Then he nodded.

"Fitz knows what he's doing. I'm only worried how D'Arcy will take it. He was closest to our mother, and those angels on the ceiling meant the world to her. Still, he was young when she died—I doubt he'd remember. Anyhow, I told you to do what you wanted. If the idea sounds good, tell Fitz to go ahead."

Stacey had only one last twinge of doubt, after the plaster was repaired and a thick coat of white wiped away the faded angels that had "meant the world" to Ellen Cameron. Then she saw the blue go up, an almost uncanny color, the exact shade of the sky just after it had been washed by the storms, and she knew she had made the right decision. Trees followed. There seemed to be a new one every day when she arrived, skeletal at first, then fleshed out with foliage, much bigger and brighter than life, but so perfectly shaded that they sometimes seemed more real than the gums on the path from the river.

She paused in the entry one morning, feeling a little dizzy as she looked up. The painted grove was nowhere near complete—not so much as the sketch of a bird graced the branches yet—but she knew it was going to be more beautiful than anything she had ever seen. The final culmination of an exquisite house . . . and when it was finished, Glenellen would be the showcase John Cameron had dreamed of for his wife.

As usual, Fitz was sprawled on his back on an

awkward scaffolding he had built himself, with paint dripping in his eyes.

"Just like Michelangelo," she called up, "painting the ceiling of the Sistine Chapel." She got no answer, but she hadn't expected one. She had already learned that that ribald sense of humor did not extend to being compared with other artists, none of whom, she suspected, the venerable Michelangelo included, quite measuring up to his standards.

He spent most of his time painting now, coming down only occasionally for tea, which she was happy to make for him. He had stuck to his vow not to touch anything alcoholic in her presence, though his eyes were often bloodshot, and she had the impression he made up for it at night.

Stacey found herself looking forward more and more to the chats they had over their "cuppa," as Fitz liked to call it. He had come to Australia as a young man, over thirty years ago, and when coaxed away from his passion for painting, proved a wealth of information about the things that made her curious.

It was from him that she learned about the girl in the portrait, which was still hanging in its niche, though everything else had been removed from the galleries and hall. She had thought it was a routine question, but for just a second he seemed taken aback by her casual: "Who is she, do you know?"

"Olivia D'Arcy . . . Cameron." A slight pause between the words. Stacey set her cup down on the table she had brought out from the parlor and stared at him curiously. "Your husband's sister," he explained. "Your sister-in-law she would have been. I take it Errol hasn't brought up the subject."

"No . . ." Stacey shook her head, understanding now why he had been reluctant to discuss it. "I didn't even know he had a sister. You said she *would* have been my sister-in-law. What happened to her?"

"Ah . . . poor, unlucky Olivia." He glanced at the portrait briefly, then took a sip of tea. "She had the misfortune to fall in love with the wrong man. A sot and a blackguard—admittedly, by the way . . . at least the chap was honest. Hardly the sort Mama would choose for her precious little darling, but Olivia might have forgiven him that. What she couldn't forgive was the fact that he had been involved with a lady of dubious persuasion."

"Persuasion?"

He chuckled at the expression on her face. "What I meant," he said gently, "was color. He had been consorting with an aborigine. No matter that there were no white ladies with whom to indulge the usual, uh . . . appetites. Such things were not done. He had lived with her openly, you see, and she was a full-blood, not just with a bit of a taint, like the man Mama had married. When Olivia found out about it—that was twenty-two years ago—she took refuge in a convent in England, where she died a short time later. Of a fever, they said . . . but I always thought it was too cold for her. She was a hothouse flower, our delicate Livy—she couldn't survive in dank stone halls."

"Perhaps she died of disappointment?" Stacey was a little scandalized at the turn the conversation was taking, but she couldn't help being intrigued.

"Perhaps." His voice had an edge of mockery, and Stacey studied him to see if he was really as indifferent as he sounded, or if Olivia's sad, romantic story had touched his heart. There was no sign of it, but then it was too hard to be sad about things that had happened so long ago.

"I don't know," she said, feeling suddenly like an outsider. "It's all so confusing. Sisters I never heard of . . . things no one tells me—or things they just hint at. Like Maude . . ."

"Maude?" He had put down his cup and started toward the scaffolding. Now he looked back, eyes much too sharp, and Stacey realized she had given herself away. "What about her?"

She was tempted for an instant to make up something, anything to hide the humiliation that came with all that jealousy and doubt. But she had already started, and there was no turning back. She had to know the truth, even if it hurt.

"D'Arcy said . . . he told me Errol was in love with

Maude . . . once. And that she's been in love with him
since she was a little girl." She could feel his eyes on
her face, riveting now, but she did not look up.

"And you're wondering," he said quietly, "if it's true?"

She forced herself to meet his gaze. "Yes I know
it's silly, but . . . yes, I am. And I thought .   you're
always so observant . . . I thought you would know."

"Did you now?" He reached up to scratch the side
of his nose, smearing a streak of green across his
cheek. "D'Arcy Cameron is a fool—and a scoundrel.
I'm flattered you have such faith in my powers of
observation, but don't you think you're asking a bit
much? I have enough trouble figuring out my own
feelings, much less those of another man. And you're
right—it *is* silly. All those things D'Arcy told you, all
the nasty insinuations I'm sure he made, happened
years ago. It shouldn't make any difference now."

No, it shouldn't, she had to admit . . . yet it did.
Now it was he who was looking away, staring off at
something on the ceiling, and she had the feeling he
knew things he wasn't telling.

"D'Arcy's insinuations *were* nasty. He said . . . he
said that Errol and Maude were lovers. Is it true?
Were they?"

There was a slight tremor in her voice, and she
knew he heard it. "Let it go, Stacey," he said as he
faced her again. "Curiosity is one thing . . . a compulsion for self-destruction is another. Take it from someone who knows. Whatever happened between your
husband and Maude Quinn—or didn't happen—is part
of the past. It can only hurt you if you let it."

The words made her feel a little better, and she
wandered over to the window, open to a clean smell of
rain-washed earth. Outside, she could hear the song of
bellbirds, aptly named, for their clear musical tones
sounded almost like cowbells in the meadow. Fitz was
right. He had only said what she had told herself a dozen
times before, but coming from him, it had more impact.

When she turned back, she was startled to see that
he had not gone to his scaffolding, but was standing in
front of the portrait, staring at it with an expression
that sent a sudden chill down her spine.

It was almost as if, for an instant, he had taken off the mask he always wore, and she could see into the darkness of his soul.

"Fitz . . . ?"

He turned abruptly. Now that his eyes were straight on, she thought she could see hatred in them, and pain . . . raw as an unhealed wound. Then it was gone and a flash of anger showed in its place.

"He ought to be shot," he said with feeling.

"He?" Stacey took a step forward. D'Arcy again . . . or Errol? Or the man who had hurt the girl in the picture?

"Whoever painted that obscenity! No one with so little talent ought to be allowed to inflict his ego on the world. Look at that—she was a pretty girl. Her face was fragile, not weak. Her eyes were pools of hope and sadness . . . and that clod has reduced them to a glassy stare!"

Stacey started to laugh as he stomped over to the scaffold, a noisy bear of a man, and climbed up. So much for intuition and little shivers up and down her spine! All that fire and fury she had sensed, all the pain . . . and it was only an artist's arrogance, piqued by the effrontery of a less-talented colleague who dared to compete in his world.

Still, it was funny, the way Errol never mentioned his sister. Stacey went back to the window, sensing from the change in light that the morning was nearly over. He talked so much about the past—now that things were beginning to relax and they dined together most evenings, she had heard more stories about Harry and Black Mick—but he rarely spoke of things within his own memory.

She had intended to ask him about it that evening as they sat down at the table on the side veranda, but D'Arcy was with them, at Errol's command, she suspected, and the conversation was strained enough as it was. She sensed that Errol was sorry for the way he had blown up at his brother—it was not altogether the younger man's fault he had lost those sheep in the flood—but the damage had been done, and while D'Arcy was civil, even witty as he joined in the repar-

tee, there was a coolness between the two men that
did not pass unnoticed.

Supper was a simple but tasty meal. Shortly after
the waters receded, Mrs. Sweeney had disappeared, as
D'Arcy had once predicted—though not with anything
of value so far as Stacey knew—and it had fallen to
her to serve the evening meal. The task had not proved
as intimidating as she feared. Meat was sent over
daily, already prepared, from the station cookhouse,
together with loaves of whole-grain bread, and with
the aid of an old cookbook she found in one of the
cupboards, she managed to whip up passable vegetables and desserts that tasted delicious, even if they
didn't always look the way she intended. Tonight they
had the usual mutton, succulently roasted with sage
and onion—"colonial goose," Errol called it, joking
that he had had it more than once for Christmas
dinner—supplemented with a casserole of tomatoes
and rice, and salad greens fresh from the garden.

Dessert was a jam roly-poly, which came out especially well, and even D'Arcy lingered longer than usual
at the table. It wasn't until later, when Errol had
poured himself a brandy and they were alone on the
front veranda, that Stacey finally broached the subject.

"Why didn't you tell me you had a sister?" she
asked.

She was surprised at the sharpness in his face as he
looked up from his glass. "Who told you that?"

"Fitz. I saw her portrait in the gallery on the second floor at Glenellen. When I asked who she was, he
told me."

"What did he say?"

"Not much." The sharpness was still there, in his
voice now, and she was beginning to be sorry she had
brought it up. "Just that she was your sister . . . and
that she went to England, to a convent, after she had
been disappointed by the man she loved. And that she
died there."

His face eased, and he leaned back in his chair,
stretching long legs out in front of him. "I'd say that
covers it—the essentials, at least. She wasn't my sister,
by the way. She was my *half*-sister. My mother's daugh-

ter, born before she married my father. He accepted legal responsibility for her, and eventually she took his name."

"Oh . . . I see." She was beginning to understand now. That faint pause when Fitz uttered her name—he would have known her first as Olivia D'Arcy. "I just assumed D'Arcy was your mother's maiden name. I suppose because she gave it to her youngest son."

"It was." He twirled the glass in his hand, looking faintly amused. "She wasn't married to Olivia's father. It was the one indiscretion of her life—otherwise she was a very proper lady. But she did it with flair, refusing to go off and have the baby in secret or send it to be raised by relatives. She must have loved the man in question. He was already married, and they say she never saw him again . . . but she didn't look at another man until after he died."

"Then she married your father?"

"Yes." He paused for a minute, his face unreadable. "I've often wondered if it hurt, being second choice. I was too young to understand while he was still alive, but I think not. I think he loved her enough so that nothing else mattered."

Stacey got up and walked over to the rail. The darkness was so penetrating she could not even make out shadows where the barn and stables stood. Second choice? Was he thinking of his father when he said that? Or of the young bride who had not been all he expected?

"You still haven't answered my question." She turned back to see that he had not moved. "Why didn't you tell me about her?"

"I suppose the subject never came up. Don't forget, I was very young when Livy went to England. Ten the last time I saw her. It just didn't seem . . ." He twirled his glass again, staring down at the amber liquid. "It didn't seem important."

It didn't seem important.

Those words were to pop into Stacey's mind again and again in the days to come. She was still thinking about them one sun-drenched afternoon when she wandered across the hillside behind the house, waiting for it to cool before tending to her chores in the kitchen.

One of the dogs was lying in a scant patch of shade, an old kelpie who knew her well enough to flick his tail halfheartedly as she passed.

Did he mean that it wasn't important because it happened so long ago? That he never thought about it because it didn't affect his life anymore? Or did he mean he didn't see any reason to discuss his deepest feelings with a woman who wasn't going to be around much longer anyway?

She followed the fence a short distance, then cut across the pasture toward a dirt path that led down to the creek. Two of the lambs looked up hopefully, then romped away when they saw she wasn't carrying a feed bucket. Rudolfina and one of the others, she thought, but there had been seven little orphans altogether, and they were growing so fat it was hard to tell them apart. It was getting late, and the shadows had begun to lengthen. Time to see if the new lettuce was ready, or plump baby cucumbers for a salad.

She wanted dinner to be especially good that night. It was the last chance she was going to have to be with Errol for several days. He had mentioned the evening before that he was going to move a mob of sheep—or a flock, as she persisted in calling it, much to his amusement—to one of the far paddocks, and she was growing more and more aware that there might not be many quiet evenings left for them.

She had just passed the place where the path forked, branching off to the surprisingly large lake that had been formed in the hollow, when she saw Errol coming toward her. If he had any thoughts about not bothering with her because she wasn't going to be around long, she had to admit they didn't show as he waved his hand and called out:

"Just the lady I was looking for. Come on, I have a treat for you. At least I think it'll be a treat. It was for me."

Stacey followed eagerly, struggling to keep up with long-legged strides as they hurried down the hill. All the way, she tried to coax him to tell her more, but he would answer only that it was a surprise and she was going to have to "wait and see." The path curved a little, dividing one more time, and she knew they were headed for the lake. A second before they got there, she realized what had happened.

The swan was back.

She had thought she would have difficulty picking it out—the other black swans all looked alike—but she recognized it the instant she saw it. The setting might have come from Fitz's painting, everything was so perfect and so still. Dusk was just beginning to fall, the water had turned to an eerie silver mirror, and the swan was a silhouette in black against soft, shimmering light.

It was bigger than the others, but it was not size alone that make it stand out. It was the sheer grace with which that sleek-necked ebony apparition skimmed across the water. It seemed to Stacey she had never seen anything quite like it. There was magic in those fluid motions, as if it were not a creature of the earth at all, but some higher ethereal being, and she knew what it was that had made Fitz want to paint it. And why everyone waited so eagerly for its return.

A bird call came from somewhere across the lake; otherwise it was so quiet Stacey could almost hear the water lapping against the shore. She was intensely aware of Errol beside her, so close his sleeve brushed her arm, and she knew, even without looking, that his eyes were not on that dark, gliding form.

He had told her once the swan reminded him of her. Was he thinking that now? Remembering the way he had felt about her . . . however briefly? There had been passion between them that single night. All the yearning had not been on her side. He had seen something in her and responded to it—and wanted to take her to his bed.

She dropped her eyes, then raised them as the swan floated nearer. An omen? she thought—as she had once before, when it had not returned. A symbol, it had seemed then, of all the things she wanted and could not have. Was it a different kind of omen now that it was back? A sign that she still had a chance?

"So very beautiful," she said softly.

"Yes," he replied, his voice as low as hers, and she sensed he was not speaking of the swan.

She was afraid to look up for fear she would break the spell. But when she did, she saw it was already broken, and he had turned away and was looking back at the lake.

"I know it hasn't been easy for you," he said after a moment. "Adjusting to Cameron's Creek. What with droughts and floods and being cooped up in the house, it must have seemed tedious at times. Before you started going to Glenellen, the men tell me you spent a fair amount of time in the barn and stable."

"I wasn't in the way," Stacey hastened to say, hoping she hadn't annoyed him. "At least I tried not to—"

"I'm not worried about that," he assured her. "I don't think the men considered you a problem. With the exception of Bluey Warren, who's so shy he loses his voice for two days if he crosses paths with a female—and maybe Bobs the bullocky, who doesn't like anyone—I think they were flattered by your interest. So was I, actually. Or pleased, I should say. I thought since you're curious about how a sheep station is run, you might like to come along tomorrow when we move the mob up the hill."

Stacey looked back at the pond, barely daring to breathe. Australia was a man's world, she had already seen that—women were never invited to "come along" and satisfy their curiosity. The swan was almost to the shore now, looking up, not curiously, as she might have expected, but knowingly. Perhaps it was an omen after all.

"Do you mean it?" she said eagerly. "I can really come?"

Errol laughed, enjoying her excitement. "You can if you can take it. But I warn you, it's going to be rough trails and a hard bed on the ground. And you'll have to be out by dawn if you don't want to be left behind."

19

Errol was exaggerating when he told Stacey she would have to be ready before dawn, but not by much. Sheep and horses and men pulled out with the first good light, kicking up a swirling haze of dust that obscured the vivid pinks and vermilions of one of the most glorious sunrises she had ever seen. The drovers had the gate open by the time she got there, and were pushing the mob through, out onto a narrow dirt road where they already formed an undulating ribbon of gray, stretching toward the horizon.

Stacey tightened her grip on the reins, holding Golden Girl in as they lingered a short distance from the gate. The horse shied, not badly, but enough to require a firm hand, and Stacey sensed she was not used to working sheep. Not that she blamed her. All around, everything seemed chaos, more heard than seen, for only vague impressions of motion came through that thick cloud of dust. The rest was noise: the drone of thousands of hooves plodding along the ground; the cries and whistles of the men, lowering sometimes to muttered curses; the constant *yap-yap, yap-yap, yap-yap* of the dogs.

Only when the last sheep had passed through the fence and the gate was secure again did Errol come over, offering to see her the first part of the way, though he warned he would have little time to spend with her later. Stacey expected him to pull in behind the sheep, but he guided her off the trail instead, picking a path between rocks and roots and holes in the ground.

"You didn't think I was going to make you follow the mob, did you?" he said with a grin. Stacey grinned back, but did not answer, for already her throat was so badly coated it was hard to find her voice, and she was relieved to know she would be at least partway out of the dust.

The wagon had gone on ahead with the supplies they would need for the four-day trek. There would be game along the way, Errol told her, and good fishing in one spot, but the tools and staples—the barrels of flour and rice and huge slabs of salt beef—would go with Bobs the bullocky, who had started his team out with the usual "Gid on yer, ye' beg-gurrr—*hi-yahh*!— I'll gi' ye' som'thin' to gid on wi' " the afternoon before. Stacey had thought, as a woman, she might be expected to ride on the wagon, and she had dreaded the prospect. But when she expressed her qualms to Errol, he only laughed, promising she could take her own horse, and telling her with a broad wink he wouldn't ride with Bobs himself!

"But's he's a damn, uh . . . a fine driver. And if the bullocks don't mind, who am I to grudge his pay?"

The sun came up slowly. Stacey could feel winter in the air at last, a welcome nippiness after the unrelieved heat of summer, and it was well into the morning before she took off the light jacket she had been wearing and draped it across her saddle. The meadows were bright with autumn wildflowers, splashes of russet and yellow, shimmering even in the clouds of dust that hovered above them.

She coaxed Golden Girl up a rocky rise at the side of the trail and paused to look out over a broad stretch of waving fields, knee-deep with silver-green grasses, and stark gray outcrops of stone. Below, Errol had just finished speaking to one of the men, and looking up, touched his fingers to the brim of a floppy felt hat as he spotted her on the hill. Stacey smiled, just worldly enough to know what kind of picture she made in the cool sunlight, and young enough not to feel immodest delight in her own prettiness. She had worn a slate-blue skirt, divided so she could ride astride, but full enough to look feminine, with a pale-blue ruffled blouse—no trim, for she sensed Errol would not approve of lace on the trail—and the jacket of somewhat darker fabric that was now lying forgotten on her saddle. Her hat was felt too, a boy's slouch hat with a smallish brim, drab gray but freshly cleaned and brushed, and perked up with a blue satin ribbon.

One of the spare horses had wandered away, unnoticed by the men as it drifted off on its own, searching for better grazing beyond the stony trail. Stacey touched her heels lightly to Golden Girl, all the prodding that spirited filly needed, and off they went in pursuit. It was difficult, driving the horses, for they strayed continually and it was necessary to gallop after them among the roots and rocks, but Stacey was glad to help. She had always loved riding, and once the men saw that she knew what she was doing, they welcomed her assistance with no grumbling or sullen sidelong looks.

The wind picked up, hissing through the trees, audible over the low rumble of hooves and the shrill barking of the dogs. A dingo followed for a short distance, keeping pace with the slow-moving sheep, never coming too close, just watching with dark, glistening eyes until it slunk away again. The dogs were on the other side of the mob, but Errol had spotted it, and Stacey sensed, as she saw him signal one of the men, that he was telling him to go after it and shoot it. The thought saddened her—it was such a lean, scruffy thing, only trying to survive. But if they didn't kill it now, she knew it would be back at night and they would lose some of the sheep.

"Why are you moving the flock now?" she asked later when Errol took a few minutes to ride beside her. "I mean the 'mob,' for heaven's sake! With all the rain, I would have thought there'd be enough grass by the creek. Or near the river if there are too many sheep for the home paddock."

"There's plenty of grass," he agreed. "For now. But we keep the herds spread out—I don't want to overgraze any one area. Besides, young grass needs a chance to get started."

"Started?" Stacey asked, curious.

"Sheep aren't like cattle," he explained. "They graze right to the ground. Once grass has a chance to take hold, it can handle that kind of close trimming. But

graze the new shoots too soon, and you're asking for
thin, weak growth. Wait till we get the home paddock
up a couple of inches—then I'll bring some of the
sheep back in.''

Everything was new to Stacey, all the details that
were routine by now for the men, and it fascinated
her, watching the way drovers and dogs worked together. They were not the prettiest dogs she had ever
seen, but they were bright and independent, like the
men who handled them: shiny-eyed black kelpies, and
rich brown kelpies with creamy chests and paws stained
by the dust to a paler brown, and a great Queensland
blue, recognizable by its size and dappled black coat.
She quickly learned to respect them, as many an Australian squatter had before her, for it was their keen
instincts and swift reactions that enabled a handful of
men to manage large properties with thousands of
cattle and sheep.

Where a man couldn't go, even on horseback, a dog
could, and several times throughout the morning she
would see a dark streak slither belly to the ground into
a deep crevice in the rocks, only to return twenty
minutes later, bullying and barking half a dozen sheep
in front of it. Though they responded to voice com-
mands, and even hand signals, Stacey noticed the men
usually worked their dogs with ear-splitting whistles
that carried above the din of the muster. Sometimes,
when the trail narrowed and the mob was too thick to
get through, they would leap up and race in seconds
from front to rear on the woolly backs of the sheep.

The first time she saw it, Stacey laughed out loud,
thinking it was some playful antic. But she soon learned
that that was a part of the working dog's stock in
trade. They were surly creatures, heaven knows, anti-
social when they wanted to be—which was most of the
time—but they were incredibly graceful too, and it
never failed to intrigue her, the way they ran lightly
across the backs of moving sheep without so much as a
break in their gait.

It was shortly after three when they stopped for the
day. They had gone barely six miles, but they had
reached the only reliable water in the area, a shallow

stream that rippled down the hillside to intersect with a weathered fence separating Emu and Koala paddocks. The men herded the sheep up to the fence, stretching out lengths of calico to form makeshift barriers on the other sides; they would bed down along the edges to keep their charges from straying and to protect them from the dingoes. Errol stayed for a while to make sure everything was all right, then chose a campsite for himself and Stacey in a small grove of gums some distance away.

The horses had to be unsaddled first, then hobbled. A strap was fastened to each foreleg with a short chain between, intended to keep them from straying too far, though Stacey, knowing how willful Golden Girl could be—to say nothing of Errol's powerful chestnut stallion—was not sure it would work. Fortunately, there was plenty of grass all around, so perhaps they would stay close to camp. While Errol went off to gather wood and make a fire, Stacey wandered down to the stream, where she scrubbed off the dust of the trail, which seemed to be an inch thick at least. The water was cool and wonderfully refreshing, and she was beginning to feel almost human again as she made her way back to camp.

She must have been gone longer than she thought. Errol had already erected the tent, which she assumed was for her, and a fire was beginning to crackle, spitting bright yellow sparks into the shadows under the trees. The warmth was welcome, for it was getting late—coolness came quickly now as the sun sank—and she lowered herself gratefully to a possum rug he had unrolled in front of the fire. Bobs had brought his wagon to the edge of the camp, but the bullocks were gone, taken somewhere for the night, she supposed, and she wondered vaguely if that was where Errol was planning to sleep. Or perhaps he would sling a hammock between the trees; he had told her that the men often slept that way.

"Well . . ." Errol squatted across from her, watching her over the dancing flames. "How did you like your first day as a drover?"

Stacey relaxed, enjoying the warmth and the closeness of him. "I think you lied to me," she said, teasing. "You promised a rough trail, and all I've had is a pleasant ride. I daresay the bed on the ground is real enough, though. And very stony ground it is, too."

He laughed, a hearty sound that drowned out the dogs and the restless stirring of the sheep. Occasionally the voice of one of the men would drift back, but otherwise they almost seemed alone in the gathering dusk. "I think I can spare you the stones. I had a feather bed packed on the wagon. You'll find it in your tent, with clean bedding on top."

Stacey shifted a little uncomfortably. He was being thoughtful, but the last thing she wanted was to make a nuisance of herself. "You didn't have to do that. I'm not some little porcelain Phyllis, you know—so fragile I'll break on contact with the ground."

"I know you're not." He took up a green stick and poked at the fire. "But there's no point suffering if you don't have to. Feather beds roll into a tidy bundle, and there was room on the wagon."

It had begun to drizzle slightly, and Errol dug out a hooded cape for her, though it was not really necessary. The thick branches overhead provided shelter. She would be dry that night, she knew. The tent was made of calico brushed with oil for waterproofing, and he had had the foresight to lay it on a bed of boughs covered with tussocks of dried grass.

She had brought her spare clothes in a carpetbag, and she pulled it up now, using it for a backrest, while Errol raked coals together at the edge of the fire to make "the best bloody billy tea you've ever had." Since Stacey had never had billy tea, "bloody" or otherwise, it seemed a safe bet, but she kept the observation to herself as she leaned back and watched the proceedings with interest.

The "pot" was no more than a smoke-darkened tin, shaped for saddle lie, which Errol filled with water and laid on some green twigs across the coals. A short time later, it was bubbling merrily, and he threw in a handful of tea and took it off to steep. When he deemed it was ready, he swung it several times in a wide arc to settle the leaves at the bottom, then poured out two pannikins of aromatic dark brown liquid.

It was indeed the best tea Stacey had ever had. She didn't know if it was the brew itself or the long day's ride, or the fact that Errol had made it for her, and she didn't truly care. It was heavenly, just to lean back and stare at the flames, and sip liquid so hot it almost burned her tongue.

Dinner was ready a few minutes later. Simple fare, cooked over the open fire, which Errol prepared himself, refusing to let her help. "You've wrestled with pots and pans enough since Mrs. Sweeney left," he told her. "And surprised me, I must admit, with some very tasty dishes. Don't you think you've earned the right to sit back and let someone wait on you for a change?"

"I didn't mind," Stacey said, warming to the praise.

"Maybe not." His eyes seemed exceptionally dark as he looked up for a second from the blackened iron pan he had been heating on the coals. "But I've been so busy I'm afraid I've taken you for granted. You're a good sport, Stacey—pitching in like that. I should have told you before. I appreciate what you've done."

He turned back to the pan, which had begun smoking in the fire, and Stacey was content to sit and watch, not expecting, or needing, any more compliments. It was enough to know that he had seen what she was doing, and that he was not as indifferent as he appeared. He had seen and appreciated . . . and perhaps he had even changed his opinion of her somewhat.

It was not an elegant feast, but it was well-prepared, and as Stacey accepted the metal plate Errol held out, she had the feeling, for all those kind words, he was still a better cook than she. Fat slabs of bacon, not sliced but left in solid chunks, had been cooked first in the iron pan; then potatoes and baby onions from the garden and seasonings she did not recognize, which added just the right savor. Afterward came thin soda cakes—"johnny cakes," he called them—light and delicious, melting in the mouth, with jam and more hot tea to finish the meal.

Stacey curled her legs contentedly, edging the carpetbag over a little as she watched Errol clean the pan with salt and an old rag. He was right after all—she had pitched in and helped for weeks, as best she could. And it *was* good after a long ride to lounge in front of an open fire and not have to worry about anything.

"I didn't know men could be so domestic," she said. "Though I should have, after that first meal you prepared for me."

"The Australian bush isn't San Francisco, you know." He stowed the pan away with the rest of the gear and pulled out a pipe and pouch of strong negrohead tobacco. "A squatter learns his way around the kitchen— or he starves to death."

Stacey laughed as he scooped out a portion of tobacco and tamped it down in the bowl. "It sounds funny when you call yourself that. A squatter. In America we think of squatters as poor dirt farmers— you know, people who claim land no one else wants by squatting on it."

"It's the same thing here . . . except in connotation. Though I've noticed some of the wealthier squatters like to call themselves 'pastoralists.' " Little lines formed at the corners of his eyes as he touched a burning stick to the pipe, releasing a pungent aroma to mingle with the smell of grass and wet earth. "We're not all dirt poor, mind you—though I must look it at the moment. Some of us have considerable holdings. Squatters in Australia tend to claim huge tracts of land as soon as an area is opened by the government. Sometimes even sooner."

Remembering what he had said about his ancestors, Stacey could believe that. "Was it your grandfather who settled Cameron's Creek?" she asked. "Or did Harry claim it first?"

"Neither, actually. It was my grandmother. Crazy Kate may have been a bit mad—I remember her as an old lady in a worn leather jacket, open at the front, with wild eyes and brazen streaks of copper in unkempt gray hair—but she was as shrewd as they come. She squirreled away everything my grandfather gave her, which I understand was considerable. They used to laugh at her, she told me when I was a boy, but she bought land from squatters all through the area—they sold it for next to nothing in those days—and had it put in her own name, too! It was all that saved us when Black Mick was caught behaving in an ungentlemanly manner on the highway and the crown confiscated everything he owned."

"She must have been a fascinating woman." Stacey leaned back against the carpetbag. Darkness had closed in all around, and the glow of the fire reflected green and gold on leaves rustling overhead.

"She was." Errol set a small pot on the fire, not the billy tin again, but another metal container filled with water. "She was the dominant figure in my childhood. Whenever I think of the station as it used to be, still unfenced, with only part of the homestead finished, I think of Kate. It was she who named me, as a matter of fact. My mother hated the name Errol, but it didn't matter; no one, even my father, ever stood up to Crazy Kate. And it was she who saw to my upbringing— strictly, I might add, according to her own rather unconventional standards. I adored her, of course, but she had my mother tearing her hair."

"Poor Ellen." Stacey couldn't help smiling as she recalled the refined lady in the portrait. The night had turned cooler, and she was grateful for the cloak Errol had brought, though the rain seemed to have stopped. The darkness was filled with comfortable sounds: the click of horses' hobbles as they grazed nearby, frogs beginning their nightly chorus in the creek, wild swans flying overhead. "It must have been very difficult for her."

"I daresay it was, though I was too young, and enjoying myself much too much, to understand." The water had warmed and he pulled it off the fire, pouring it with an equal amount of wine into a small pannikin, which he handed to her. " 'To ward off the rheumatiz,' as Kate would have said—or just a pleasant way to end a meal." She noticed that he poured his own straight, with no water to warm it, but he sipped from a similar container.

"I often thought," he went on, "that that's why D'Arcy was her favorite. By the time he was born, you see, Kate had been dead for some years. He was her own baby, to do with as she chose . . . her first son, in a way, for I had never really been hers."

"Did that bother you?" Stacey took a sip of the wine, feeling her blood begin to warm. "That she doted on him more than you?"

"No. Oddly enough, I hardly noticed . . . or perhaps not so oddly. As I told you, my strongest bonds were to Kate. Besides, it always seemed to me, even then—it's amazing what children pick up on—that she could never quite love D'Arcy the way she wanted." He put the wine aside, almost untouched, and took up his pipe again, making a strong masculine picture in the firelight. "My brother was dark-skinned, you see . . . the aborigine blood again. It's not so much a taint here, but the D'Arcys were from England, and I think the strangeness offended them."

"Yet she married your father. Knowing he had native blood."

"So she did." Errol took a long, thoughtful draft on his pipe. "Did I say there was only one indiscretion in her life? I wronged her. That was the second . . . though with my father, the taint didn't show as much. His skin was almost milk-white, and while his eyes were black, his hair was somewhat lighter than mine."

The fire had nearly gone out, and he reached forward, poking it back to life, though Stacey noticed he did not throw on any new wood. Everything in his manner indicated that the conversation was over, and she made no effort to pursue it, recalling how reticent he could be when it came to his past. The wine was taking effect, and she felt strangely dreamy as she got up and wandered over to the edge of the ring of firelight. Everything was still now, the world seemed clean and new . . . the air was so crisp it almost hurt to breathe it in.

She was surprised to feel tears in her eyes, and she reached up surreptitiously, brushing them back, trying to pretend it was the smoke, though she knew that was not true. It had been so pleasant, so natural, sitting with him like this, as if they really were husband and wife. It was hard to believe she didn't belong . . . and all because of that one stupid mistake she had made after Grandfather forced her into a marriage she thought she didn't want.

"Grandfather . . ."

She was not aware that she had whispered the word aloud. But she must have, for suddenly Errol had set his pipe down, and there he was standing beside her, and he was turning her until she knew that he could see the tears on her lashes.

"Did I say something wrong?" His face twisted with a hint of humor, but there was only tender concern in his voice. "Here I thought I was entertaining you with tales of my eccentric family . . . and all the time I was upsetting you. Or are you tired from the ride?"

"No . . . it's not that. It's just . . ." Stacey broke off awkwardly. How could she tell him she had been thinking of him . . . and the thing she had done that now kept them apart? "Talking about your family . . . well, it reminded me of mine. My . . . my grandfather died shortly after I left San Francisco. I didn't even know it until I heard from Olga—my sister—weeks and weeks later."

"Ah . . . the letters from home." Errol nodded slightly, as if she had explained more than her tears just now. "I remember how unhappy you looked the day the mail came, but I assumed it was homesickness. I wish you'd told me, dear. I might have been able to help."

Stacey shook her head. "There was nothing you could do . . . and I didn't want to talk about it. It's just . . . Oh, Errol, I'll never forget the way he looked standing in front of the house the day I rode away. I was so angry . . . I thought he had tricked me—he *had* tricked me!—and I wouldn't look him in the eye, much less speak to him. I wanted to write after I got here. I *tried* to write, but I didn't know what to say. And now it's too late."

"Stacey . . ." Errol put his hands on her shoulders, looking deep into her eyes, pools of dusky gray in the shadows. "We all have regrets. You can't spend your life looking back. God knows, I wish I had been closer to my parents . . . or spent more time with D'Arcy after I returned from England. He was only nine. He needed a man's influence in his life—a brother, if not a father—but I was too preoccupied to see it."

He dropped his hands and went back to the fire, caught up in his own thoughts now. Stacey followed after a minute, crouching beside him on the possum rug as he continued.

"I should have given him more responsibility—early on. Hindsight is an amazing thing, isn't it? He was still a baby when Father made out his will. Everything went to me on the assumption I would provide for him. It seemed perfectly natural—I was only nineteen myself at the time. But it must have been humiliating for D'Arcy as he grew up, having no legal position on the station. And I was always too busy to teach him anything. I expected him to learn for himself, you see—as I had—forgetting that he isn't me. I tried to make up for it later, tried to give him the responsibility all at once, but I suspect it was too much . . . and too late."

Stacey, remembering the way D'Arcy had reacted to the one disaster she knew about, was inclined to agree. "He was so angry when you scolded him about the sheep. Or maybe 'angry' isn't the right word. Maybe he was just lashing out. He was too inexperienced for what you expected of him, but it must have been humiliating all the same, failing like that."

Errol looked up so sharply she regretted her words. For just an instant, it almost seemed as if that half-hearted defense of D'Arcy had angered him, as if he did not like even the sound of his brother's name on her lips. Then, whatever it was disappeared again.

"Maybe," he agreed slowly. "The point is, I can't go back and remake my relationship with D'Arcy. And you can't go back and mend your fences with your grandfather. Besides . . ." His voice softened, and he was almost smiling, "You're too young—and too pretty—for tears. I'm sure, even without that last letter, your grandfather knew you loved him. And I'm sure he loved you . . . very much."

"I know that." Stacey picked up a leaf from the ground, still dry, for it was beneath the trees, and crumbled it absently in her fingers. "I do know, really, but . . . it isn't just the past that troubles me. It's the future too. With Grandfather gone, I feel like there's no place I belong. I was a little afraid of him—I knew he'd be furious if I didn't do what he wanted—but he would have taken me back in the end. Now I can't ever go home."

She was aware as she spoke that he was watching her. Looking up, she saw his eyes intently on her face. It had begun to rain again, heavier than before; she could hear little droplets pattering in the leaves overhead and all around her on the ground.

"Is that what you want?" he said very quietly. "To go home?"

"What I want?" She stared at him numbly for a moment. There was only one thing she wanted, and that was the one thing she dared not say. "Does it really matter what I want?"

"Yes." His voice was still quiet, so deep it vibrated. "It matters very much, what you want."

Say it, a little voice in the back of her mind urged her. Say you love him and want to stay with him . . . and you'll do anything to keep him from sending you away! But she was afraid to speak the words, afraid that even broaching the subject out loud would mean an end to her tenuous hold on the only world she cared about.

"What I want and what I'm likely to get don't seem to be the same thing nowadays," she said. "It was so much easier when I was a little girl and only had grandfather to twist around my finger. Besides, you're wrong. It really *doesn't* matter. Even if I wanted to, I couldn't go home . . . not anymore." She got up slowly, feeling a little groggy—from the wine, she supposed, or the long day, or the sadness that had welled up inside her. The rest of the camp was silent. Not a sound came from the men in sleeping rolls beside the fence; even the sheep seemed to have ceased their restless stirring. "It's getting late. I think it's time to go to bed."

He rose too, raking the last of the coals into a neat red pile. His eyes were thoughtful as he looked at her.

"You're right," he said after a moment. "It is time . . . for bed."

The tent seemed almost unnaturally empty as Stacey entered it. She had brought a lamp with her, and she was vaguely aware as she set it down that it should have seemed cozy . . . the shimmer of yellow light on glossy oiled cloth . . . the soft even sound of the rain on slanting walls. Why, then, could she see only the shadows? Feel only the loneliness?

They had been so close tonight, closer than she dared to dream. But much as she wanted it, much as she prayed for it, closeness never went that extra step to intimacy.

She stripped off her clothes, shivering a little as she took her nightdress out of the bag. The same sheer white gown she had worn that one time he came to her bed . . . much too frothy for camp, but the laundry never seemed to get done without proper servants, and it was all she had that was clean. She was conscious as she drew it on of the feel of the fabric, soft against her skin—achingly sensual—and her body swelled with the sweet, half-defined yearning that, once roused, she sensed would never be stilled again.

Resisting the impulse to pull out a mirror, she tugged at the pins in her hair, releasing it to tumble in wild tangles down her back. What did it matter if she looked pretty now? If she looked more beautiful than she ever had in her life? There was no one to see.

She heard a sound in the doorway and, turning, saw the flap move. A hand came in, then the oiled calico parted and Errol was stepping into the tent. In spite of herself, she felt her heart jump. He looked so strong in the flickering lamp glow, so intensely masculine, shoulders stretching the rough fabric of his shirt, damp hair spilling onto his forehead.

"Did . . . did you want something?"

His lips moved, an ironic half-smile as he slipped inside, letting the flap fall behind him.

"A man usually wants something . . . when he comes to his wife at night."

<unreadable>. What is or <unreadable> <unreadable> be in <unreadable>
to come life-ask, he <unreadable> <unreadable> <unreadable> <unreadable>

The <unreadable> <unreadable> <unreadable> <unreadable> <unreadable> <unreadable>
<unreadable> <unreadable> <unreadable> <unreadable> <unreadable> <unreadable>

20

"His . . . wife?"

For a moment, Stacey could only stare, half-wondering if she had heard him right. He looked so casual, pulling back the tent flap, so completely at ease as he secured it against wet winds that threatened to tug it from his grasp. "Did you say *wife*?"

Amusement showed in his dark, rugged features. "How you utter that word, 'wife,' as if it didn't apply to you. We *are* married, I believe . . . though I have that only by hearsay. I wasn't there, as you will recall. But you assured me the proxy ceremony had taken all the legalities into account."

"Yes, but you said yourself . . . you told me it wasn't binding because you hadn't authorized your brother to speak for you. You said if I wasn't pregnant, you were going to repudiate it and send me back to my grandfather!"

"I said a great many things, it seems." His face twisted wryly. "I had hoped you weren't going to hold them against me. Was I wrong?"

"I . . . I don't know." Her voice dropped, soft and deep in her throat. "Everything is so confusing, I hardly know what to think." The last thing she had expected was for him to come to her tonight, yet there *had* been clues. The way he had been looking at her these past few days . . . the subtle intensity in his manner all evening as he sat across the fire from her. "It's hard to answer when I don't know what you're asking. Or what you expect of me."

"No . . . of course you don't." He stepped away from the entrance, crouching because the sloped calico walls were not high enough to stand erect. Stacey held her breath as he sat beside her on the edge of the mattress. "You said before that it didn't matter what you wanted . . . but it does. It makes all the difference in the world. I was asking then what you wanted for the future, what kind of life you longed for in the days to come. I'll ask the same thing again—but only for tonight—and hope you trust me enough to tell me."

The rays of the lamp softened his strong male features, making his face so gentle she was almost tempted to tell him that all she wanted, all she had *ever* wanted, was to have him take her in his arms again. But there was nothing gentle in those dark, challenging eyes.

"You mean . . . right now? This very minute?"

"This very minute." He seemed to sense her tension, for he leaned back, just slightly, as if he knew how threatening it was, that sheer masculine aura he exuded. "If you could have anything in the world, if tonight could be any way you wanted, what would you choose?"

"If I could have anything I wanted, *anything*, then . . ." She felt her cheeks burn, and she knew she was blushing, but she couldn't let herself back down. Once before she had not spoken when she should, and she had nearly lost him. She was not going to let a sudden bout of shyness spoil her chances now. "Then I'd choose that same night all over again . . . the night you spent with me. I'd have everything exactly the way it was then."

"Exactly?" He raised one brow, enjoying her reaction.

"Exactly." She felt his eyes on her and faltered. "Well . . . until the part where you got angry. I know I was wrong, Errol, not telling the truth in the beginning. I know I should have, but—"

"Shhhh!" He touched the ends of his fingers to her lips. "No words now . . . no apologies. You wanted it exactly like that night, remember?" He lowered his hand, letting it linger tantalizingly close to the neck of her gown. "There will be time for apologies later . . . if you still want them."

And she would. Stacey knew that. She would want to throw herself into his arms, telling him again and again how sorry she was, knowing at last that he would forgive her. But he was right. All that was for later. Now she could think of nothing but the feel of his hand as he laid it, oh, so gently, on her throat, slipping inside the lace edge of her collar.

"What . . . what are you doing?"

"You did say *exactly* like that night, didn't you?" There was laughter in his voice, at least she thought there was, low and husky. But all she could feel was the warmth in his fingers and the little tremors that had begun to shiver all over her body.

"Yes . . . but . . ."

"The first thing I did was take this little button . . . just like this . . . see, love? . . . and slip it out of its lacy nest." His hands were busy undoing the button, easing the fabric apart. Lowering his head, he buried his mouth in the pulse that was beating wildly at the base of her throat. "And this button . . ." he murmured, teasing the next pearly orb loose, following again with lips that seemed to know just what effect they were having. "And this one . . . and this . . . and this . . ."

The air was icy in the tent. Stacey sensed the coldness as he finished with the last button and eased the gown off, letting it tumble to the floor. But every inch of her flesh felt hot beneath his hands, his lips . . . those black, burning eyes that seemed to sear into her, branding her once and for all as his.

"There, love." He was still half-teasing, but his voice was rough with desire. "That's it, that's good . . . not quite like the last time, eh? Last time, you turned timid and pulled away because you thought you weren't big enough . . . here." He laid his hand on her breast, cupping it lightly but firmly, and Stacey felt a warming sensation run through her.

"I remember," she said, arching her body closer. "And you said that men were known to be disappointed when a woman took off her corset and her breasts flopped to her ankles."

"Her waist, minx!" He was laughing again, a deep masculine sound; she was sure of it now, sure for the first time that her hold on him was as compelling as his on her.

He began to move his hand slowly, deliberately, easing it away from her breast, playing with the slender flesh above her ribs, the rounded swell of her belly, her hips . . . tarrying briefly on thighs that longed to part. Stacey barely recognized the sound that came out of her lips, a soft, almost animal cry as his mouth found her neck again, etching a trail of kisses along her shoulder, across her breast, bold tongue darting out to tease first one engorged nipple, then the other.

Then suddenly that same hard mouth was on hers, bold and demanding. She did not even feel him leave her breast; she knew only that he was kissing her, and she was kissing him back with all the hunger she had been trying for weeks to suppress. His hand was between her legs now—how could he have moved it without her knowing?—and he was toying with her, as he had before, manipulating, challenging, not cautiously this time, but boldly, sure of her desire for him and the way she would respond.

She had forgotten how sweet it could be, the pain that filled every corner of her being until she felt as if she were going to burst. She had missed him so much, yearned for him so much; she had thought she knew exactly how it would be if he touched her again. But she had forgotten the aching that came with the passion, forgotten the helplessness, the sense of being swept away beyond herself. All she could do was hold on to him, digging her fingers into his arm, only half-aware of the male hardness of his body, the searing wetness of his mouth, as he brought her swiftly, skillfully, to the rapture that was somehow as new and unexpected as if it had never happened before.

His hand remained for a moment, motionless but warm between her legs, possessive. A strong gesture, masculine and faintly arrogant, telling her that he knew he had satisfied her and was pleased with himself.

"Well?" His voice was faintly hoarse, as if he, not she, had just come from the peak of pleasure. "Was that what you wanted? Was it like the first time . . . exactly?"

"Not . . . exactly." She dared to let her eyes sparkle as she looked up. He had propped himself on one elbow beside her on the mattress. His shirt was open at the neck—strange she had not noticed before—and familiar sensations stirred again as she glanced at the dark tangles of hair curling nearly to his throat. "Almost . . . but not quite."

"Oh?" He sensed the teasing in her tone and matched it with his own. "It wasn't the same?" His hand was resting on the inside of her thigh, moist with the residue of her own passion, but she was so comfortable with him she wasn't even embarrassed.

"No, not the same . . . Better."

His lips did not move; he didn't make a sound, but she knew he was laughing, and suddenly she was laughing with him. It *was* like the last time, she thought as she raised her hand, letting sensitive fingertips run across the slightly coarse hair spilling out of his shirtfront. It was like it, but it was different too, and much, much better now that she knew what to expect and was not the tiniest bit afraid.

"I think you have on too many clothes," she said, surprised, but secretly pleased with her own boldness. "Last time you were more suitably attired."

"If I had known the terms you were going to set— that tonight was to be *exactly* like before—I would have brought my dressing gown." His eyes dropped to the floor, where her pretty white nightdress lay in a crumpled heap. "You, it seems, had more foresight."

Stacey smiled, recalling the necessity that had forced her to bring that particular garment, and determined not to let anything as mundane as laundry enter the conversation. "It seems I did . . . but fortunately your carelessness hasn't done any harm. You didn't wear the robe long anyway, as I remember." She was already beginning to move her hands, daring her fingers to play with the loose neck of his shirt, eyes questioning as she did. She got the answer she expected.

"I made free with your buttons a while ago. It seems only fair that you should do the same with mine."

The words were not necessary. Everything in his manner told her he liked what she was doing. Even before he finished speaking, she had worked the top

button out and was starting on the second. He made
no effort to help, letting her do everything herself.
Her hands moved daringly until they neared his waist;
then at last they faltered, and he came to her aid,
jerking the final button loose himself, grunting with
impatience as he unfastened his belt and trousers and
cast them brusquely aside.

Stacey was surprised how right it felt, having him
there, half-sitting, half-lying beside her on the bed,
sharing the pillows she had propped behind her. He
was completely naked now, all body hair and bronzed
skin, except for the white parts where the sun had
never touched. She did not even feel self-conscious
when her eyes drifted down to see that he did indeed
want her as much as she had assumed.

Her fingers twisted in the thick masculine curls on
his chest, and she dared, tentatively, to explore the
body that was still new to her. Every pore, every
coloration, every sturdy male sinew seemed wondrous
and precious. It amazed her, the way a man was
designed so perfectly to complement a woman. His
shoulders were broad, contrasting with her own slender form; his chest strong, rippling with muscle, un-
yielding when he pressed it against her softly rounded
bosom; his hips, lean and hard, fit exactly into her
womanly curves.

She had not even been aware that her fingers were
following her thoughts, outlining every powerful muscle on his chest, tracing the thin line of hair that ran
down his stomach. Gasping with surprise, she realized
suddenly what she was doing. But it was too late, for
he had already reached down and caught her hand in
his.

"Don't stop now, love." His voice was deep in his
throat, and Stacey could feel his desire drawing her
toward him. "Men are not so different from women—
they like to be touched too. I want you to touch me,
Stacey . . . everywhere.

"I . . . I want to." A faint flush rose to her cheeks,
and she felt awkward for the first time since he had
taken her in his arms. "Especially if it pleases you,
but—"

"Then, do . . ." He tightened his hold on her hand, urging but not forcing. "Don't ever be afraid to please me, sweet . . . or yourself. There is no shame in lovemaking. The things that happen between a man and woman are good and natural. Don't be afraid to trust your instincts."

"You're sure?" she said hesitantly. "It's all right?" But even as the words slipped out, she knew it *was* all right. Nothing she could do now would be too bold, too wanton.

Hardness met her fingers first, then warmth, surprising warmth—she had not known it would be like that, almost as stimulating for her as for him. Is this what love is all about? she thought, understanding at last. Giving and sharing . . . enjoying every part of each other?

"Last time," she whispered, "you were so eager you couldn't wait. Do you remember?"

"How could I forget?" He said it lightly, but his voice was heavy with longing, and Stacey could feel slow tremors running through his body. "I wanted you so much I couldn't take time to be gentle . . . as I had promised."

"I didn't want you to be gentle," she said. She was still touching him, still aware of that potent male hardness in her hand, not threatening but exciting, provocative. "I didn't need your gentleness then."

He drew her closer, confident hands sliding down her back, cupping her buttocks. "And now?" he whispered hoarsely. "Do you want me to be gentle now?"

"No." Stacey was conscious of the pressure of his fingers, hard, bruising, as he held her taut against him. "I don't want gentleness now—I want your strength . . . and your passion."

They came together in a single fluid motion, her hips surging up as his thrust downward, her hands eager now, unashamed, helping guide him into her. There were no more questions, no doubts, no fears, only sweet, compelling sensations as he set a familiar rhythm, throbbing, carrying her once again outside herself. The same pleasure he had given her before, she had come to recognize it now—the same physical exhilaration—only it was a hundred, a thousand times more intoxicating, sharing it with him.

Instinct moved her now, her body understanding what her mind had barely grasped. Her hips seemed to have a will of their own, writhing, twisting, responding to every hard, driving motion as he pushed again and again deep into her yielding softness. Then, just as she was sure she could bear it no longer, she felt that last shuddering convulsion, and for one brief, breathless moment, their flesh seemed to join before they sank back heavily on the bed.

The gentleness came afterward. This time he did not pull away, but held her in his arms, easing his weight off her, lying beside her on the thin mattress. So good, she thought as she let her head sink to his chest, moist with sweat but still warm from their lovemaking. So good . . . being with him like this.

The rain had stopped, but little droplets fell from the trees, making a faint pattering sound on the roof, and the frogs had begun their chorus again, somewhere by the creek. Otherwise everything was silent, and Stacey almost had the feeling that nothing existed beyond the smoky golden glow that filled the inside of the tent. Errol's arms were tight around her; he seemed to cling, as if, like her, he was afraid to let go for fear all their newfound happiness would vanish in the night.

Or was it she who was clinging, and he was just too kind to push her away? To her surprise, she found herself giggling, a hopelessly inappropriate reaction, but she couldn't help herself.

"What, woman?" He pulled back, looking stern as he studied her in the lamplight, though she could see laughter forming in little lines around his eyes. "Does my lovemaking amuse you? Don't you know a man expects to have his passion taken seriously?"

"*A* man?" Stacey traced the outline of his mouth, coaxing full, sensuous lips into a smile. "Generalizations—coming from you? Aren't you the one who told me that men are not a single entity, always looking for this and that and never the other thing?"

"Good God!" He held her at half-arm's length,

pretending to scowl. "Are you going to remember everything I say? What a nasty little habit! Do I have to watch my words for the rest of my life for fear you'll throw them back in my face?"

For the rest of my life? Stacey snuggled in his arms, liking the way that sounded. She hadn't been at all sure, when he came into the tent, that he had more than a single night's pleasure in mind . . . nor had she truly cared. She had wanted him enough to accept whatever he was ready to give without thought of the future. Only now that reason had returned, she couldn't help wondering what it would be like to feel secure at last.

"Does that mean you accept me as your wife?" she asked hesitantly. "You're not going to send me back?"

"Send you back? What the devil are you talking about?" He caught her chin between his thumb and forefinger. "Did you think I would come here tonight—do *this*—if I was planning on getting rid of you?"

"I . . . I didn't know," she murmured, averting her eyes.

His hands were on her brow, brushing back damp curls; she could feel him kissing her, lips lingering briefly where hair met skin. "I know I've been rough on you—I have a way of letting my temper get the better of me. But do you really believe I'm capable of using you like that?"

"No-o-o," she admitted. "Not *using* exactly. But men . . . well, I have heard that men get carried away sometimes by . . . by physical sensations."

"Who's generalizing now?" His arms were still around her, making her feel warm and safe. "There *are* men who behave like cads and use nature as an excuse, but not me—I hope. I was tempted, I admit. You are a sexy wench, and it was all I could do sometimes to keep my hands off you. But I made myself stay away until I was ready for the promises you deserved to hear. . . . Ah, silly little Stacey, don't you know I would never have sent you back?"

"But . . ." She pulled away, peering intently into his eyes. "You said you were going to. That first night. You were very emphatic about it. If I hadn't reminded you I might be pregnant—"

"If you hadn't reminded me," he said, laughing softly, "I would have had to eat crow in the morning."

"Crow?"

"Or cockatoo, whichever is tougher. The latter, I suspect." He eased her back on the pillows, smiling as he leaned over her. "Long before the sun came up the next morning, I was already regretting my hastiness. Fortunately, I didn't have to come up with some flimsy excuse to keep you here. You saved face—for both of us—and gave us time to get to know each other, which I would have insisted on from the beginning . . . if I hadn't been so all-fired eager to get you into bed."

His eyes seemed to darken, warming her blood again, reminding her how thoroughly he had just made love to her.

"Put yourself in my place, sweet. I was angry that night. My pride was hurt—and I am not a man who lets go of pride easily. It was hard for me to accept the fact that you had belonged to another man first. Even harder because you lied about it."

"Oh, Errol . . ." Misery swept over her as she recalled that terrible night. "If only I could go back and do it all over again. It was a stupid lie, I know—"

"It *was* stupid," he agreed, "but I understand. You don't have to keep justifying—"

"But I want to. I *need* to tell you how I felt. You did promise there'd be time for apologies later."

"And there will . . . if you insist." He kissed her forehead again, then her temple; then his tongue was teasing the tip of her ear and it was hard to concentrate. "But I don't require your apologies . . . or want them. Stacey, love, do you think I don't know how young you were, or how frightened you must have been?

"I *was* frightened," she murmured, remembering only too clearly the way she had felt when she first realized how much she cared for him and how desperately it would hurt to lose him. "But that's no excuse."

"If it isn't, it will do for now. Unless, of course. . ."

His voice changed subtly, and she knew even without looking that he was watching her intently. ". . . unless there are more secrets you want to share with me."

Stacey stiffened. D'Arcy's face came to her, eyes black and mocking, like Errol's sometimes, but with no compassion in them. There was still one secret between them, only she would be a fool to blurt it out. Besides, wouldn't it just make things worse between the two brothers?

"No," she said softly. "No . . . secrets are the last things I want to share now."

"Good." He was kissing her again, lips blazing a hot trail down the side of her neck, sinking to the slender cleavage of her bosom. "I can think of something much nicer to share . . . can't you?" He had begun to circle her breasts, using his tongue, teeth pausing to inflict playful little nips. Stacey sighed half-expectantly, wondering if he was teasing. It hardly seemed possible he could want her again so soon.

"What would you have done," she asked huskily, "if I had told you before—when you asked—that I wanted to go home? Would you have sent me?"

"No." He was laughing as he lounged full length beside her. Lean, masculine muscles rippled against her body, a distracting temptation.

"And later," she persisted. "When you came to the tent? If I had told you then I wanted you to leave, what would you have done?"

"Tried harder, of course." Strong hands moved sensuously down her back, caressing her buttocks, her thighs, pressing her close against the provocative contours of his body, leaving nothing to the imagination. It was hard to believe he was ready for her again.

"Tried harder to do what?"

"Why . . . to seduce you, of course."

III

GLENELLEN

21

The rainy season was over by the time they moved into the limestone palace on the hill. The air was dry again, but crisp, with an early-morning coldness that left one's breath hanging in little white clouds, and Billy Two was talking about another drought, though no one seemed to take him seriously. The kangaroos had gotten bolder. They came right up to the house now, begging for crusts of bread, and though she knew Errol did not approve—they were terrible pests, he said, competing with the sheep for grass—Stacey couldn't resist coaxing them closer.

The house was even more spectacular, now that the first round of decorating was over, and despite the affection she had formed for the homestead, Stacey was happy to find herself in large comfortable rooms. It was midafternoon, and she sprawled out on a massively proportioned sleigh bed, feeling wonderfully decadent as she stared up at rays of sunlight splashing across the pinkish-beige ceiling. She had closed off the original bedroom, planning to redo it later, and the master suite was now in the opposite wing, under the old nursery, which she had had converted to quarters for the maids. Their own nursery, when she and Errol had children, was going to be nearby, not halfway across the house!

Not that it looked like she was going to need it soon.

She sighed, stretching her legs out on the roomy bed. The children had not been coming as fast as she had expected. Errol was the soul of patience, reminding her that "these things take time—and I'm not in an all-fired hurry to start a family." But he was a man who would want tall, strong sons to carry on his name, and she was beginning to worry that she might disappoint him.

She sat up, pulling the sheet over her naked breasts, even though she knew no one would intrude on her solitude. That was the one household rule Errol insisted on: the servants were not to come into the bedchamber for any reason after it had been made up in the morning. He wanted privacy to be alone with his bride whenever it struck his fancy.

And, she thought, blushing slightly, it seemed to strike his fancy with rather startling frequency—though, in truth, she not been inclined to object.

She smiled to herself, not even realizing it, as her eyes took in the room. Unlike most of the downstairs, it had been completed to her satisfaction, and she was pleased with the results. The beige carpet was flowered, but not too boldly, and the pattern in the wallpaper so subtle it was barely visible. Deeper rose-tan curtains had been thrown open—the sun was always welcome in the winter—and the furnishings were light and graceful, more Empire than Victorian, for Errol hated overdone carvings and curlicues. It was a nice room, she decided as she got up and made her way languidly to the dressing table, pretty and feminine, but simple enough so a man could exist in it comfortably.

She hesitated as she caught sight of herself in the mirror. Even a few weeks ago she would have been embarrassed by her own nudity, but now, under Errol's influence, she was comfortable with her body. She had begun to fill out, she noted with satisfaction. Her hips were a bit too round for fashion, but Errol seemed to like her that way, and her breasts were getting so plump she almost looked pregnant, though she had had three disappointments now in as many months.

She pulled a simple white dress out of the wardrobe—the one she had worn that first night for dinner—and draped it over the back of a chair beside the dressing table. She did not particularly care for it herself; it was too childish for her taste, but it was Errol's favorite, and she knew he would be pleased to see her in it when he got home.

It felt a little strange, having time to sit in front of the mirror in the middle of the day, brushing and rebrushing her long black hair until it gleamed. Finding servants for the new house, surprisingly, had not been a problem. It looked as if the days of rooting in the kitchen garden and firing up the black-iron cookstove were gone forever. Errol paid excellent wages, half again the going rate, and while money alone could not attract a quality staff, that and the reputed elegance of Glenellen brought a surplus of applicants. Stacey had chosen an English couple, Butler, ironically, for the butler, Mrs. Butler as cook, and under their capable supervision everything ran so smoothly she almost felt as if she were a guest and not the mistress of the house.

They even had a laundress again, thank heaven. Pegeen, the bright-eyed Irish girl who had left shortly after Stacey's arrival—to get married, it now seemed— was back, several months pregnant, with a story of a husband who had gone north to Queensland to find work on the cattle stations. Errol had been too kind-hearted not to take her in. Ordinarily he didn't employ women with families, for he noticed that quarrels broke out more frequently when there were children in the servants' quarters, but this time he made an exception, and neither he nor Stacey regretted it. Pegeen was a hard worker, and efficient, and linens and clothes were beginning to look almost the right color again. Besides, her broad freckled face and hearty laugh took away some of the loneliness and made the days pass more quickly.

Stacey picked up her dress, fluffing the wrinkles out of the skirt, but made no attempt to put it on as she continued to stare at the mirror. Her body was faintly flushed, and she could see red marks on her breasts, the residue of recent rough caresses. Glenellen was the most beautiful place she had ever lived, but it *was* lonely sometimes, when Errol was off in the paddocks, and it seemed funny, having all that space just for the two of them.

"You aren't unhappy, are you?" he had asked a short time before. He had just dismounted from his horse, and they were walking toward the house, supposedly for lunch, though the raffish look in his eye warned her he might have another kind of repast in mind.

"Unhappy?" She paused, looking up through sooty lashes.

"Pegeen is a lively girl, but even if she weren't busy, she'd hardly be sufficient company. I know you must hunger for the 'society' you left behind. I had hoped to throw a gala fete, you know, when we opened the house—an introduction to the 'best people' of the bush. But decorating the ballroom took longer than I thought. It would be impossible to get everyone together now. Once shearing starts, no one thinks of anything else."

Stacey smiled. "So I've noticed." The shearers had begun arriving several days before, a motley crew in rag-bag clothing, some on horseback, some in wagonettes, some, surprisingly, even on foot. No sooner had the first of them bedded down in the bunkhouses than bleating mobs of sheep appeared in crowded pens around the long metal-roofed wool shed. "It looks like it's going to be chaotic. When does it begin?"

"Tomorrow morning. A day early, but everyone's here, and I like to get a jump on things if I can. So you see, your party's going to have to wait. I had no idea it would take so long for everything to arrive from Sydney."

"Well . . . never mind. We did have a gathering, even if it wasn't the 'gala fete' you promised. Why, there must have been three dozen people—including the Anglican minister, which gives an air of respectability, don't you think?" Her voice must not have been as bright as she hoped, for he gave her a thoughtful look as he slipped an arm around her waist and drew her toward the rear veranda.

"Hardly the crowd you must have longed for—and deserved. You did a beautiful job decorating, my dear. I must remember to compliment you more often. Three dozen is not an appropriate audience for all those efforts, especially when one of them was an elderly minister who kept looking down his pince-nez. Still, that's probably two and a half dozen more than you thought lived in the area."

"At least." Stacey leaned a little closer, responding to the pressure of his arm. "And truly, it *was* nice, even if it wasn't big."

Surprisingly, it had been nice. Stacey smelled soil and sheep and dried tussock on his sleeve as they moved up the step of the veranda. Distances were vast in Australia, and she had been amazed at how far some of the guests had come to pay their respects to Errol and make her feel welcome. Maude had been there, looking pale, but a little plumper, and D'Arcy, of course, and old Martin Quinn—whose eyesight *was* failing, but who was nowhere near senile, making Stacey think that he might have been an excellent chaperon after all. At any rate, the lovers had taken advantage of one of the minister's infrequent visits and were now husband and wife. It had been a shock, coming home from driving sheep to find them already married. Errol had been furious; irresponsible, he called their behavior, but Stacey couldn't help being secretly pleased as they took over the old homestead. It was a relief, not having to live under the same roof with D'Arcy— and knowing that Maude would be too busy to call!

Only Fitz had not shown up. Stacey paused at the top of the steps, not noticing as Errol threw her a quizzical look. It surprised her a little, though she knew it shouldn't. Any other artist would have wanted to be there to hear the *oohs* and *aahs* as each guest entered the foyer and looked up at his masterpiece on the ceiling. Only Fitz Blackburn wasn't "any other artist," and she had a feeling there was only one opinion he really cared about.

"You're smiling." Errol slid his hand from her waist, easing it under her arm, fingers resting just at the edge of her breast. "If you're remembering the party, then perhaps you weren't disappointed after all."

Stacey could not resist throwing him an impish look. "How could I be disappointed," she said demurely, "when the handsomest man there was my husband?"

One brow arched up. "Are you always so agreeable?"

"No." Stacey laughed as she twisted out of his grasp,

flitting toward the house. "You'd better enjoy it while you can."

"Minx!" He reached out with both hands, pulling her back. "You make my blood boil, and you know it! You've always known it—right from that first afternoon when you looked at me with sultry eyes and cast your witch's spell."

"Did I indeed? And *how* was I supposed to know, pray tell, the way you received me? If I stopped to think at all, which of course I didn't"—she tossed her head prettily, black curls catching the sunlight—"I would have thought you despised me."

"Ah, but I didn't. I lusted for you . . . passionately." His hands were much too bold, there on the porch—anyone might pass by—but she couldn't bring herself to rebuke him.

"You mean you took one look at me—silly, frivolous little bonnet, bird wings and all—and said to yourself: I must have this woman!"

"No." He grinned. "I took one look at you and said: What a silly, frivolous little creature. I had better get rid of her at once."

"Then when . . ." He had moved closer. She could feel his breath on her cheek, intimate as a kiss.

"Later. After I was unspeakably rude, and you answered back with as tart a tongue as I'd ever heard. I knew then I was lost."

"Right then? While you were still being rude?" She knew he was teasing, but there was sincerity in his tone, and she couldn't help being flattered. "What was going through your mind then? When you first realized you wanted me? What were your exact thoughts? Or don't you dare tell me?"

"Dare?" He pulled her against the wall. Shadows half-hid them from the yard. "I didn't think—I felt . . . *this*." Taking her hand, he pressed it against his groin, bulging and unmistakably hard. "That, exactly, is what was going through my body . . . my mind wasn't working at the moment. You have that effect on me."

Stacey tried to squirm, protesting halfheartedly that they shouldn't, that someone would see, but it was hard to sound convincing when she wanted him as much as he wanted her. He *had* desired her that first day. She had sensed it in the arrogant gaze he cast up and down her body, pretending to a scorn that was belied by the heat in his eyes. And she had desired him too, though she had been too naive to realize it.

"Don't pull away," he said, his voice hard, almost rasping. "Never pull away, love—I don't like it when you do."

"But . . . they really *will* see," she said weakly.

He laughed, confident as her body swayed against him, enjoying his mastery over her. "I doubt it. The servants won't come out while we're here. They have no more desire than you to be embarrassed. And the men are busy with preparations for shearing. Besides, if one of them saw us, he'd only wink and boast about the bawdy bastard he works for." He was still laughing, but softly, a low sound, deep in his chest. "You are my wife and I want you *now*." He shaped his hand around her buttocks, sliding it between her legs with a suddenness that sent hot tremors through her.

She heard the little moan that came out of her mouth, felt her legs turn to jelly as her body molded itself against lean, hard muscles, and she knew she was completely, inescapably his. If he had torn her dress off right there, in the bright Australian sunlight, if he had dragged her down to the planking at his feet, she would not have done a thing to stop him . . . or wanted to.

But he released her instead, laying a hand on her back—she could feel his fingers vibrating through the thin fabric of her dress—and they went inside together, racing each other in their eagerness to get upstairs.

Stacey shivered a little as she turned away from the mirror, embarrassed by the softness in her face. Even now the sensations were intense. The bold way he had touched her on the porch . . . the wonderful tenderness of the hour that followed . . . the sweetly sexy compliments he had whispered in her ear when they were done.

She started to take up the dress, then changed her

mind and flung herself back on the bed. She was too
caught up in feelings and moods to face the world.
How sinful it felt, lounging in bed all afternoon. Even
Grandfather, who had raised her to be catered to by
servants, would be shocked at her laziness. Doubly
shocked if he knew what she was thinking.

Or perhaps not. . . .

She let her head sink luxuriantly into the soft down
pillow. Like most women of her era, she had been
raised to believe that even the lustiest male had a
different standard of behavior for the females he cared
about. His wife, his sister, his daughter—they were
supposed to be prim and demure. Yet how could she
forget those wonderfully romantic stories of Grandfather's elopement with the beautiful Natalya, who, even
years after her death, could bring a faraway look to his
face? They had always marked their anniversary from
their second wedding, the religious ceremony, never
the original one, and it occurred to her for the first
time to wonder how many months there would have
been between *that* occasion and her father's birthday.

She had always thought she was most like Grandfather. Everything about her seemed a reflection of him,
his strength, his spirit . . . his pigheaded stubbornness.
She closed her eyes, enjoying the warmth of the sun as
it spilled across her face. Now it seemed there might
be something of the passionate Natalya in her too.

Errol cut across the corner of the home paddock,
horse's hooves kicking up a cloud of dust as he passed
the bunkhouse on his way to the wool shed. A lone
man was seated on the porch, rickety stool tilted back,
feet propped up on the rail. His appearance was typi-
cally disreputable: a half-week's growth of beard, a
sweat-stained jersey, and fraying pants tucked into his
socks.

New this year, Errol thought, taking the man in
with an expert eye as he slowed the stallion to a walk.
He had never seen him before, but there was no
mistaking the fact that he was a shearer and not a
roustabout. Even seated, his back looked stooped,
and his arms were abnormally long. His pack, or swag,

rested beside him on the floor, a carefully rolled possum-skin bundle, strapped in three places.

Errol raised his hand, waving a casual greeting. The man nodded back, but made no other move, and Errol rode on. Some of the men were friendly, cadging a drink or a smoke—they'd talk your ear off if you let them—but for the most part, shearers were a breed apart and did not mingle with the station owners.

They were, in a way, the most important workers on the station, though they were there for only a few weeks. Every year at the same time they would begin to appear, a seasonal migration on parched roads cutting like faintly marked ribbons through the vast savannas. One might be a farmer, working during his slack season; another a tough little Cornish emigrant, also from the farm; or a shop assistant saving for a store of his own; or a factory hand; or just a footloose "sundowner," making enough during the season to keep from settling down the rest of the year.

Errol could still remember what it had been like, seeing them as a boy. They had seemed unutterably romantic then, bold, carefree figures, but the passing years had stolen the glamour from threadbare coats and stiff boots and blistered feet. The fortunate few had horses, perhaps even wagons, but all too often they were "footmen," trudging through the midday heat with resigned and dusty faces.

And all too often, he thought grimly as he dismounted and hitched the stallion to a rail, the same men came back year after year, older but no wiser, last year's stake gone in a game of cards or a rousing drunk that had lasted for a month.

The wool-shed pens were full when he reached them, and he nodded with approval as he ran his eye across a sea of yellowish gray, so thick in places it looked like a carpet. Any other time, he would have supervised the muster personally, spreading himself thin as he rode from paddock to paddock to make sure everything was going smoothly. But with a new wife and a new home, he had decided it was time to give up some of his responsibilities, and a competent overseer had been placed in charge, with more limited duties going to D'Arcy.

It was satisfying, if not altogether flattering, to see how well things were going without him. Mustering the sheep was almost as important as shearing itself, and while to the casual eye it might seem simple, it was in reality a well-organized operation. Orders had gone out weeks before, and sheep from the far paddocks were brought in on a tightly regulated schedule, with fresh mobs timed to arrive as others, newly shorn, were being moved out. Any mix-up or delay could cost dearly. All the incidental workers, the roustabouts and tar-boys and sweepies, were paid by the day—whether anything was going on or not. And while the shearers were compensated by the head, they had to buy their own food and pay their own cook, and it didn't make for a pleasant atmosphere if they sat around without work.

He turned slowly, taking in all the pens as he mentally counted the sheep, assessing the damage that showed in thin scraggly coats from the year-long drought. His lips twitched unconsciously, and he leaned back against the split rail, recalling, irrelevantly, the way Stacey had looked when he left her, alone in the rumpled linen of an extra-wide double bed. She had surprised him that afternoon with the depth of her passion. He had feared, once the novelty wore off and she was used to having the needs of her body satisfied, she would not be quite so eager to see her husband ride home in the middle of the day. Instead, her appreciation of him seemed to be growing . . . and her skill in lovemaking, which was becoming surprisingly abandoned.

A familiar sensation throbbed in his groin, and he turned back to the fence, not wanting the men to see and guess, all too rightly, what he was thinking. It had been roguish of him, teasing her mercilessly that way on the veranda. He had known she was embarrassed—even though he had looked around first to make sure no one was there—but he hadn't been able to resist. And he hadn't been able to keep from reveling in the completeness of her surrender.

Damn! He rammed his fist against the post. Ordinarily his mind was extra keen during shearing—not the smallest detail escaped him. Today he couldn't even remember the number of sheep he had just counted! He had never had a woman of his own before. There had been affairs, of course, attachments, some deeper than others, but never a woman who was always there, always in his bed, whenever he wanted her, and the distraction made it hard to concentrate.

He shoved away from the fence, more in control now as he went over to the shed to see if the preparations for tomorrow were complete. A man was just coming out of the wide, blanket-draped side door. The sun was behind him, throwing his face into shadow, but there was no mistaking that shock of red hair.

Jack O'Rourke. The shearers' representative. Errol frowned slightly. Every year the men elected one of their number to speak for them. A dangerous policy, to hear the other squatters tell about it—it smacked of unionism just when that blasted AMA, the Amalgamated Miners' Association, was organizing the shearers—but Errol persisted, feeling it kept grievances to a minimum if the men had a way to air them.

He called out, something between an order and a greeting, and O'Rourke stopped. He was an unpleasant-looking man with thick lips and pallid, unshaven cheeks, but when he was young, he could outshear anyone, and even now only the cockiest young gun challenged him to a contest—usually to his regret. Errol didn't like him, but he respected him, and he knew the men had made had made a good choice.

"Well, Jack, how's it going? Everything all right?"

"Seems ter be." If Jack O'Rourke ever smiled, Errol hadn't heard about it. "Ain't got nuthin' ter complain about . . . yet."

Errol grinned. "Maybe if we're lucky it'll stay that way, eh?"

"Mebbe," O'Rourke replied, but he didn't sound convinced.

Errol continued up the steps and into the shed, where he took a few minutes to look around. D'Arcy had been in charge of the setup, with one of the more experienced men checking up on him, and it looked like everything was in order. The place had an air of expectancy. The floor gleamed in the dim light—years of lanolin had given it a high sheen—and he could almost hear a buzz of activity on the long, empty shearing board. The smell of the place was like the smell of nothing else on earth: wood and grease, leather and wool.

He glanced up at the sky as he left the shed, noting with satisfaction that it was clear. Not a wisp of cloud showed in all that shimmering blue. The dryness had been worrying him lately—the rains had ended too abruptly; another drought so soon could be disastrous, but the last thing he needed now was a downpour. The men wouldn't shear wet sheep. The old-timers believed they'd be poisoned, especially after a long drive when the yolk was thick in wool, and even the newer hands were afraid it would cause rheumatism. Nothing could clear the shed faster than a cry of "Wet sheep! Wet sheep!" echoing down the board.

Not that there'd be any risk of that tomorrow. He had left his hat on the fencepost when he went inside. Now he put it on again, tilting it over his eyes as he looked one last time around the pens. Everything seemed to be ready. It was going to be a good shearing; he could feel it in his bones. He was whistling as he headed back to the place where he had left his horse.

He was halfway there before he realized he wasn't thinking about the shearing at all. He was thinking about Stacey again . . . and wondering how she was going to feel when she saw it all for the first time.

22

Stacey heard the wool-shed yards before she saw them.
It was barely midmorning, but the shearing had been
under way for some time, and a dull, dreamlike drone
drifted across the paddock. She had left her horse at
the homestead stable and was covering the rest of the
way on foot. The ground was cold, even through sturdy
boots, but a faint breeze was warm against her cheek,
and she knew spring was on its way. All too soon the
heat would return, and she would long for the chill of
August again, but now the sun felt good.

The din increased, breaking into individual noises as
she neared the shed. The bleating of the sheep and
their hacking coughs, almost human at times; the sound
of hooves pounding on the hard earth; the cries of the
men and the constant, rhythmic barking of the dogs;
and beneath it all, a faint *slap-slap*, *slap-slap* she could
not identify. With the sounds came the smells of a
bush station: dried grass and greasy wool, tobacco
from the men's pipes, and the dust that drifted up in a
golden-ocher haze.

She hesitated, a little bewildered as she looked
around. Everything was a blur of sound and motion,
yet there must be some order behind it, for the men
seemed to know what they were doing. The last of the
mobs had been placed the afternoon before in a series
of yards, and sheep were being driven through them
now, a river of gray wool emptying into a long runway, just wide enough for one at a time. At the end, a
dark-complexioned man worked a heavy wooden gate,
swinging it back and forth, forcing them first to one
side, then the other.

A short distance away she spotted Errol, talking to a

man with reddish hair and a rather bloated face. He turned his head as he moved away, watching the even flow of sheep through the runway, and just for a second Stacey forgot everything else. He seemed to have lost his hat, for he was bareheaded, and the sun caught in dusty black hair, making it glisten like jet. Strength vied with muscular grace as he paused briefly, surveying his land and his animals with the mien of a prince looking over his realm, and she sensed a kind of confidence that would have seemed arrogant in a lesser man.

How can I love him so much? she thought helplessly. How can my life be so wrapped up in him, when only a few months ago I didn't even know he existed?

Errol turned, almost at that moment, seeing her where she stood a little uncertainly beside one of the fences. He had not expected her so early, and he was a little surprised at the thrill of pleasure that ran through his body, though he couldn't help remembering that his last thought yesterday when he left had not been of the shearing but of her. Now, as then, he found himself wondering how she was going to react to the bustle and excitement he had always found so stimulating.

She looked especially pretty, the little vixen. Had she dressed deliberately to entice him? Probably. It was he who had talked her into man-tailored shirts, like the one she was wearing now, a creamy gold cotton, just loose enough to be proper, but tight enough to show off a slim torso and high young breasts. And it was he who had sent to Sydney for denim pants, the first she had ever worn. She had tried them on under protest.

"I look like an American cowboy," she had said, laughing as she darted off to sneak a look in the long oval mirror with its dark mahogany frame.

"An American maybe," he had agreed. "But a cowboy? Hardly." If anything, the pants made her look more womanly, accenting an unexpected sultriness that was becoming more apparent with each passing day. And, as he had reminded her, "They're more practical for riding—or coming down to watch the shearing."

Practical indeed, he thought again as he crossed over to join her at the fence. But fetching too, and he was glad she hadn't been too inhibited to exchange her corsets and petticoats for the more casual attire of the bush. He considered, just for a moment, telling her how much she pleased him. Then, knowing where that line of conversation had a habit of leading, and recalling the busy day that lay ahead, he decided for safer ground.

"Confusing, isn't it?" He put one foot up on the lower rail as he leaned forward to watch. "I grew up on the station, but I can still remember, as a boy, wondering what was going on . . . and being too proud to lose face by asking. Of course Cameron's Creek was smaller then, and things were easier to figure out."

"Well, *I'm* not too proud to ask." Stacey laughed as she looked over, glad he had stopped to chat. She had been afraid he was going to be too busy to spare time for her. "I'm especially curious about that man over there." She pointed toward the dark-skinned man who was still swinging his gate. "What on earth is he doing?"

"Drafting . . . separating the sheep into pens. They're bolted one at a time down the race or passageway toward those two openings at the end. Watch now—as a new sheep starts into the race, old Bert'll look up to check the markings on its ear. If it's a ewe, he'll swing the gate across the opening on the left, forcing it to the right. If it's a wether, it'll go the other way."

"A wether?" Stacey had heard the term before, but she hadn't wondered until now what it meant.

"The equivalent of a steer. A boy who isn't a boy anymore, so to speak. We keep only the rams we need for breeding."

Stacey looked back at the gate, fascinated at the deft agility that almost made the task look simple. Now she recognized the slapping sound she had heard before. "They're coming so fast—it must take great concentration."

"More than you realize. Not only is Bert separating the sheep, he's counting them as well—and he won't be off by more than a head or two at the end of the day. I tried drafting myself once, when I was young enough to be cocky. I've learned to respect the men who are skilled at it."

"I should think so." Stacey studied the man more closely now that she knew what he was doing. There appeared to be five or six sheep in the run at any given time, but everything was happening so fast it was hard to tell. Bert's eyes moved constantly. Now they were watching the end of the race where a sheep was just coming in, though it was hard to imagine he could see its earmark in all that dust. Now they were on the gate and he was swinging it sharply to one side. Now they darted back to the end again, flicking over every sheep on the way, taking in its exact position—and all that in a fraction of a second. And he was counting as well!

It took all her effort, even to watch, and she was exhausted as she looked away. "I can't help noticing how dark he is—yet no one seems to mind. Do they always get along so well in Australia, the mixed bloods and the whites?"

"That depends on what's been mixed into the blood," he said easily. "We've come to terms with our native population, perhaps because we've had to. Labor is in short supply here. But you won't find us side by side with a Chinaman or an Indian or an American Negro. Most of the men say they'll only work with an aborigine—or a Maori from New Zealand. And I suspect that's because they know the latter wouldn't be allowed in the country."

Stacey laughed. "You sound cynical."

"Not cynical. Realistic. Anyway, Bert is no *myall*, no wild black running around in nothing but a shirt or a smelly old skin. He's more white than colored, and he's a damn fine drafter. The men know that, and they can live with it."

A woman cut across the yard, carrying a bundle and something that looked like a billy of hot tea to one of the men. Glancing around, Stacey was surprised to see several other women there too. Australia was a man's country, and even in busy times, like lambing, she had not been aware of the workers' wives. But perhaps shearing was different.

"Isn't the owner's wife supposed to do her share too?" She laughed at the puzzled expression on his face.

"Her share of what, love? Drafting?"

"Hardly. It makes my head spin just to watch. But I notice women bringing food to some of the men. Are they in charge of cooking for the shearing?"

"Only on some of the smaller stations. Here all you'll see is an occasional wife bringing lunch to her husband or son. The shearers hire their own cook— they pay him well, so they have plenty of choice—and the station cook feeds the rest of the workers, with a little help this year from Mrs. Butler. You found a gem in that woman. Without Maude, I didn't know how we were going to manage."

"Maude?"

"She always comes over—we shear the Mirandola sheep at the same time—and takes care of the domestic arrangements. Makes sure the bunkhouses are ready, sees to extra help for the station kitchen, that sort of thing. But now that she isn't feeling well . . ."

His voice drifted off, and Stacey looked over, not liking the funny feeling in the pit of her stomach. There was something about Maude that seemed to bring out his protective instincts—she couldn't help remembering that day in the back of the wagon when he had cradled her in his arms. And it was all so silly! There was nothing wrong with her! She was just enjoying being a bride and not caring about anyone else.

"She looked fine at the party we gave."

"Do you think so?"

His eyes were on her, dark and quizzical, and Stacey turned away, confused. She *had* looked fine, pale perhaps—rather *too* pale—but she had put on weight, and surely that was healthy.

"Yes. She looked perfectly all right to me. And very pretty."She tried to keep her voice teasing, but she didn't quite manage. "You must have thought so too. You hardly took your eyes off her all evening."

"If I was watching her"—a subtle emphasis on *if*—"it was because I was worried about her. I didn't approve of that hasty marriage. And by God, I still don't!"

Stacey hated the way she was feeling, but she couldn't stop herself. It had been weeks and weeks since she had been jealous of Maude. But then, it had been weeks since she had seen her, too.

"Why not?" she asked cautiously.

"Why not? Because she's overdoing, that's why not. She very nearly came down with pneumonia from that nasty dunking in the creek. She still hasn't recovered. If my brother had any consideration . . ." He broke off, lips tightening. "But then, consideration isn't D'Arcy's strong suit, is it? Especially when it comes to women."

Irony cut through his tone, and Stacey felt the tightness in her stomach turn into a knot. That same old friction every time D'Arcy's name came.

She always wanted him. Wasn't that what he had said that morning in the willow grove by the dry creek bed? *She always wanted him . . . and she got him.* Dear heaven, why did those words keep coming back? Why did they haunt her? Because they had been so firmly planted? Because of the malice in D'Arcy Cameron's heart?

Or because some instinct deep inside told her they were true?

She turned back to the fence, rather too hastily, not wanting Errol to see the disturbed look on her face. It seemed to work, for he said nothing as he left, only that he was going to check on a few things and she could go into the shed and watch the shearers if she wanted.

But then, she thought uncomfortably, maybe he had been too wrapped up in his own thoughts to notice.

Errol *did* care about her. She knew that. His desire for her was very tangible, and very flattering. He could not have faked the passion that glowed in his eyes every time he looked at her—nor would he have been deceitful enough to try. Only, physical passion wasn't love, and God help her, love was what she wanted. Not just his body, but his heart as well, and his soul, and every waking thought—

A shout came from across the yard. Suddenly dogs were yelping and a group of men hurried off to one side—why, she had no idea, but it was enough to break into her thoughts, and in spite of herself, she started to laugh. Stacey Cameron, you are a first-class ninny! she told herself as she headed toward the shed to take up her husband's invitation and watch the shearers. Just a short time ago she would have been thrilled to have his passion. All she had wanted then was not to be sent home. Now she was fussing because everything wasn't absolutely perfect. Because her husband might—just *might*—be in love with Maude . . . or have been in love with her a long time ago.

And all because a man with the scruples of a snake had told her so!

She went around the corner to the front of the wool shed. No one was in sight—only a boy wtih a pair of pants two sizes too big, and he was gone in a flash—and she sensed that the men had finished their break, their "smoke-o," and gone back to work. The shed was a large rough-sided building several feet off the ground, with room underneath for a number of pens. A flight of steps led to a wide door hung with an old wool blanket that had been pulled open and tied to the side.

Stacey stood for a moment in the doorway, getting her bearings as her eyes struggled to focus. After the winter brightness, the shed seemed almost unnaturally dark, a long tunnel with a burst of sunlight spilling through a door at the far end. The only other light flashed here and there through what appeared to be chinks in the walls.

It was a relatively new shed, but several seasons' shearing had given it the look of something that was old and had been used too long. The same smell Errol had noticed yesterday was more pronounced now, punctuated by an odor of human sweat. Years of greasy wool had stained the floors and walls, and every plank and post was polished to an oily glow. The center and one entire end were dominated by the shearing board, long enough to accommodate two dozen men, and it was here that most of the light was concentrated. As her eyes adjusted, Stacey realized that what she had taken for chinks were in reality ports or openings that led to the catching pens, twelve in all, one for each pair of shearers. Other openings led to chutes through which shorn sheep were ejected into still another series of pens, to be checked, counted, and credited to the man who had removed their thick woolly coats.

Stacey stepped into the shed, following the shearing board but staying close to the wall so she wouldn't get in the way. She had to take care how she walked, for the floor was surprisingly slick. The chaos outside was repeated here, if somewhat more compactly, and broomies and roustabouts and tarboys were racing back and forth, arms filled with baskets and fleeces. The light shimmered from behind, forming a halo effect around shearers crouched in various positions. Their backs were so stooped Stacey could almost feel them creak and stiffen, and muscular arms were premanently elongated.

One seemed to be faster than the others, and Stacey angled into a position where she could see him better. It was the redheaded man she had noticed before, and she watched, intrigued, as he denuded first one sheep, then another, with deft, impersonal hands. He worked with an unbroken, almost mechanical rhythm that showed no strain, though his sleeveless flannel singlet was saturated, and perspiration poured in glistening streams down his face.

After she had watched for a time, she began to pick out a pattern in his movements. Reaching into the catching pen, he would grab one of the sheep by the forelegs and drag it bleating and protesting onto the board. A second later, the struggling ceased, and a burly forearm showed sweaty against yellow-gray wool as the animal lolled back, almost comically, like an overgrown baby sitting on his lap. The belly wool came first, frothing cream inside, and locks from the legs fell sticky with burs and paddock grass onto the floor. Then the sheep was between his knees, limp like a sack of grain, and he was beginning the long cut, hand swift and sure as he cleared the left flank. The right side was next, another smooth motion, and suddenly the fleece was off, a solid piece, and the boy was racing down the board with it, holding it like a woolly blanket over his head.

What was left, Stacey thought, laughing out loud, was the saddest, scraggliest-looking creature she had ever seen! Rather like a peeled orange, with just enough spirit left to let out a pathetic little bleat. The man shoved it toward the port, prodding with his knee to urge it down the chute and into the pens below. Then his arm was out again, and he was hauling another sheep onto the board.

"That's a real mean one 'e's got there," a rough voice said, chuckling in her ear. "Last one in the pen, ya can bet on that. Ya like to leave the last fer th' other bloke, but it don't always work out that way."

Stacey looked up to see a young man with brawny arms and shoulders grinning down at her. One of the roustabouts, no doubt. "What do you mean?" she asked, curious.

"Well, missus, it's like this. Two shearers workin' outta the same pen, ya gotta figger the other bloke's gonna go fer the easy one. If there's a 'rosella'—an old ewe with most o' the lower wool wore off—'e'll take that first. Pretty soon, all that's left is a bunch o' blokes with wrinkles stiffer'n an ol' boot with a beard."

"A boot . . . with a beard?"

His grin broadened, showing a missing tooth at the side of his mouth. Any other time he knew he'd be chewed out for lying down on the job, but he'd already noticed the boss was softheaded when it came to his young wife. And an ear-bash beat working any day, especially when the lady was a looker like this.

"This stiffest, wrinkledest of all, we call 'im the cobbler—'cause 'e sticks to the last."

Stacey laughed in spite of herself. It was a dreadful joke, but he was so good-natured, it was impossible not to like him.

Lunch break came a short time later, or dinner as the men called it—"lunch" was at four or four-thirty, and the last meal in the evening was "tea"—and while Errol was too busy to join her, he made sure she had plenty of Mrs. Butler's good English bread, with a pot of wild-lemon marmalade and thick slabs of cold mutton.

The sun beat down on the metal roof, and by afternoon the shed was uncomfortably hot. The shearers continued their work, backs painfully bent as their hands disappeared in a sea of wool. Occasionally a kneepad would be nicked or a blade would sink too deep in a flank, and the tarboy would come running with his bucket of kerosene or lampblack to paint on the wound. But for the most part, a scrawny white sheep replaced a fat gray one every five minutes or so, with not so much as a splotch of crimson.

By the end of the day, though Errol could give her only a few minutes at a time and none of the other men, even her garrulous young roustabout, was inclined to talk for long, Stacey had at least a rudimentary idea about what happened to the wool after it was stripped from the sheep. First, it was sorted into three categories. The bellies, which were still in one piece, but badly matted with burs and grass seeds, were checked for stains and tossed into one bin. Leg locks and other odd pieces that landed on the floor were swept by the broomies into another. The fleece itself, the largest part of the clip and the most valuable, was brought to a special area for skirting—removal of dirt-encrusted edges and tangles of herbage—then rolled in a great furry ball.

The wool classer took over next, standing behind his "table," an odd-looking openwork shelf rather like a grate. He was a smallish man, all neck and no chin, with a face that didn't invite questions, and Stacey was careful to stay a distance away. Twenty or thirty fleeces lay like woolly eggs all around him; on either side, piece pickers were busy at their own tables, and wool rollers worked in front.

As Stacey watched, he unrolled a fleece and ran his hands through it, feeling the texture and thickness. Fingers tested for strength, tugging at the flocks and separating loose ends, which fell through the grate to the floor below where they were swept up and sorted into yet another bin marked "table locks." If a fleece was fine and even in length, with a staple of about two inches, it was classed as "first combing" and would fetch a good price; if it was coarser and stronger, still long, but with more waste and unevenness, it was "second combing." Shorter wool was baled separately and labeled, according to quality, either "first clothing" or "second clothing."

It surprised Stacey to discover that the classer was employed, not by the people who were going to buy the wool, but the station owner himself.

"Isn't that . . . awkward?" she asked as Errol came over to stand beside her at the end of the day. "I mean, sellers aren't likely to make the most objective classers. Besides"—she had already seen the presses, where the wool was tamped into bales, about a quarter its original size, and sewed up in rough sacking— "once everything's been bundled, you can't tell what's buried in the middle. What's to prevent an unscrupulous squatter from labeling the wool 'first combing' and stuffing in anything he wants?"

"Nothing at all—the first time." The bell had just sounded, and the shearers were finishing, knee-deep in a foam of wool as they prodded the last sheep into the chutes. "A man gets a reputation in this business. Sell first combing once and deliver second, and see how well you do next year. That's why I look over the classer's shoulder all the time, surreptitiously of course— he may look like a moth-eaten mouse, but he doesn't like having his judgment questioned. I don't blame him. He's the best in the business. But one mistake, and a man could be ruined for years."

Stacey was surprised, as they walked out together, to feel how tired she was. It had been exhausting, just standing on her feet all day, and she could imagine how it must be for the men, especially the shearers. Behind them, the shed was quiet. Dusk had fallen, and the woolly gray backs of the sheep that had been moved in for the next day's shearing could barely be distinguished in pens across the yard. Somewhere beyond the mountains the sun was setting, and a streak of red-violet blazed across the sky.

Errol had stopped to give instructions to one of the men. Now he joined her again, smiling as they started toward the stables.

"You look like you sheared a few dozen sheep

yourself," he teased, brushing a smudge of dust off the side of her nose.

"I feel like it," she admitted, grinning easily. "How do the men manage anyway? Crouched over like that for hours at a time—swinging the sheep around as if they weighted a pound or two at most? I lost count, but they must shear at least a hundred a day."

"That depends on the man." It was getting dark, and he took her arm to keep her from stumbling on the unfamiliar track. There was a full moon rising; it would be an easy ride to Glenellen, but he had left D'Arcy in charge, with some misgivings, so he could escort her back. "Figure an average of five minutes a sheep, an eight-hour day with a couple of twenty-minute smoke-o's, and you come up with somewhere between seventy and one hundred sheep per man. That's an average, though. A 'gun shearer,' a crack man, can manage two hundred and up with no problems. Then there are the 'dreadnoughts'—a handful of men who shear over three hundred a day."

"Like the man with the red hair?"

"Jack O'Rourke? No. He's good—no one here can touch him—but his record is somewhere around two-fifty. Which, incidentally, is all I want. Most of the squatters like fast shearers, the faster the better, but I don't figure it's worth the cost. Too many 'crackers' leave a pile of dead and badly maimed sheep wherever they go."

Stacey, remembering the amount of blood she had observed in even a carefully run shed, couldn't help agreeing. They were passing the yard where the newly shorn sheep had been penned, and she stopped to watch as the boy drove the last of them in and tugged the gate shut. They moved with odd jerking motions, poor little lamblike creatures, and she felt a little guilty laughing, but she couldn't help herself. Now she knew where the expression "sheepish" came from—they all looked as though they were embarrassed, being caught outside with their clothes off!

"What happens to them now?" she asked.

"Nothing very strenuous. A bath of sheep-dip, which hurts their dignity more than anything, but rids them of ticks and other vermin—then out in the shorn-sheep paddock with them." He didn't add that they would be watched carefully for the next few days. If it turned cold, without thick wool coats to protect them they would lie down and freeze; the only way to save them then was to light fires or set the dogs to keep them moving. "Weather permitting, we'll open the gates soon, and you'll see how eager they are to get out."

"I can believe it." She looked back at the sheep milling in the yard, spindly toothpick legs sticking out of scrawny bodies. "I thought nothing in the world was a pathetic as a cat who'd gotten into a disagreement with a skunk and had to be bathed. Now I know better."

She was still watching the sheep, engrossed for the moment, and Errol had a chance to study her profile, undetected in the dusk. The light that would have subdued anyone else only made her more vibrant, turning dark hair to shadow and emphasizing the pink in her cheeks. It surprised him all over again, how beautiful she was. If he had been able to pick the woman he wanted, if he had selected every feature, every characteristic, he would have chosen exactly the opposite. And he would have been wrong.

"I like your spirit, lady," he said suddenly. "And your patience. You must have expected a mansion, but when you saw the homestead you didn't say a word. You turned a little squinty-eyed maybe, but you didn't say anything. It's not an easy life for a woman. Drought and flood, lambing and shearing—and not a complaint through any of it. I think you deserve a reward."

She turned back, lips curving impishly. "Another diamond pendant?"

"If you want. Diamonds or rubies or pearls—you name it. But I had something in mind I thought might please you more. What would you say, after shearing is over and things are back to normal again, if we spent a couple of months in Sydney?"

"You'd take me to Sydney?" Visions of white houses came to mind, set in vibrant green hillsides, and proper carriages on real city streets, and glittering balls and people to talk to at last. "But you said . . . you told me before that you didn't like going to Sydney."

She could have bitten her tongue off the instant the words were out. What was she doing, giving him a chance to back down, when she was fairly drooling at the thought of lights and music and well-stocked shops?

He seemed to read her thoughts, for he started to laugh.

"I told you the social scene in Sydney didn't appeal to me—and it doesn't. But I have to go there periodically, and I don't see any reason why we shouldn't linger awhile. I do have business to tend to, as I believe I mentioned—I think I can keep myself occupied while you go out and see how much of a squatter's fortune you can spend in an afternoon." The eagerness on her face was so transparent, he couldn't keep from smiling. He had forgotten how young she was, and how lonely it must be for her here. "Besides, if the chitchat bores me, I have a feeling it will delight you, and it's your turn to have your way. This is compromise, my love—at its sweetest. You have spent three seasons at Cameron's Creek to please me. I believe I can spend one season in Sydney to return the favor."

Compromise? Coming from Errol Cameron? Stacey looked up, trying not to let him see that her eyes were sparkling through carefully lowered lashes. "Compromise" hardly seemed a word he would be in the habit of using. But then, even the strongest man could sometimes be sensitive . . . and it wasn't a quality she wanted to discourage.

"I think," she said softly, "it's a lovely idea. I can hardly wait to go."

23

Sydney was at its best in the spring. Even the boxiest houses took on a cheerful look with riots of red and pink roses showing through iron grillwork, and azaleas rambled over open lots, so profuse in places, they seemed to grow wild. Recent rains had watered the streets, holding down the dust, and the air was so crisp, glimpses of the cove in the distance glittered like cut glass.

Overhead, the branches of a flowering tree swayed in the breeze, and Stacey smiled to herself as she stepped out on the shallow balcony that opened off her bedroom. Fragrant pink petals floated down, forming a soft carpet all around. She had expected Errol to take her to a suite in one of the hotels—Petty's perhaps, for it seemed to be the finest in the city—but when they arrived, she had discovered to her surprise that he had rented a house on Macquarie Street where she could look down from her private balcony and see the *beau monde* of Sydney passing to and from the governor's residence.

If she liked, he had told her, laughing at her eagerness when she saw the comfortable furnishings and tasteful, if understated moss-and-burgundy decor, he might consider buying it for her . . . though he had his eye on a small, elegant mansion on Darling Point, less conveniently located, but infinitely more fashionable. Most of the married squatters kept houses in Sydney, and indeed, a number of wives spent the entire winter there, leaving their husbands in the country to visit when they could. Not, he informed her with a hint of sternness in his tone, that he expected that from her.

He had not, after all, gotten married to have a wife he saw only at odd intervals during the "social season."

Stacey, who had been warmly enclosed in his arms at the time, had not been inclined to murmur the slightest protest. It was hard for her to imagine any woman wanting to be away from her husband that long, social season or no. But then "any woman" wasn't married to handsome, dashing, and very sensual Errol Cameron.

Her eyes turned dreamy as she recalled the slow-moving train that had brought them to Sydney. Three days, three wonderful days, locked up in a private compartment, opening the door only occasionally, and then only enough to let in the tray the porter brought from the dining car. It was like the honeymoon they had never had—a special world lovers entered only once in a lifetime—and Stacey had thought, when they reached their destination and society and business closed in, it would all be over and they would live like an ordinary married couple. But miraculously, Errol had continued as attentive—and passionate—as ever.

The clock made a faint tinkling sound, and Stacey looked back into the room to see that it was already half-past four. Time for Errol to return, for he had been gone the entire afternoon and he never left her alone more than a few hours at most. Pressing matters required his attention, he had told her that noon over a light lobster salad, then added with a knowing wink: "I'm sure you'll find something to keep yourself occupied until I get back."

Occupied, indeed! Stacey laughed as she looked back at the bed, where a colorful garden of new gowns, pink and gold and lavender and magenta, was sprawled across the rose satin coverlet. The delivery from Farmer's had been waiting an hour before, as the carriage pulled into the drive from a new round of shopping, and she hadn't been able to resist tearing off the wrappings and holding them up, one by one, in front of the mirror to see if everything was really as pretty as she had remembered. Errol had been joking when he said she might try to spend his entire fortune in a single afternoon, at least that was what she thought at the time, though now she wasn't so sure. The wardrobe she had brought from San Francisco, which had been waiting when they arrived in Sydney, was perfectly adequate—not only was it still in fashion, it was actually *avant-garde*, for Australia was easily two years behind in style—but Errol, generously, had insisted she buy anything she wanted.

"You were born to be spoiled." He grinned when, after the weakest protests, she had given in.

"I think I was," she had to admit. "If not *born*, then surely raised." First Grandfather had indulged her shamelessly; now it appeared her husband was out to do the same. "But can we afford it?"

He laughed, captivated in spite of himself by the one quality that had disconcerted him most—her extreme youthfulness. "Oh, I think I can manage to pay the bills without going to the poorhouse . . . for a year or two at least. Go ahead. Explore the shops in Sydney to your heart's content. Don't deny yourself anything—except jewels. I want to choose those for you myself."

His eyes slipped to the diamond at her throat, and Stacey sensed it pleased him to see how often she wore it. "I don't really need any more jewels," she said. "I have my share of my grandmother's, after all, and the diamond. But I must admit I love it when you bring me presents."

She was absolutely shameless, she thought, feeling the tiniest bit guilty as she stepped over to take a closer look at the spill of tarlatan and tulle and watered silk across the bed. She would be hard put to find an occasion to wear all of the new dresses while she was in Sydney, and she couldn't imagine needing half a dozen ball gowns at Glenellen! Farmer's had been her downfall from the moment she discovered it. She had already known the name, for it had been stamped on numerous packages of rolled-up carpets and swatches of upholstery material that had arrived at Cameron's Creek; but what she hadn't known was that it was an immense, convenient establishment, divided into departments that supplied absolutely everything. You went to one department to choose fabric, then to another where wonderfully clever seamstresses could make anything from even the scantiest sketches, then another to find shoes, and another for gloves, and yet another for a bonnet to complete the outfit.

Well, at least she hadn't succumbed to the temptation of having bird wings put on this time! The bonnet that peeked out of its box on the dresser was a silly bit of fluff, all ribbons and ruffles and fantastically colored silk roses, and she knew Errol would smile when he saw it, but he would like it too, and that was what counted.

A puff of breeze came in the window. Stacey went back out on the balcony again. The sun was low, slanting obliquely, but the air was still warm. She had changed again, the fourth time since she had come home—it was hard to leave all those dresses alone—and was wearing a deep pink lawn, sprigged in lighter pink and trimmed with French satin ribbons in yet a paler tone. It amused her a little to imagine what Errol would think when he came and saw her framed in the doorway—a picture by some romantic impressionist: *Girl in Pink Dress Under Flowering Pink Tree*.

There had been an almost fairy-tale bliss to their days since they had come to Sydney. It was, although she was not capable of understanding it at the time, the kind of happiness that comes with youth and innocence, having about it a carelessness that is never quite achieved again. It was almost as if, leaving everything behind—D'Arcy and Maude and all the doubts and suspicions—their love had grown and blossomed until it was as bright and beautiful as the flowering spring trees. Everything would be so perfect, she thought moodily, if only . . .

If only . . .

Stacey turned her head slightly, drawn by the bed with its impromptu billow of fabric and lace. She and Errol had been closer than ever. Not a day had gone by they hadn't made love, not a morning or an evening when he hadn't drawn her into his arms and shown her again how much he wanted her . . . and yet still she hadn't conceived. Her hand slipped up, fingering the little diamond that throbbed in the pulse at the base of her throat. What if there's something wrong with me? she thought nervously. What if I can't bear a child?

Certainly Errol hadn't seemed worried about it when she had confessed again, that very morning, how concerned she was. "Pregnancy isn't like spontaneous combustion, you know," he said with an easy laugh. "It doesn't always happen—*poof!*— like that!"

"I suppose so, but . . ." Stacey sighed. She knew he was right, but it had been months now, and it was hard to control her feelings. "I wish . . . I just wish it would!"

He heard the tremor in her voice, and his face turned serious. "You expect too much of yourself, love. Every little girl who gets married doesn't have a baby in nine months—and I wouldn't want you to. This is our time to be together, to get to know . . . and enjoy . . . each other. It's not good to start a family too soon."

"But what if . . . what if it doesn't ever happen?"

"If it doesn't," he said calmly, "it just doesn't. But I think it will. And after all, you have to admit"—he nuzzled her neck suggestively—"I'm doing everything I can to bring it about."

Since they were in bed at the time, and since the actions that followed were appropriate to the words, Stacey forgot her cares for a time. But later, as she was thinking back, his reassurances were nowhere near as soothing as he had intended. Quite the contrary. With all that passion, a baby ought to be in sight, and still nothing had happened. For all his cavalier comments, Errol Cameron did want a child, she knew that—it was his desire for a child that had induced him to let her stay that first night when he was so angry. If time passed and she couldn't give him one, what then? What would happen if, year after year, he looked at her and saw only a barren field in which his seed had been spent in vain?

She stepped over to the balcony rail, shaking her head a little, as if to clear the cobwebs out of her mind. Errol was right. It *was* silly to worry after only a few short months. She was young and healthy; she would conceive in time. She was only making things worse, fretting like that—and trying his patience too, she'd warrant, though he was being wonderfully understanding about it.

The street was beginning to fill with people. The fashionable of Sydney had turned out for a late-afternoon stroll, and the narrow sidewalks were brimming over with color, the softer fawn and gray of gentlemen's breeches setting off the vivid lilac and turquoise and crimson of the ladies. In truth, it was ungrateful to complain; Sydney had been a constantly changing kaleidoscope of delights, and she had loved every minute of her stay. One afternoon Errol had taken her to the North Shore, hiring a private yacht, though she would not in the least have minded the charming little penny ferry; another day had been spent on the beach at Manly; still another morning was set aside for riding one of the new steam-trams, a great puffing, snorting contrivance that had alarmed her on first sight, but proved great fun once she got used to it. There were balls in the evening, where Errol proved not merely as good a dancer as his younger brother, but much better, and rowing contests on the Parramatta River, and strolls through the beautiful Botanical Gardens, where Stacey sometimes got the flattering feeling her handsome husband was every bit as eager to show her off as she was to be seen on his arm.

One day, at lunchtime, he took her for a midday bathe at the Natorium on Pitt Street, near the Redfern Railway Station, where a freshwater plunge could be had for nine pence, hot seawater for a shilling. Heaven knows what Errol paid, for somehow he managed to bribe a scandalized attendant in one of the private therapeutic rooms to let them go in together.

"Have you no shame?" she said, giggling as the door grated shut and they were alone.

"None whatever," he replied, and proceeded to show her an entirely new, but definitely therapeutic use for the dingy gray high-sided tub.

Culture had not been ignored either. Stacey had been surprised to learn that Sydney, far from being as provincial as she had expected, had theaters with everything from Shakespeare to burlesque, and concerts and ballets and even an occasional Italian opera company, offering a most presentable *Travatore* or *Norma*. Still it was the art that intrigued her most, and under Errol's guidance she discovered a whole generation of painters she had never seen or even heard of. John Glover, with his luminous water scenes and classically graceful gums; Eugen von Guerard, capturing the distant softness of the hills; Conrad Martens and the harbor at Sydney, a study in sun and haze and sea; all bringing their own subtle interpretation to the landscape, making the country come alive in new and exciting ways.

None, however, was as dynamic as Fitz Blackburn, and Stacey smiled to herself as she thought again of the sweeping mural on the dome at Glenellen, or the exquisite *Silver Swan* that was still hanging over the mantel at the homestead, for the parlor had not yet been finished to that artist's exacting standards. She couldn't wait to see the look of utter astonishment on all those faintly bored faces when they came into the gallery one day and saw his work for the first time!

The air had turned cooler, just in the last few minutes. It was not yet dusk, but the sun was slipping behind buildings on the far side of the street, and there was a distinct chill to the shadows that swept across the balcony. Stacey was about to go inside when she caught sight of a woman on the opposite curb. She was just standing there watching as a carriage passed . . . pretty and undeniably feminine in a blue silk dress.

The *same* woman?

In spite of herself, Stacey moved closer, hands tensing around the rail. Yes, of course it was—she must live somewhere nearby. Distance and diminished light emphasized her prettiness, giving a subdued impression of delicate features and abundant red-gold hair.

Stacey closed her eyes for a moment, wishing she had started inside a second sooner. It was funny, she could remember every detail of that afternoon she had first seen the woman. It had been about the same time then, too. Carriages were rumbling past, and the sidewalk was crowded with men in top hats and women in bright spring dresses. She and Errol had been among them, chatting about something—she couldn't remember now what it was—and she had looked over to catch him staring straight ahead with a startled look on his face.

More curious than alarmed, she had turned to see a woman in a blue-green taffeta dress. Just for an instant she seemed familiar, though Stacey was positive she had never seen her before. The woman must have noticed them too, or more accurately, Errol, for she paused briefly, blue eyes narrowing in what looked like recognition. Then they flitted past, focusing on something beyond, and Stacey realized she had imagined it all. The woman, clearly, did not know who Errol was, and he didn't know her. Yet there *had* been something in the way he looked at her before . . .

The woman had already gone by before Stacey realized what it was. Turning, she caught a glimpse of slimness and peacock silk and almost unnaturally bright hair, and suddenly she knew.

Maude. Her body stiffened and she was aware of a sinking feeling in her stomach. The woman looked uncannily like Maude. Her figure, her coloring . . . even her walk. And Errol had stopped to stare as if he had seen a ghost from the past! Stacey could have wept. Even here, even in Sydney, where she had been so sure she had him all to herself, he could not keep his thoughts from Maude.

She sighed softly, watching from the balcony as the woman lifted her skirt and began to cross the street. Stacey had covered her reaction well that afternoon. Errol had not seen, she was sure of that. She had been smiling when she turned back, and talking of something else. She had not been ready yet to confront him with her jealousy, fearing that he would admit it was true . . . or that his protestations would sound weak and unconvincing. But here alone, on the balcony, with no one to see, it was hard to pretend she was not afraid.

Now that the woman was closer, Stacey could see

that she was not as pretty as she had appeared before, or as young. She must have been wearing makeup, for her lips were almost as vivid as her hair, and deep lines showed in the dry skin that stretched across her cheeks. Nor did she really look that much like Maude. The similarity had been fleeting, the kind of quick impression that came and went in a flash.

But it had been there. She had noticed it—and Errol had noticed it. And did it truly matter whether *she* was young or not? Pretty or not? It wasn't this painted woman with her brittle parchment skin that left Stacey feeling suddenly ill. It was that split second's resemblance to Maude.

Like it or not, she was going to have to come to terms with the possibility that this was the one true love of her husband's life. The one obsession he could not forget, no matter how he tried.

If only she were carrying his child. Stacey turned miserably, slipping back into the room, closing the doors behind her. She knew Errol desired her, she had had ample proof of that—if only she could give him a son too, then she would not be so afraid.

The new dresses were still sprawled across the bed, frothing over in an untidy tumble, but it no longer gave her pleasure to look at them. It was another Stacey who had taken such delight in frivolous things. A shallow young girl who grew up in San Francisco, her grandfather's pet, and never gave a thought to anything beyond the next party and the next ball gown and whatever pretty bauble she wanted at the moment. It was an altogether different Stacey who had returned to Sydney with her husband on the train.

And that Stacey only wanted him to come home and take her in his arms and tell her that he loved her more than anything else in the world. And that he would be as devastated as she if anything ever came between them.

Errol leaned back in the open carriage. The light was just beginning to fade, and shadows stretched across the road from great blocks of wool warehouses on either side. The traffic of the day had abated some-

what, and the area was already beginning to take on
the abandoned look of a business sector at dusk. A
cart groaned past, massive canvas-wrapped bales
swaying precariously as the cursing bullocky maneu-
vered his team around the corner and out of sight.
Coming from the railway terminus at Redfern, Errol
judged by the direction, and probably headed for the
docks.

The coachman slowed as they approached a cross
street, glancing over his shoulder, but Errol raised the
tip of his walking stick and gestured him on. The man
would be surprised, no doubt; a gentleman of means
usually ended the day at his club with a glass of brandy
and a smoke. But it was getting late, and Errol had no
desire to detour. He had spent too much time in those
stuffy chambers as it was—he had taken lodging there
on previous trips into town—though he had to admit it
came in handy for business. Most of the large landowners belonged to Warrigal, which was getting a
reputation as the "squatter's club," but the Australian
was the oldest and the most exclusive, and it had been
a feather in his cap, to say nothing of a tribute to his
wealth and proper English education, that he had been
asked to join. Ordinarily he liked stopping there. It
amused him, strolling past the doormen in their elegant livery and thinking that the descendant of a bushranger and a common pickpocket was among that elite
membership. Today, however, he had other things on
his mind.

He glanced idly at the buildings as they rolled past,
noting that lights were beginning to show in some of
the windows. That's what comes of having a beautiful
young wife, he noted wryly. It made a man soft. He
forgot all about affairs of business and powerful con-
nections to be made at the club and thought only of
getting back to a rented house where a tepid cup of
tea and not a bracing brandy would be waiting.

Still . . . He smiled faintly as he spotted an acquaintance in a passing hansom and tipped his hat in
greeting. There was something to be said for tea, after
all, especially in the company of a charming woman. It
had been a thoroughly satisfying afternoon. He had

made what promised to be an excellent investment and brought another to fruition, yet neither had given him the pleasure he now felt as going home—to Stacey.

Streetlights were beginning to go on as the carriage turned into George Street. The darkness had grown thicker, and orbs of gaslit yellow glowed dull against a faintly pinkish sky. George Street had always fascinated him; he disliked being a part of the social scene, but he enjoyed looking down on it from the vantage point of a passing carriage. The day was just ending, and the area was swarming with people. The fashionable of Sydney had finished their day's shopping and were strolling arm in arm along the sidewalks, and commercial workers jammed into omnibuses and tramcars for the long trip home. Store windows displayed everything imaginable: jewelry and corsets, illustrated books from London and ladies' bonnets trimmed with purple lace, silk-backed satin draperies, rosewood writing desks, bootbrushes and lampwicks and imported Parisian perfume, and the latest in novelty quack medicine, whatever it was that season.

He called impulsively to the driver, stopping in front of a jeweler's with which he was slightly familiar. He had seen a trinket in the window the other day in passing, a Siamese-sapphire brooch, not expensive but pretty, and it occurred to him that Stacey might like it. He came out a few minutes later, not with the pin after all—he had not liked its looks on closer examination—but with a bracelet, also Siamese, the deepest, reddest rubies he had ever seen, set with small, perfectly matched pearls.

It was nearly dark by now, and he urged the coachman to hurry. He had been longer than he intended. He had the feeling Stacey would be worried. They had turned off George by this time, and the streets were narrower, but brighter and livelier. Garish lamplight fell on a gay profusion of fruit shops and oyster saloons. Long rows of stalls were thronged with young people eager for a taste of ice cream or ginger beer, and housewives elbowed through the crowds, large baskets of mutton and fresh vegetables balanced on their hips. The voices of hucksters carried, shrill above the general din, even after the carriage had passed the market, and Errol could hear the sound of a barrel organ somewhere in the distance.

He felt the long velvet box in his pocket and thought of the expression on Stacey's face when she saw it, and in the darkness he smiled. He remembered the way she had looked that first time he saw her. Standing by the mantel in an absurdly heavy gown with all those petticoats and little frills up to her neck, and his first thought had been: God, she is so young!

And she *had* been young. He eased back in the carriage, stretching long legs out in front of him. A little girl sent to share a man's bed. But she hadn't minded too much, as he recalled, and neither, once he got used to the idea, had he. It still worried him sometimes—youthfulness had a disconcerting way of bordering on childishness—but it delighted him too, and he was frank enough to admit it. He liked going home and having her thrust her lips up for a kiss; yes, and having her feel in his pocket too, sometimes— the little minx—to see if he had brought her a present. He liked her eagerness and her excitement at anything new, the way she lived every day for itself, with no thought of what lay ahead.

Young, indeed. Yet youth brought with it vitality and joy and a zest for life that almost made him feel seventeen again when he was with her.

She was so different from the wife he had imagined for himself. He had had a picture of her, a visual image in his mind. Skin like Stacey's, but with brown hair, not black, pulled back in an old-fashioned knot at the nape of her neck. He had been so sure then what he wanted; every detail had been precise in his mind. A woman who was calm and sure of herself. A woman with a soft-spoken voice and cool hands, soothing at the end of a stressful day. A woman who would know him as well as she knew herself, and understand the need for peace in his well-ordered life, and teach him the gentleness and patience he had never had time to learn. Instead, he had gotten a girl, with all the impulsiveness of youth, and all its insecurities, and his life was less peaceful than ever.

And—if he was going to be completely honest—the idea of a gentle, soothing existence no longer held quite the same appeal.

Gaslight glowed a warming welcome as the carriage rolled up in front of the house. The door was closed but not locked, and Errol let himself in after dismissing the coachman. He never rang for the servants when he returned. He liked the independence of coming and going himself, no butler to greet him—"Good evening, sir" . . . "Will that be all, sir?"—with pinched English tones coming through his nose.

He found the shelf for his hat, then flipped his cape on the peg beneath and started up the steps, restraining himself from taking them two at a time. He had promised Stacey they would go out for dinner—a new restaurant had opened near the cove, reputedly the best in town—and he supposed she would already be decked out, in a new gown no doubt, with her hair done up in whatever was the latest fashion.

Too bad, he thought as he reached the top landing and headed down the hall. He would have liked to help her dress—he always enjoyed those little husbandly tasks, like fastening the hooks in the back—but then, perhaps it was for the best. The way he was feeling now, it might make them late for dinner. At least he would have the pleasure of slipping the ruby bracelet around her wrist.

24

But Stacey wasn't dressed when he came into the bedroom. She was seated on a stool in front of the dressing table. As she rose to face him, Errol could see that she had on a negligee, some sort of flimsy fabric that moved with her body. She had not done her hair yet. It was loose, the way he liked, hanging to her shoulders, and her eyes had a faintly pinkish cast. Almost if she had been crying, though no doubt that was the light.

"And here I thought I was going to be late." He set the velvet box down and removed his coat, arranging it on the back of a chair. "I expected to find you dressed and ready—and tapping your toes on the floor."

"You *are* late," she replied, working her lips into a pout. "There was no point getting dressed—I had no idea when you'd be back. It really is unfair, you know, staying away so long. I'm a bride, and brides hate being alone."

She was trying to tease—Errol knew it—but she couldn't keep a trace of petulance out of her voice, and suddenly he was irritated with the youthfulness that had enchanted him before. It seemed to him he had been remarkably attentive. He had devoted far more time to her than most new husbands would, and he had been bolting up the steps just now to be with her.

"I'm sorry," he replied coolly. "I'm afraid my business took longer than I expected. I do have to make money, you know." He cast his gaze pointedly over the profusion of finery on the bed. "I assume the bills for all those pretty froufrous will be coming in posthaste."

Stacey's chin tilted up. "Did it ever occur to you I

might prefer my husband's company to a roomful of new gowns?"

He raised one brow slowly. "I am sorry," he repeated somewhat stiffly.

"No . . ." She came to him then, standing so close it was hard not to take her into his arms. "I'm the one who's sorry. I didn't mean it that way. Truly I didn't. I was just concerned when you didn't come back . . . and I missed you. Is there anything wrong with a wife's missing her husband?"

"If there is"—he relented, drawing her into his embrace—"you won't hear about it from me. But don't you think it might have been wiser to at least start your toilette. Not that I don't think what you have on is delightful, mind you . . . but you do take longer to dress than I. We wouldn't want the restaurant to be closed by the time we got there. You were looking forward to going out tonight."

"Oh?" She lowered her lashes, knowing it was a gesture that appealed to him. "Was I?"

The warmth of her was palpable against his chest, the scent of her hair in his nostrils a distinct distraction. "So you told me when I left this afternoon. The new place is becoming quite famous for its lobster. And I know how you adore lobster . . . and just a sip of champagne."

"I also adore cold beef with Cook's special mustard sauce, and maybe a light green salad . . . which is what I ordered for tonight."

"Because I was late and you didn't know what time I'd be back?"

"No. Because I wanted to. I thought you'd want it too . . . unless of course you're getting bored with me." Her lips pursed slightly, pink and inviting. He might almost have thought she had rouged them if he hadn't been close enough to see better. "I'm having it sent up to the room on a tray. But don't worry, I told the maid not to bring it till we rang."

"How very clever of you." His hands slid down her back slowly and very deliberately, seeking the supple firmness of her buttocks. He was already hard for her. He knew she could feel it as he drew her tight against

him, and he knew it excited her . . . as her responses
always excited him. "Do you know . . . you have very
round, kissable lips."

"Yes," she replied. Her arms were around him then,
and that round, kissable mouth was on his, and suddenly nothing else in the world existed. He liked it
when she took the initiative—this boldness was new in
their relationship—and he held himself back deliberately, letting her urge him, tease him toward the bed.
Waves of fabric billowed up, a drowning sea of skirts
and bodices; then everything was on the floor, cascading in all directions, and they were together as they
had both wanted, forgetting everything else but the
urgent need that surged and encompassed them.

Afterward, Stacey was strangely still. Errol could feel
the difference as he held her in his arms, and for the
first time, he sensed he had not satisfied her. Usually
she was clinging at a time like that, touching every part
of him, covering moist chest hairs with a thousand tender
little kisses. Instead she was subdued, almost as if she
had retreated into herself, forgetting he was there.

He laid his hand on her face, a light, possessive
gesture. Where is she now, he wondered . . . so far
away from me?

It took a moment; then he realized. The baby again.
She had been worrying a lot about babies lately. Funny
. . . he had always thought he wanted children—he
did want children—but if she were to turn to him now
and tell him she was pregnant, a part of him would be
reluctant. He loved being with her like this, touching
her whenever he wanted, not having to be concerned
about hurting her or the child she was carrying. He
was not ready to let go of that yet.

He shifted his weight, propping himself up on one
elbow. "Is this my passionate little Stacey, who could
never bear the caresses to end? And you asked if *I* was
getting bored with you."

She looked up, silver-gray eyes misty with shadow,
and Errol realized suddenly that he had been wrong.
It wasn't that he hadn't satisfied her—it was that she
had been more intensely, more completely satisfied
than ever before.

"No," she said softly. "I am not bored with you." The corner of her mouth moved just faintly, an unconscious half-smile. "But that reminds me—you didn't answer my question before. Are you, perhaps, getting bored with me?"

"Hardly. I might be bewildered by you sometimes— and out-and-out exasperated. But I don't think I'll ever be bored."

"You're not sorry you didn't send me back when you had the chance?"

"No." He looked at the froth of silk and lace on the floor and started to laugh. "God help me, it will probably be the ruin of me, but no, I'm not sorry I didn't send you back."

He took her in his arms, and they made love again, slowly, languidly, with all the easy tenderness of two people who are sure their happiness will last forever and they have all the time in the world. Later, as they lay in each other's arms, Errol recalled the little trinket in its velvet box on the table, but it didn't seem the time to give it to her, and he amused himself thinking how he would hide it among the racks of toast on the breakfast tray in the morning. And Stacey, unaware of its existence, and totally uninterested in jewels at the moment, thought only how safe and warm it was in his embrace and how complete her love for him was.

She had no way of knowing that her fragile happiness was to be shattered in the morning.

The sun was already streaming through the open terrace window when Stacey woke the next day, feeling lazy but deliciously content. It surprised her a little to look over and see an empty place beside her on the bed. Errol was usually there to greet her with a morning kiss, though she could hardly blame him. The clock on the Italian marble side table was already chiming nine. He must have been ravenous.

She threw on a dressing gown, not the lacy negligee she wore when they were alone, but a more modest peach-colored silk, and hurried out into the hall. She had expected to find him in the breakfast room, by the big bay window with the *Morning Herald* propped in front of him, and she wasn't really looking when she got halfway down the front stairs and realized suddenly that he was there, standing in the foyer.

He must have heard her approach, for he turned. His face was pale, as if all the blood had drained out of it, and he was holding a piece of paper in his hand.

"A telegram," he said tersely.

Stacey's heart thumped in her chest. Telegraphy had reached such a state that a cable could be sent across the Atlantic to London, then via India and the Suez to a ship that would carry it to Australia, and her first thought was of home and her sisters. Then she got a better look at his expression.

"From . . . Cameron's Creek?"

He nodded grimly. "It just arrived. Maude needs us. We have to get back at once."

Maude? Stacey stood at the base of the steps and looked around the brightly sunlit hall and tried not to feel sick inside as her mind turned over what he had said. Except for a few unwelcome reminders, she had thought she was free of Maude in Sydney. But one word from her, one helpless, fluttery appeal, no doubt, and he was ready to go running back!

"What . . . what do you mean? What can she need you . . . *us* for?"

"She's ill." His voice was controlled, but Stacey could have sworn she heard a catch in it. "Oh, what the hell! Why do I say it like that?" He held out his hand, thrusting the paper toward her. "Here. See for yourself. She isn't ill. She's dying."

Stacey took the telegram, squinting down at faintly inked block letters, struggling to make them out. It wasn't from Maude, after all. Mrs. Butler had sent it. Maude had just given birth to a son—and neither mother nor baby was expected to live.

"But . . . I don't understand." She had moved over to the door to take the telegram. Now she held it up to the window, as if somehow daylight could make things clearer. "It doesn't make sense. Maude has only been married a short time. She couldn't have carried a child to term—or anywhere near it. Surely Mrs. Butler must have meant she had a miscarriage. Unless . . ."

She gaped at the telegram, stunned.

"Unless of course she was pregnant when she wed." Errol's voice was sharp. Stacey looked up to see that he was already on the steps, staring down with dark, ironic eyes. "That is what you were thinking, isn't it? Does it shock you so much? That a woman might take a man to her bed before the marriage vows had been uttered? But then, I forgot . . . you're hardly in a position to judge, are you?"

Stacey stepped back, recoiling as if he had struck her. He *hadn't* forgotten. He would never forget the indiscretion that nearly tore them apart. And he had reminded her of it intentionally just now, knowing it would hurt.

"That's not fair. I . . . I was just surprised, that's all. I had no idea . . . it never occurred to me she was pregnant." And yet it should have. The clues had been there. The hasty, impulsive marriage . . . Maude's sudden indisposition . . . that extra plumpness around her waist. "But it doesn't surprise you, does it?" She was beginning to understand, more than she wanted to. "You knew all along. You guessed before this . . ."

"Of course I guessed. I'm not exactly naive. I should never have left—I knew she might need me—but she wouldn't hear of our giving up the trip to Sydney."

"*She* wouldn't hear of it." Stacey felt as if the whole world were falling apart. Not only had Errol guessed that Maude was pregnant, he had discussed that most intimate matter with her! And the trip that had given so much joy, apparently, was at *Maude's* instigation!

"I daresay she was relieved to get rid of me," he went on. "She was probably afraid I'd confront him with it. And I would have, too, the bastard, if we'd hung around!"

There was little doubt who *the bastard* was. "You're talking about D'Arcy, of course. Your own brother, whom you despise." She knew she was on dangerous ground—he always reacted badly to any mention of D'Arcy from her—but she couldn't stop her tongue. "That sounds a little strange, coming from you. D'Arcy may have bedded Maude, but as you pointed out yourself, that can hardly shock either of us. He *was* her fiancé . . . and he did marry her."

"Yes—after he'd gotten her pregnant, damn him! My brother is a user, he always has been. Only this time it was Maude who got hurt."

Stacey blinked back a sudden sting of tears. D'Arcy *was* a user. Who knew that better than she? But when it came to Little Miss Innocent, Errol had a blind spot. Stacey had done exactly the same thing—and he had been all too ready to condemn! What made her Jezebel and Maude the Virgin Mary?

"It seems to me," she said tartly, "it takes two for what they did."

She thought for an instant he was going to slap her. As long as she lived, she would never forget the look on his face. He took a step forward, then stopped, clutching white-knuckled at the banister.

"She's dying, for Christ's sake! Do you have to be petty and childish now?" He seemed to pull himself together. Stacey could almost see the muscles unwind as he eased his grip on the rail. "If it's any concern of yours, she was in love with him. God knows why, but she was—no doubt she still loves him for the little time that's left her—and he had no compunctions taking advantage of that. Anyway, there's no point going over all this. We're wasting time. I expect you to get dressed, madam, and throw what you need in a bag. There's a train leaving Redfern a little after noon. We're going to be on it."

"But we can't go back!" Stacey gaped at him in dismay. Maude *was* dying—in the confusion of the last few minutes, she had somehow lost sight of that—and she couldn't let her die in Errol's arms. She didn't dare take the chance. The bond between them, whatever it was, was already too strong. "There's nothing we can do. Honestly, there isn't. We'd only be in the way. And I . . . I don't want to go back."

"You don't *want* to?" His eyes narrowed, and Stacey had the uncomfortable feeling he was seeing her for the first time. "You don't want to go back to your responsibilities . . . or you don't want to leave Sydney? Because you're having too much fun!"

"N-no, of course not." She knew how it must sound, as petty as he had said, and self-centered, but she couldn't let him go back to the woman he might be in love with! "It's just that . . . well, there's no point. We really *would* be in the way. Besides . . ." She cast around in her mind, searching for something, anything, to hold him back. "It takes three days to get there. If the telegram is right and it's truly urgent, we'd be too late—"

"Too late to do anything but bury her? You may be right. But, by God, if there's nothing else I can do, at least I'm going to do that! I've known her all her life—*cared* about her all her life. I'm not going to turn my back on her now."

Cared? Stacey's heart broke at the pain in his voice. Cared . . . or loved? "Maude is married to your brother," she reminded him harshly. "Have you forgotten? He's the one who should be at her bedside, not you or I. She has her own home now, Errol . . . her own life. We don't belong there."

"She's still family, and family is what counts. We're going to stand by each other now if we never have before. My place may not be at her bedside—or yours, heaven knows—but we belong in the homestead if she needs or wants us. I can't believe even you are too immature to acknowledge that." He started up the stairs, turning as he reached the top. "Twenty minutes, madam—I think you can be dressed in that time if you set your mind to it. The maid will pack your bags."

Stacey stared at him helplessly. His face was cold, but his eyes were burning, and she was more terrified than ever of letting him see Maude again. Things had a way of happening when someone was dying; she had read about it in cheap novels, and she knew it was true. One last moment for Errol to take Maude in his arms . . . one last chance to declare his love, right there in front of everyone. . . .

"No!" She felt her heart tighten in her chest. "We can't go back. Not now! I mean . . . it would be foolish going all that way when we're not even sure it's necessary. Why don't we wait and see what happens?

Then, in a few days, if things are really as bad as they seem . . . well, then of course we'll go back."

His eyes darkened as he looked down at her. "*I am going this afternoon*," he said pointedly. "You, I suppose, will do what you want. The house is paid for till the lend of next month. You may as well stay. I don't really care."

I don't really care. Stacey stood alone in the hall after he was gone, trying not to cry, but it was hard when she was so young and everything seemed to be tumbling down around her. He didn't care, he had said, and she had the terrible feeling he meant it. All he cared about now was Maude; and nothing else—no *one* else—mattered.

The morning streets were just beginning to come alive. Through the tall windows on either side of the door Stacey could see carriages rolling by, and an occasional pedestrian. Maude had had a child. For the first time the reality of that sank in, and suddenly she felt barren and empty inside. So long . . . she had been trying so long to get pregnant . . . months and months it seemed, and Maude had done it just like that! Errol had been kind about it, of course—he had said it didn't matter—but he had to be comparing her with Maude. And finding her inadequate one more time.

The sun was bright and the window felt warm as she ran her fingers down it. She hated the envy that was tearing her apart—an ugly, unseemly emotion!— but she couldn't help herself. Maude was dying. She ought to feel pity now, horror at the young life being snuffed out, but all she could think was that Maude had conceived a child and she hadn't. And Maude hadn't even been married at the time!

A flash of turquoise showed through the window. Stacey looked up to see a slim stylish figure on the walk across the street. The same woman again? she wondered with a shudder. But then she looked closer and realized she had been wrong. Only the color was the same, a vivid blue-green. Otherwise, she didn't look like that other woman at all . . . just as the other woman hadn't really looked like Maude. Illusion, that was what it was. Illusion and doubt. And fear.

She remembered suddenly the wives Errol had told her about. The ones who stayed in town season after season while their men worked on stations in the bush and outback. Was that what lay ahead for her? The house had been paid for for a month at least, he had told her . . . no doubt the arrangement could be continued if that was what they decided. A nice genteel separation . . . like all those other couples who had married too quickly and learned to regret it.

And that *was* what would be decided, she realized bitterly, if she let him go back alone.

But if she went with him . . . She turned slowly from the window, letting her hand drop to her side. If Maude really was dying, as the telegram had said, if Errol got there in time to take her in his arms, if the words she dreaded so much were spoken—what was going to happen to her marriage then?

But what choice did she have?

Stacey looked back up the stairs, seeing nothing but emptiness in the hall above. Five of the twenty minutes he had given her were gone. If she stayed behind, he would never forgive her. Their marriage would be over for sure. If she went back, at least she would have a chance to fight for it. And her marriage to Errol—her love for him—was worth fighting for.

He was in his dressing room when she found him, packing shirts and underwear quickly and efficiently in an open leather valise. He did not look up, but she knew he sensed her in the doorway.

"I'll be ready in fifteen minutes," she said quietly. "I'm going with you."

25

The room was uncomfortably silent, with only a pair of lamps casting flickering semicircles of warmth into the brooding shadows. Maude had redecorated the homestead, and a sofa and chairs were clustered around a red-patterned carpet, making a homey grouping in one corner of the large front salon where Stacey sat alone. It was a hot night, dry with the drought that had set in again. The windows were open, but not so much as a crackle of wind or a frog croaking by the creek drifted in to break the stillness.

Looking up, she saw Pegeen standing awkwardly on the fringe of light. Mrs. Butler had been there earlier, but she had gone back to Glenellen, leaving the Irish washermaid to tend to the tea and bring out biscuits and sandwiches as required.

"Will you be needin' anything, mum? I could bring a nice cuppa—that'd make you feel better, sure."

"No, Pegeen, thank you." Stacey shook her head slowly. She hadn't realized how tired she was, but the last thing she wanted in all that heat was a cup of tea. "Why don't you take one of the comfortable chairs back to the kitchen and try to get some rest? There's nothing you can do here."

"All right . . . but don't you be worryin', mum. There's a bit o' Irish in that lady in the bedroom, an' faith if the Irish aren't tough. It'll be all right—you mark me words."

Stacey smiled wearily. Why did people always think they had to say things like that, even when they weren't true? "No, Pegeen," she said softly as the girl disappeared into the darkness again. "No . . . everything isn't going to be all right." She had a terrible feeling, sitting there in that empty room, that nothing was ever going to be right again.

She rested her head against the back of the velvet-upholstered chair and tried not to think of that long, uncomfortable train ride from Sydney. They had barely make it to the station in time, and she had had to share her compartment with three other women and a colicky baby who cried all the way, making it impossible to get more than an hour or two's sleep. Errol himself had managed only a hard wooden seat in one of the lower-class carriages.

Not that he had complained, but then, he rarely did. He had been polite but distant those few times he came to check on her or bring the lunch or dinner he had purchased from vendors on the platform. There had been little conversation between them. He no longer seemed angry, but Stacey sensed he was disappointed, and she felt as if she had been shut out of his feelings.

Well, she thought, looking back on it, maybe it was for the best. If they had been closer then, if he had been tempted to confide in her, he might have confessed his passion for another woman. And words once spoken could never be called back.

She sighed softly, glancing at the window. Small panes of glass were dark mirrors in the lamplight. They had reached the platform in town to find the American buggy waiting; Mrs. Butler had arranged to have it stabled in town at the same time the telegram was sent. It had already been dark when they arrived at the homestead, but the moon was bright enough to see, and the sprawling structure glowed a ghostly gray-white as they pulled up in front. Mrs. Butler had come to the door to greet them, sagging lines showing for the first time in her round, sturdy face. The baby had been a boy—a fine, bonny lad, she called it—but too little to come into the world, and they had buried it the morning before last. The doctor had appeared a second later, and Errol had followed him into the bedroom without so much as a glance back at Stacey. He had been there ever since.

Four hours. Stacey got up and went over to the window, pushing it farther open. Not a breath of air came into the room. He had been there four hours without coming out once. She could hear noises somewhere in the rear of the house, and whispers, and she realized that the doctor had gone back for a cup of tea.

The doctor had slipped out, and Errol was alone with . . . whom? The friend he was losing? Or the woman he loved?

A movement caught her eye, quivering in the darkness. Squinting, she stared through the window. The moonlight was vivid, but the veranda lay heavy in shadow, and it was a moment before she made out the vague outline of a man's head and realized D'Arcy was there.

D'Arcy?

It surprised her a little, now that she thought of it, that she hadn't seen him before. She had been so wrapped up in her own concerns, her observations of Errol and his reactions, she hadn't wondered, or cared, where D'Arcy was. He had always been a strange one, sociable when he chose, but lonely at the core. She was aware of his pain—he was like a wounded animal, stalking back and forth—but she couldn't bring herself to feel anything for him.

His place is at her bedside, she had told Errol that fateful morning the telegram arrived. Only D'Arcy *wasn't* at her bedside. He was out there on the veranda, all by himself . . . and Errol was with Maude.

She looked back through the window, but D'Arcy must have wandered around to the other side, for she could no longer see him. She had sensed grief in that taut, pacing figure, and the fear the kept him from going to his wife. But she had sensed anger too, and she could almost feel him hating his brother.

The door to the side hall opened. Turning around, Stacey was startled to see Errol standing there. The doctor was still at the back of the house. She could hear his voice, conversing softly with Pegeen. Surely they wouldn't have left Maude alone?

"She isn't . . . ?" she asked, alarmed.

"No." Errol shook his head. "She just woke up a few minutes ago. She's been asking about you."

"Me?"

"She wondered if you'd come back with me. It seems she knows my wife better than I do—it didn't surprise her in the least to think you remained behind." His lips twisted wryly, but Stacey sensed more irony than bitterness. "She wants to see you."

"To see . . . me? But why?"

"Why, indeed?" The irony was clear now, but he sounded almost gentle, not angry. "Perhaps she's grown fond of you. Anyway, she does . . . and I think it's the least you can do.'

Stacey nodded vaguely, feeling strangely clumsy as she headed toward the door. Errol stepped aside to let her pass. She half-expected him to follow, but instead he went back into the parlor, leaving her alone in the shadowy hall.

The door to the small master bedroom was open, and faint rays of light seeped out. The smell of sickness was almost suffocating, the close, stale odor of a room that had been shut up, the acrid sweetness of disinfectant, and it was all she could do to force herself to go on.

The instant she crossed the threshold, she knew. It was not sickness she had scented in the hall outside; it was death. Maude was lying in the center of the wide double bed, looking small and oddly doll-like, with her head propped up on the impersonal whiteness of the pillows. Her skin was pale, almost translucent, the way it had been that afternoon she got soaked in the creek, and deep blue veins throbbed at her temples. The bed linen had been straightened, and a thin comforter came up to her breast, providing an unexpectedly garish splash of color. On it, her hands were folded, so limp they already looked lifeless.

In that split second, Stacey realized that she had never truly believed Maude was dying. Mrs. Butler had believed it when she sent the telegram, Errol believed it when he read it, but somehow she had thought it was all a mistake. An exaggeration. The way it had been after Fitz pulled her out of the creek, and Errol had held her in his arms all the way back to the house . . . and the next morning she had been weak but much, much better.

"Maude . . ."

It was barely a whisper, but the woman on the bed heard. She turned her head, and Stacey could see that her eyes were open.

"You mustn't . . . mind so much," she said weakly. "For me."

"Sh-h-h-h." There was a chair by the window, and Stacey moved it over and sat next to the bed. "What a way to talk! Anyone would think you weren't going to recover, the way you're going on. We've all been worried about you, but the doctor is here and—"

"Don't . . ." Maude tried to raise her head, but she didn't have the strength. It seemed to Stacey she sank even deeper into the pillows. "Don't . . . pretend. . . . They've always told me, you know . . . I shouldn't . . ."

"Shouldn't what, Maude?" The room was almost unbearably hot, but all the windows were closed, and Stacey could feel perspiration drenching her bodice. "What did they tell you you shouldn't do?"

"A baby . . . said I shouldn't have a baby . . . that this might happen . . . but I didn't care . . ." Something in her face changed, and just for an instant she almost seemed to smile. Her hair was plastered moistly to her head, as if she had been feverish before, but she looked almost unnaturally cool now. "He is beautiful . . . isn't he?"

Her voice was so soft, Stacey had to lean closer.

"He?" she asked, puzzled.

"The . . . baby."

The baby? Stacey stared at her, feeling suddenly sick at heart. They hadn't told her about the baby! He had been buried nearly two days, and Maude thought he was safe and cooing in a cradle somewhere in the house.

"Yes . . . yes, of course," she murmured awkwardly. Why hadn't someone prepared her for this? Someone should have told her what Maude expected, what the baby had looked like, what color hair he had had, so she would know what to say. "He's . . . he's the most beautiful baby I've ever seen. He's all red and puffy, of course, but newborns are like that. He's going to be very handsome when he grows up."

"Like his father. . . . D'Arcy . . ." Her voice trailed off. Stacey sensed she was trying to speak—her lips were moving, but nothing came out—and all she could do was sit there and watch. Was Maude trying to say that the boy would grow up to look like his father, D'Arcy? Or was she asking where her husband was?

"I'm sure D'Arcy's proud of him too," Stacey said, prattling in her nervousness. "Of course he is—that's where he must be now. Checking on the baby. He probably doesn't know you're awake. When he finds out, he'll come right away."

"No . . . you're pretending again . . ." Her voice faded, then came back in disjointed phrases, and Stacey knew she was getting weaker. "Always a coward . . . poor D'Arcy. . . . It's hard . . . too hard for him."

Poor D'Arcy? All Stacey could think of was the way he was cowering alone in the shadows on the veranda. She couldn't imagine what it was that had ever made her think he was bold and dashing! "And you forgive him?" she said incredulously. "For not being with you now?"

"I've already forgiven . . . more than that."

Her eyes half-closed, as if the lids had turned to lead. Stacey made a move to get up, thinking she was too tired to talk anymore, but Maude raised her hand limply.

"Don't go . . . not yet . . . need to tell you . . ."

She made a fluttering motion, and Stacey, sensing what she wanted, took her hand. It was cold as ice, though the room seemed to be getting hotter by the minute. "What is it, Maude? What are you trying to tell me?"

For a minute she thought the other woman had not heard her. Then her lips began to move.

"I . . . know," she said softly. "I *know*."

Stacey's body went stiff, and she looked away, unable to meet that quietly probing gaze. She knew, Maude had said—she knew! But she couldn't possibly know *that*!

Oh, please, she thought helplessly—please, *please*, don't let her have guessed the truth about D'Arcy and me. Not now, when she's dying. It would be too cruel!

But when she looked down again, she knew her
prayers were futile. Everything in those blue-green
eyes reflected the truth Stacey had tried so lo.., to
block out of her own mind.

"I know . . . everything," Maude said. "I knew that
day . . . on the dock. . . . When the ship came in and
I saw you beside him . . . I knew."

Oh, sweet heaven! Stacey had never wished anything so hard in her life as she wished now that the
floor would open and swallow her up. It was bad
enough, what she had done, but to think that Maude
had known it all along! And that it was tormenting her
on her deathbed!

"You mustn't say things like that. Please, you mustn't
even think them!"

"No . . . it doesn't matter . . . it never has. . . ."
She seemed feebler, but she forced herself to go on, as
if she had to finish what she was saying. "I've always
known . . . about D'Arcy. . . . You weren't the first
. . . but it never mattered. . . . Just a physical thing . . ."

Stacey felt for a moment as if she were going to faint.
Just a physical thing? She tried to pull her hand back,
but Maude was clinging and she couldn't get away. "You
really *did* know, then. All along. And yet you were
kind to me. You went out of your way to be my friend."

"I was afraid . . . when I saw you. . . . But then he
came to me . . . and I knew he loved me."

Rememberance flooded back. That afternoon on
the dock. D'Arcy leaping down the gangplank, clasping Maude in his arms. The look on her face, how
strange it had seemed then. Not excitement at all . . .
more like triumph. But that, of course, was what it
was. Triumph that he had returned to her!

"Of course he loved you. I think he always has, in
his way. There was never anyone else. Not truly. You
were the one in his heart." She felt a faint pressure on
her hand, and she sensed, guiltily, that Maude was
trying to comfort her.

"I wasn't afraid for me, later . . . but you."

"You were . . . afraid for me? But why?" Why
should Maude have cared one whit for the woman
who had tried to steal her fiancé?

"You were . . . so young . . ." Beads of sweat were standing out on her forehead now, and Stacey could see bright spots of pink in her cheeks. "I was afraid . . . he had hurt you. . . . Then I saw how strong you were . . . and I knew you were going to love Errol. . . . You do, don't you? . . . Love him?"

"Very much," Stacey said quietly. She was confused by the turn the conversation was taking, but somehow it seemed important to reply. "I love him more than anything else in the world."

"Then . . . everything is all right."

Her eyes drifted shut even before she had finished, and Stacey felt the pressure loosen on her fingers. For an instant she was frightened; then she looked down and saw Maude's chest rising and falling beneath the gaudily patterned quilt, and she knew she was just asleep. She eased her hand back and rose slowly, every muscle aching as if she had been sitting in the same position for hours.

Errol was alone in the parlor when she returned. She found him by the window, pacing, she sensed, though he was standing still when she opened the door. He asked a question with his eyes, got the response he seemed to expect, and without speaking, went to take his vigil in the room she had just left. Stacey went back to the chair where she had been sitting before and sank into it. Her legs were suddenly so wobbly she couldn't have stood a second longer.

Everything is all right, Maude had said. Just like Pegeen a short time before, as if saying things could make them happen. Only more than ever, she was sure that the world was falling apart.

All she had to do was love Errol—that was what Maude had said—and nothing else mattered. And perhaps, for Maude, that would have been true. Certainly she wasn't possessive in her love. It had been surprisingly easy for her to forgive the acts D'Arcy had committed—what was it she had called them, "just physical things"? Mere sexual dalliances that weren't important because they involved only his body and not his heart.

But Maude was a different person. She lived her life

by a different code; her values, her reactions, her very
feelings were different. There was gentleness in her
heart, but there was wildness too—Stacey had sensed
that the first time she saw her—and freedom was as
important to her as love. She had allowed D'Arcy
freedom for his infidelities, those little "physical things"
that didn't count. . . . Had she allowed the same freedom for herself?

Stacey pulled her feet up, curling her legs around
her on the broad seat of the chair. It would be easy for
someone like that, someone who thought sexual indiscretions didn't matter, to have an affair with another
man. Only, if that man was Errol, mightn't it have
mattered to him?

She turned her head, startled to see the painted
swan in its dark wood frame above the mantel. The
light had a shimmery effect, giving the silver back-
ground an etheral glow, and the swan was a black
silhouette that almost seemed to be gliding out of the
canvas. Like the spirit soaring from the body, she
thought, staring at it, fascinated. Wild and free, ready
at any moment to take flight and leave nothing but the
ghostly iridescence of the water in its empty wooden
shell.

Dying. Maude was dying. She repeated the word over
and over, even whispering it out loud, but she couldn't
make it mean anything. She had had no experience
with death. She came from a time and a culture where
families gathered together in moments like that, where
deathbeds left no room for privacy or loneliness, but
she had been very young when her father died, not
much older when she lost her mother, and she had
been shielded from that final reality. She had no frame-
work now, nothing to help her understand or recognize what was happening. She sensed dimly that she
ought to feel something, anger or pity—something!
—but all she could think was that Errol was with her,
and he was holding the same cold hand that she had
held before.

The sweat seemed to chill on her body, making her
clothes clammy and uncomfortable. She looked up at
the swan again, dark and still, and thought what se-

crets it must know, if only it could talk. The whole house seemed full of secrets tonight, with shadows closing in and no sounds of life from outside. But the only secret that mattered was the one behind that closed door into the hall.

The friction between Errol and his younger brother . . . she had a feeling that was the key to the whole thing. Whether D'Arcy was right or wrong, whether there really had been something between them—whether they actually were lovers—plainly he believed it, and he hated his brother for it. D'Arcy was arrogant, but he wasn't stupid. Would he have believed so strongly if he didn't have some basis for it?

And there were other things too. She stirred slightly, settling her feet underneath her. Things she had noticed for some time and stored away in her mind. The look on Errol's face when he had cradled Maude in his arms in the back of the wagon, as if he had been terrified he was going to lose her then. His irrational anger when he found out she and D'Arcy were married, though he had know for years it was bound to happen. And that woman on the street in Sydney. He had stopped dead in his tracks and stared as if he had seen a ghost—and all because she bore a faint resemblance to Maude.

"Oh, God . . ."

She leaned back in the chair and closed her eyes, but she couldn't drop off to sleep. It was hard to sort things out when she was tired and confused and didn't know what to think. All she knew was that the doctor had come and gone again, and Errol was alone in that room with Maude, and he would not leave until she died.

26

It was over in the early hours of the morning. Stacey was still sitting in the same chair when she heard the hall door open. Even before she looked up, she knew she was going to see Errol. And she knew what he was going to say.

"She's gone."

His voice was heavy, but controlled. Stacey scanned his face, searching for some sign of emotion, but nothing showed. It was as if he had prepared himself before he came out, setting his features in a deliberate mask, and she could only guess what he was feeling.

"I'm sorry," she said quietly. "I know how much you . . . you cared for her. And I'm sorry I tried to keep you from coming back. I was wrong. You would never have forgiven yourself if you hadn't been here."

If he heard what she said, he gave no sign. His shirt was rumpled, and he reached down automatically, tucking it into his trousers as he glanced at the window that opened onto the veranda.

"Someone has to tell D'Arcy," he said heavily.

"Oh." Stacey moved numbly, wriggling her feet out and planting them on the floor. "Yes, of course . . . he ought to know." It was funny, she had forgotten D'Arcy again. But for all his cowardice, for all that he hadn't been there when his wife needed him, he had to be hurting now. "I'll do it. I think he's still on the veranda. He was a while ago anyway."

Errol's eyes clouded as he looked back. "There's no need for that. It's my place as his brother. I'll tell him myself."

"No." Stacey shook her head firmly. "It will be easier for D'Arcy, I think, coming from me."

"I daresay it will." His face relaxed, and for an instant she almost thought he was smiling. "We haven't grown to be the best of friends over the years, my brother and I. Very well, then—if you are willing."

She thought he was going to go back into the bedroom, but he turned instead and made his way toward the rear of the house. She could hear the sound of leather boot heels echoing along the covered passage to the kitchen. He was back a minute later with the doctor, and the two men disappeared into the hall as Stacey opened the front door.

Outside, in the paddock, moonlight shimmered almost day-bright on parched silver grass, but the veranda was so dark she could hardly see where she was placing her feet. The silence was eerie. The drought had dried the creek, and even the wild dogs were still. The air was hotter than usual. Ordinarily at least a breath of breeze stirred in the hours after the sun went down, but tonight there was nothing.

"D'Arcy?"

She called his name in a hushed tone. No answer came, but she hadn't really expected one. If he were there, she would have heard him breathing in the stillness. She tried again on the side veranda, with no better luck, then started down the steps.

She had just reached the bottom when she saw him. The yard was an open expanse, sweeping from the homestead to outbuildings some distance away. There had never been any trees near the house; she had noticed that the first time she rode up in a rented carriage, but she hadn't questioned, simply accepting it, as she accepted so many other strange things in this strange new land. Now it made it easier to spot him. Someone had left an old crate overturned at the edge of the drive, and he was sitting on it, staring at mountains that were a deep purple blur on the horizon.

The only sound was the rustling of her petticoats. He looked up when she was still a few steps away, and she saw his face in the moonlight, and knew that he understood why she was there.

"Oh, my dear . . ." she said awkwardly, "I am so sorry."

His hand jerked back, an odd, abrupt motion. "Are you indeed?" A funny sound came out of his throat, and she realized to her horror that he was laughing. "I should have thought you were waiting for something like this. She was a very pretty rival, and a wily one. You must be glad to have her gone." A stench of brandy mingled with the heat and dust, and Stacey took a step back.

"You're drunk." Waves of disgust flooded over her. "Your wife was in there dying, and all you could do was sit on an old crate and swill brandy!"

"Of course I was 'swilling brandy,' as you so prudishly put it. What the hell was I supposed to do? Read a rousing adventure novel? Or bed down for a cozy night's sleep in the bunkhouse?"

"You could have been inside with your wife. Didn't it occur to you that she might have wanted you? Might have needed to hold your hand? My God, D'Arcy, did you stop to think, just once, that she might have been afraid, dying alone?"

"Alone?" He gave an little snort, somewhere between a laugh and a sob. "She wasn't alone. You know that as well as I. She was with the only man she every wanted or needed! My brother. Errol."

Stacey felt something tighten inside her. That insane jealousy again—it was becoming an obsession. "You don't know what you're saying. You're angry and hurt, and trying to lash out—"

"Dammit, it's true! Hide from it if you want—if you can—but . . ." He half-rose, than sank back with a low moan. "Lord, Stacey, why are you doing this? I don't want to spar with you. If you can't understand, just let me be. I know you're not fond of me—"

"And whose fault is that?" She was stung by the unexpected rebuke. "What have you ever done—"

"Mine, mine, I admit it—all mine! I know I used you badly. I was a brute—I'm always a brute with beautiful women. I don't blame you for despising me. But you did like me once . . . didn't you?" He looked up, face twisting suddenly into an echo of his former charm. "Just a little? And I have been better these past months. You have to admit that."

"Well . . ." Stacey stared at him. It was amazing, the way he changed. Savage anger one minute, almost boyish wistfulness the next. "Let's just say you haven't been any worse."

"I did love her," he said softly. "Truly I did . . . with all the unrequited passion of a trashy romance. That's no excuse, you're thinking, and I suppose you're right. But it seemed like a excuse at the time. You have no idea how it hurts, loving someone and knowing that person will never love you back. Do you know what I was doing just now?"

"No. . . . What?"

"I was thinking what she was like when she was a little girl. Lord, she was such a pretty thing—her hair was redder then. I used to call her 'copper-top' and she pretended to get angry, but I think she liked it all along. She would flirt with me sometimes, and I would be so damn flattered. I tried to be blasé, but oh, God, I was! Then she'd go off and flirt with my brother, and I'd get so mad I wouldn't speak to her for days."

He fell silent, brooding again, though his voice had been almost cheerful for a second. In spite of herself, Stacey's heart went out to him.

"She *did* love you, D'Arcy. No matter what she may have done, she did genuinely love you. I was with her an hour before she died, and I know."

"Did she say she loved me?" He glanced up sharply. Stacey caught a mixture of sarcasm and hope in his eyes. "Did she actually say, in so many words, that she loved me?"

"No-o-o-o . . ." Stacey hesitated. It was strange, thinking back, that she hadn't. But then, she had been so weak, and there were other things to talk about. "No, but she didn't need to! I could see it . . . feel it . . . every second I was with her. She loved you very much. With all the love in her heart."

"Are you saying that to convince me—sweet little platitudes to comfort the bereaved—or are you trying to convince yourself that your husband has been faithful? That he hasn't been romping in the hay with my dear departed bride?"

"No! How can you say such a thing?" Stacey gaped

at him in shock. No matter what he thought, this wasn't the time to indulge his evil suspicions. "You aren't much of a man, are you, maligning your wife like that? She just died a few minutes ago. Dear heaven, she isn't even cold yet! And she died giving birth to your son!"

"My son?" He jumped up from the crate and began to stalk back and forth, pacing off a small square like a tiger in a cage. "*My* son? Do you really think it was my son that left her bleeding her life away on the sheets in there?"

"Of course it was."

"There's no 'of course' about it! Are you so naive? Or are you pretending because it's convenient? That wasn't *my* son they put in a box in the ground two days ago. It was your husband's."

"Errol's?" The warmth drained out of her body. It was all she could do to stand there and gape at him. Maude carrying Errol's baby? That would explain D'Arcy's strange behavior—if it were true. But it couldn't be! "I don't believe you. I don't believe anything you're saying! You're lying."

"Am I?" He whirled suddenly, eyes glowing out of deep, shadowy pits. "Do I look like I'm lying? You said before I wasn't much of a man, and maybe you were right. Certainly I didn't father my wife's baby."

"But you can't mean . . . That's . . . that's . . ." Stacey heard herself stammering as she tried desperately to collect her thoughts. "That's ridiculous! You can't *know* something like that. Even if Errol did have an affair with Maude—and I'm not agreeing for a second that he did—you slept with her yourself before you were married! Don't forget, I heard you that night in Sydney."

"Clutching at straws?" He propped one foot up on the crate and leaned forward. "That night in Sydney was a long time ago. Maude hasn't exactly been . . . generous with her favors since then. The doctor told me the morning the boy was born that he was a seven-month baby. And seven months ago, Maude was being coy and virtuous. You see, I really *was* sleeping in the guestroom all those nights at Mirandola when you thought I was such a rake."

There was no denying the bitterness in his voice, and Stacey found herself recalling the one time she had met Maude's father, and how she had thought then that he might have made a good chaperon. D'Arcy might be mistaken, but she didn't think he was lying.

And how could a man be mistaken about something like that?

"Maybe . . . the doctor was wrong. It does happen, doesn't it? Doctors aren't infallible. Maybe he just thought it was a seven-month baby and it wasn't."

"Doctors aren't wrong about things like that. Husbands, maybe. But doctors? Never. God help me, I hoped—I really *hoped*—until then."

"But surely you thought the baby was yours when you married her. You did know she was pregnant, didn't you?"

"Oh, yes." He swung himself upright and started to laugh, a harsh, staccato sound. "I was so damned proud when she told me. I thought I'd just proved my virility. God, what a fool! Even later, even after I started to wonder, I didn't let myself think about it. Then he told me, the son of a bitch, it was a seven-month baby, and I knew I hadn't been with her, that way, seven months ago. And your husband wasn't exactly sharing *your* bed at the time."

"No!" Stacey shouted it, trying to drive away the ugly doubts he was sowing in her mind. "No. It isn't true. It can't be true!"

"Deny it if you want . . . I don't care." He sank onto the crate again, dropping his head in his hands. Stacey stared fascinated as his hair tumbled in a dark cascade over his fingers. From somewhere nearby, a sound broke the silence, a sharp clanging like metal against metal. "God knows, it doesn't matter. Don't you understand, I don't give a damn what you think. Or do. It doesn't change anything for me."

Stacey stood for a second, listening to the noises that reverberated through the night, wondering vaguely what they were, not really caring.

"Oh, God . . ." she whispered. "Please . . . please . . ." She knew she was pleading. She could hear it in her voice. *Even if you have to lie*, she was begging him, *say it isn't so*! But his eyes, when he looked up, were too full of his own misery to see her pain.

"Just go away," he said hoarsely. "I don't care whether you believe me or not. Your precious husband's in his own private hell now, and so am I. Go away and leave me alone."

Stacey turned, too numb even to protest as she made her way slowly toward the veranda. The metallic sound continued, ringing and rhythmic. Like workmen in the barn . . . but why would workmen be out so late?

Could it be true? That unspeakable thing D'Arcy had said? Plainly he thought it was. Always before, there had been a little room for doubt. Always before, the things he said—the ugly insinuations he made—were intended to hurt her. But this time he hardly seemed to know she was there.

Only . . . could a man be sure a baby wasn't his? Not for the first time, Stacey cursed the rigid Victorian conventions that kept women in such ignorance about the most elemental facts of life. Could a doctor really know about a seven-month baby? Were there set stages of an infant's development, so much at six months, so much at six and a half, so much at seven? Was there no margin for error at all?

Oh, God, what if it was true? What if the baby really *was* Errol's?

She reached the steps and caught at the railing, hanging on as she started to climb. Her legs were shaking so badly she was afraid she would fall if she let go. Had another woman's body responded where her own had failed? Had Maude been Errol's secret mistress—and had she borne him a child?

Stacey paused partway up the steps, just beneath the shadow of the roof. She had thought her love for Errol was enough, that he didn't have to love her in return, as long as he wanted her and accepted her in his life. She had thought all she had to do was to get through this terrible night without anything being said out loud, and then they could go back to the way they were and start pretending again. Now she was not so sure.

You have no idea how it hurts . . . loving someone

and knowing that person will never love you back. But she did know. She knew very well—and, oh, it did hurt.

What if the baby they had buried was Errol's son? The only son he would ever have? What if she never managed to conceive herself? Would she be able to sit across the table from him, night after endless night, and make polite conversation and know that she could not give him the one thing he really wanted? That his heart belonged forever to a memory?

The sounds from the barn intensified, clanging sharply into the night, and Stacey realized suddenly what they were. The coffin. Errol was out there, alone . . . and he was making Maude's coffin.

A man had come to the door once—she remembered it clearly—just after the floods last year. His face had been expressionless, like the faces of all the drifters who camped by the creek. He had asked for medicine for his little girl, who was sick, but he brought it back a short time later, saying the child had died and requesting wood for a coffin. Errol had offered to build it for him, but the man had refused.

"How can you let him do it himself?" Stacey had cried, appalled, as the man disappeared into the night. "It must be agonizing."

"The child is his," Errol had replied, shutting the door. "And the grief. There are things a man has to do for himself."

Was that what Errol was doing now? The sounds vibrated through the darkness, biting into her bones. He hadn't asked about the baby, not as far as she knew . . . but perhaps the full force of that loss would come later. Was he assuaging his grief now with those hard, rhythmic blows of the hammer? Was he trying not to think that he had just lost the only woman he would ever love?

She sank down on the steps and buried her head in her hands and tried to cry, but the tears wouldn't come.

IV

INTO THE
MORNING . . .

27

The last streaks of crimson were fading from the sky the next morning as the little group of mourners made its way slowly toward the Cameron graveyard. Maude had been dead only four hours, but the brutal heat that was already turning the dawn world into a furnace left no time for flower-draped corpses in front parlors and weeping friends and family. If a body was not disposed of immediately, decomposition set in, and bloated flesh swarmed with flies and maggots. The stench was so vile it took away the last illusion of dignity.

Stacey followed a short distance behind the men who were carrying the coffin. They moved easily, but then, Maude had been a small woman, and they must have found their burden light. There had been no time to send for the minister, and it was Errol who came directly behind the pallbearers. A small black book was clasped in his hands. Stacey had never seen him pray before, but the leather was worn, and she sensed it had seen similar service.

There were no public cemeteries in the bush. The dead of Cameron's Creek were laid to rest on a shallow hill just above the last of the stagnant billabongs in the creek. A handful of scraggly gums lined the narrow plot of land. Dust coated their trunks and drooping leaves, turning them a ghostly gray. The wind had picked up, not cool, but almost unbearably hot, and puffs of fine sand crackled like static in the air.

The grave had already been opened, and the men laid the coffin inside, heaving and grunting, with no special ceremony. Stacey stood a little apart from the others and thought what a lonely spot it was. Perhaps on a balmy spring morning, with the rich moist smell of growing things, and the leaves a soft murmuring green, it might be pretty. Now it seemed achingly desolate.

There were surprisingly few graves. Stacey glanced around, half-surreptitiously, glad for something to occupy her mind. Perhaps a dozen wooden crosses rose from the barren earth; they had probably been painted once, but wind and weather had worn them down until the names were not even legible. Workers who had died on the station, she guessed, or drifters who had happened by—men without families to know or care where they had come to rest. The Cameron graves were clustered together at one end. That would be Kate's in the center, with a block of heavy gray stone that Stacey sensed would not have pleased her at all. John Cameron had a simpler marker, tasteful, more in keeping with the landscape. Beside him, an improbable flight of carved marble doves marked the final resting place of the beautiful Ellen.

Off to one side, almost out of the burial area, she spotted a small mound of earth, covered with a parched veneer of vegetation. There was no cross, no marker, not even a row of plain stones to fringe the border. The little girl who died last year after the floods? Stacey stood and stared at that empty place, and tried to imagine what it was like for a mother to watch her menfolk bury her child in a stranger's soil, and get back in the wagon and ride off again.

"I am the resurrection and the life, saith the Lord: he that believeth in me, though he were dead, yet shall he live."

Errol's voice broke the stillness, repeating the unfamiliar words of the Anglican service, and in spite of herself, Stacey's attention was drawn to the grave. As she turned and saw him standing there, she felt all the fear come back like a hot wind in her face. He looked so tall and remote, in his white shirt and dark workman's pants with a black string tie at his throat. Only a few days ago he had been her husband, generous and attentive, needing only the flimsiest excuse to draw her into his arms . . . or his bed. Now he was a stranger as he stood beside that gaping grave and read the last words over a woman who might have been his mistress.

"We brought nothing into this world, and it is certain we can carry nothing out. The Lord gave, and the Lord hath taken away; blessed be the name of the Lord."

Why does it have to be *Errol*? she thought as his voice droned on, only sound now, not words taking shape in her consciousness. It was all perfectly proper—as owner of the station, it was no doubt his place to officiate in the absence of a clergyman. Hadn't she noticed herself the prayer book had been used before? But it tore her heart that it was he who was speaking now, he who was uttering those last tender farewells . . . and she didn't even know what he was thinking!

The wind gusted, stinging sand into her face and whipping her skirt so fiercely she had to hold on with both hands. The sky had been darkening almost imperceptibly. It hardly seemed like dawn at all, but dusk drifting into night. Errol was stooping by the grave now; the dirt was in his hands, and she heard a dull spattering sound as it landed on the coffin. "Unto Almighty God we commend the soul of our sister departed," he was saying—but was that what he meant? Was he saying good-bye to his sister, his friend, the little girl he had known since she was a baby and watched grow up? Or was it the best and most beautiful part of his life he was burying?

Stacey had bowed her head with the others. Now she looked up through thick lashes, trying to read something—anything!—in his face. But whatever he was feeling, it was well hidden, and all she could see were clear, hard eyes and a wide jaw set in taut lines.

His face had been expressionless, too . . . the man who had come to beg a few crates to make a coffin for his child. There had been no sign of pain, no grief, no anger, but she had known it was there, beneath the surface, eating at his heart. Was that what was happening to Errol now? Was his pain so deep he could not let it show?

She tried to look around again, but her eyes were blurred and the other mourners were a haze. There were precious few of them, a true bush funeral where time and distance made all but the grimmest essentials impossible. Maude's father had not come; he had been ill the last few days, and it had been decided that the hasty night journey from Mirandola would be too much for him. D'Arcy, at least, had pulled himself together and was standing beside Errol, immaculately dressed in a clean white shirt, but so dazed, she half-suspected he was still too drunk to know what was going on. The rest were servants or those of the men who had found time from their busy chores to attend. Maude had been a favorite. They would miss her laughter and willful spirit, and they stood a respectful distance away, in shabby but mended clothes, dusty hats in their hands, looking awkward as men always did at the double mysteries of childbirth and death.

The dust swirled suddenly, eddying around the little group, and the wind began to howl, low and keening. A flash of white seared through the darkness, followed almost immediately by a resounding crash. Heat lightning? Every eye, even Errol's, looked up, and Stacey knew what they were thinking. The drought had left every living thing a dry, brittle shell, and dryness made the land a tinderbox that could erupt into flames at any time.

The wind eased, as if that single outburst had been enough to release nature's pent-up violence. After a second, Errol lowered his eyes to the book again, and Stacey heard him go on.

"Earth to earth, ashes to ashes, dust to dust; in sure and certain hope of the resurrection unto eternal life, through our Lord, Jesus Christ."

Such finality . . . as if it were really over. As if the earth had been filled in above the coffin, and Maude and everything she stood for gone at last, and they could forget.

Only they wouldn't forget. Stacey knew that now, with a certainty that sent chills through her, even in the sweltering heat. She had hoped and rationalized and pushed her suspicions to the back of her mind, but she could ignore them no longer. Errol would never forget Maude, not if he loved her—and Stacey could no longer hide from the truth. There was no going back to things the way they used to be. She could not be the spoiled young bride again, enjoying the trinkets her husband brought home and spending his money in all those wonderfully diverse shops in Sydney, and trying to pretend that was all there was to life.

She loved this man she had married. Loved him with a passion that was deeper than anything she had ever imagined, and she knew now there had to be honesty between them or everything was a sham. It wasn't enough to have his fondness, his indulgence. It wasn't enough to know he would never send her away. Love didn't exist in a vacuum. It was meant to be shared; otherwise it would wither and die, like dried grasses in the drought. She had to know the truth . . . even if it destroyed her.

And there was one person who could tell her.

The sky had turned a deep tawny color by the time she reached the small, roughly built cottage and dismounted, looping Golden Girl's reins over a rail in front. The wind was erratic, whipping clouds of dust around scanty shrubbery, and the horse pawed skittishly at the ground.

"Fitz? Are you there, Fitz?" She clutched her dress as she scurried around the side, toward the open porch where the artist worked. The wind blew her voice away, and she called again, louder: "Please be home, Fitz—I need you."

A heavy gust threatened to carry her away, and she grabbed at one of the support poles. The porch was so empty it looked abandoned. A sturdy table stood against the far wall, but there were no chairs, and neither beer bottles nor teacups nor artist's paraphernalia gave the place a lived-in look. For an instant she panicked; then she realized Fitz would have moved everything inside. The wind was howling so fiercely, he probably hadn't heard her.

She paused at the door, conscious that there was still one moment to turn back. One last moment to

untie her horse and leap into the saddle, and no one
but her would ever know she had run from the truth.

But she would know it, and she could not live with
it. She pounded with her fists on the door, flinging it
open and stepping inside.

The room was gloomy with shadows. The only light
seeped in through filthy windows on two side walls,
and at first Stacey could not see. Then her senses
picked up everything at once. The clutter she had
missed before was abundant here, porch furniture
jammed together, papers and sketchpads and heaven
knows what strewn across the floor. A reek of liquor
mingled with the smell of dirt and oil paints. Fitz was
at a small table in the corner, his arms flung out in
front of him, head resting clumsily on top of them. A
whimper came from below, and Stacey looked down
to see the dust-colored cat she had noticed before
peering out from between two oversize boots.

"Oh, no, Fitz—please. You can't be drunk. I have
to talk to you."

The wind died down as she forced the door shut. He
seemed to hear, for he raised his head groggily.

"What, my pretty?" His voice was so thick it was
hard to make out. "Does your hot-tempered husband
know you are here?" He looked around, shaking his
head, as if trying to get his bearings. "Damnably
dark—is it night already?"

"It's not night," Stacey said, exasperated. "It's morning. Much too early to be in such a state! I think the
whole world's gone mad. Everyone is drunk today."

"Everyone?" His lips twisted coarsely, and he gave
her a ribald wink. "And still morning? Are you sure
you have your facts straight, lady? *Everyone* is drunk?"

"Not everyone," she conceded. "Just you and
D'Arcy. He was so bad last night he could hardly
stand. I doubt he's any better now."

"Well . . . perhaps there's reason for that." He
seemed to sober slightly. His eyes were bright as he
gazed out of the shadows, but his face was splotched
and ruddy. "They buried her this morning, didn't they?"

Stacey nodded slowly. Something cold and hard
seemed to settle inside her. She wished now she hadn't

come, but she knew she wasn't going to turn back. "I want the truth, Fitz. I need to know."

"The truth?" He picked up a bottle and held it to the light, squinting ruefully at the state of its contents. " 'Tis strange, but true; 'for truth is always strange, stranger than fiction.' Don't recognize it? . . . Well, never mind. What is truth anyway but illusion? One man's truth is another man's lie—and no one knows the difference. Who are you to preach the truth to me when you don't even know what it is?"

Stacey stared at him helplessly, wondering if he was really as drunk as he seemed. She had thought she caught a glimmer of awareness in his eyes, but it was gone now, and he was sweeping his hands across the table in clumsy, searching motions.

"She was a beauty, wasn't she?" he said abruptly.

"She?"

"The lady they put in the coffin this morning. Or is 'lady' quite the word? I've always had a weakness for beautiful women. I wasn't there, you know. I hate seeing them fed to the worms. Beastly little slimy things. Damn, where is that glass?" He was groping again, knocking small objects off the table. The cat, startled, leapt out and scampered across the floor. "I left it here. It couldn't have walked away."

"How can you talk like that?" Stacey strode over to the table and leaned forward. "She's dead, Fitz. She gave birth to a baby—and they buried her next to him an hour ago. That's hardly a matter for coarse comments."

"You find my levity repulsive? What I find repulsive is the travesty of a ceremony that was no doubt uttered over her this morning. Probably by your husband. He plays the minister nicely when no man of God is around. 'Ashes to ashes' and 'life everlasting' in the same breath. Hedging his bets, don't you think? Religion is playacting. Haven't you discovered that yet? And hypocrisy. You wanted the truth? All right, I'll give it to you. The truth is: nothing lasts forever. Nothing beautiful. Nothing ugly. That's all there is to it." He found the glass and angled the bottle against it, trickling out a thin stream of whiskey. "And if the worms bother you . . . well, they'll be food for worms themselves in the end, won't they?"

Stacey shivered as he held the glass up, amber liquid glowing in the feeble light. The wind had started up again; she could hear loose boards banging against the sides of the house. "You can't mean that. You don't know what you're saying. It's . . . it's too awful!"

"It's you who don't know what you're saying." His eyes seemed to burn as he raised his head, and for just a second, looking at him, Stacey was frightened. "There have been other times and other beautiful women . . . and other funerals I have missed. Don't be so quick to judge when you don't understand." He flicked his fingers against the glass. "All these aren't strictly self-pity. . . . Or perhaps they are."

He lifted the glass, but Stacey reached out, holding him back. A few more drinks and she wouldn't be able to get anything out of him.

"I want the truth, Fitz."

"Ah?" His eyes turned murky. "There it is. That word again. Nasty word—truth. Everyone always thinks they want it, and no one really does."

"I told you before." Stacey tightened her hold, digging her fingers into his arm. "I *need* to know the truth. About my husband and Maude . . . and what happened between them. And I think you can give it to me. Unless you're too drunk."

"*Too* drunk?" He laughed shortly. "It doesn't work that way. Don't you know I'm just drunk enough so you'll get it out of me if you push? Dammit, a man loses all sense when he's got enough liquor in him! If *you* had any sense you'd get out of here before this goes any further. Why do you keep asking?" Hair tumbled around his face, dark in the shadows, and the white streaks stood out in his beard. "Why do you ask . . . when you know you don't want to hear the answer?"

"Oh, my God . . ." Stacey stared at him, barely daring to breathe. "It's true, isn't it? . . . everything I feared. You wouldn't mind so much if it weren't."

"Yes, it's true." Something seemed to go out of him, and he collapsed into the chair, looking small and suddenly older. Stacey had let go of his hand, but he made no effort to drink. "You mustn't blame him . . . it was mostly her doing. I don't think any man could have gotten away once she set her cap for him."

The wind had subsided; the boards outside stopped flapping, and the room was so still Stacey's voice sounded unnaturally loud. "D'Arcy said . . . he told me once she always wanted Errol. Right from the time she was a little girl. And in the end, she got him."

"Well . . . he was right." He raised the glass, taking a hefty gulp. The liquor soothed his throat, warm as it went down. "I told you that other time you asked—I warned you to let go. I thought you were going to do it. But you didn't."

"No . . ." The silence was almost oppressive now. The smells of the room were stale and nauseating. "But all that happened a long time ago. It's over now . . . isn't it?"

Fitz set the glass down. "Is that what you want me to say?"

"What I want . . . is to know."

"No, that isn't what you want, but it's too late now." The bottle had got his tongue, and there was no way he could hold back. "It *is* over . . . now. With her death. But I don't think it would have been over any other way."

"You mean he was with her even after he married me?"

"Of course he was with her. Don't look at me with big sad eyes like that. Why did you start this blasted business if you couldn't take it? They were together right up to the time of her marriage, maybe even after. I don't know, and I don't give a damn."

"Then . . ." Stacey swayed weakly, catching hold of the back of a chair by the table. "It really was *his* baby? Errol's?"

Fitz's head jerked up. "Who told you that?"

"D'Arcy. He guessed—he *knew*—when the doctor said it was a seven-month baby."

"D'Arcy . . . ?" He leaned back again, half-whistling through his teeth. "The poor stupid bastard. I never cared for him, but he must be writhing in purgatory now. Ah, but there's an end to purgatory, isn't there? And I don't think there's any end for young Mr. Cameron."

Stacey sank down in the chair, not even feeling the wood beneath her. "You're sure, aren't you? You're not just guessing—like D'Arcy was. You're *sure* the baby Maude bore was my husband's."

"She was sure of it, which is more to the point. Maude always liked an audience—she had a way of saying more than she should. She may have wanted Errol all those years, but she knew he wouldn't marry her. She'd been promised to D'Arcy the day she was born."

"I know," Stacey said numbly. "The will. D'Arcy told me all about it."

"The will?"

"His father's will. Errol was given the property, and D'Arcy was to have Maude. It was a strict condition— Errol would lose everything if he didn't abide by it. That was why he couldn't marry Maude himself."

"Maybe." Fitz shifted uncomfortably, squirming in his chair. "That might have been it, of course. But maybe it was just that she was committed to someone else. Your husband has a strong, if somewhat misguided sense of honor. At any rate, since she couldn't have him, she made sure she had his child."

"You mean she did it on purpose?" Even as the words slipped out, Stacey realized with a rush of horror they were true. Maude stopped sleeping with D'Arcy—and a short time later she was pregnant! She'd been trying to conceive, and she wanted to make sure it was Errol's.

And now she had him forever. Darkness seemed to fill the room, tangible and brooding. She was dead, and she had him forever, because she had borne him a son and Stacey could not. Because it was her baby, and his, buried beside her in that desolate cemetery, and it would be a bond between them forever.

Dropping her head in her hands, Stacey began, soundlessly, to weep.

"Damn!" Fitz sat across from her, a big awkward bear, staring at splashes of jet-black hair spilling across the table. "Damn." He moved clumsily, spilling the glass as he laid his hand on her head, coaxing her to look up."I didn't mean this to happen. God as my witness, I never wanted to say those things. . . . I wouldn't have done it if you hadn't caught me drunk. Never catch a man drunk if you don't want to find out what he's capable of."

"No . . . it wasn't your fault." Even through her tears, Stacey could see that he was genuinely distressed, and she almost felt guilty. "I asked for the truth. I had to know."

"And now you do?"

There was something almost ironic in his tone, but it was lost on Stacey, she was so wrapped up in her own unhappiness. "Yes," she said softly. Fitz would never deliberately hurt her. He was her friend; he had been, from the beginning. Besides, what reason would he have to lie? "Yes, now I know."

28

"I want to go home." Stacey tilted her chin up as she faced her husband in the brooding midday darkness. The neat phrases she had rehearsed over and over on the way back vanished from her mind, and all she could do was blurt out the words. "I've been thinking about it all day, and I want to go home!"

"What the devil are you talking about?" Errol had just come out of the house and was standing in the scanty shelter of the portico, a brown leather jacket in his hands. The storm was getting worse by the minute. The sky was twilight-gloomy, and shadows made his face look gaunt and worn. "And where have you been? I thought you were inside. You know I don't want you out in weather like this."

"I . . . I had someplace to go." Stacey felt her heart sink. He hadn't even realized she was gone! He had been so caught up in feelings about Maude, he hadn't seen her running down the hill from the graveyard like all the demons in hell were after her. "There was something I had to do. But that isn't important now. Didn't you hear—"

"Dammit, it is important! You know better than that. We talked about the heat storms—I've described them to you often enough." He shook out his jacket as he spoke and began to put it on. The air was hot, but the wind had a way of driving sand into a man's skin, and he needed the protection. "I told you very specifically that I wanted you to go inside if something like this came up—and stay there. You could have been risking your life on a day like this."

"Well, I wasn't." Stacey tried to sound more convincing than she felt as she glanced back at the yard. It was eerie, the way the clouds massed, heavy and brownish-gray with no hint of rain at all. "I know my way around now. Anyway, that doesn't matter. We have to talk, Errol. You must have heard what I said. I want to go home."

He turned slowly, poised in the act of putting one arm through his sleeve. "What do you mean . . . you want to go home? This *is* your home now. Glenellen. And you *are* here."

"I mean my real home. Where I come from."

"San Francisco?"

His eyes were buried in valleys of darkness. Stacey couldn't see their depths, but she had the sudden feeling he knew what she was thinking, and all her courage left her. She had planned everything so carefully. She couldn't stay with him. Their whole life together had been a lie. It was humiliating, the way he had treated her—it would be doubly humiliating now that she knew the truth—and she thought she had figured out exactly what she wanted to say. But when he looked at her like that, intense and unfathomable, it was easier to evade.

"Just . . . just for a visit. San Francisco is so different. It's in the hills, you know, on such a pretty bay. Everything is cool and green. I can't help missing it."

"You mean . . . you're homesick." He finished putting on his jacket, looking almost casual as he buttoned it up, but his eyes never left her.

"Yes, I'm homesick. That's it." Stacey clutched at the flimsy rationale. Better to let him think that than deal with the truth. Better for both of them to pretend it was just going to be a short stay. Later there would be letters, diminishing in frequency, and the references to coming back would grow fewer and fewer. "I haven't seen my sisters for a long time. We were very close—though I didn't realize it at the time—and I worry about them. Especially Zee, the youngest. I want to see them again. Surely you can understand that."

He was still watching her, she could sense it, looking down from the top of the steps to where she was standing, but she couldn't bring herself to meet his gaze. "This is hardly the time I would have chosen to leave," he said slowly.

"Oh, but it's the best time! Don't you see?" She knew her voice sounded forced, but she had to convince him. "It's so awful here now. The drought and the dust . . . and these terrible dry storms, all clouds and no rain. This would be the perfect time to get away."

"For you, perhaps . . . but you must be aware that I can't leave now. Two droughts in a row have taken their toll on the station. We would have had to come back from Sydney soon anyway. And then, of course, there's the danger of fire."

"Yes, I know. You have to be here to protect the land. I understand that. But . . . couldn't I go alone?" She looked up at last, trying to gauge his reaction. "Honestly, it would be better that way. You could come later . . . if you wanted. You'd hate being there all the time anyway. It would be so boring, just me and my sisters—and all that 'girl talk.' You wouldn't enjoy it at all."

He paused briefly, toying with the top button of his jacket. "Didn't you tell me," he said thoughtfully, "that you couldn't go back again? That with your grandfather dead, there'd be a new head of the family— one of your brothers-in-law you didn't like?"

Stacey gulped nervously. He isn't going to let me go, she thought. He sees what I'm doing, and he doesn't care—not really—but his pride won't let a woman walk out on him!

"Not my brother-in-law. The father of a potential brother-in-law. And it doesn't seem to have worked out that way. The last letters I've had are promising. It looks like the two Richards—my older sisters' husbands—are standing up to him. So there'll always be . . ." She hesitated. *There'll always be a refuge for me.* Only she didn't dare say it. If he didn't already know what she was up to, that would give her away for sure. "So . . . it'll always be comfortable for me to go back. Zee hasn't even been pushed into marriage yet, and it looks like she's having second thoughts. That's another reason I want to go back."

"Well, I'm afraid it's out of the question." There was as much finality in his tone as the words. "I can't let you go alone, and it's impossible for me to escort you now. "Unless, of course"—he paused, studying her pointedly—"you had another escort in mind."

Why was he looking at her that way? As if he expected something. "No . . . no, of course not . . ."

"Then it's settled. Maybe next year. But there's too much to do now. We'll talk about it later." He started down the steps, leaving Stacey at the top to stare after him.

"But . . . you can't just say no and walk away!" Frustration turned to anger, bursting inside her. He had been lying, right from the beginning. She had lied too, one little lie, and he had made her pay for it dearly. And all the time, he had been making love to another woman—and fathering a child by her! Now he was trying to tell her what she could and couldn't do! "It's not your choice to make. If I decide to go to San Francisco, I will—whether you like it or not!"

She was rewarded by a faintly surprised look as he reached the ground and turned back. The wind was almost savage now, whipping dark hair away from his face. "That, I'm afraid, is impossible. I am your husband. You will do as I say."

"Will I, indeed?" She tossed her head, looking more like a little girl than the independent woman she intended. "You may be my husband, but you are not my master or my sole support. Don't forget, I'm an heiress in my own right. Grandfather left me well-off. I can take my own money and buy my own ticket, and there's nothing you can do about it!"

"Nothing?" A look of weary amusement crossed his face, and Stacey realized she had made a mistake. "You have a quaint idea of the role of women in today's society, madam. The money is yours, I grant, but it was left in my charge, as your husband. You can't touch it. Maybe in San Francisco, with those brothers-in-law to act for you. But here in Australia . . . ? You have to have *my* permission to spend a cent."

Stacey stared at him, aghast. Of all the things she

had imagined, this was the worst. It ought to have been so simple. A little playacting on both sides . . . a polite pretext that the separation was "only for a while." Was he really going to force her to stay? And all because of his pride!

Or perhaps—a little bit—his passion too. She *was* his wife, and clearly he liked having her in his bed, though that was as far as it went.

"You mean you'd keep it yourself? You wouldn't let me have it—even though it's Alexander money, and my grandfather left it to me?"

He gave her a last long look as he turned away.

"That's precisely what I mean."

The wind whipped the dust up, driving it into Errol's face. He lowered his head as he hurried down an incline and across the open stretch of land that led to the stable. Overhead, the clouds had rolled together, forming a billowy mass with the elusive darkness of rain, but he had lived in the bush too long to be fooled. You could feel a rain cloud even before it blew across the horizon, smell the moisture in the air. All he smelled today was dryness, and the gritty dust that coated every hair in his nostrils and made it hard to swallow.

Damn! What was there about women that made them turn contradictory at the most inopportune times? He hadn't been fooled for an instant, all that prattle of Stacey's about wanting to go to San Francisco for a "short visit," fussing over the littlest sister. He had seen the misery in her face and the way she avoided looking at him, and he knew that life in Australia had suddenly grown too hard and she was hungering for the comfort of home. But he was blasted if he knew why.

Or even, he thought, turning his collar up, if it was Australia that had disappointed her—or the man she had married.

A bolt of lightning shimmered across the sky, breaking into jagged streaks of multiveined brightness. The land was clearly illuminated for an instant; then everything dissolved in muddy purple again. The storm was intensifying. They had been lucky that time. No tell-tale flashes of red-gold in the darkness pinpointed spots where fires had broken out. But if it went on . . .

Errol dug his hands in his pockets and hurried toward the stable. It was one storm or another, it seemed—on his land or in his life. He could still see Stacey, the way she looked that morning, childlike and vulnerable, standing beside the open grave. He had had the feeling she wasn't thinking sadly abstract thoughts about death and the transience of life. Hell, whom was he kidding, telling himself he didn't know why she was leaving him? He knew perfectly well. He just didn't want to think about it.

A makeshift lean-to had been erected as a henhouse on one side of the stable, only temporary, but he'd never had time to build anything better. The door was bulging slightly, and he put his shoulder to it, prop-ping it with a length of board. Faint clucking sounds came from within, and he knew that the hens were settled on their roosts, riding out the storm, heads tucked down as thin films of dust drifted over them.

He had been so sure for a while that everything was going well. The wind seemed to ease, but he stuck close to the wall. Certainly, they had been happy in Sydney. Stacey had been like a little girl, excited at everything, and pleased, he thought, with him. At least she had welcomed him enthusiastically the many times he came to her bed. But that, of course, was the big city, with all its lights and glamour . . . and this was an isolated station at the other end of the world.

The stable door groaned as he pushed it open, and he stepped into a haze of dusty lanternlight and familiar smells. He liked the outbuildings, liked working with the horses and the farm animals, and he always felt more at home here than in the parlors and game rooms of the main house. Had it been a mistake, taking Stacey to Sydney? He had intended it as a diversion, a reward for her patience and remarkable lack of complaining through the last, long drought and the flooding that had followed. But she had barely had time to adjust to life on a great sheep station—she had

just started to take an interest in lambing and why the
mobs were moved from one paddock to another and
what went on during shearing. Had it been a mistake,
giving her a taste of theaters and concerts and elegant
restaurants, only to snatch them back again?

A rusty lantern was hanging on the far wall, its light
filtering down to where Golden Girl stirred restlessly
in her stall. Her coat was still sweaty, and Errol noted
with a frown that dust was caking on it. The boy
hadn't gotten to her yet; he would have to speak to
him in the morning. Strange, Stacey usually took care
of the mare herself. He ran a hand along that fine
sleek neck, then found a comb and began to curry her
down. Faint traces of foam showed at her nose, and
her eyes were wary, but he felt only a slight quiver as
he worked her over. Stacey must have ridden her hard
and fast . . . and she must have had more than a little
on her mind.

Maybe he had been too hard on her. He moved
briskly and efficiently, grooming the horse with strong,
smooth strokes. She had loved being in Sydney, and
he had loved it too, enjoying the pleasures of the city
with only a little uneasiness at the thought of responsibilities left behind. She had looked so hurt, that last
morning when he berated her. Damn his foul temper
anyway! It hadn't been unreasonable, wanting to stay.
Immature perhaps—but then, she *was* young. And
wasn't it her very youth that so charmed and entranced him?

Why the devil had he expected her to react any
differently? Family obligations—he had thrown that in
her face. But what did obligations of any kind mean to
a girl that age? All she saw were parties and excitement, and who could blame her for not wanting to
leave that and come back to a house of death? Maude
wasn't even *her* family. She had tried to be kind, but
she had been ill much of the time and Stacey had
barely had a chance to get to know her. It hadn't been
fair, asking her to give up everything for someone she
hardly knew.

Fair . . . or, as it turned out, wise.

He finished tending to the mare and put the comb

back in its place, throwing one last look around before heading for the door. The horses were uneasy; they couldn't keep their heads still, but they were no more distressed than usual during a storm. There was nothing else he could do, no reason to stay. Ordinarily he would have made a round of the home paddock, checking everything there, but the men knew their jobs, and the sheep had a way of huddling together on the ground while the heat and dust blew over them. Besides, he had more important things to do.

The lightning flared up again, just as he opened the door. It seemed to come from everywhere at once, a starkly dramatic sight, beautiful and grotesque at the same time. The sky was a velvet backdrop, dark and eerie, as flash after flash of sheer white arced across it. Thunder boomed continuously, each new clap melding into the last until all he heard was one vast roll.

What was it she had said? It's so awful here . . . the drought and the dust and the storms. It wasn't awful—it was terrifying. No wonder she wanted to get away.

He stood in the doorway, waiting as the final flashes faded and the storm seemed to lose some of its force before darting across the open space to the house. He couldn't let her go, of course. There was already a rift between them—he had sensed that all too clearly a few minutes ago when she wouldn't look him in the eye—and rifts that were allowed to continue had a way of deepening. Whoever said that absence makes the heart grow fonder had been a fool. Absence made the heart forget.

He couldn't let her go . . . but maybe he could compromise.

Stacey was still in the entry hall when he returned to the house. She looked more like a little girl than ever, sitting on the stairs, knees tucked halfway up to her chin as she leaned against the curving wall and stared at the ceiling. The storm seemed to be ending. Savage winds were dying away as quickly as they had come, and the clouds had already drifted past. Murky light seeped through the windows at the base of the dome, and Fitz's painted jungle seemed to be ablaze.

Errol lingered a moment in the doorway, waiting for her to sense his presence and look up. When she didn't, he went over and sat beside her.

"I didn't mean to be so rough on you. I'm sorry."

The light gave her face an almost elfin solemnity as she turned. "For what?"

"For quite a bit, I'm afraid. I hope you aren't going to make me list my transgressions. It wasn't very kind of me, dragging you from Sydney when you didn't want to come. You're right—it *is* awful here. If you'd like to go back, you can. As a matter of fact, I think it would be a good idea."

"Back?" Stacey looked at him, puzzled. "You mean . . . to Sydney?"

"I should have suggested it before. I would have, but . . . well, my temper has a way of flaring up. I *am* your husband. I do demand obedience. But not unreasonable obedience. San Francisco is out of the question, but there's no reason you shouldn't go to Sydney."

You. Stacey did not miss the subtle emphasis on that word. For just a second, when he sat beside her, she had thought he was going to take her in his arms, and she had dared to hope, illogically, that everything was going to be all right. Now she saw that he was only proposing a different kind of separation, one more acceptable in his circles—the wife properly ensconced in her villa in town and the husband off tending to whatever it was he tended in the bush.

"You won't be coming with me then?"

"I can't. You know that. As long as the drought continues, I have to stay here. But there's no reason for you to stay too. Dammit, with all this dryness, you shouldn't stay! You've never seen a bushfire, but I have, and believe me, you'll be safer in Sydney. I'd feel much better, knowing you were there."

"I see." Stacey rose and went down the stairs to the marble-smooth floor below. The windows beside the door were clear now, and the world was returning to normal. It looked almost like daytime again, though the dust had still not settled, and a brown haze hung in the air. He would feel better, he had said, with her gone. There it was, out in the open at last. She had gotten what she wanted—*almost* what she wanted—but there was no savor in it.

"Sydney seems very far away now."

"I suppose it does." He was aware of a tremor of surprise in his voice. That was not what he had expected to hear. "But I can't imagine you're averse to the idea. All those shops you love so much are right there waiting."

"Oh . . . I don't think it's going to be quite the same." She twisted her lips in a deliberately ironic smile. "I can hardly buy out the stores when I can't touch a cent of my money, now, can I? Why, I'll probably starve on the train. I won't be able to get off at any of the stops for a hearty meal, or even pick up a loaf of bread from a vendor on the platform."

He acknowledged her words with a wry grin. She had a point, the minx, and plainly she was going to drive it home. "I always keep a little cash on hand. I think I can spare you some. Starvation, at least, will be averted."

"Carefully doled out of my inheritance, I assume?"

"If you prefer it that way. Or a gift from a husband who doesn't particularly like eating his words. It should be enough to tide you over for a few days. After that, my agent will contact you with all the spending money you need. And, of course, you can charge anything you want in the shops."

The meaning was not lost on Stacey. She could have all the money she wanted, his or hers—as long as she spent it his way. There would not be enough for even a steerage ticket on a steamer to San Francisco if that was what she decided to do. "Very well, then, perhaps I will. Go to Sydney, I mean . . . as you suggested."

"I'm, uh . . . I'm glad. It'll do you good." He started to get up, then sat down again, feeling uncharacteristically awkward. He was aware that he was begging for the first time in his life, and he wasn't even sure what he was begging for. "You can leave in the morning if you want. The way the weather's been going, that would probably be best."

"Yes, I guess it would." She did not look back, but continued to stare through the window. It was funny,

the way things changed, all of a sudden. Now that the
storm was over, the paddock looked strangely serene.
It was almost a relief, the way things had turned out.
She had been sorry, when she came into the house,
that she had been so impulsive before. She was not at
all sure she wanted to go to San Francisco; she was not
even sure she really wanted to leave him. It was hard,
when he was sitting there, looking caring and concerned, and she remembered how much she had loved
him and all the dreams she had had of their life together. But she had to have time to think, and Sydney
with its gaslights and crowds and carriages rolling past
the house day and night was hardly the place for that.

"I think I will leave in the morning. . . . . First thing."

Only she wouldn't go to Sydney. She didn't know
where she was going, or how she would manage, but
somehow she had to find a place to herself. A place
where she could work things out and decide what to
do.

And she couldn't tell Errol what she was planning
because she knew he'd try to stop her.

29

Morning comes gently to the islands and coral reefs off the coast of Queensland. The air is cool with the last lingering memories of night, and dawn fades slowly. Life is just beginning. Geckos scurry along the shore, and silver gulls swoop down, landing on spindly legs as the first splashes of gold spill across the sand. It is a world of magic and serenity, and only the man—or woman—who comes quietly and alone can capture its fragile beauty.

For Stacey, who had never imagined such a world, it was like waking in the middle of a dream, with everything so slow and languid it hardly seemed real. She had gotten up before sunrise, as had become her habit in the week and a half she had been on the island, and the light had been barely bright enough to see as she made her way from the cottage to the leeward beach to greet the day. Now she stood ankle-deep in sand and listened to the cries of the gulls as the sun rose in a shimmering glory of color. It was low tide, and the brilliant aquamarine water was so clear she could pick out every pebble and grain of sand on the ocean floor.

. Wrasse Island had come as a surprise. She didn't know what she had expected, something denser, she supposed, with tropical vegetation and the kind of heat and humidity that made little beads of sweat stand out on her forehead. But the water here had a soothing coolness; even the sand was cool, especially in the mornings when she dug her toes into it, and except for stands of mangroves with their odd, stiltlike roots, there was only a sparse cover of shrubs and undergrowth. A fringe of sand ringed the entire island, widening to a pleasant beach on the leeward side,

and coral formations stretched out in extensive underwater flats, waiting for her to explore. All in all, she
thought contentedly, the perfect place to relax and
take stock of her life.

Strangely enough, it had been Fitz who found it for
her. She hadn't left the first thing in the morning after
all, but had delayed her journey two days, which gave
her one last chance to visit the artist in his hilltop
studio. She had gone reluctantly, not because she
really believed he could help her, but because it suddenly occurred to her that she had no place else to
turn.

She had found him red-eyed and short of temper,
dragging the rough-hewn table back from the interior
onto the open porch. He had had the good grace to
appear shamefaced, and Stacey sensed that he remembered all too well what he had revealed in his drunk-
enness the day before, and regretted it, though she
noticed he made no effort to soften his words.

He did try, halfheartedly, to talk her out of her
plans. But when he saw that she was determined, he
sat down and penned a letter of introduction to an old
friend, Matthew Duncan, who owned a small private
island—"You can walk around it in an hour," he had
emphasized—on what he casually referred to as the
barrier reef. Duncan had been shipwrecked there as a
youth, and had been so enchanted, he returned later
to build a cabin, which he used for sketching and
scientific study. Now that he was married and had a
family to care for, the place was virtually abandoned,
and Fitz was certain he would be more than happy to
lend it to the friend of a friend.

"But are you sure you want to do this?" he had
said, holding on to the letter one last minute. "Running away is easy. It's not always so easy to go back."

"I'm not running away," Stacey retorted, only half-
lying. She wasn't running—she was trying desperately
to find herself. "Anyway, I've thought it over very
carefully. It's what I have to do."

"I suppose you're right. You haven't much choice,
have you?" He met her eyes briefly, and Stacey felt
herself crumble inside as she remembered once again

what he told her and how much it had hurt. "All the same, I hope you know I'm sorry."

Stacey wriggled her toes in the sand, shaking off the memory. A gentle breeze wafted across the beach, and she flicked her hair over her shoulders. The shadow of a reef heron drifted past; sunlight played on pure white feathers as it landed on a ledge of stone jutting out of the water. It was a beautiful, cool morning, and it would be foolish, dwelling on unhappy thoughts just as the world was waking and everything seemed to be in harmony with everything else.

As it turned out, she hadn't needed Fitz's letter after all. It was still packed in her case in the one-room cabin, along with most of her other things. She had thought, when she got off the Sydney train at the next station and headed back in the opposite direction, that all she had to do was find the small coastal town Fitz had named. But when she arrived, she discovered to her dismay that the Duncans had migrated inland.

Fortunately, Wrasse Island was still uninhabited. A few well-chosen inquiries had led her to a Portuguese family—lighthouse keepers and pearl divers, if she understood their garbled English—living on a nearby island. A letter would hardly have been necessary, even if they had been able to read it. They had simply looked at her expensive dress and lace-trimmed bonnet, and accepted without question her right to go anywhere she chose. For a small sum, they agreed to ferry her to the island and drop a supply of food on the beach every afternoon. She had given them a few small coins in deposit; the rest she would pay when she left.

She still felt a little twinge of guilt when she thought about it. Most of her money was already spent; it had gone for fares and meals, and she was not at all sure she would have enough to pay up. But she had to have a place to be by herself, and she was ready to live one day at a time.

The waves lapped lightly against the shore. The ocean was as still as glass, with only the tiniest ripples. Stacey had brought a pair of thin-soled shoes with her, and she slipped them on now, wading out into the water. She had to move carefully, for the stones and shells were sharp, and she didn't want to break off fragile pieces of coral that had taken years to form.

Only a small part of the life of a coral reef showed from shore; the rest was teeming underwater, and there was no way she could see it without wading to her waist and plunging in. Fortunately she was a good swimmer. Grandfather had made sure all four of his girls were reasonably athletic, and she and Zee especially had taken to the sea with a zeal that sometimes alarmed him, particularly when they went out over their heads and started to fight.

The water was sparkling with a gemlike clarity. Only the faintest reflections floated on the surface to distort the soft colors and intricate patterns of a vast garden of coral beneath. It fascinated Stacey, thinking that all those prettily colored gems she had seen on jewelers' counters were not lifeless pieces of stone at all. They **were** living things, or the skeletons of living things, **who** had the ability to take calcium out of the water and form the rocklike shelters in which they had lived. As each tiny coral polyp had died, another had built its home on top, until eventually a structure of beauty and astonishing complexity had been formed. But they were delicate, these little creatures and the "houses" they had left behind. Storms and sunlight could destroy them, or crown-of-thorns starfish, or the footsteps of one careless human along an otherwise deserted shore.

Something moved in the water, and looking down, Stacey saw the fragile tentacles of a sea anemone floating on the current. It was hard to tell what color it was; absorbed sunlight gave it a warmish hue that blended into the sand. A brilliant yellow butterfly fish flitted past. A pretty creature, but almost comical, looking as if it were swimming backward with a great false eye near its tail.

Stacey had always thought of fish as shadows in the murky waters of a pond, or sleek silver-gray objects that sometimes appeared on platters in fancy restaurants with their heads on, which had made her cry as a little girl. Here they came in a rainbow of color. The little butterfly fish were the first she had learned to recognize, and she would always be partial to their distinctive stripes and chevrons, but others stood out too, and she enjoyed putting names to shapes.

Angelfish came in a number of varieties. She still had trouble telling them apart, but it was easy to pick out some of the boxfish—the males in gaudy blue and yellow, the females a blander green with reticulated sides—or the red emperors, or brown-and-white-spotted sweetlips, or the boldly orange-striped clown anemone fish, aptly called, for she could never look at them without laughing. Her special fondness was for the wrasses, perhaps because they were so pretty, perhaps just because the island had been named for them. They were more parrotlike than the parrotfish, at least the males, in startling shades of pink and blue, though it amused her to realize that they had not started out that way. Like many species on the reef, wrasses were hermaphrodites, beginning life as drab females and changing later to males when the need arose. An odd system, but practical, for even in small groups there was no possibility of one sex or another being depleted.

Stacey paused knee-deep in the water, glancing back at the shore, now some distance behind. A gull skimmed across the horizon, dipping low, then angled up again, and everything was still. The peacefulness of the setting, the sense of being utterly alone on that vast stretch of sand and sea, was an almost tangible presence, relaxing every muscle in her body, easing the hurts of her heart.

It was funny, the way things happened sometimes. She had thought, when she came, that she was going to agonize over her decision for weeks, that no matter how long she worried about it, she would never quite know what she wanted to do. But she did know. She had known almost the instant she stepped off the boat. She was just putting off thinking about what it meant.

She had to smile as she recalled the expression on the face of the Portuguese boy, Paulo, when he put her ashore that first afternoon. He was fourteen—fourteen and a half, he made a point of saying—and to him the idea that any woman would be on an abandoned island by choice was unthinkable.

"You no wanna be alone, lady," he had said, eyes dark and frankly wide. "W'at you gonna do, all by self? No good, woman alone on island."

"Actually, Paulo," she had told him, laughing, "it's very good indeed. That's why I came. I was looking for someplace quiet and serene."

"Quiet, sure." He had ignored that other word, which he didn't understand. "But much better for two, yes? Tell you w'at. My father, he no busy now." His face had taken on an avid look, and Stacey realized suddenly that, to him, she had the forbidden appeal of an older woman. "I come. Keep you company, yes?"

"Keep me company, no," she had replied firmly, turning away so he wouldn't see the laughter she couldn't quite suppress. She had never been an "older woman" before, and she was finding it distinctly amusing. "I'm sorry, Paulo. I appreciate the offer, but I really do want to be alone."

And she had been—in a way. Stacey glided into the water, a little surprised at how cool it felt against her skin. She had been alone . . . yet she didn't feel alone at all. Perhaps it was because there was so much life around her, in the air, the sea, burrowing into the sand itself. Or perhaps it was just because she was beginning to come to terms with her feelings at last.

The tide was coming in, and she was careful to stay close to shore, not letting herself drift too far out. It was only sensible, being cautious; there was no one to see if she got into trouble, or hear if she called for help. She had been so unhappy when she left Cameron's Creek. She had been afraid of life and everything it held, when she should have been reaching out and grasping with both hands! Flipping on her back, she floated above the submerged coral beds, eyes closed against the sun. It was so still here. Still, but not quiet. Not with the cries of the birds, and the wind whistling through the mangroves, and the waves lapping against the shore. Was it just the lack of human sounds—the intrusion of man in the world of nature—that made it seem so tranquil?

She found a shallow spot and stood up, shaking water out of her hair and the thin chemise and pantalets that were all she was wearing. It was good not to be afraid anymore. Good to look at the beautiful crystalline water and think that it was exactly the color of Maude Quinn's eyes and not feel a terrible knot of envy inside. She could remember Maude now, her spirit and her generosity—even her beauty—and feel only a normal human sadness at her death.

And Errol . . .

She waded back to shore and flopped down, still dripping, on the sand. She could think of Errol too, and the fact that he had loved Maude, and it did not tear her apart as it had before. She would always regret that she had never been the passion of his youth, that she was not the one pure dream in his heart, but it was a regret she could come to terms with. There was more to life than passion and daydreams. Love came in many guises; she was just beginning to understand that. There was the love Errol had known with Maude, but there was another kind of love too, a love that came from living together and growing together, and changing and striving . . . and sharing.

And she had something to share with him. She looked out at the water, faintly rippling, with streaks of mirror brightness. She had known for several days now, but she had kept it half a secret, even from herself. A secret that came from the past, but belonged to today and tomorrow . . . and would change her life forever.

She jumped up impulsively, laughing as she ran back to the ocean. The sand had caked on her arms and legs, and her hair was so badly matted she had to jump in again and wash it off. She swam aimlessly for a while, diving beneath the surface to see how many new fish she could spot, but the sun was already well above the horizon, and after a while she forced herself to come out. Her hair might be dark, but her skin was fair, and the heat was getting fiercer every minute.

She paused just long enough to twist her thick tresses into a braid down her back. The lacy undergarments covered her body, but just barely, and already she could feel them beginning to dry, clinging as they did to every provocative feminine curve. Anyplace else, she would have been horribly embarrassed, dressing so flimsily, but here she felt free and wonderfully abandoned. And, after all, there was no one to see— not as long as she stayed away from the beach when the afternoon tide came in and the Portuguese boy delivered her rations. She wouldn't put it beyond him to linger for a few minutes in the hopes of catching a glimpse of his tantalizing "older woman."

And what a glimpse it would be, too, if she forgot and was careless!

She was still chuckling as she made her way back the scant quarter of a mile to the cottage Matthew Duncan had built. In that blazing tropical light it was impossible to stay out for long. Even in the shade of the shrubs that bordered the beach, reflections glistened off the sand, turning her nose an unfashionable scarlet and making the skin peel off. Besides, her hair was too heavy for a plait down her back, and she was longing to get inside and pin it up.

The cottage was located in a cool spot, almost in the center of the island, beneath the bushy, spreading branches of a mature black mangrove. It was rustic at best, little more than a shack, but the roof was sturdy enough to resist even the most torrential downpour, and in that warm climate a few chinks in the walls hardly mattered. The furniture was sparse: a table and a pair of chairs, a cabinet with the rudiments of dishes and cooking equipment, a single chest of drawers, and low shelving along the walls. The bed was nothing more than stout cords lashed across a crude frame and covered with a thin quiltlike mattress, but the sun and surf were so exhausting, Stacey hardly noticed the discomfort in the four or five seconds it took her to fall asleep.

She hadn't bothered to close the door. A faintly musty smell blended with the tang of salt air as she stepped inside. No effort had been made to decorate the place, at least not in any conventional sense, but it had a comfortable, homey air. The storm shutters were open, spilling sunlight across a tamped earth floor, and fishing nets had been draped along the walls, with shells of varying colors and shapes arranged in the folds. Whatever Matthew Duncan had done with his life in later years, clearly he had once been a scholar. Shelves were crammed with books and scientific instruments, and the overflow was heaped in a clutter on top.

It was the books that fascinated Stacey most. She had never read anything but novels before. It hadn't occurred to her that dry-looking treatises with their small print and overlong words—and neither handsome hero nor spirited heroine to move the tale along—could be even remotely interesting, and she had turned to these only because the lamplit nights were long and there was nothing else to do. But once opened, they had introduced her to a whole new world of knowledge and abstract ideas, and she found herself reading them as avidly as any romance of her adolescence.

The air was warmer now, and she sat at the table, guessing at her appearance as she wound the long braid around her head, for there were no mirrors in the cabin and she hadn't thought to bring one with her. It was from the books that she had first learned about the reefs and islets, how they had been formed and what kinds of creatures lived among the coral and the seaweed and the sponges. Matthew Duncan had been an artist as well, and sheaves of illustrations were jammed in with the books on the shelves. Fading pen-and-ink for the most part, but watercolors too, meticulously labeled illustrations of fish and sea life that enabled her to understand much of what she saw when she dived beneath the water.

She had taken some of them out, the prettiest and the most interesting, and tacked them up in the few spaces on the walls that were not covered with shells and netting. One in particular never failed to intrigue her. It was a dainty fairy basslet, drawn so skillfully, its subtle pastel hues barely dulled by time, that it almost seemed to be swimming out of the paper toward her.

Obviously Matthew Duncan had had more than a passing acquaintance with the pen and brush. She recalled vaguely the look on Fitz's face when he had spoken of him—a kind of faintly veiled derision. Duncan had been a man of talent. If he had pursued it, he would have been capable of creating an undersea mural as compelling in its own way as Fitz's jungle diorama on the sweeping dome at Glenellen. But he had given it up, and all to raise a family and make a decent living and have something material to pass on to his children. Placing human considerations before art would always elicit contempt from Fitz Blackburn, though she sensed it might have brought a touch of envy too.

She made herself a light lunch of tropical fruit and cheese, topping it off with a piece of sweet cake left from dinner the night before, and settled down at the table to read a book she had found yesterday on one of the shelves. A smell of mildew greeted her as she opened it, and brown splotches obscured some of the words, but she struggled over them anyway, lost for a while in the silent world of the sea. It was well into the afternoon by the time she finally set it down and marked her place with a scrap of paper. Wrapping the last of the fruit in a faded blue bandana, cowboy-style, she went out and followed a narrow sand ridge to a leafy stand of mangroves.

The sun was at an oblique angle now, glinting through thick branches, and afternoon shadows emphasized the tall, twisting root structure that never failed to intrigue her. The trees ran all the way to the ocean, straggling onto the beach at one point, and when the tide was in, they almost seemed to settle on the water. But here, all that could be seen was a jungle of man-high roots, like dozens of gnarled talons, so dense only glimpses of sky and sea came from behind.

Ordinarily Stacey would have taken a book with her, but today she felt dreamy, and finding her favorite spot in a generous patch of shade, she stretched out and let her mind drift off in directions of its own.

Secrets. She smiled to herself as the word flitted across her mind. Secrets . . . the very thing she had been thinking about before. Now, as then, a warming sensation went through her. She remembered the silver swan, hanging on the wall in the old homestead, and how she had looked up at it the night Maude was dying and thought about all the secrets it could tell. It seemed such a dark concept then, frightening and sinister. Now she had secrets of her own, and everything was different.

The air was beginning to cool, a subtle change, and she finished the fruit and wandered over to the windward beach. It was no more than a hundred yards or so from where she had been lying, but it took a quarter of an hour to get there, for the mangroves were too thick to penetrate, and she had to go around.

Late afternoon was her favorite time on the ocean side of the island. The gulls were thick overhead—she could hear their mewing mingled with the wind—and the ocean broke in great thundering rolls on the shallow beach. The tide had been in and was going out again, and a wall-like mass of coral was just becoming visible, churning in a froth of yellow foam. To Stacey, watching, it made a breathtaking sight, violent perhaps, but the violence of nature somehow seemed less brutal than the violence of man. She could understand now why the straits between the islands had proved so treacherous to mariners . . . and the terrible awe they must have felt the first time they looked over the rail and saw waves breaking against obstacles that had not even been there a moment before.

It seemed to her a microcosm of the country itself, this little island with its placid coves and sheltered lagoon and wild windswept outer beaches. Australia, too, was like that, a land of contrasts—frost-cold in winter and sweltering in summer, arid here and steamy there, lively and crowded in the city, and so desolate in the outback it could drive a man mad with loneliness. Or perhaps it was just that life was like that, with its ups and downs, and pleasures and sorrows, and sweet perfect moments that made all the hardships bearable.

It was an hour or two before sunset, and the shadows were already lengthening as Stacey left the windward beach. She considered for a moment heading toward the other side of the island to pick up her supplies, then changed her mind. The tide was still going out. If the boy, Paulo, had decided to hang around, as she half-suspected, he might still be there, dipping his paddle aimlessly into the water while he pretended to do something or other with the boat. She could just imagine the expression on that dark, slightly impertinent face if he looked up and saw her strolling in her chemise on the beach! The package, wrapped in paper first, then canvas tied with cord, would be safe where it was. There were no predatory animals on the island, and even the greediest reef heron could hardly rip through that.

Not that she thought Paulo would be any trouble. A brown finch fluttered onto a nearby branch, eyes bright and curious as it peered out of a funny dark-banded face. The boy was fourteen and a half, and small for his age. She could handle him if she had to, but she'd rather avoid the unpleasantness. Besides, it would be silly, taking chances when she was alone on the island.

She had just rounded the last stand of mangroves and was heading for the cabin when she saw what appeared to be a footprint in the sand, coming from the direction of the leeward beach. She paused, frowning slightly as she gaped at it. Rather large, not like a smallish boy at all . . . but then, she hadn't looked at his feet.

A flicker of alarm ran through her, and she forced it back, laughing at her imagination. A footprint, indeed! More like an impression, and a vague one at that. She didn't know what kind of creature could cause such an indentation, but plainly it wasn't a man. Not on a deserted coral island.

But a minute later, when she came in sight of the cabin, her heart contracted again, this time for real. Was that a light shining in the window? She stopped where she was, staring at the illusion, waiting for it to go away, but it didn't. Not the sun reflecting off something inside at all, but a lamp flickering steadily. As if someone had lit it to welcome her home.

So . . . she wasn't alone after all.

30

A ray of sunlight slanted through the trees, blending with the soft glow from the window in a burst of gold. Stacey felt her mouth go dry. Had she misjudged the boy after all, the hints of lewdness she had seen in his eyes? Had he not tarried harmlessly, as she imagined, but beached his small craft and come inland, searching for the cottage where he knew she would be alone and unprotected?

She repressed a shiver, trying to think sensibly as she started forward again. She was being irrational. The house must have been used occasionally in the last few years; it wouldn't have been in such good condition if it had been abandoned. No doubt Matthew Duncan, reasonably assuming it to be empty, had offered it to a friend.

Or perhaps, she thought wryly, he had come himself, and she was going to have to explain what she was doing on his property.

The door was open, as she had left it, but the interior of the cabin was shadowy, and she hesitated on the threshold. A funny smell greeted her, something that hadn't been there before, sour and vaguely unpleasant. For a minute she could see nothing. If it hadn't been for the light on the table in the corner, she would have thought she was imagining things. Then she heard a faint scuffling sound, and turning, she saw a man silhouetted against a dusky window on the far side.

Not the Portuguese boy at all; she could see that at a glance. And not Matthew Duncan either, for all that she had never laid eyes on him. This man's head had

an arrogant tilt to it, and thick black hair tumbled over
finely chiseled features.

"D'Arcy Cameron! What are you doing here?"

Her surprise seemed to amuse him. He laughed
softly.

"I could say I was passing through the neighborhood, just by chance, and decided to drop in. But then
. . . I rather suspect you wouldn't believe me." The
words were faintly slurred, and Stacey realized what it
was she had smelled before. Whiskey. He must have
brought a supply with him, for a half-empty glass
stood next to the lamp on the table. "The truth is, I
came to find you. If you think it over, I'm sure you'll
know why."

His voice dropped. Even in the shadows, Stacey
could feel his eyes running boldly up and down her
body. For the first time, she remembered that she was
wearing nothing but clinging lingerie, which left little
to the imagination.

"How . . . how did you know I was here?" she said,
stammering. Her eyes flicked around the room, gaug-
ing the distance to the chair where her dress was
carelessly draped. To get it, she would have to go by
him, and he would never let her do that. "I didn't tell
anyone where I was going. I wanted to be alone. As
you can see, I'm hardly prepared for company."

"On the contrary . . ." He moved closer, drifting
into the lamplight. She could see his face clearly now.
There was none of the open lasciviousness she had
expected. Only a kind of weariness and pain that was
even more unsettling. "I think the outfit is charming
. . . but then, you always look charming, no matter
what you wear. That fabric does have an interesting
way of, uh, emphasizing, doesn't it? You've filled out
a bit in the last few weeks. Sydney must have agreed
with you."

His eyes were caressing her again, not flirtatiously,
but with a deep, aching hunger that sent shudders
down Stacey's spine. He was drunk. So drunk he was
reeling slightly; yet he had none of the drunk's usual
sloppiness and lack of control, and she was reminded

once again that she was alone on the island. There was no one to come to her rescue. And this was no small-ish fourteen-year-old she had to handle.

"What *are* you doing here, D'Arcy?" she demanded, fighting to keep her voice steady. She didn't dare let him see how frightened she was. D'Arcy had a bit of the bully in him, and bullies were emboldened by fear. "And don't tell me again I'll know if I think about it. I don't believe you know yourself, for all those lewd insinuations!"

"Ah, but they weren't insinuations." He took another step, smiling at the look on her face. "At least they weren't intended as insinuations. I would have thought you understood, but in case you have any doubts, let me spell it out. You and I were lovers once. I have come to revive that delightful association."

"Lovers?" Stacey gaped at him. "You call that one encounter 'love'? It was lust at best on your side . . . and total unconsciousness on mine."

"Not quite total. But that's hardly the point. That one encounter, 'love' or not, did take place. You and I have been together. And we are going to be together again . . . this afternoon."

Stacey gasped. The man's audacity was amazing. Even intoxication couldn't account for it. He had come all that way to find a woman he had to know didn't want him anymore—and he wasn't even making an effort at pretense!

"You're certainly frank." She forced herself to meet his gaze. "But I wonder at your conceit. I did think you were charming once, but I was very young and didn't know any better. I assure you I have no such feelings now. I thought that was perfectly clear. Or doesn't it make any difference to you?"

"You're still very young. And I think you do have feelings, you just won't admit them. I think you want me as much as you ever did . . . maybe more, since your precious husband disappointed you. But you're right about one thing. It doesn't make a difference. I am going to have you this afternoon, whether the idea appeals to you or not."

Stacey backed away, feeling the doorframe behind her. She caught hold of it with one hand, gripping to keep from trembling. "You're mad," she whispered hoarsely. "You have to be. Otherwise you'd never try anything like this. You can't get away with it."

"Can't I?" D'arcy saw what she was doing, and his eyes checked out the door, searching the open area beyond it. He seemed to be reassured, for he relaxed, leaning against the wall. A seashell came loose from the decorative netting, breaking with a clatter on the floor. "Who's going to stop me, pray? You told me once before, when I got a little amorous for your taste, that you were going to scream. I took you at your word . . . then. This time, my pretty, you can scream all you want, and no one but the birds and the fishes will hear."

"Oh, God . . ." Stacey cast her eyes at the shattered pieces of shell, wondering if they were sharp enough to use as a weapon. But they were almost under his feet. She'd never reach them in time. "You *are* mad. Your wife was just buried, not two weeks ago. Have you no grief at all? No pity or common decency? Can't you even wait for the grass to grow over her grave before forcing yourself on another woman!"

"My wife?" He broke out in a harsh laugh. "My *wife,* you say—and talk of decency in the same breath! There was nothing decent about that woman, God help me. Grieve for her? I did grieve, all the long, sad time I loved her. Grief is a stupid emotion, don't you think?"

He leaned forward, eyeing her cannily, like an animal. Madness was just a word she had used before, an expression of her own helplessness, but she realized now it was true. He had been drinking, but it wasn't alcohol ruling his passions. He was insane with grief and despair, and years of the very real pain Maude had inflicted upon him. But, oh, dear heaven, he was going to take that pain out on her!

"You still didn't answer my question." Keep him talking, a little voice at the back of her mind urged.

Keep him talking while you figure out what to do, how to get away. "How could you know I was here? I didn't tell anyone where I was going. Even Errol thinks I'm in Sydney."

"Obviously you told *one* person." Cunning showed in his eyes, a kind of gloating, and Stacey sensed that he liked talking about his cleverness.

"One person?" she prompted.

"Of course. Your buddy—Fitzhugh Blackburn. The great and noble artist my brother grovels in front of, for all that he despises the sight of him."

"Fitz? You went to Fitz? And he told *you* where I was?"

"A lapse in judgment, I daresay." A flicker of annoyance crossed his face, and Stacey knew she had, dangerously, wounded his pride. "He was feeling pangs of conscience, I suppose, for letting you go off on your own. He had to tell someone, and I was the logical choice. He could hardly mention the fact to brother Errol, when he was the one you were running away from."

He paused, staring out of the shadows. His breath came in a sigh, and the smell of cheap whiskey grew stronger.

"Well, weren't you, pretty? . . . Running from him?"

"N-no-o." There was a faint quiver in her voice she couldn't control. "No, I wasn't running. Not from him. Fitz told me . . . he told me that everything you said was true. But I wasn't running! I needed time . . . a place to work things out. And I did. I understand now, and I can live with what happened. Errol is my husband. I am going back to him."

"Really?" The word was brittle with derision. "Very noble of you, if it's true. But forgive me if I doubt it. For God's sake, Stacey—he wronged you as much as me! I have tried to live with it. For years I've tried. Take my word for it, it doesn't work." Suffering haunted his eyes as he looked up, and for just an instant Stacey felt herself waver.

"It will work for me. It has to . . . because I love him."

"Love has nothing to do with it. Don't you know that yet?" His face softened, and he reached out with both hands. Stacey sensed he was trying to appeal to her now, courting her as he had once courted in San Francisco.

"It's too late, D'Arcy. Way too late for that."

"It doesn't have to be. Think about it. We've always been second choice, Stacey, you and I. And you always will be if you stay with Errol. We could be first choice with each other. You loved me once. Don't deny it, I know you did. You could love me again . . . if you tried."

Stacey watched helplessly as he stood there, hands extended—as if he really cared! There would be no reasoning with him. She knew that with a terrible, blood-chilling certainty. Reason was beyond him. Her only hope lay in the frighteningly open space that surrounded the house. And she was going to have to grasp it, quickly, before it was too late.

"You're wrong," she said boldly. "I couldn't love you . . . even if I *did* try. Nothing on earth could ever make me love you—or want you—again!"

She whirled abruptly, before he could react, racing out onto the barren stretch of sand that led away from the house. It had grown darker in the few minutes she had been inside. Afternoon shadows were deepening into dusk, and just for an instant she dared to hope that night would be her ally. She knew the island so much better than D'Arcy. With no light she would have the advantage.

Only it was easily an hour from the first trace of dusk until night actually fell! She ran along the stand of mangroves for a few yards, then started toward the leeward beach, not for any reason, just because that was where she went most and her feet were used to the way. An hour until darkness . . . and even then, how dark would it be? Hadn't there been moonlight last night, spilling cool and blue-white through the windows onto the rough wood floor?

Her toe jammed against a rock, throwing her off balance. Pausing for a fraction of a second, she listened to the sound of footsteps, frighteningly close. D'Arcy may have been startled by her sudden flight, but not for long. Thank heaven he didn't have Errol's superb physical conditioning, or he would have caught her by now. Or perhaps it was just that terror lent speed to her feet.

A path appeared in front of her, and she took it, a narrow course cutting through dense banks of shrubbery on either side. There were no choices now. She had to go straight ahead. She couldn't have pushed into the tangled undergrowth even if she tried.

If only the island weren't so flat and treeless! Stacey continued to run, not knowing what she was going to do when she reached the beach, knowing only that she had to keep on fleeing. There wasn't a man-high hill anywhere, or a cave or crevice, or even a respectable grove of trees. There were only the mangroves, and with their thick, twisted roots, they were impossible to get through.

No hope. She knew that as she reached a small clearing halfway between the house and the beach. No hope on a tiny island with no other occupants—and nowhere to hide. D'Arcy was sure to catch her when her strength ran out. She could hear him clearly now, hear the rough stumbling sounds that drowned out her own light footfalls, and she sensed he was angry. Running had accomplished only one thing. It had made him so furious he was going to enjoy hurting her!

She didn't see the smooth slab of stone until her feet were on it. She didn't even know it was covered with a slick layer of sand until she slid out of control, arms flailing wildly, and plummeted to the ground. The pain was instant and sharp. Her hands were rubbed raw, and she knew she was badly bruised as she struggled frantically to her feet. But it was too late. D'Arcy was there, only a step behind. Even as she managed to get up, coarse male hands grabbed her wrists, pulling her toward him.

"No, please," she gasped helplessly. "Please, *please* . . . don't do this. For pity's sake . . . I'm your brother's wife!"

The wrong thing! She knew it the instant she heard that sharp intake of breath and recalled how intensely his animosity for Errol had always been.

"Dammit, bitch! I gave you a chance before, and you didn't take it. Now we're going to do it my way . . . and to hell with your sweet sensibilities."

He wrenched her arms down, fingers gouging into her flesh. Stacey could feel his mouth searching for hers, crude and sour-smelling. She twisted her head to the side. His hands seemed to be everywhere at once. No matter how she tugged and fought, she couldn't get away. They were pawing her neck now, her shoulders, trying to loosen her chemise as she struggled grimly to free herself. A ripping sound rent the air, and she felt a sudden rush of coolness, telling her that the soft skin of her breast was exposed to his lewd gaze. He was like an animal now, hardly human anymore. Those groping fingers found her breast, clutching roughly . . . not enjoying, but claiming. Then they were slipping down, capturing her buttocks, grossly forcing her against him.

Stacey shuddered with revulsion as she felt the coarse proof of his masculine demands, threatening and deliberately insulting against her belly. Bitterly she realized it was not yearning that filled him how, not even raw, crude lust. It was a deeper, crueler passion. When he looked at her, when he felt her trembling in his arms, it was Maude he was seeing, Maude he was feeling, and what he wanted now was not to possess but to punish.

She pressed her hands against his chest, trying one last time to push him away, but it was no use. He was stronger than she, much stronger. She felt that even before she felt him forcing her slowly, inexorably, to the ground.

Nausea welled up inside her, and she opened her mouth, not even recognizing the harsh sounds that spilled out. There was no point screaming—no one was on the island to hear—but she screamed anyway. She couldn't give in without resisting, and that was the last resistance left her. Then the earth seemed to rise.

She felt it hard and gritty against her naked back, and she knew it was over.

Damn him. She closed her eyes and held her breath, trying to block out her senses, as if somehow, by not feeling, she could make this terrible thing cease to happen.

For a moment it almost seemed to work. The pressure lessened—she could have sworn it did—and the brutal weight of his body was gone, as if suddenly he had relented and let her go. For an instant she thought she had fainted again, as she had that last terrible time he had used her, and it was all a merciful illusion. Then she recovered enough to realize it wasn't illusion at all. He *had* let her go. She was alone on the ground. She could not feel the heat and sweat and bruising pressure of his body anymore.

Slowly she opened her eyes, half-hopeful, half-afraid of what she was going to see. D'Arcy had moved a short distance away. He was on his knees now, or half on his knees, working his way clumsily to his feet. He had unfastened his trousers, and the part of him that was hanging out was still hard and menacing. As she watched, fascinated and horrified, it shriveled out of sight.

It was a moment before her eyes went farther and she saw a second figure looming in the shadows.

"Errol!"

She thought at first the cry was hers. Then she saw D'Arcy's lips move, and she realized that that shrill, high-pitched sound had come from him. He had one foot planted on the ground and was just starting to rise when Errol's hands came out, grabbing his shirt front, jerking him up. A second later, a fist smashed into his face, and he was sprawled on the ground again.

"Bastard!" The word came through clenched teeth, low but intensely audible as Errol stood over his younger brother and glowered down at him. D'Arcy sat up, rubbing his jaw, looking somehow drunker than he had before.

"Dammit," he murmured thickly, "I didn't do anything I haven't—"

"Shut up—and get to your feet!" There was enough force in that rough male voice to command obedience, and D'Arcy did as he was told. "I ought to kill you for this. If you weren't my brother, I would—and by God, if you stay, I may anyway! There's a boat on the beach, back there where I left it. I suggest you find it and get the hell out of here."

He waited, not moving, every muscle tense. D'Arcy gave him one last look, then stumbled down the path and vanished into the dusk.

Only when he was out of sight did Errol turn back to Stacey.

"And now, madam, what is the meaning of this?"

31

Stacey huddled miserably on the ground, staring up at Errol in the shimmering twilight. Something hot and fiery flared out of the darkness of his eyes, but his voice was edged with frost—almost as if he thought she had been lying on the ground with his brother by choice! Surely he saw that she had been fighting for her virtue. He must have heard her cries for help!

Or had he?

Stacey clutched at the fragments of her chemise, trying to cover her nakedness, but it was too badly torn. She *had* cried for help, but that was earlier, when D'Arcy first forced her down. She had lost all sense of time in the struggle that followed. If she had screamed *before* Errol beached his boat, he might not have heard.

And by the time he got there, she was lying motionless, her eyes closed to block out all awareness of him! Might not that have seemed like acquiescence?

"I didn't want him to do those things to me," she cried unhappily. "I was trying to get him to stop. I swear I was! I was fighting as hard as I could."

"I know that." His voice relaxed somewhat as he squatted beside her. Compelling hands took hold of her arms, half-drawing her up. "I have eyes to see— and ears to hear. I am well aware that that was no token struggle you were putting up. But I am aware, too, that you came here without telling me . . . though apparently you saw fit to inform my brother."

"Oh, God . . ." So that was it. He was hurt. Perhaps he was even jealous because he thought she had informed D'Arcy of her plans. Only that was the wildest kind of misunderstanding. "I didn't invite him here.

I would never have asked him to come. He's the last person in the world I wanted. Please, you have to believe that!"

For one terrible, frightening moment, she thought he didn't. His grip had contracted, and he was holding her suspended off the ground. She could feel anger throbbing in powerful masculine hands, and she was sure with a rush of despair that he was going to hurl her back. Then suddenly his body was against her, so taut she could feel every contour and quiver. His arms, instead of rejecting, caught her in a vise so tight she could not have gotten away even had she wanted to.

Was that his mouth that clamped on hers, tongue scourging, probing—or had her lips gone searching for him? Stacey would never know. She knew only that all the fury and tension of a moment before had exploded in a sudden burst of passion, and his hands were exploring her, every bit as rough and bruising as D'Arcy's, but ardent, and oh, so exciting.

She barely felt the grating texture of the sand beneath her. All she was aware of was the intense masculinity of Errol's body as he tore his clothes off, the lean hardness of muscles she had grown to savor, the coarse texture of his chest hair against her own soft, yearning breast. Then he was inside her, penetrating, deeply, urgently, and all her fears, all her doubts, were gone in one last sweet surge of sensation.

When at last he eased out of her body, it seemed to Stacey she had never been so drained in her life. Or so utterly fulfilled. She half-expected him to be brusque after the way he had given in so abruptly to his passions. But when she looked up, she could have sworn she saw laughter in his eyes.

"I had forgotten how you inflame my senses," he said, resting a hand easily and possessively on her breast. "You have a thoroughly devilish way of making me lose control—and blast you, temptress, I suspect you do it on purpose."

"Maybe," she said honestly. "But I would have thought, before, you were too angry to be tempted." She couldn't help remembering the terrible iciness in his voice. She knew she ought to berate him for frightening her, but it was hard when his hand was on her breast like that, playfully tweaking the nipple.

"I thought so myself," he admitted. "But you do have a way of making me forget everything else. Only . . ." His fingers hesitated, lying still for a moment as he studied her seriously. "If you didn't want D'Arcy to come, why did you tell him you where you were? You must have known he'd follow . . . and what he would want when he did."

"But I didn't tell him," she insisted. "I would never have told him. The only person who knew was Fitz. D'Arcy wormed it out of him."

"Fitz?" Errol frowned quizzically.

"I had to go to someone. Fitz was the only person I could think of. And he did help—it was he who found this place for me. It belonged to a friend of his, Matthew Duncan, a naturalist and artist. I think they own a cattle station in the interior."

"Yes . . . that makes sense." He rolled over on his back and stared up at the sky, which was just turning the deep, rich blue of a tropical night. "I had heard that one of the Duncans was artistically inclined, though I didn't know Fitz was acquainted with him. By God, madam, have you any idea how I felt when I cabled my agent in Sydney to watch out for you, and he cabled back that you weren't there! I was frantic. Then when D'Arcy took off abruptly, I was sure he was going to meet you."

"You mean . . . you followed him?"

"With a certain degree of difficulty, yes. He had half a day's start on me, but fortunately he made no effort to cover his tracks. I couldn't have been more than an hour behind him when I hit the coast. I managed to find a big-eyed Portuguese kid who admitted to ferrying him out here, and I scared him into giving me directions and a boat."

"Thank heaven you did," Stacey said fervently. "And thank heaven Paulo was so easily intimidated. If it had been his father, you might have had a bit more persuading to do. And if you had come along even a few minutes later . . ."

Just the thought was enough to make her tremble. Errol moved closer, holding her for a minute in arms that were strong and protective. "Don't talk about that now," he said huskily. "Don't even think about it. It's foolish, worrying about what might have been. Nothing happened. That's all that matters. The only savage male lust you have to satisfy now is mine . . . and I get the feeling that isn't totally unwelcome."

He had begun to move his hands again, so softly and tenderly at first Stacey sensed rather than felt them. Now he was circling her breasts, toying with them, slowly growing more demanding. A shiver ran through her body, quivering all the way to her toes as she felt him lower his lips, touching the nipple his hands had been teasing before, using it in ways that were so familiar to her now. His tongue darted out, tracing a provocative course around the areola, running down her belly, lingering at last on the warm moisture between her thighs.

If he had taken her right there, again on the sand, with no preliminaries, no words of tenderness, it would not have surprised her, nor would she have been disappointed. Instead, he picked her up in his arms and carried her back through the twilight, naked and longing, to the hard narrow bed where he satisfied his own hunger and hers, taking her again and again until they were both spent.

It was well into the night, and the moon was so high the windows were black with shadow when he finally rose and wrapped a sheet like a lavalava around his waist, though Stacey had made no effort to clothe herself. The lamp was almost burned out, and he filled it again, taking time to relight it before he came back and sat on the edge of the bed.

"What I meant to do when I found you," he said, lips twisting wryly, "was talk. You seem to have distracted that little thought right out of my mind . . . temporarily."

"Temporarily?" Stacey felt her heart sink. Everything had been so beautiful for a while, so perfect, she had almost forgotten there were problems between them. "Isn't it enough . . . just being together like this? Doesn't it prove that I . . . Oh!" She broke off as an unpleasant thought hit her. She had been sure before, when anger turned to lovemaking, that he accepted her version of the story. But what if that was just his strong male passions? "You still don't trust me, do you? You think I asked your brother here."

"No. I believe you when you say you didn't. I don't think you're lying about that. But I still don't understand. Why did you come in the first place? All by yourself?"

Stacey shifted a little on the bed, half-sitting as she leaned back against the pillows. "I had to. I didn't want to, but I had to get away. I couldn't stay there any longer."

"You *couldn't*?" She started to move, but he put out a hand, holding her back. "I knew something was wrong. I could feel it, the day of the storm . . . after we buried Maude. But I had too much on my mind to think about it then. Or ask if I could help."

"There was nothing you could have done," she said simply. "I needed to get away and think. I had to work things out for myself."

"But why? You were happy with me in Sydney— there were no thoughts of running away then. What happened, after we came back, to change all that? Did I . . . ?" he took a slight pause, willing himself to go on. "Did I fail you in some way?"

It was a difficult question for a proud man. Stacey recognized it, and her heart ached for him. He hadn't failed her. Nothing he had ever done or said had failed her in any way. It was only her own unrealistic expectations that let her down.

"It wasn't that. I didn't leave because you didn't please me." She took a long, deep breath, hoping against hope that somehow, even now, the painful words would not have to be spoken. But there had been too many deceptions between them—and deceptions were lies, with the power to hurt. "I left because of her. Maude."

"Because of . . . Maude?" He looked genuinely surprised. "You mean . . . because she died?"

"No. Not because she died. Because she lived . . . and loved . . . and you were in love with her."

There. It was out. She had spoken the words at last, though if he recognized the terrible truth in what she was saying, she had to admit he didn't let it show.

"What the devil are you talking about? Me in love with Maude? Where did you get an idea like that?"

"It's not an 'idea.' I know it! I've known for a long time, though I didn't want to admit it. I'm not blaming you, darling—truly I'm not!" Now that she had started, she couldn't stop, and the words came spilling out, one on top of the other. "She was so beautiful. How could you help yourself? And it all happened before you met me . . . at least most of it. I don't mind, too much, that the affair continued after . . . well, after I arrived. I wasn't your wife then. Not really . . . not like this."

"Are you saying you think I was *sleeping* with Maude?" His dark eyes narrowed inscrutably. "All the time I was married to you? You seriously believe that?"

"Not all the time, no. Just at the beginning. When you were . . . disappointed and thought you were going to send me back."

"And you kept it inside. You didn't say a word. To anyone. My God, if you thought that, no wonder you left! Why didn't you ask me? I could have told you it was a flight of fancy."

"You . . . deny it then?" Stacey eyed him warily, not wanting to let herself hope, but unable to avoid it. "That you loved her?"

"No, of course I don't deny it. I loved Maude very much. But I was never 'in love' with her. She was like my little sister. I was a doting older brother. When she was still a toddler, I used to ride over to Mirandola and play with her . . . and read stories that seemed unutterably silly, just to amuse her. In many ways I was closer to her than I was to D'Arcy, but it was a sibling fondness—nothing else. I have only been in love, deeply and truly, with one woman in my life. I thought you knew who that was."

Stacey closed her eyes, leaning back against the bed pillows. There was so much sincerity in his voice; it would be so easy to pretend, if only she could. There were reasons for a complete reconciliation now, secret reasons, not just in her heart, but deep in her body as well.

Only there were reasons for honesty, too.

"That's not what D'Arcy told me," she said, looking up again. "He told me that you and Maude were lovers for a long time. He knew, right from the beginning—she flaunted it in his face."

"And you believe him?" She had known he would be angry—he always was at the mention of D'Arcy's name—but she was totally unprepared for the coiled tension in his body as he leapt up and paced over to the window, staring out at the darkness. "You take his word over mine—even after what just happened?"

"He was telling the truth. Oh, Errol, I could see it in his eyes. I heard the pain in his voice. I didn't *want* to take his word—I tried not to. For months I tried! But he wasn't lying. He believed every word he said."

"I daresay he did." The anger was gone as he turned back, a tired, self-mocking look on his face. For the first time, Stacey noticed the faintest touch of gray in the black at his temples. "That's my fault, in a way. Maude never had eyes for anyone but D'Arcy. She worshiped the ground he walked on . . . but that didn't make her blind to his faults. Nothing that came easy ever appealed to my brother. He liked a challenge, the thrill of the chase, I suppose, though he hated it like hell when he lost! As long as she was sweet and adoring, he didn't know Maude was alive. But let her flirt with someone else, me, for instance, and he fell all over himself trying to win her back. So she flirted— and like an ass, I let her."

"Yes . . ." Stacey thought about the look on Maude's face that day on the docks—and the way she had always forgiven D'Arcy his dalliances, if only he came back to her. "It could have happened that way."

"It *did* happen that way, and it was as much my fault as hers. More, because I was older and ought to have known better. I didn't realize, until it was too late, how badly her little game was going to damage my relationship with my brother. And I had no way of knowing you would be hurt by it too."

Everything in Stacey wanted to believe him. She wanted it desperately, but there were too many questions still unanswered. "You were so angry when you found out that Maude and D'Arcy were married. And that he had gotten her pregnant. It was as if you couldn't bear the thought."

"I couldn't." He moved over to the table, where the half-empty whiskey glass was still sitting, a painful memory of what had gone on earlier. "Maude was seriously ill before you arrived. She was just getting over it when she came to meet you at the boat. The women of her family have always been fragile—her mother and grandmother both died in childbirth—and she still hadn't recovered her strength. She should have waited at least a year before getting pregnant, but D'Arcy couldn't have cared less! All he wanted was his own pleasure, and the ego gratification of fathering a son."

"Well, he didn't get that, God help him." Now that she was safe and D'Arcy was no longer a menace, Stacey could almost feel sorry for him. "He said that the boy wasn't his. The doctor had told him it was a seven-month baby, and he hadn't been with Maude—hadn't been sleeping with her—seven months ago."

"The doctor was a damn fool!" Errol picked up the glass and headed toward a slop basin in the corner. "I wanted her to go to Sydney, where she'd get better medical care, but she wouldn't leave D'Arcy. She might be alive today if she had. It was more like an eight-month baby, it was just very small. She stopped sleeping with D'Arcy when she suspected she was pregnant. She didn't want to take any chances."

Stacey caught her breath. It all sounded so logical. It would be so easy to believe, if only . . .

"Fitz told me everything, Errol. I went to him, before I left, and he said that D'Arcy was telling the truth. He didn't want to admit it, I could see he didn't. But he was drunk and I badgered it out of him. He said you and Maude *had* been lovers . . . and it was still going on when I came to Cameron's Creek!"

"Fitz Blackburn said that?" His eyes glowed like

burning coals as he whirled around, the glass still unemptied in his hand.

"I don't think he would have if he'd been sober. I think he hated betraying you—and hurting me. But he did, and once spoken, there was no calling the words back. I had to believe it then. What reason would Fitz have to lie?"

"The best reason in the world," Errol said slowly. "Revenge."

"Revenge? Against me?"

"No, against me—or rather the Cameron family. Do you remember the story he told you once about my half-sister, Olivia, and how she fled to a convent in England because she had gotten involved with a man the family considered unsuitable."

"Yes, of course . . . but it didn't seem to matter much. He said it so flippantly. Perhaps because it happened a long time ago. Or maybe he didn't know her well."

"Oh, it mattered." His hand was not quite steady, and he lowered the glass back to the table. "And he knew her very well. You see, Fitz was the man she was in love with."

"Fitz? But—"

"None other. He may seem jaded and self-sufficient, but there's a soft spot under that tough hide, and I think he really loved her. But Livy . . . well, Livy was a lady of convention. After they told her about some of his indiscretions—that was my father, I suspect; he always did the dirty work—she packed her things without a word and went back to England. She died there a short time later."

"And he blamed *you* for that?"

"Hardly. I was a child at the time. But he blamed the family. And hated us. It must have been eating away at his insides all these years."

And that afternoon, with storm clouds hovering in the sky, drunk and off guard, it had finally gotten the better of him. Stacey recalled the way he had looked at her the next day, and how he couldn't meet her eyes. She had thought then he was embarrassed because he had slipped and told her the truth. Now she realized it was a much deeper shame.

"And you supported him all these years? You gave him a house and everything he needed? Knowing how he felt about your family?"

"The man has talent. That has never been an issue between us." He moved back to the window, looking out at a silent moonscape of scrub and sand, dreamy and unreal in the night. It was the kind of picture Fitz Blackburn could have painted to perfection.

When he turned back, his face was relaxed and he was smiling.

"So you see, love, you have been mistaken all this time. It was you, and only you, in my heart. And it always will be."

"Oh, my dearest . . ." It was all she could do to keep from holding out her arms. Strangely, it didn't disturb her that he was lying again. If anything, she loved him more for caring enough to protect her. But the truth didn't frighten her anymore. He might not have had an affair with Maude—certainly it didn't seem he was the father of her child—but there had been more than "sibling fondness" between them. "I might almost believe you . . . *almost*"—there was more teasing than reproach in her voice—"if it hadn't been for that woman in Sydney."

"Woman? In Sydney?"

"You probably don't even remember. She passed us on the street one day. She had on a bright turquoise gown—the color Maude always used to wear—and she looked so like her, just for a second, it was almost uncanny. You turned absolutely ashen. As if you had seen a ghost."

His mouth dropped open, and she thought for a minute she had him. Then, to her amazement, he threw back his head and laughed.

"How my sins come back to haunt me. I looked as if I had seen a ghost, foolish little wench, because I had. A ghost from my rather rakish past."

"You . . . knew her."

"Intimately, I'm afraid. You don't look shocked. Well, good. I haven't exactly led a monastic life. The lady in question married quite well in later years. That sort of thing isn't unusual here, but she has, uh . . .

quite a history. Most of her male 'friends' don't tip their hats on the street, especially when they're with their wives. I'm embarrassed to admit I seem to fall into that category. At least I wavered when I saw her—and she, kindly, passed on without speaking. And incidentally, except for the color of her hair, which is quite different now, she doesn't look the least like Maude."

Stacey started to laugh, softly, under her breath. The woman *hadn't* looked like Maude. Not really. Just her coloring, and something in the way she moved. Hadn't she thought herself, when she got closer, that there was hardly any resemblance at all? And apparently Errol had been close enough to see very well indeed.

The laughter brimmed over, filling the room with sound. A mistake. The whole thing had been a series of silly mistakes! And if she hadn't had the courage to confront her fears, she would be living with them still.

"Do you remember," she said impulsively, "that first night when you were so furious—and I had to point out that I might be pregnant so you wouldn't send me away?"

"I wouldn't have anyway. Surely you believe that now. I would have found some way to back down in the morning . . . and keep you with me."

"I know . . . but I was thinking . . ." She held out her hand tentatively. "It was the possibility of my being pregnant that kept us together then . . . and it's the certainty of it that made me sure, no matter what happened, I wasn't going to leave you now."

He took a step toward her, hesitating just at the edge of the bed. "You mean . . ."

"Yes. I am carrying your child."

32

They spent the next two weeks on the island, a wonderfully lazy interlude, as sweet and perfect in its own way as the honeymoon days in Sydney.

Perhaps even more perfect, Stacey thought dreamily as she lolled on the sand in the rising morning warmth and stared at a wisp of cloud trailing across the sky. That had been a stolen happiness, with doubts and fears hidden in the corners of her heart. Now, for the first time, her marriage seemed complete, and she was secure in her husband's love.

Errol must have sensed her contentment, for when she looked up, he was leaning over her, smiling. He had just come in from the ocean, and water dripped off his jet-black hair, trickling down the cleavage of her naked breasts. Neither of them bothered to wear clothes now. It seemed foolish when they were alone on the island. Besides, all those layers of fabric just got in the way of their unashamed enjoyment of each other's bodies.

"You look as if you were miles away," he said teasingly. "Lost in pretty daydreams."

"My daydreams were pretty," she conceded. "But I wasn't miles away. I was right here . . . with you."

She took his hand and laid it on her breast, half-wishing he would stir her with the spontaneous ardor of his caresses, but knowing he would not. Ever since she had told him she was pregnant, the mood of their lovemaking had changed, no less sweet now, but considerably gentler, with none of the wild roughness she had come to relish. It's almost, she told herself, amused, as if he thought I was made of glass and would shatter on contact.

"The women in *my* family are not the least bit fragile," she had told him once, daring to tease. "You don't have to treat me like a little porcelain figurine." He had agreed, laughing, but she noticed he continued to hold his passions in check. And because she knew he was concerned about her and the child—and because she knew it meant he loved her—she did not protest again.

The weather continued fair, with only fluffy trails of white showing occasionally in the sky, and while Stacey knew it boded ill for the interior, where rain was fast becoming a desperate concern, she could not help enjoying the balmy warmth of their sultry island paradise. To her delight, she found that Errol liked the water almost as much as she. They were well matched. He was the more powerful swimmer, but she was suppler and quicker, and more than once she found herself outdoing him. At first she was afraid he would mind; she had always been taught that a woman never, under any circumstances, tried to beat a man if she wanted him to care for her. But she soon learned that Errol Cameron's ego did not demand being best at everything. Here was a man secure enough in his own masculinity not to fear a challenge from her.

Nor did he seem to mind her superior knowledge of the island and the complex forms of life that existed in that silent coral world beneath the sea. If anything, surprise was mixed with pride when he discovered that she had actually waded through those books and drawings on the shelves and absorbed much of what they contained. Stacey loved sharing what she had learned with him. She loved pointing out the cowries, with their exquisitely colored shells, and telling him that each species had a distinct and identifiable pattern of its own. Or the startlingly pink sponges, no bigger than a man's fist and pocked with tiny craters, but so efficient they could filter thousands of liters of water through their bodies in a single day. Or whimsical butterfly fish, bright yellow with dark circles near their tails, false "eyes" to confuse predators into striking in the wrong place while they swam off in the other direction. It gave her great satisfaction to see the look on his face as she regaled him with fact after fact, proving, if she still needed to, that she was hardly the bubble-headed little flibbertigibbet who had appeared in his parlor one steamy afternoon in a ruffled gown with a bonnet made of dead birds.

It also gave her great satisfaction when his eyes strayed from the water, as they were doing now, and she knew he was not thinking of false eyes on butterfly fish at all, but the way her breasts had begun to ripen, and the sensuous curve of her hips . . . and long coltish legs, parted just slightly to reveal a soft patch of down glistening with a residue of moisture from the ocean. One surreptitious look was enough to confirm the desire it was impossible for him to conceal. It didn't even matter that he wasn't going to follow through on the impulse that was so plainly on his mind at the moment. There was more to love than passion—she was just beginning to understand that—and the tenderness and concern he showed now were things that would last throughout their lives as their marriage grew and deepened. There would be time for passion later. Time for the excitement and wild abandon they both savored so much. Now it was enough to lie next to each other and feel so close it was almost as if there were no separation between them.

Still, she couldn't resist a teasing glance at that visible proof of his very flattering feelings. "I think perhaps," she said wickedly, "you have more on your mind right now than fish."

He grinned obligingly. "Actually, my mind *was* on the fish, in a way. I was thinking that you seem to know a great deal about wrasses and parrotfish and fairy basslets . . . and very little about men. Did you really think I could be so, uh . . . fervent with you if my heart belonged to another?"

"Well . . ." Stacey pouted prettily. He was right, of course. She had leapt to all sorts of silly conclusions, on the flimsiest evidence. But it was unfair of him, pointing it out like that! "You are a very virile man."

"And to believe I fathered Maude's child? That was really farfetched."

"You *were* awfully concerned about her. The minute you got that telegram, you had to go rushing back, even though there was nothing you could do. It didn't matter how I felt. What *I* wanted. All you had to hear was that Maude was pregnant and having trouble giving birth, and you went running home to her."

"I didn't hear she was having trouble," he reminded her with maddening logic. "I heard she was dying. Of course I wanted to be there. And I already knew she was pregnant, remember? Do you seriously believe, if there'd been a ghost of a chance that child was mine, I would have left her and gone off to Sydney . . . with you?"

"No-o-o," she had to admit, feeling a little foolish. It all sounded so reasonable, now that fear wasn't clouding her thinking.

"And why would I have sent for you in the first place?" he went on, pressing his advantage. "Maude wasn't married to D'Arcy yet. If I loved her, I would have courted her. Openly . . . and with everything I had. It might have been a lost cause—she was so obsessed with D'Arcy—but I would have given it a hell of a try."

"Oh, but you couldn't." At least on that one point, Stacey was sure of her ground. "You would have lost Cameron's Creek if you had. And I sometimes think that station means more to you than any woman in the world. Your father was very explicit about it. In his will."

"His will?" Errol looked puzzled as he picked up a fragment of shell, running his thumb along the edge.

"D'Arcy mentioned it one day. He said you got everything material, the land and all that, and he was to have Maude. It seemed funny to me, but apparently one was contingent on the other."

"I see." His voice was quiet. "It never occurred to me before, but I can understand why he thought that.

D'Arcy was nine when our father died. The will did leave everything to me. Just the land, incidentally, there was nothing else. It was understood that I would look out for my brother. I realized, in later years, that that was a clumsy way to handle it, but it seemed practical at the time. There was a letter, too . . . a reminder that it had always been my mother's wish that Maude and D'Arcy wed. But there was nothing binding about it."

He was silent for a moment. Then he tossed the shell onto the glassy surface of the ocean, watching as little ripples spread in broadening rings.

"I must have thought, even then, how unfair it was, leaving D'Arcy at my mercy that way. I wasn't aware of it, but I must have, because I brought him into Father's study and read the letter to him—and made it sound very official and important. I daresay he got it mixed up in his mind."

"Yes . . . I daresay he did." Stacey trailed her finger in the sand, tracing out an idle pattern. She had been thinking so much of herself lately, it hadn't occurred to her that the misunderstandings might reach far into the past and hurt her husband in ways she hadn't contemplated. "What's going to happen now? With D'Arcy? Will you be able to go on as before?"

He turned his head, giving her a long, contemplative look, and Stacey felt a chill pass over her. Just for a second it almost seemed as if he were waiting for her to confess the last of her secrets, to tell him that it was his own brother, D'Arcy, who had taken her to bed.

But that was only her guilty conscience. The look was gone when he began to speak.

"I don't know," he said thoughtfully. "I should have considered it, I suppose, but it's been easier to push it out of my mind. No . . . I don't think I can, but fortunately there are options. Mirandola will be his soon, and I can always deed over a portion of Cameron's Creek. Or I could buy him out, which I suspect he'd prefer, and he can find something for himself in Sydney. But that will be up to him as much as me. I'll have to have a talk with him when we get back."

A talk. . . . Stacey realized suddenly what it was that had made her feel cold before. D'Arcy had more to lose than she, but if he got angry—if his hatred flared again—would he remember that? She was no longer afraid for herself. She knew now that Errol would never reject her because of something in the past. But it would hurt him deeply, and she could not bear the look of betrayal in his eyes when that final, ugly truth came out.

"What are you going to say when you confront him? Are you . . . are you going to berate him for what he did to me?"

"Don't you want me to?" The dark questioning look came back, briefly but intensely, and Stacey had an eerie feeling he was trying to see through to her soul. "The man almost raped you. My God! Do you want me to just walk up to him and hold out my hand and pretend nothing happened?"

"No-o-o . . . of course not." Stacey faltered in her confusion. What she really wanted, when she thought about it, was to see her husband smash his fist into D'Arcy's arrogant face again. But if he provoked him . . . "I don't want you to pretend everything's all right. But I . . . I don't want you to quarrel either! Oh, Errol, there's so much bad blood between you as it is. I don't want to be the cause of more violence."

"The violence is already there," he reminded her quietly. "It's going to come to a head sooner or later."

"Maybe . . ." She shivered. "But not now. Now I just want to forget about D'Arcy, and all the unpleasantness . . . and everything that isn't you and me."

"Well, then . . ." His face relaxed, and he started to smile as he drew her into his arms. "I think that could be arranged . . . for a while at least."

Stacey felt a slow tremor run through his body, hard and rugged, hinting at passion just beneath the surface. His lips were hot on her cheek; now they were playing with the pulse that throbbed at the base of her throat, and she moved her mouth to find his, every thought gone except the hope that he was going to take her there, on the sand, as he had that first impulsive afternoon.

But impulse was no longer a part of their lovemaking, though she knew he hungered for it as much as she. Gently, so gently it hardly seemed he was the same man, he coaxed her to her feet and led her back to the small house and now-so-familiar bed where with aching tenderness he made her his again. Afterward she lay in his arms and listened to the sound of the breeze in the trees outside and thought how little it mattered whether his passion was wild or gentle. The satisfaction was the same, and the closeness and the love, and she was happier than she had ever been in her life.

Their days on the island evolved into a pleasant pattern. Swimming in the morning, exploring the mysterious undersea world that never failed to intrigue them both. Then a light lunch in the cottage; an afternoon with a book beneath the trees; slow, languid strolls on the beach in the evening. The nights were long and lamplit, spent not so much in passion as intimacy, with time to get to know and love each other even more.

Matthew Duncan had been a man of varied tastes, and Errol found books of poetry mingled where Stacey had missed them among the dry scientific volumes on the shelves. He opened them, and from the mildew-scented pages picked out old favorites, introducing her to the world of Byron and Shelley and Keats. Stacey, whose knowledge of poetry had been limited to romantic jingles, was entranced. Night after night, she lay in the moody shadows and listened to the dreamy sound of her lover-husband's voice—"She walks in beauty, like the night of cloudless climes and starry skies, and all that's best of dark and bright meet in her aspect and her eyes"—and wondered how it was that a poet who had been dead so many years could touch her so deeply.

She had been shy at first, but after a while she picked up the books herself, sensing it pleased Errol, and choosing the poems she liked best, read aloud to him. She was a little surprised at first that he had a passion for something so delicate. She hadn't thought that men who spent most of their lives outdoors, among other men, would like poetry—or at least admit to it. It didn't seem to go with the strong-male image. But then, images were for people who needed them. Errol Cameron didn't have to put up a facade.

There's so much about this husband of mine I didn't know, she thought as she lay beside him on the bed, feeling his even breathing against her cheek. So many things she had yet to learn. They would have problems in the future—there were things that still had to be faced—but for now, it was enough to be with him and know he loved her. Their idyll on the island might be short, but it was as sweet as anything she had ever known, and she intended to relish it to the fullest.

She was not the only one who felt the sweetness of that brief stay. Errol, for his part, was finding pleasures he had not dreamed of on the wide, windswept beaches of an islet that, only a few weeks ago, had been a dot on the map. He had never taken the time to be idle before, to do nothing but relax and enjoy himself. There had been school holidays, of course, but they had been filled with cricket games and polo matches and other lively activities. And since he had returned to Australia, chores and responsibilities had consumed much of his time. Even in Sydney, there had been wool auctions to go to, and agents to meet, investments that had to be checked out. Now, for the first time, there was nothing that absolutely *had* to be done, and he was feeling the surprising exhilaration of his newfound freedom.

"You're a bad influence on me," he teased one afternoon as he and Stacey shared a basket of tropical fruit in the shade of the mangroves. "I've never been so lazy in my life. I'll have completely forgotten how to work by the time I get back to the station."

"Then I'd say I've been a *good* influence." She looked up through dark, impossibly long lashes. "You work too hard as it is. It's time you learned to play."

Errol leaned back on the sand, reveling in the laughter that danced in her eyes. She had always been pretty, but maturity was bringing a new softness to her beauty, and it never ceased to amaze him that this enchanting creature was his wife. "You've certainly brought a change in my lifestyle. I have to admit that."

"Well, I should hope so." She tried to look shocked, but she was still too young to it carry off. "It seems you've led a wilder life than I imagined . . . at least if *she* was any indication."

"She?" He must have looked more confused than he realized, for Stacey started to laugh.

"The woman you snubbed on the street, of course. In Sydney. What was her name?"

"Fanny," he replied, feeling a little guilty at the memory. "When I knew her at any rate. "Now she's Mrs. Frances Deberham—for all the good it does her. If her husband were alive, it would be different. Money has a way of influencing even prudish morality, and Walter Deberham was a very wealthy man. But he died two years ago, and I'm afraid, as the saying goes, she simply 'isn't received.' "

"Which means, of course, the ladies cut her dead."

"The gentlemen too," he said, squirming as he recalled his own very ungentlemanly behavior. "It's a bit disconcerting to come face-to-face with one's own 'wicked' past. A damn shame, too. Fanny was always a kind woman. She doesn't deserve the treatment she's getting."

"Well, then . . ." Stacey plucked a mandarin orange out of the basket and held it tentatively in her hands. It seemed to Errol there was a distinctively mischievous gleam in those captivating gray eyes. "I'll have to do something about that. Maybe I'll call on her the next time I'm in Sydney . . . and leave my card."

"Good Lord!" Now it was Errol's turn to look scandalized, and the expression was considerably more genuine. "It would be just my luck she'd be at home and the two of you would spend a delicious afternoon comparing notes. No, you'll do nothing of the kind! I absolutely forbid it. Do you hear me?"

"Oh, I hear . . . but if you think I'm going to obey, just because you order me around in stern masculine tones, you have another think coming. Are you by any chance under the misconception that I'm one of those docile little women who do everything their husbands say?"

Errol groaned mockingly. He loved her spirit. He absolutely adored it. And heaven help him, she knew it. "What did I do to deserve a wife like this?"

"You pampered me shamelessly," she said, smiling sweetly. "You encouraged me to think for myself. And you didn't even pretend to be annoyed when you found me reading books and learning things you didn't know. Now you're going to have to bear the consequences of your own rash actions."

"Am I, indeed?" He tried not to grin, but it was hard when she was looking so prettily smug. He might pretend he wanted an obedient wife, but secretly he was pleased with her feisty independence. She would not call on Fanny Deberham, of course. It would be too awkward, for both of them. But he wouldn't have to cut her if they passed on the street again, and he was proud of Stacey for that. He would be the envy of every man in Sydney when they found out, though he'd wager not a one of them would admit it to his wife! "Very well, then. When we get back, you may do as you choose, and I will learn to live with it. But right now, you are mine . . . and I can do anything I want with you."

It was a safe challenge, for they both knew, right now, their desires coincided. Nor would she have defied him, Stacey thought, snuggling into his arms, even if they didn't. She had already pushed him far enough. She had only been half-teasing when she said she didn't intend to be a docile wife, and he had known it, and his male ego had taken it remarkably well. Now it might be time to feed it, just a little.

"You are right, my love," she said softly. "You *can* do anything you want with me. I am powerless to resist."

They might have stayed happily on that island paradise forever. Certainly, if Stacey had had her way, thoughts of leaving would never have crossed their minds. But while Errol didn't say anything, she noticed that he found excuses to put his clothes on every afternoon and head for the leeward beach just as Paulo was delivering their daily rations. And the Portuguese boy, wanting to earn a few extra coins, made it a point to find out what was going on in the world outside. The news he brought was always bad. The drought continued, worse than ever, and bushfires were beginning to leave great charred swaths across the country.

And every day, when Errol returned, the expression on his face was a little more tense.

Finally Stacey could stand it no longer. She loved being on the island, loved these days alone with him, but she knew she was being selfish. Errol had been more than generous, dallying all that time with her. She had accused him once of loving the station more than any woman in the world, but she had been wrong. He loved her enough to let go of everything that mattered to him. Now it was her turn to do the same.

"You're worried about Cameron's Creek, aren't you?" she said as he came up the path from the beach that final afternoon. "You want to go back."

He held out his hand, taking hold of hers as they walked together the rest of the way to the house. "I am worried, yes . . . but I won't ask to return. Not if you don't want to."

"Oh, but I do." His hand felt warm, and Stacey held on tight. There was so much on the station she wanted to avoid. Not just drought and the threat of fire, but D'Arcy and that last, guilty secret she was going to have to confront sooner or later. "I want very much to go home. Paradise is pretty . . . but it isn't real. It's time to get on with our lives."

"You are very beautiful."

Errol studied her silently for a moment in the drenching rays of island sunshine, drinking in her loveliness as if he had never seen her before and never would again.

"You're right," he said at last. "It *is* time to go back. The station needs me. But you could stay on for a while. It's going to be dangerous if the fires come too close. You might be better off here."

"No." Stacey touched her fingers to his lips. She loved him for the sacrifice he was making, but it was a sacrifice she could not accept. Didn't he know that danger held no terror, as long as she was with him? "I am your wife, my darling. You can't leave me behind. Whatever happens, I am going to be at your side."

V

HOME

33

It was late afternoon when they returned, almost the same time of day as that first journey to Cameron's Creek, and the hired wagon from the livery station in town jolted roughly over the same rutted track. The landscape looked much as it had then. Parched earth was crisscrossed with deep cracks, and a vague wind sucked the dust up, obscuring purple mountains in the distance. Only the feeling was different.

Stacey straightened up in the wagon seat, looking around as she picked out landmarks she had missed before. A slightly worn path to the left—that led to a small farm belonging to a man named Harpur. Stacey had never met him; he had been invited to the gathering at Glenellen, but he had been too conscious of station and class to accept. To the right, a gentle slope rose, slightly back from the road, crowned with a grove of dusty eucalypti. Fitz Blackburn's place. And just beyond, masked by the hill, the dry stream that flooded into a river in the rainy season. It was there that she had seen the hauntingly beautiful swan, as compelling in its own way as Fitz's silvery blaze on canvas.

It was all so familiar, and despite the desolation, so beautiful. Stacey stared at the dry soil and the dust and the mountains, and wondered how it was possible to love a place that was so terrifyingly, awesomely empty. But love it she did, and she realized with a little tug at her heart that a part of her would have died if she had had to leave it forever.

"We're almost home." She laid a hand on Errol's arm. He turned briefly to look at her. Dust had settled on his hatless head, dulling the magnificent jet of his hair, and even his eyelashes were pale, but his eyes were bright with anticipation.

"We'll be there within the hour. I'd go faster if I could, but Angus MacDouall has never been known for the horseflesh in his stable. This nag can barely manage a slow walk. We wouldn't want to kill it by forcing it into a trot."

"No." Stacey smiled. Australians were notoriously hard on their mounts; they rode them long and fast, and roadsides were littered with the carcasses of animals that had not made it. But Errol had never been like that, and she loved him for it. "No, we wouldn't want to kill the horse."

They arrived, as Errol had predicted, a few minutes short of an hour later. Pegeen was waiting for them at the front door. She had spotted them from the window and rushed out, wiping her hands on a soiled white apron.

"Sure 'n it's a fine day for a house when the master 'n mistress come home," she greeted them with her rich Irish brogue. "It's been lonesome without you, 'n that's a fact. Not that you don't look like the islands were agreein' with you." She turned to Stacey with an approving glance. "You're bright as a new penny— and doesn't it do me heart good to see you lookin' so fine?"

"I feel like a new penny," Stacey agreed with a laugh. The sun was so strong, her face was shining. She could hardly wait to get to all the creams and cosmetics in her vanity table so she would look pretty for Errol again. "But it's good to be back. How are things with you? Are you feeling all right?"

"Fit as a fiddle." Pegeen smiled, showing a gap between exceptionally white teeth. She was visibly pregnant again. Her husband had come back from Queensland, but only long enough to get her in the "family way," as she liked to put it, before taking off again. But if she resented the fact that she was merely an interlude between riding and ranching and carousing with his "cobbers," it didn't show in her broad, good-natured face. "It'll take more 'n a wee one comin' to get me down. I've never been sick a day in me life, and the good Lord willin', I won't be startin' now."

"There were no problems on the station?"—Errol's voice, coming from behind, quiet, but with enough emphasis so both Stacey and Pegeen knew it wasn't a casual question.

"No more 'n you'd expect, sir, considerin' the weather. The men respect the foremen you put in, and that's good—though we have been a bit shorthanded, 'n not just in the paddocks. The station cook left. No reason a'tall, just up 'n took off. Mrs. Butler's down there now, feedin' the men. Butler, too, though you'd think it was beneath his dignity, the way he holds up his nose when he walks into the cookhouse." Her own nostrils twitched, showing plainly what she thought of Butler and his airs.

"Well, leave them for the time being," Stacey said impulsively. Pegeen started to protest. The Butlers' place, after all, was in the main house, a man could be sent in a minute, but Stacey held her off. "Feeding the hands is more important. I can supervise the maids myself—and I'm quite a passable cook. I learned to work wonders with omelets on the island, which is good, because eggs are all we're likely to get in this heat."

They did send a man, however, to fetch one of the boys from the main stable behind the homestead to take charge of the hired carriage. Stacey was a little surprised to note that Errol made no effort to go himself, though he must have been eager to speak with the men. He claimed he was tired from the journey and there was nothing he could do that late in the afternoon anyway, but she knew better. He was not going to the homestead because D'Arcy would be there. And he was not ready to face his brother.

So much bitterness, she thought helplessly, as she stared at his face, unreadable in the afternoon shadows. So much anger . . . and hatred that might never heal. The friction between Errol and his brother had begun long before she arrived—those conflicts had nothing to do with her—but every time she thought of the rage on his face when he came into that clearing and saw D'Arcy trying to rape her, she couldn't help feeling at least partially responsible. She had not caused the rift, but she had deepened it. She loved her husband, and she knew he loved her, but she had brought much pain to his life. And unless she could figure out a way to avert it, there was more pain yet to come.

The weather seemed to mock them in the days that followed. Clouds appeared every morning on the horizon, thick and black, as if to taunt them with the rain that never materialized. This time, Errol didn't talk of feeling the moisture in his bones, like an old hatter when he got up in the morning, and Stacey sensed it was for a very good reason. Because there was no moisture to be felt.

"But that doesn't mean it isn't going to rain," he assured her, not wanting her to worry. "Sometimes it happens that way. You might feel the rain weeks ahead. You can almost taste it in your mouth. Or it might come out of nowhere, when you least expect it . . . and when you need it most."

It was not the drought itself that had everyone worried now. It was the very real danger of fire. Stacey didn't know if the threat was more acute than it had been before, when she first came to Cameron's Creek, or if it was simply that she was more aware of it. Perhaps a little of both. Certainly the lush vegetation that had sprouted everywhere in the heavy rains last season left plenty to burn.

Errol had already warned her that a fire could start anywhere. A bolt of lightning might ignite a dried-out shrub . . . or a man could get careless. All it took was a thoughtlessly lighted pipe, a campfire improperly extinguished, a spark from a native's firestick, even a broken bottle left in brittle grasses with the sun glinting through it. Or it might be started by nothing at all. A dead tree, standing in the searing heat day after day, exploding spontaneously in a burst of flame.

"I think perhaps I was wrong," Errol said a few days after their arrival. He had come in to find her alone in the front parlor with its long blue-violet draperies. "I should have insisted you go to Sydney in-

stead of returning with me. It would have been safer
. . . especially now, with the baby coming."

"I wouldn't have gone, even if you'd ordered it."
Stacey tossed her head, trying to look brighter than
she felt. "Besides, you make it sound as if I were *very*
pregnant and already as big as a barrel! The baby isn't
due for months. Why, I hardly show at all."

It was a slight exaggeration. She *had* begun to show.
She was aware of a new bulkiness as she ran her hand
along her waist, as if to emphasize her point. She had
been so eager to get pregnant. All she had wanted was
to bear a child. Now suddenly it occurred to her that
she was going to be fat and ugly for months.

Errol did not miss the expression that flitted across
her face. In spite of himself, he had to smile. "You're
right, love. You hardly show. But what I do see makes
you more beautiful than ever."

Like Stacey, he, too, had been surprised at his reaction to her pregnancy. He had thought children weren't
important to him. A goal for the future, yes, not an
immediate need, and he had been satisfied with his life
as it was. Now, as he looked at her and saw the
thickening waist she was at such pains to hide, he was
filled with an overwhelming love for his unborn child—
and an urge to protect the woman who carried it in her
body. But he needed her too, and he knew he would
be desperately lonely without her, so he let the subject
drop and allowed her to stay.

The weather continued to hold. The dust storms
Stacey remembered only vaguely from the past were
alarmingly frequent now, and with their brooding darkness and sudden streaks of lighting came a fear that
was never completely absent. Although she knew, in-
tellectually, that there were many ways a fire could
start, it was lightning she feared the most, perhaps
because it was the most visible.

And the most terrible, she thought early one afternoon as she stood in the parlor window and shivered at
the sheer force of the elements. Inside, the room was
as dark as dusk. A pair of lamps flickered feebly, their
faint yellow glow barely detracting from the gloom.
Outside, the world had turned an eerie purple. Huge

forks of lightning seared one after the other across the
sky until it seemed to be veined with white. Great
crashes of thunder shook the room, and Stacey longed
to run upstairs and hide her head under the bedcovers,
but she was so mesmerized she couldn't move.

She had learned from experience to recognize the
pattern of the storms. They came quickly, out of nowhere. First, the sky turned a deep tawny color, lumi-
nescent, almost pretty, if it hadn't seemed so ominous.
Then the wind began, a hot, burning sirocco. Lacy
rounds of dried vegetation danced like tumbleweeds
across the earth, and clouds of dust swirled up until
the sun was blotted out. Then the darkness came, and
the thunder, and all she could do was wait and watch
at the window.

The storm ended an hour later, ceasing almost as
abruptly as it had begun. The wind died down. The air
was so still, it was almost visibly stagnant, and dust
seeped slowly back to the earth. The sun was a red-
orange ball, with a twilight haze around it, though it
couldn't have been more than three in the afternoon.

Stacey turned back to the room with a sigh. It was
lighter now, and the lamps looked strangely out of
place. A bare space showed above the mantel, which
had been painted deep gray to blend with the softer
pearl tones of the walls. Errol had been urging her to
hang something there. "That blasted artist is never
going to consider this room good enough," he had
muttered, referring to the way Fitz found one reason
after another to keep his silver masterpiece at the
homestead and not bring it up to the main house. But
Stacey had held out, knowing instinctively that the
swan would be a perfect focal point for the understated elegance of the room. She could almost see it
now, stately and arrogant, looking down on dim circles of light and deep violet draperies and polished
floorboards, covered with a thin film of dust.

At least the storms had accomplished one thing.
Stacey glanced back at the window. The dust had
almost completely settled. Only a faint yellowish haze
dulled the sun. In that weather, everyone stayed close

to home, and she didn't have to worry about D'Arcy finding an excuse to ride over to Glenellen.

Not that she truly feared him. D'Arcy had no hold over her anymore—Errol loved her enough to understand and forgive, no matter what had happened—but she couldn't keep her heart from stopping every time she looked up and saw a horseman approaching, usually just another of the many drifters who had been coming around with increasing frequency lately. She couldn't keep the truth from Errol forever. She realized that now and was resigned to it. But how could she add to his burdens when he was already so worried? If only D'Arcy, in a fit of anger, didn't tell him first!

Oh, please, she thought helplessly. Please let Errol stay away from the homestead until this is over and I can somehow find the right time—the right way—to break it to him myself.

She had been a little surprised when she learned that D'Arcy had elected to remain at the homestead. She would have thought he'd prefer the more comfortable surroundings of Mirandola, which, as Maude's widower, would soon be his. Martin Quinn had never recovered from the illness that kept him from his daughter's funeral; indeed, he was rumored to be on the brink of death. The last thing Stacey would have expected was for D'Arcy to observe the niceties and stay away.

Nor would she have expected Errol to leave the old man alone when they could nurse him better at Glenellen.

When she broached the subject, however, he shook his head. "Let him be, love. Good medical care at best would prolong his life a few weeks. He's been slipping in and out of consciousness since Maude died—I doubt he even knows she's gone. It would not be a kindness to revive him so he can die in grief."

D'Arcy's name, Stacey noticed, had not been mentioned in the conversation, and she had been careful not to bring it up herself. Whatever feelings Errol had for his brother were deep and hidden, and she was no more ready than he to face them. Yet his antagonism toward the other man who had set the stage for that ugly scene on Wrasse Island seemed to have abated.

"You've forgiven Fitz?" she asked one morning, startled to discover that a wagonload of supplies had just been sent to the artist's cottage. "For all those terrible lies?"

"Hardly," Errol replied dryly. "I will never forgive, but I can, in a way, understand."

"Then . . . you're going to let him stay?"

"Maybe. I haven't made up my mind." He stared up at the blank space over the fireplace, then turned to her with a piercing look. "Would you mind so much if I did?"

"No-o-o." She knew she ought to—Fitz had behaved abominably!—but it was hard to forget the torment in his eyes that awful, drunken afternoon . . . and the sheepish way he looked the next day. "No, I wouldn't mind. He's a dreadful scoundrel, but he does have a way about him. And he really is a good painter."

"He has talent," Errol admitted grudgingly. "His work isn't good—it's brilliant. That was always enough before. I never fooled myself into endowing him with any of the saving graces, like compassion or honor. Or decency." His lips twisted wryly. "Though I did think for a while he was going to be decent with you. Perhaps he would have, if the hatred hadn't run so deep."

"What was she like?" Stacey asked impulsively. "Your sister?"

"Livy? It's hard to say. I was a child when she went away." He sat down on a silk-upholstered chair over which a dustcover had been thrown for protection. "She was a pretty thing, I remember that distinctly. Fragile-looking, like a flower that only blooms for a day, then dies. Straitlaced, too—and pious. I sometimes think that was what appealed to Fitz. They say opposites attract, you know."

"Yes, but . . . piety?" Stacey stared at him skeptically. "I can see how a man like Fitz might be *intrigued* by piety, even awed by it. But attracted? That seems out of character."

"Well, perhaps he saw her with an artist's eye. The surface was very beautiful . . . all the things that showed. Underneath, I suspect she was rather shallow. It's hard to tell with people like that. Do their thoughts and feelings run so deep you just can't detect them? Or can't you find them because they aren't there?"

"Do you think he would have been happy?" Stacey said curiously. "If Olivia had stayed and married him?"

"No." He smiled again. "It would take a woman of spirit and complexity to keep Fitz Blackburn interested." He paused, teasing. "Someone like you. Even then . . . no, I can't see him relaxing and enjoying himself. Unhappiness is something he carries around inside. He would have found it anyhow, one way or the other."

It was the last casual conversation they were to have for some days, though Stacey was not aware of it at the time. Less than an hour later, ominous rolls of black appeared on the eastern horizon. At first, she barely noticed, thinking only that the dust clouds were encroaching again. Then they thickened and intensified, and masses of birds soared out of the center, all flying in the same direction.

Smoke. That was smoke she saw. The dreaded fires had come at last.

The news was confirmed minutes later when a stranger rode into the yard, stopping just long enough to tell them what had happened. Three fires had broken out separately, all to the east, near the farm where Ned Harpur eked out a precarious living. The alarm had already gone up. Men were gathering from as far away as town. There was precious little they could do against the bush fires that spread like sheets of flame across the earth, so fast even the swiftest horse could not outrun them, but they had to try, and they would. There were no class distinctions now, no differences between rich and poor. The fires threatened all alike, and all would pitch in and help where they were needed.

Errol was already in the yard, preparing to join the others, when Stacey reached him. He had just finished saddling his horse. Not the thoroughbred he usually rode, but a stocky, thick-legged gray gelding. Steadier

and less skittish . . . easier to handle in the smoke and
heat and the primitive fear of the flames.

Stacey's heart leapt into her throat as she looked up
and saw him, tall and lean on his mount. They were
just beginning to grow close—their lives were finally
coming together. She could not bear to think that she
might lose him now.

"Be careful," she cried helplessly. "Please—don't
do anything foolish!" He nodded briskly, but she knew
he had not really heard. His mind was on the task
ahead. There was no room in it for anything else, and
despite her anguish, Stacey would not have had it any
other way. He was going to need his wits about him.
His chances would be better if he didn't have to worry
about the woman he left behind.

The next hours were the longest of Stacey's life, and
the most exhausting. Just as class distinctions melted
away in the menace of a bushfire, so did distinctions of
sex. Australia might be a man's domain—women might
be excluded from much of a station's activities—but
there were times when every hand was needed, and
this was one of them. Some of the more robust wives
were saddling horses and hitching up wagons themselves to carry water and tools and provisions to their
men. Others took the places that had been vacated by
the stablehands and kitchen boys.

Mrs. Butler was still down at the homestead, han-
dling the cookhouse virtually alone, with only a couple
of workers' wives and what maids Stacey could spare
from the house. Butler himself was out on the firebreaks. Stacey would have liked to help, but Errol had
forbidden her to leave the house. There was no guarantee of safety anywhere in a raging bushfire, but
Glenellen, high on its hill, with no trees around and all
the dried grasses shorn, was at least less vulnerable
than anyplace else. He didn't want her taking unneces-
sary risks, for herself or their unborn child.

Fortunately, the kitchen at Glenellen was big enough
to be of service. Stacey kept Pegeen and one of the
maids with her. Butchered sheep were brought in, and
together they cut them up and set them roasting in
black iron ovens in the already overhot room. Sweat

poured into their eyes, and the smell of smoke and searing mutton fat was so nauseating, Stacey had to put her hand over her mouth to keep from retching. Pegeen, worried, urged her to go upstairs and lie down.

"You mustn't forget there's a wee one on the way," she reminded her. "You won't be doin' yourself any good, 'n that's a fact, you keep on like this."

Since Pegeen had a "wee one on the way" herself, and was showing no signs of slowing down, the argument lost much of its force, and Stacey kept on working. She did agree, however, to leave the freshly killed meat to the others and busied herself instead turning barrels of flour into mountains of dough for bread. She felt a little guilty at first, thinking she had chosen the easier task, but she soon learned better. There was nothing easy about baking bread in such quantities. Her arms and shoulders ached as she beat and kneaded, and punched the dough down, and kneaded again, and shaped it into dozens and dozens of loaves, until she was so tired she would have wept if she had had the strength. She had not known it was possible to be so exhausted and still stay on her feet.

Even in the small butler's pantry where she was working, the air reeked with smoke. Outside, it was almost unbearable. She could feel it clinging in her nostrils when she took a short break and went out to peer anxiously at the horizon; the taste was there every time she swallowed. Fear was in the air. Animals fled across the paddocks: terrified kangaroos and wallabies and emus; wild pigs with singed patches smelling like roast meat; hundreds upon hundreds of lizards and snakes.

Ashes were visible now, floating in black chunks on the deceptively light wind. Later she would learn that they had drifted even onto the decks of ships miles out at sea, but now she was aware only of the fires that created them—and the fact that her husband was somewhere close to those searing flames.

Don't think about it, she told herself grimly as she went back into the pantry. Don't think about anything! Just keep your mind a blank, and do what you have to! She dug her hands up to the wrists in a pile of dough and began to knead again. *Slap-knead, slap-knead, slap-knead*—over and over again. Anything to keep from worrying about Errol. From wondering if he was safe . . . and alive. . . .

It was nearly forty-eight hours before he finally returned, so bone-weary he could barely drag himself through the door and sink down on the wide circular stairs in the central hall. The wind had died down, mercifully, and the fire was mostly contained, with only scattered patches left to burn themselves out. The men were taking turns coming home to sleep for a few hours before going out again.

"We lost Harpur's place," he said. His voice was so hoarse from smoke Stacey could not even recognize it. "The house, the barn, the livestock—even the damn fences! We only managed to save the horses and one of the wagons."

"And the family?" Stacey thought about the woman whose first name she did not even know. And weren't there four or five older children, and a baby still in arms? "Were they—?"

"No, thank God. Billy Two got them out in the wagon. He's a maddening rascal, no good for fighting fires, but by God, that boy can drive!" He leaned back, eyes half-closed in exhaustion. When he opened them again, Stacey saw discouragement for the first time in their depths. "Harpur's taking it well, poor devil—there's a lifetime of work in that place, and he's not a young man anymore. I don't know if he'll have the stamina to start all over again."

Or the resources, Stacey thought, wondering if in all those years Ned Harpur had managed to save a single penny, and doubting it. Her heart ached, not just for him, but for Errol too. She knew he had to be thinking of his own land, and all the sweat and passion and dreams that had gone into it . . . and wondering how he was going to feel when the wind picked up again and those same devastating flames swept toward everything he loved.

And they were going to. Stacey knew that with a sudden, chilling certainty. Errol had been lucky too long. The station had not been touched by fire during the last prolonged drought, and it had been spared so far in this one. But no man's luck lasted forever. The flames were bound to come their way sooner or later.

Next time, when a drifter rode into the yard with news, it would be of a conflagration nearer and more urgent. Next time—or the time after that—when the winds changed and the fire flared again, it would be heading toward Cameron's Creek.

34

It happened three days later. There was no need for a stranger to come riding into the yard this time to tell them the fire had started up again. They could feel it in the savage heat that turned the earth into a furnace, smell it in the acrid odor of fresh smoke. It was shortly after dawn, but they had been up for some time. Errol had gone down to check on the horses at the stable. Stacey had just thrown a robe over her nightdress—she always slept in something now, in case she had to get up in a hurry—and was crossing the hall toward the veranda when she realized something was wrong.

The instant she opened the door, she knew. There was no mistaking the density of the smoke; great belching puffs of black, not just in the east now, but the south as well, and though she could not see the flames, she could feel them getting closer. The sound of hoof-beats drew her over to the side of the veranda, just in time to see Errol take the gray gelding out of the stable and ride across the yard. If he realized she was there, he gave no sign. He simply touched his heels to the horse's flanks and disappeared in a cloud of smoke and morning haze.

He had not even waved good-bye.

Stacey felt her eyes sting with tears. He might be riding away for the last time—she might never see him again—and he hadn't even turned to look . . . or let her look at him.

Angry with herself, she forced her thoughts back where they belonged. Self-pity was the last thing she needed now. Others were struggling in the fields at that very minute . . . risking their lives! Who was she to stand around like a pampered princess while there were things to be done?

Hurrying upstairs, she pulled on an old pair of workman's pants—her own were much too tight now—and tied a cord around the waist instead of a belt to hold them up. Her hair she worked quickly, if somewhat untidily, into two braids, which she coiled peasant-fashion around her head to keep them out of the way.

When she returned downstairs, she expected to spend the rest of the day in the small, stifling butler's pantry. But it soon became apparent that cooking, and even eating, were luxuries for which there would be little time in the hours to come. What provisions the men already had were going to have to last them until the fires had run their course; soon, Stacey suspected, they would be living on tea and sugar, if indeed there was any sugar left. The women had set up a portable field kitchen several days earlier, but that could not continue much longer, nor would they be using the precious wagons to ferry food to the fields. Now that the flames were ominously close to the little village of workers' huts behind the homestead—the smoke was especially thick in that direction, Stacey noted grimly—they would be coming back to evacuate their children and whatever little of their possessions could be saved.

For the first time, Glenellen itself was threatened, and Stacey knew what it was like to feel helpless and vulnerable in the fires that raged all around. The air was so hot, paint blistered on the shutters, and sweat and soot clogged her skin until she longed for nothing so much as a cool, perfumed bath. The ashes that floated toward them were live now, smoking and smoldering where they landed.

At least the house was relatively secure. Limestone blocks not only cooled the interior but also were impervious to the threat of fiery embers. Even the steeply pitched stable and outbuildings were roofed in whitewashed tin and could deflect a considerable amount of sparks and burning debris before overheating so much the framing below was threatened.

Only the back veranda was in any real jeopardy. It had been gracefully constructed in what Stacey thought of as plantation style, all wood with a gently sloping roof to catch the shade and channel the breezes. Fortunately, it was quite small, constituting less than a quarter of the house, and she was sure they'd be able to protect it.

Before she could give the necessary orders, however— or even think what they were—Pegeen had already picked out that one vulnerable spot and taken charge. By the time Stacey got there, she had dragged a barrel of water from one of the huge cisterns Errol had had the foresight to erect near the house, and was dipping blankets and torn halves of sheeting into it. A ladder had been propped against the corner support pillar, and the one maid Stacy had kept in the house was perched halfway up, wailing at the top of her lungs that she was terrified of "bein' so high" and couldn't go any farther.

Poor Dollie. If she hadn't been so anxious, Stacey would have had to laugh. She was a willing little thing, head and shoulders above the usual Irish waifs who had converged on the Australian domestic scene, but she was so frightened now, even a sharp tongue-lashing from Pegeen had no effect.

"For heaven's sake . . ." Stacey caught the hem of her skirt and dragged her down. "Just grab the blankets when Pegeen gets them wet. No, you can't trade places—her belly is so big, she'd never maneuver the ladder! Climb as high as you dare and hand them up to me."

Stacey had no head for heights herself, but the situation was urgent, and there was no time to think about anything else as she scrambled across the roof, beating back the embers as they fell. It was not as frightening as it had looked from below. The roof was flat enough to find her footing, once she got used to it, and the coals did not ignite immediately, so she didn't have to rush precariously back and forth. Still, it was exhausting. The smoke was so thick, it was hard to breathe, even with a dampened scarf around her face, and after a while she felt faint and had to force the frightened maid to take a turn spelling her.

Dollie was still hesitant, but her mistress's courage shamed her somewhat, and she allowed herself to be bullied reluctantly up the ladder. Once there, if not exactly nimble, she did as well as could be expected, and between the two of them, working in short shifts, the women managed to keep the roof intact.

The danger came in spurts. The wind was more capricious now than it had been in past days. Sometimes it whipped around them, driving heat and ashes sharply into Stacey's face as she scurried after fallen cinders. Other times, it almost seemed to abate, and she actually had a minute to sit on the roof and look around.

The fire seemed to have gotten worse. Smoke rose steadily, blacker in some places than others, and now and then she thought she caught a glimmer of flame, though it disappeared before she could be sure. A warm glow lay on the horizon, like the last blood-red of dusk. Only she was facing south . . . not west.

Except for the airborne ashes, their hillside seemed to have escaped the worst of the menace. The grasses had been shaved to the ground weeks before; the stubble had long since died and blown away, and naked earth gave the fire no place to take hold. She could still recall how barren the land had looked, that first time she saw it—and how strange it seemed that no one planted trees for shade around the buildings. Now she knew why.

They kept the fire off the roof for the rest of the morning, but it was increasingly hard work, and both she and Dollie were so tired sometimes they could barely raise their arms to beat the wet blankets down again. When one of the men rode up with orders from Errol to check on them, she had him take an ax and cut the structure down. Later, perhaps, she would remember and regret the pretty latticework that had softened the coldly formal lines at the rear of the house. Now it was just a relief to drag the broken pieces inside where sparks couldn't get at them, and sink exhausted into a chair in the parlor.

She had no idea what time it was. Somewhere around noon, she supposed, but the shutters had been closed across the windows, and the light that filtered in from the hall was not enough to illuminate the hands on the delicate porcelain clock.

They would be safe for the time being. Now that the worst danger had been disposed of, Stacey could be reasonably certain of that. All they had to fear was the smoke—she could feel it oozing through cracks in the heavy shutters—and they had managed the smoke quite nicely outside with their water-drenched scarves. Surely, if they survived that, they could survive anything.

But . . . Errol?

Stacey got up restlessly and wandered over to the window. One of a pair of shutters had been left ajar so she could look out. Every muscle in her body ached. They would survive in their stone house on the hilltop, but what of Errol in the fields below? Where was he now? What was he doing? What terrible risks did he feel he had to take?

She leaned her head on the windowpane; even the glass was feverish now. Was he ever, ever going to come riding back up the hill? Was she ever going to feel his arms around her again?

The smoke was thicker at the base of the hill. The men were scattered in small groups, trying as best they could to defend the land. It was discouraging work. They cut firebreaks as fast as they could, and hauled wagons of water with balky oxen over badly rutted tracks, and struggled through the smoke and dust and unbearable heat, but all their efforts had little effect. Nature was in charge now, not they. The fire would run its course.

The wind was more constant here. It fluctuated somewhat, but never completely stopped, and Errol sensed it was girding for a wild sweep over open plains and up the gently wooded slopes. Every time the smoke died down in one place, it started up in another. He squinted his eyes, bloodshot and tearing, trying to make out a pattern in the haze. A number of small fires seemed to be forming steadily in the south. If that continued, they would be cut off from the half-dried river, their only source of water.

"Ye'll take a cup o' tea, Mr. Cameron?"

Errol glanced around to see a stout, ruddy-faced woman behind him. Sarah Cooper was one of the two or three wives still running the makeshift kitchen where he had stopped, not so much for sustenance as a chance to talk to the men as they drifted in. She was no longer young; her boys were teenagers, out fighting fires with their father, and she had no little ones at home to protect. Soon, he suspected, she would be alone there.

Not that it mattered. Errol grimaced slightly as he reached out to take the metal cup she offered. There was no more flour for damper, and the stewpot had already been watered more than once to stretch the greasy mutton.

"Thanks, Sarah." The cup felt unpleasantly warm as he wrapped his fingers around it. What was there about Australians that made them insist on their tea steaming hot? "The men have been coming in, have they? Taking advantage of the kitchen?"

"Not so as ye'd notice. A few here, a few there, but its' a long way to fill a billy. Stew's not a thing ye carry off in yer pocket."

Errol nodded. The bread Stacey had labored over was long since gone, and there were no more of the American-style sandwiches that had proved so handy. "Still, I'm glad you're here. It isn't much, but God knows how long this is going to go on, and men can't work forever on an empty belly." He paused, smiling tiredly. "If I were a gentleman, I would have thanked you long ago for sticking it out with the rest of us."

"If a few polite words was what it took t' make a gentleman," Sarah replied, "there'd be a passel more of 'em in this world." She wiped her hands on a stained homespun skirt and started back toward the fire. "Anyway, where else would I be?"

Where else indeed? Errol thought as he watched her lumber away. It seemed bizarre somehow, a cookfire in the midst of all those raging fires in the fields. Cooper was with the others, her boys were there too; what choice did she have? Australia was hard on its men—they toiled and went without and died before their time—but it was even harder on the women. Men at least could fight for what they held dear. Women could only watch . . . and wait.

A fleeting thought of Stacey came to him, alone in the house on the hill. She, too, was watching—he knew she was, anxiously by her window, watching and waiting—and he knew she was afraid.

The tea was cooler now, and sweet with sugar. It grated on a smoke-rasped throat as he took a sip. He found it hard to swallow, but he made himself finish, not because he wanted it—he was beyond thirst by that time—but because he knew he needed the liquid in his system. He had just set the cup on the ground and was going back to where he had tethered his horse when he became aware of a rider approaching.

The man was so encrusted with soot, it was a moment before he recognized him.

"Harpur." He greeted him briskly. There was no time for pleasantries, even had the other man encouraged them.

"Cameron." Harpur swung from the saddle, keeping a hold on the reins as he started over toward the cookfire. He looked older than his fifty years. Sweat streaks showed skin that was unnaturally pale, and Errol could see he was exhausted. "What's happenin' your way? You bin down—"

He broke off as another rider appeared. Bluey Warren, coming at a good clip from the east. Even before he dismounted, they were joined by a fourth man, whom Errol knew only as Barstow. He had a small spread on the opposite side of the town road from Harpur's, still intact as far as they knew.

The men went together to the fire. Sarah Cooper had already thrown a handful of tea in a billy and was pouring it out when they got there. Errol, knowing both tea and sugar were in low supply, waved his aside as he hunkered down with the others. Young Warren seemed to have lost some of his shyness and was almost talkative, even though Sarah and one of the other women were standing there frankly listening. Barstow, by contrast, was a morose man; he spoke mainly in monosyllables, at least in the presence of the local "gentry," among whom he obviously included Errol, but he managed to get his point across.

None of the news was encouraging. The fire seemed

to be spreading in all directions. The two older men swore they had never seen anything like it. Mirandola had been struck early that morning. Flames had already consumed the barns and outbuildings—the house itself was probably gone by now. If the wind held and the fire continued, the homestead would be next.

"Wish I could tell you diff'rent," Harpur said grimly. It was he who had just come from that direction and seen the men riding away after giving up Mirandola. "Don't look like there's nothin' kin be done t' save either one of 'em. Sorry, lad—that's jest the way it is."

Errol did not waste time bemoaning the obvious. The homestead dated back to the first Cameron occupancy of the land; it had always been there, the one constant in his life. It would leave a void when he lost it.

But loss was a part of floods and droughts and fire. A man in Australia learned to accept it.

"I foresaw that possibility yesterday," he said quietly. Ned Harpur had lost everything too, and he was still there. "I had the men move what livestock they could. The barns at least are empty, and the stables—and the sheep are mostly on those rises across the creek. The dogs . . ." He hesitated, recalling suddenly that someone had told him Harpur's prized kelpie had perished in the flames. The man would as soon have laid down his own life as lost that dog. "Hell, they'll take better care of the sheep than I could. We left the gates to the paddocks open. With any luck, the dogs'll herd them away from the flames. God knows, they haven't the sense to move themselves."

"Nuthin' stupider 'n a sheep," Barstow agreed, chuckling suddenly. "Stone the crows, all they do is mill round in a circle! Round 'n round—till the flames come in 'n roast 'em alive!"

It was a major, if somewhat ghoulish, concession, the longest speech the man had ever made in Errol's presence. Any other time he would have recognized and enjoyed it. Now he had too much on his mind.

"I don't like the way things look in the south. Over

there by the river. If it gets much worse, we're going to be in trouble."

"Bin thinkin' the same thing m'self," Harpur said, looking worried. The three men moved a short distance away, leaving Bluey Warren alone with his "cuppa cha" by the fire. "If it gits too bad, there ain't no point holdin' on. A bloke'll not mind riskin' his life when there's somethin' to be gained. But you don't risk it fer nothin'. Best to cut your losses and run."

"Bloody right,' Barstow agreed dourly. "We'll be riskin' our lives fer nothin', that's a cert, we can't git t' water. Mebbe we're riskin' 'em fer nuthin' now."

Cut your losses and run . . . Errol glanced up at the heavy veil of smoke that hid Glenellen and its hill from his sight. He could give up the homestead if he had to, and the livestock . . . the graceful house that had been his mother's dream. But Stacey was in that house. His beautiful, precious Stacey. And if the flames surged between here and there, he wouldn't be able to get to her.

He couldn't afford to wait much longer to decide what he wanted to do.

"I have to know how bad it is. With all this damn smoke, it's impossible to see. There's a hill right over there. From the top, you can get a picture of what's happening."

"Good idea." Barstow nodded. Errol was accepted now; gone was the restraint between them, but neither man had the time to realize it. " 'Least that way, we'll know what we're up agin."

"I'll go." Harpur hooked one foot in the stirrup and started to mount. "I bin workin' this land so long, I know it like the back o' me hand. Even in the smoke, I'll find the way."

"No.' Errol spoke quietly, but there was force in his voice. "I'm familiar with that hill myself—I used to play there as a boy. It's my land that's threatened, Harpur. I have to do this."

The older man gave him a sharp look. "It isn't just the smoke that's a danger now."

"I'm well aware of that. And I'm going. Leave young Warren here. I'll send him out with a message when I get back."

Harpur nodded. Arguing would only waste time, and time was precious. The wind could pick up at any moment. He, too, had noticed that subtle tension in the air and, like Errol, was expecting a gale.

"All right, then, Go if you must, but take care, lad. That blanky hillside's thick wi' old gums, dry as tinder in this heat. The wind starts up again, you could be riding into a death trap."

"I know that, Ned." He used the other man's first name without thinking. "But it's got to be done. That's the only way we're going to find out what's going on. And I'm the one who's got to do it."

The gelding was pawing the ground when he got to it. The scent of fear was nearer now; its eyes were rolling, and a vein stood out, throbbing on one side of its neck. Steadier than the stallion maybe, Errol thought grimly—but not the horse he would have chosen for what he had to do. He cast a backward glance at the place where Harpur was standing by his own much steadier mount. He would have liked to ask for the loan of it, but a man's horse was as much a part of him as his dog in the Australian bush, and that was a thing one did not do. Tossing the reins over the gelding's head, he hoisted himself into the saddle and rode away.

Behind him, the two men were looking at each other with uneasy eyes. The kitchen camp was quiet now. Bluey Warren had wandered off by himself, and the women were nowhere in sight.

"Ya shouldn't o' let him go," Barstow said glumly. "He's a boy yet—wet behind the ears."

"He's no boy," the other replied. "He's a man, and has been for a long time. But he's wet behind the ears when it comes to fire."

"Short on sense too, it looks like. You ought t' of gone yourself. You know the wind better'n anyone. It starts t' change, you smell it b'fore the first blade o' grass moves. You'd o' got back all right. Or me."

"Didn't hear you offerin'," Harpur said dryly. "Mebbe if you had, he'd o' let you. Ain't nobody like to miss a crusty old bachelor like you."

"Don't seem right," the other agreed, unruffled. "Bonzer wife like that, waitin' there t' home. What the bloody hell's he doin' takin' chances? Damn fool pride, you ask me."

"A man's gotta have his pride," Harpur replied calmly. The horse raised its head, whinnying restlessly, and he laid a hand on its neck. "Can't live wi'out your pride."

Barstow was inclined to agree, but not in words. Verbal agreement was something he had never indulged in. He liked the Cameron heir, despite his education and fine speech and fancy clothes sometimes. Young Errol had guts—Barstow respected that. He didn't cry when things went bad, and he had the courage to do what he had to.

"Still, he's a bloody fool."

"Well . . ." Harpur swung a leg over the horse's rump and eased himself into the saddle. "There's still time. Mebbe he'll make it back all right."

"Mebbe." Barstow cast a dubious look at the sky. The smoke had rolled into thick gray clouds and was moving alarmingly across the horizon. "But it don't look good."

"No," Harpur admitted. "It don't look good at all."

It was Stacey, ironically, who first saw the puff of gray in the southwest and realized that the fires had veered their course and were heading in new directions. She was standing by the window again, as Errol had pictured her, and for just a moment she was almost reassured—the new outbreak seemed so much farther from Glenellen.

It was some minutes before she recalled the geography of the area and realized suddenly that Fitz Blackburn's cottage was right in the middle.

Fitz. Her first thought, strangely, was not for the man himself, but for that landscape she had once seen on an easel, and the roomful of beautiful, disturbing, haunting canvases in back. Errol had urged him to place them in a museum, where they could be protected and properly maintained. She remembered that now so clearly. But Fitz, being Fitz, had refused—and for no better reason than that he didn't want to.

Stacey turned back into the room. She had extinguished the lamps to cut down on the heat, and shrouded chairs loomed like gray-white ghosts. The blank space over the mantel glowed eerily in the shadowy light that seeped in from the hall. The space where *The Silver Swan* was to have hung—if the room ever measured up to Fitz's exacting requirements.

Only it never had, and the painting was still in the homestead, itself in danger. . . .

Strange. Her eyes closed heavily, and she had to force them open again. She ought to hate Fitz. She had tried to hate him in the days that followed their return from Wrasse Island, where she had learned of his treachery, but somehow she couldn't. Perhaps Errol was right. Perhaps his brilliant talent *was* enough. Or perhaps it was just that there was something in his rakish eyes and boisterous laughter that made her like him in spite of herself.

She glanced back at the window. The gray was denser now in that direction, almost black, as if night had fallen several hours early, and she found herself thinking again of the paintings that must already have been damaged by smoke, and hoping that Fitz was not in the small cottage but off somewhere fighting fires with the men.

But Fitz was in his cottage. At the same moment Stacey was looking out her window, he was standing in the doorway of the open porch and staring down at flames clearly visible near the base of the hill. The fire had been working slowly up the slope. The wind had died down, and the air was almost stagnant, rippling only with the savage heat.

It had begun a short time ago, on one side of the hill, leaping crazily to the other, with a gap between. Now two arcs of flickering red-gold were burning their way together, sheer walls of flame that threatened to cut him off. A swath of yellow-brown still showed between, wide enough for a man and a swift horse to get through, if he had still had a horse.

But the horses were gone, and the chickens and the milk cow. He had opened the barn door that morning and driven them out to take their chances in the field.

The look of the fire fascinated him. He felt no fear
as he stood there mesmerized by its steady progress.
The flames had colors in them that he had never seen
before, bright, glowing, infused with light—colors no
artist's brush could capture. There was a violence in
those pretty tongues of fire that called to something
deep inside him, a savage thrill that seemed to crackle
with the audible crackling of the flames . . . a kind of
excitement he had sensed in his dreams but never
known before.

Like the violence in his paintings.

He laughed aloud, enjoying the sound as his eyes
drifted over to the working easel, where his canvas
was so blackened with smoke that the subject was no
longer identifiable. It had been a study of the river,
painted from memory. That same memory enabled
him now to see it as it had looked the afternoon
before, when he laid his brushes down. It was a deceptively soft piece, like all his works, with hazy outlines
and luminous tones—but a pair of carrion birds glided
across the robin's-egg sky, waiting to swoop down and
devour.

It drove them mad, the way he kept his paintings in
the storeroom, Cameron and Martin Quinn, and that
bloody art critic who came up from Sydney . . . and
Maude with the blue-green eyes that would laugh no
more. They didn't understand, not even the dark-
haired bride, though he had thought sometimes she
caught a glimmer when they were working together in
the house. Why the devil should he care what happened to his paintings after he was gone? What comfort would it be to have a parade of idiots marching by
and gawking in some musty museum?

Something brushed his leg, and he looked down to
see a ball of sooty fur. "Here, what do you think
you're doing?" he grumbled, startled. The little
scrounger had gotten so dependent, it was turning to
him instead of trusting its instincts. "That's what comes
of feeding a cat. A bowl of milk is one thing, me
cobber, but salvation you're going to have to work out
for yourself." He gave a rough shove with his boot—no
point coaxing it to hang around until it was too late.

"Better get going while you can. Another minute, and all you'll be good for is a turn on the barbecue."

The fools! They thought paintings were possessions, bits of canvas and daubs of oil to hang on the wall and look at. His paintings were a part of him—a living, breathing extension of himself, with spirits and souls of their own. They were not *things* to be owned; they were separate and alive in their own right.

And everything that was alive, everything that breathed and loved, and laughed and wept and hoped, died in the end and was gone.

Olivia . . .

He had not thought of her for a long time, yet not a day went by when something in his heart did not remember—and miss—her. She had been so lovely, a fragile, captivating will-o'-the-wisp. They thought he had not known how empty she was. They thought he had not recognized the piety that was in reality prudishness, the shallow manners that masked a shallow mind. But he had . . . and he had not cared. There was depth enough in him for both of them, and intelligence, and talent. That was not what he had wanted from her. What he had wanted—what he had *needed*—was her cool and placid beauty.

He stepped over to the other easel, still mysteriously draped in ash-darkened cloth, and pulled off the cover.

The exquisite face that stared out at him was so lifelike it almost seemed to breathe. The lips had just parted, teasing, not quite a smile yet; the soft irridescent eyes were wide and ingenuous, delicate somehow—as if they had just caught a glimpse of pain. Fair hair blew in a rising wind, and the cheeks were faintly flushed.

Blast that fool of a charlatan who had tried to paint her! He hadn't seen anything at all but features. He hadn't seen the softness and the timidity, the hopes, the longings, the dreams of romance in a young girl's heart. But Fitz had seen, and loved . . . and captured it all on a square of canvas.

The portrait was his best work. He knew that objectively, with none of his usual vanity. The best of everything he had done, and it had never been seen by other eyes—and never would be. He had always vowed to himself that it would die when he died, that it would never be shared by any man, or woman, on earth. Exactly how this was to be accomplished, he had not known. Fitz had never been a man to bother overmuch with details. He had simply known that it was so. . . . And now it was.

He would have made her happy. They thought he wouldn't, but they had been wrong about that too. He would have loved and cherished her, coming to her bed only occasionally, when he could no longer stay away—not with his usual rough passion, but gentleness and even humility. There would have been other women, of course. Fitz Blackburn was a virile man, and he had no illusions about his capacity for fidelity. But they would have been whores, in the bawdy houses in town. Olivia would not have minded that. She might even have expected it. It was the accepted price a woman paid for not having to indulge her husband too often.

Nor would she have minded the women in his past. They could have told her anything they wanted about anyone they wanted . . . except that she was black.

He rested his hand on the edge of the table, drawing it back as he felt the heat. The one thing they could have said that would have turned her against him. John Cameron's doing, of course—Ellen wasn't clever enough for that. Livy had withdrawn into herself when they told her; she had simply closed like a morning flower in the midday sun and refused to see him or speak to him again. Lips that had touched a black woman's would never touch hers, she was telling him with that terrible hurt silence . . . and the body that had lain beside a black woman's through long, sweltering nights would never lie beside hers.

He draped the cloth back over the portrait. No reason for it—no one would be coming that way—but it was a habit, and over the years, habits had gotten harder to break. The cat was gone now. He couldn't see it anywhere under the table or along the walls. Maybe it had taken his advice and scurried down the hill. He hoped so. He didn't like cats, never had, but he had gotten used to the little beggar.

Oh, Livy, Livy . . . He had wanted so little from her, and so much. She could have sat in her room all day and tried on the baubles he would have sold his paintings to buy for her, and only come down to smile at him in the evenings. She had been his hope, his salvation, his only joy in a life that had known no other delights, and he had yearned for her as a man crawling on his hands and knees through the burning desert yearned for swaying palms and the cool deep wells of an oasis.

With her, there had been a reason for living. Without her . . .

He went back to the doorway. The air was still strangely calm. The fire was burning higher now, halfway up the slope, broken only in one place. The smoke was suffocating; his eyes stung with it as he stared down, fascinated, at two points of flame creeping closer and closer together.

A little time yet . . . a chance for one mad dash to try to get through . . . then it would be too late.

He did not move.

35

The wind had almost completely died away. The sounds of the fire were hushed on the shallow hilltop where Errol sat on his horse, but he could still hear them, faint snapping noises like electricity on a dry winter morning. The leaves on the nearby trees were motionless, barely quivering in a reddish haze that drifted up from the plains below.

The calm before the storm? he thought, wondering why that old cliché popped into mind, yet knowing it was true. Something was about to happen. The air was too heavy. He could feel it pressing against his chest when he tried to breathe.

He ran his eye across the landscape, assessing damages and dangers at the same time. The situation was not as bad as he had feared. Great bands of black swept cross the earth, stretching as far as the horizon—thousands of acres had been destroyed—but the worst of the flames had passed, heading toward the mountains. The way to the river was open.

If only the calm held . . .

He clenched his jaw as he tightened his hold on the reins. The horse beneath him was nervous, scenting something new in the air, as he himself had scented, not knowing yet what it was. Isolated patches of flame still showed, vivid red in places—the danger was not over by any wild hope—and smoke rose in thick dark pillars from the earth. He didn't like the look of that haze over by Fitz Blackburn's place. There was a clump of trees in the way, but it looked like the entire hill might be on fire. Damn Fitz, he hoped he had had the sense to get away, but with someone like that you never knew. And the paintings . . .

He blocked the thought of the paintings out of his mind. There was no time now to grieve for the art he had nurtured with his money and his forbearance, and which every fiber of his being told him was already gone.

The smoke was thick near the homestead too. Errol felt something tighten in his chest as he stared at it. The patches of red were alarmingly close. Harpur had been right. They were going to lose it, and soon. The grasses were too dense leading to the house, and there were shrubs that should have been cut.

D'Arcy? For the first time that day, it occurred to him to wonder about his brother, and the thought made him unaccountably nervous. He hadn't seen him since the fires started. Not that he had tried to seek him out—the anger was still too fresh in his heart—but he was aware that the men had noted his absence.

"Ain't seen hide nor tail o' the young toff," he had overheard one of them saying the afternoon before. No names, but Errol hadn't needed a name to know whom they were talking about.

"Tail's all you're like t' see," someone else put in. "Movin' fast—in the wrong direction."

The others chuckled. "Prob'ly in town," one of them said. "Swillin' a pint at the bar . . . and laughin' at us fer riskin' our bloody skins."

Errol's neck burned red at the memory. He didn't want D'Arcy there. The younger man would only be in the way. He was about as much use in an emergency as Billy Two, whom Errol had sent back to Glenellen with orders to keep the wagon ready. But he hated it that his own brother was a coward, and that the men had noticed and pitied him for it.

At least Stacey seemed to be safe. He glanced back at the hill where Glenellen rose out of the haze like a castle from the clouds. A great ribbon of burned earth, two miles wide at least, separated it from the main body of the fire. Even if the wind started up again, the flames would never leap that barricade.

Stacey . . . The heat was torturous; rivulets of sweat ran down his neck and drenched the open collar of his shirt. The most precious thing in his life, and the best. Stacey and their unborn child. A son to carry on his

own fierce passions . . . a little daughter, the image of
her beautiful young mother.

He had never thought it mattered before, a child to
perpetuate his name and genes. Vanity, he would have
called it. Foolish vanity, to think you could live your
life again or see yourself reflected in another. But it
was not vanity at all. It was the natural yearning of
every man to leave something good and lasting behind.

A hint of breeze blew across the hill. Reaching up,
he rubbed a weary forearm over his brow. He ought to
be getting out of there. The wind could start again at
any time. When it did, he couldn't afford to be caught
with a rocky precipice to the rear and the only way
down that tinderbox of dried leaves on the slope in
front of him.

He raised the reins, then hesitated, eyes caught
hypnotically by the homestead buildings, tiny dots of
black in a patch of yellowing grass. The fire was already closing in; a breath of wind was all it would take
to whip it into raging violence. Part of his life was
about to go up in flames, the memories he held most
dear—his parents sitting down to dinner in full formal
dress, his grandmother telling stories on the side veranda, his pretty young bride in the parlor that first
afternoon—and he couldn't even afford the luxury of a
moment to mourn their passing.

He found himself hoping that the men were right
and D'Arcy was in town. He wouldn't like to think he
had remained behind at the homestead, out of stubbornness or pride, or whatever the hell it was D'Arcy
was capable of feeling. He had not forgiven his brother
for what he had done. He hated him with all the
hatred in his heart, but he loved him too, with the
same passionate intensity, and he could not bear to
think of his perishing in the flames.

Suddenly everything seemed to erupt around him.
The sound came first; that was what he had been
tensing for, though he had not realized it. A wild
whoooosh, like the bellow of fire up a chimney, only a
thousand times louder—and then the wind was hurtling at him, so strong it ripped his shirt and nearly
wrenched him from the saddle. The horse reared,

terrified, and would have bolted if he hadn't had so tight a hold.

No warning. It had come from nowhere, with absolutely no warning. The flames that had been smoldering a minute before leapt up, and Errol could see them dissolving into a solid mass at the foot of the hill. Treetops shimmered suddenly, blazing like torches in the night, and then everything turned a vibrating blood-red. The wind seemed to shift capriciously, holding the flames back one second, flinging them forward the next.

Too late to get away. Errol felt a knot tighten in his throat. He should have run while he could. Now it was too late. The trees were aglow, luminous wreaths of crimson; he could smell the pungent aroma of burning euclyptus. The heat was so intense, the air seemed to be on fire. A gum exploded, cascading a burst of brilliant sparks, an awesomely beautiful sight, if fear hadn't made him numb to everything else.

Three kinds of fire blazed in the bush. There were grass fires, sizzling across the savannas, scorching everything—buildings and crops and sheep—in their path. And there were scrub fires that flared up in a high wind, sweeping uncontrollably over the earth. But the fires men dreaded most were the crown fires, raging in oak and gum and wilga, leaping from treetop to treetop like liquid red lightning, at speeds neither man nor horse could match.

And this was a crown fire.

He could hear the roar of it now, deafening in his ears. He could feel it searing his skin. The horse wanted to run. It was all he could do to hang on to the reins, and God help him, his own instinct was the same! But the base of the hill was solid flame; the trees were beginning to catch, showering sparks in a gaudy fireplay on the earth below. And behind was a sheer rock wall!

Only one thing could save him now, and that was the wind. He set his lips in a taut line as he felt it whirling around him, threatening to change—*promising* to change—but always remaining the same. If he was lucky, if it altered its course, the fire would be sucked away and he and the horse would be saved. If it stayed . . .

Every muscle in his body tensed. A whim of the wind, a quirk of nature . . . chance alone was going to decide his fate. He wanted to run. God, how he wanted to run! Like the horse, he longed to turn and charge down that slope, racing as fast as he could. But running wasn't the answer. No man ran from a fire like that.

He laid his hand on the horse's neck. Not for comfort—nothing could comfort either of them now—but because he needed that sense of closeness with another living thing. The wind would change and he would live . . . or it would hold, and he would die. It was as simple as that, and he thought again of Stacey and the child he might never see, and he was glad at least that something would survive.

The heat was even more relentless at the homestead. It had been unbearable from early in the morning. Now, as D'Arcy sat brooding in the oversize front parlor, it was so intense he couldn't bear the sweat-soaked shirt on his back. Taking it off, he tossed it irritably on the floor. Light seeped through the windows, giving the room a reddish glow. The furnishings Maude had taken such trouble to arrange were no more than shadows in the gloom.

The men in the fields had been wrong. The last place D'Arcy Cameron would have chosen for himself was a rough male bar with a pint of Aussie ale. He was not a man's man. He never had been. He was more at home in fashionable salons, with pretty ladies and light, flirtatious talk. A man like that belonged in London, or at least in Sydney—not here on the frontier where he would never fit in.

He started to get up, then sank back on the couch. The leather upholstery prickled annoyingly against his skin. Nor had he stayed away from the fires because he was a coward. He was not afraid to battle flames with the others. It might have given him a sort of primal satisfaction, pitting his strength against the savage strength of nature. He might even have been good at it, if he had known what to do—if anyone had ever bothered to take the time to teach him. But he was damned if he was going to go down and let Errol sneer and hurl abuse at him!

So he had stayed at the homestead. Not because he chose to be there, but because there was no place else he wanted to go. He wished now he had thought to bring a fresh supply of tobacco from the storeroom. It was crazy, in all that smoke, wanting to draw more into his lungs, but he did. Maybe he just needed something to do with his hands. Something to occupy himself while he was sitting there waiting.

He had always been so smug—Errol, with his education and cultivated manners and absolute perfection at everything he did! D'Arcy could remember going to a cricket match with him once. He must have been twelve or thirteen at the time. He had been beside himself with excitement. It had been an important game; he didn't recall what it was now, but it had been held in Sydney, and he had been so proud, sitting there beside his big brother, waiting for everyone to notice how grown-up he was.

Only no one had paid the least attention to him! Not a one of the men who came over. Nor Errol either—he was so swelled up that they remembered he himself had played in England. And been damn good at it, too. But then, Errol was good at everything.

"You mustn't mind so much, little brother," he had said with that bloody condescension of his as they had left with the rest of the crowd. "You'll learn to play cricket yourself one day. Then everyone will make a fuss over you."

Only Australians didn't play worth a shit! The English teams always got the better of them! And it had already been made clear to him that he was going to have an Australian education. *Errol* was the one to go to England. *Errol* . . .

It was not that he minded so much about the cricket. He had never been particularly athletic; he would not have been good at it anyway. But he minded terribly being second best, always coming up with the short end of the stick, never having anything but his brother's leavings.

Even Maude . . .

He jumped up and paced over to the fireplace. Even his own wife had preferred his brother to him! He raised his hand, sweeping the candlesticks violently off the mantel. She had been in that house such a short time, yet everything there reminded him of her. Fascinating, beautiful, treacherous Maude—she had been in love with Errol since she was a child. She had flirted outrageously with him, even when he, her rightful fiancé, had been there. She had never had eyes for anyone else.

Blast! The wound was still open and bleeding, and he lost all sense of logic, as always when it came to his brother. He had thought once that he had finally gotten the better of him—when he bedded the innocent young bride. But even then he had been wrong. Stacey, that little bitch, had stopped giving a damn about him the instant she saw his brother!

His eyes flitted back, catching sight of the painted swan in its mahogany frame over the mantel. Dark and silent, it seemed to be staring down, laughing at him . . . as everyone had laughed all his life. Fitz Blackburn, the great and wonderful artist, had touched his brush to canvas, and everyone thought it was brilliant!

Damn him! His eyes narrowed as he glowered at the painting. Damn him, damn him, damn him! He had behaved as despicably as D'Arcy. Errol had every bit as much reason to hate him. Wasn't it he who had filled Stacey's head with all those lies and sent her to the island? But, no—Errol kept him on anyway! Errol disdained to speak to his brother, he made a point of staying away from the homestead—but he sent wagonloads of food and supplies to Fitz. And all because he liked his stupid pictures!

He clutched one of the candlesticks and was about to hurl it across the room when suddenly there was a loud crashing noise. Like glass shattering . . . as if he had already propelled the heavy piece of brass through the window.

Then he saw that the glass *had* broken, forced inward by the pressure of the heat. Glitter-edged shards splashed sharp and jagged across the floor. Dropping the candlestick, he went over and stared with hypnotic fascination through the window. The flames had reached the road and jumped across. The paddock was a sheet of fire. He could feel it hot against his skin, burning his lungs with every breath he took.

It was the first he realized that the fire was so close. He had been inside all day, and the view from the window, when he bothered to look, showed nothing but smoke. Now suddenly he sensed his danger, and with it came a surge of fear, sweeping the last reason from his thoughts. He ought to be running—he knew he ought to be running!—but he stayed where he was, feet glued to the spot, feeling, irrationally, that he had to save something from the house.

There was no reason for it. He had not been happy there. He hated the house, yet now that it was about to be destroyed, he had a compulsion to salvage something. Without thinking, he seized on the first thing he saw—the painting he both envied and despised, hanging in its place above the carved wooden lintel.

He could not have said himself why he did it. He was behaving irrationally now, reacting solely from instinct; and as always in his life, instinct played him false. It was the one thing in that house he hated most—the one he would have cared least to save—but he found himself tugging it loose, grappling with the heavy frame, dragging it down the hall and out the rear door into the yard.

The fire was not visible there, but he could hear it, a terrible roar, closing in on the front of the house. He started to run, clumsily, for the painting threw him off balance. The stable was nearly a mile from the house, but somehow he managed to reach it. Gasping for breath, he kicked open the door and gaped into the empty interior.

He was bitterly aware of his folly now. It was going to be all he could do to save himself. What the hell was he thinking, carting Fitz's canvas swan across the fields? Carrying it inside, he buried it impulsively in a pile of hay at the back of one of the stalls—a kind of mad instinct he still did not understand—and raced for the door again.

A slight sound caught his ear, and he hesitated, looking back for a second. Then it came again, louder this time, and a woolly head peeked out from the straw.

Stacey's lamb. He started to laugh, raspingly, half-hysterical. Stacey's stupid pet, now a young ewe. What was that ridiculous name she had called it? Rudolfina! It must have escaped the kelpies and wandered inside. Well, that would be an end to one of the lady's little toys. Everyone knew sheep were too dumb to run from a fire. It would lie down and die where it was, and somehow he felt it served her right!

The wind was a raging gale when he got outside. The same wild gusts that whipped across the hilltops had reached the plains, and he knew suddenly that that one vindictive second had cost him dearly. The flames had churned up. He could feel them all around, half-hidden in a veil of smoke. Then the world seemed to explode behind him, and whirling, he saw a solid wall of fire.

Fear burned like the smoke in his throat and chest. There was nothing he could do now but run. Run from the stable, where he would be trapped inside . . . from the house and barn and sheds, which would do little to feed the flames but seemed the greatest danger now. The creek bed beckoned ahead, nearly dry, but with a few stagnant billabongs and the willows along the bank that had been so cool in his youth.

He was running now, as fast as he could. Not looking over his shoulder. There was no time to look, but he knew the fire was just behind and gaining . . . and he kept running, though he thought his lungs would burst. . . . Running and running and running . . .

36

"What did you say?"

Stacey's eyes widened with fear as she stared at the man in front of her. She had just been coming out of the house when he rode into the yard; now she was standing on the lower step of the portico, facing him. He was so disheveled, he looked as if he had been in the saddle for days.

"Jest that the damage looks real bad, ma'am." The man glanced around, searching in vain for a place to hitch his horse. All the posts were some distance from the house. "The wind seems to've died down. 'Least that's the way it looks. I ain't seen nothin' like this fer mebbe thirty years. The paddocks are black as far as you kin see. Some bloke, Harpur, 'as already lost his place—"

"No." Stacey's mouth was dry with smoke and anxiety. "Not the land—I don't care about the land! You were saying that the men . . . some of the men have been hurt . . ."

"More'n half a dozen, near as I can make out." He shuffled his feet awkwardly, staring down at the toes of his boots. It was hard to look at her when she was frightened like that. She was a pretty thing, even with smudges on her cheeks and black hair tumbling every which way over her brow. Judging from the look of her, she was expecting a little one, maybe her first. "I wish I was carryin' better news. One of the men from town's dead already. I saw 'em bringin' the body back. Another's burned real bad, I hear—don't expect him to last the day. Even Mr. Cameron hisself's bin hurt."

"Mr. . . . ?" Stacey swayed dangerously. The world seemed to whirl around her, blackness and terrible gray clouds, blotting out the sun. "Did you say Mr. Cameron?"

The man stared at her curiously. The Cameron place was several miles down the road, an old homestead that had been added onto over the years until it was a comfortable, rambling structure. What could a Cameron have to do with this woman in her elegant limestone palace with columns across the front?

Unless, of course, it wasn't her husband the lady was worried about.

"Yes, ma'am," he said cautiously. "I heard that not more'n half an hour ago, when I was ridin' in from town to see if I could help. I met some men on the road. The worst is over, they say, unless the wind starts in again. Only it come too late fer Mr. Cameron."

"But . . ." Stacey fought the weakness and nausea that rose to her stomach. "Which Mr. Cameron? Please—*which* Mr. Cameron was hurt?"

"Beggin' yer pardon?" The man gaped at her blankly.

"Please," she said again, desperately this time. The air was hot—beads of perspiration stood out on her forehead—but she felt cold as death inside. "I have to know. Was it *Errol* Cameron the men told you about? Or D'Arcy?"

"Ma'am . . ." The man shifted from one foot to the other as he held on to the reins. He had met a Mr. Cameron once, when he had stopped at the homestead, and despite his youth, the man had impressed him. He had been sorry to hear he was hurt. It hadn't occurred to him there might be a brother or a cousin of the same name, though it should have. Cameron's Creek was by far the largest holding in the area. Who but a Cameron would have built that castle on the hill? "I don't know, ma'am—I didn't even know there was two Mr. Camerons. I didn't think . . . well, it jest didn't jump into my head to ask."

"Then . . . you can't tell me?" Stacey tried to force her mind to focus. A Cameron man had fallen to the flames—a Cameron man was lying on the ground, he might be dead or dying at that moment—and she didn't know who it was! "You said he was hurt. Badly? Did the men tell you that?"

"Yes. Real bad—they said he was hurt real bad. Matter o' fact, I got the impression—" he caught himself, seeing the pain and the fear in her eyes. He ought to tell her, she had a right to know, but he couldn't bring himself to hurt her any more. "Never mind, it was only an impression. I might o' got it wrong. Mebbe it isn't as bad . . ."

He went on speaking, but Stacey didn't hear. She was halfway down the path by the time he finished. All she caught were the words "bad, real bad," and she knew suddenly what she had to do. Errol had ordered her not to leave the house, but that was before she learned that he might be hurt! Surely he wouldn't expect her to stay there now, just sitting, waiting for someone to bring her the news! Besides, the man in the yard had said the worst was over. If she was lucky, she'd make it down the hill without mishap, and along the road to the homestead and the rise beyond it . . .

And if she was lucky, when she got there . . .

She forced the thought out of her mind as she reached the stable and shoved the door open. The smell of smoke was as strong inside as out; she could feel the fear of the few animals that had been left in the stalls. Only four of the horses were still there: a pair of hard-mouthed piebalds that were usually hitched to the wagon, Stacey's own Golden Girl, and the spirited stallion Errol had left behind. They snorted softly when they saw her, eyes rolling wildly in the light of a lantern hanging from one of the posts. It was hard to guess which would be most reliable if she hitched it up and forced it outside.

Probably none of them. She heard a sound, and turning, saw Billy Two perched on a bale of hay at the end of the stable. He looked like one of the animals himself, with great wide eyes and dilated pupils. The steadiest of the horses had already been removed. If the stallion handled well in a fire, Errol would have ridden it himself, and the piebalds, while good enough for harness, had never taken to the saddle. That left only one choice.

"Get Golden Girl out of her stall," she said brusquely

to Billy Two. "And help me put a saddle on her. I have to go down the hill for a while to . . . to see what's happening." When he did not obey, she led the horse out herself, dragging it through the open door with one hand, struggling to manage the heavy saddle in the other.

The next minutes were a blur in her mind. Somehow— she would never know how—she got the saddle on the horse's back, though Golden Girl was fighting and rearing so badly it was next to impossible. Billy Two was beside her suddenly. He must have been even more terrified of her impetuosity than all that dense smoke settling like storm clouds in the sky. Stacey barely heard his anxious: "No, missus, what you do? That fellow, 'e no bin good for ridin'. Mr. Cameron, 'e be very angry."

Mr. Cameron might well be angry, Stacey thought as she gave the cinch one last sharp tug. But Mr. Cameron could be hurt—or dying—and she had to go to him.

She didn't even notice that the stranger who had brought the news was there until he spoke.

"The boy's right, ma'am. The best horse is skittish enough, it comes to a fire. That one—well, you won't get half the way."

Stacey felt her heart sink. The man was right, she knew he was—but what could she do? "Golden Girl is one of the best horses we have. I've been riding her for months. She's an excellent mount."

"For frolics across the meadow, mebbe. But a horse that's good fer frolickin' ain't always good fer nothin' else." His eyes lowered, taking in her condition, which was even more obvious now. "Whyn't you let me go, ma'am. I know about where t'look. Over there, near where the homestead . . ." He hesitated, holding back for a second, then went on. "Near where the homestead used to be. It went up in flames, mebbe an hour ago. There's a creek runs along there toward a hill where a man can git a view if he has to. I'd be back in an hour or two. No more 'n that."

An hour or two! Stacey stared at him. Did he really think she could survive an hour or two, not knowing whether her husband was dead or alive? "No, I have to go myself. I can't wait that long! Don't you understand? I have to!"

"Take my horse then." He was beside her, pressing the reins into her hands. "She's no beauty, but she holds steady, you keep a tight grip. You'll have a chance with her."

Stacey eyed the mare warily. Gray, like the horse Errol had ridden, with stocky legs and a thin, unkempt mane—but at least it was standing still. Nothing but its eyes were moving. She didn't like the idea of riding a horse she wasn't familiar with under circumstances like that. But she liked the idea of her own temperamental mount even less.

"I'll take good care of her." She grabbed the reins and tossed them impulsively over the horse's head. "I'll bring her back safe, I promise." Then, before she could think what she was doing, she swung into the saddle and headed for the path.

The horse was not graceful, but it was surefooted and surprisingly swift, and she reached the base of the hill and had crossed the dry creek in less than twenty minutes. Signs of the fire showed intermittently here. The earth ran beige, then black, then golden beige again, the demarcations strikingly straight in places, as if they had been drawn with a ruler and charcoal. The flames had been capricious in their violence, leaping back and forth, burning a wide swath of grassy soil here, sparing another there.

It was not until she came out on the town road that she found herself in the area over which the worst of the fire had swept.

The devastation was utter and terrible. Everywhere she looked the earth was black. Blackened hills rose out of blackened plains, and the skeletons of blackened trees were eerie silhouettes against a deep gray sky. Here and there, tongues of flame sputtered out, startling flashes of red, the last death throes of tall gums still afire, their hearts not yet burned out. Lacy patterns of shiny black showed where shrubs had once stood—so delicate they looked as if the first puff of wind would blow them away—and wisps of smoke curled in a low fog over the ground.

Like a nightmare, Stacey thought numbly as she turned her head to look around. Everything was distorted and unreal. A grim, surrealistic canvas, splashed with a mad artist's brush! Fitz Blackburn could have done justice to such a scene. There had always been hints of madness in his paintings. Only they were just hints, like crows on the sunrise-pink branches of a flowering tree—this was all around, as if the madness had escaped and was running wild.

Stacey looped the reins around her hand, tightening her hold, though the horse had given her no trouble yet. Overhead, smoke massed in thick black clouds, seeming, as always, with the cruel illusions of the bush, to promise rains that would not come. The aftersmell of the fire was distinct and unpleasant. Ashes, like the inside of an old fireplace, and singed fur, and an aroma of roasting flesh. A wallaby darted out of nowhere, looking dazed for an instant before turning and hopping back again, going around and around in circles in its terror. It had been so close, Stacey could make out burned patches on its side.

Others had not been so lucky. Carcasses could be seen, black and rigid along the road, unavoidable, though she tried not to look. A dingo that had not run fast enough; it was lying now with one leg stiffly in the air . . . another wallaby, or a small kangaroo, caught in the undergrowth . . . charred bits of things that were no longer identifiable but had only hours before been living creatures.

The silence was so intense, it was unnerving. Stacey had not expected that; she had never heard the bush so quiet. Occasionally a tree would crash joltingly to the earth, the last reverberations echoing into emptiness until they finally died away. Then the only sound was the steady crunching of the horse's hooves.

If only Errol was safe. Smoke and ashes caught in her throat, choking her so she could hardly breathe. She didn't even know if the man who had been hurt *was* Errol—it might be his brother—or if the injuries were as serious as the stranger thought. She might ride up in a panic and find one or the other of them sitting on a fallen log with a bandage on his arm or his leg, and nothing worse than a few bad bruises!

It was only her fear, after all, that made her so sure the worst had happened. And fantasies of fear had nothing to do with reality.

The horse hesitated, and she prodded it forward, a little surprised at how well it responded to her signal. She was glad now she hadn't been too proud to accept it. The smoke and smells were enough to spook any mount, especially one as high-spirited and unruly as Golden Girl. An animal screamed somewhere nearby, crying out again and again, a terrible, piercing, almost human wail of pain, and Stacey felt the fear tighten in her heart.

Errol might be in pain too. He would not be screaming—he would never let himself cry out—but he might be in pain, and there was nothing she could do! She could go to him, she could hold him in her arms, if that would help, if he even knew she was there. But there was no way she could stop the pain . . . or spare his life.

Oh, dear heaven. She closed her eyes for a brief second, letting the horse find its own way along the path. She loved this man so deeply; her life was so entwined with his. She tried to force herself to dwell on the happy times, tried with the superstition of a small child to cling to good moments, as if somehow that would make everything all right. But all she could remember was the way he had looked that first night when he stood in the doorway of her bedroom and told her he was sending her back to her grandfather . . . and the anger in his eyes the afternoon the telegram arrived in Sydney . . . and that awful, ugly suspicion in her own heart as she stood at Maude's funeral and tried to read something comforting into his face. All the silly moments that had come between them, all the time they had wasted, time they could have spent touching, clasping, loving each other. Now it might be too late.

If only it wasn't Errol. If only it wasn't her husband who had been hurt . . . who might be dying—or dead!—at that moment. If only it was D'Arcy!

A loud snapping noise broke into her thoughts. Turning, she was just in time to see a bright flare as the last core of resin burst in a nearby tree. Flames flashed for one brief, dazzling instant, then clusters of luminous sparks floated all around, settling harmlessly on the burned-out earth. The horse shied, but she tugged at the reins and it quieted again.

It was a terrible thing to hope that a man was dead. She knew it was wrong, she despised what she was doing, but she couldn't stop herself. She bore no animosity toward D'Arcy. She did not hate him anymore. She could even pity his pain, if indeed the pain was his, but she could not help hoping it was he lying somewhere dead on the ground. If it was D'Arcy, her life would go on.

If it was Errol . . .

He heart caught in her throat as she rounded a curve and noticed a small group of men just ahead. They had not seen her yet, but she was intensely aware of them. They were huddled together on the side of the road, heads down, not looking at anything, not talking, just standing there, as if waiting for someone to come.

Then she saw the thing lying on the ground a short distance away, and she felt as if her heart had stopped.

The men spotted her at almost that moment. They turned, eyes startled, and Stacey's blood ran cold as she saw them glance uncomfortably at each other. If that sooty pile of something was not what she thought, then why were they milling around, silent and clearly avoiding it? And if it was D'Arcy—only D'Arcy—would they be staring at her that way?

She gripped the reins so sharply the horse pulled back. Yes, of course they would. They were only station hands, not used to dealing with the boss's wife, and they could not know she had no liking for her husband's brother.

Which one is it? she longed to cry out. *Which man lies there on the ground? The husband I love . . . or his brother?* But her throat was dry and she could not get out the words. Nor would it have done any good if she could. It did not matter what they said. They could tell her anything, but she had to see it for herself.

Numb inside, she dismounted, one foot moving automatically in front of the other. She was vaguely aware that one of the men had broken away from the group and was coming toward her, but she brushed him back with a wave of her hand. She had to know, once and for all . . . and she could not hear it from someone else's lips.

Then she was there. She was alone now; she knew it without having to turn and look. The man behind her had stopped, respecting her privacy, she sensed. She wavered for a second, then forced her eyes down.

"Oh, my God . . ."

The one thing she had not considered. The one thing of all those terrible imaginings that had not even crossed her mind. That she might look down at the man on the ground—and still not know.

That he was dead, she had no doubt. There was no life in that sprawling form. He was lying on his chest, arms flung out at awkward angles, head twisted to one side so half his face was visible. Stacey struggled with a wave of nausea as she stared down. His features were badly distorted, the flesh so swollen and engorged it was almost flame red—he must have died in terrible pain—and she could not pick out anything she recognized.

A little sob slipped out of her lips. How could she have forgotten how physically alike they looked? Errol was taller, but lying on the ground, height didn't matter. Otherwise they were the same, the same broad shoulders, the same tapering waist, the same lean hips and thighs. Then her eyes went back to his face, and she noticed the one feature that set the brothers apart.

And at last she knew.

37

D'Arcy!

She caught her breath, holding it, not even daring to move. The man on the ground was D'Arcy! His features were unrecognizable—he must not have shaved for days, the stubble was so thick on his cheeks and chin—but a dark line still showed across his upper lip. And only D'Arcy had a mustache.

Thank God. . . . The words were mute in Stacey's heart, coming out only in a long, quivering sigh. She had a vague sense that she ought to be feeling something for that twisted body on the blackened soil. Shock, compassion, horror—*something*. But all she could feel was a flood of relief that it was D'Arcy, not Errol, and her husband was alive.

"Ma'am . . ."

Turning, she saw that the man behind had stepped closer. A spate of tears rushed to her eyes. Embarrassed, she blinked them back. She was not crying for the dead man, but for herself, and the fears that had seemed so dark before . . . and the sheer, utter joy that her world had not been shattered.

"I . . . I'm all right."

"You shouldn't o' come, ma'am. That ain't no thing fer a lady t' see. Best you step back now."

Stacey stared at him blankly for a minute. It was hard to focus through the tears on her lashes. Then, beneath all that soot and grime, she recognized young Bluey Warren. The shiest of the men—and the only one who had had the courage to come to her.

"I *am* all right. Really I am. But . . ." She shuddered as she threw a last glance at D'Arcy's body. "You're right. It isn't something anyone should see, lady or man. How . . . how did he die? His face looks as if he were in terrible agony."

The young man hesitated, shoving his hands awkwardly in his pockets. He knew how D'Arcy Cameron died, of course; they all did. It was not an unfamiliar story in the bush, though he had never seen it before. The man must have been running from the flames—they came at lightning speed sometimes—and there was that billabong in the half-dry creek, right in front of him. He wouldn't have been thinking, just going on instinct. And instinct wouldn't remember that the water had been heated to boiling by the flames.

"Death by fire is never easy," he said gently. "But it, uh . . it looks worse sometimes than it is."

Stacey nodded weakly and turned, moving a short distance away. The same dull ebony sprawled in every direction, a charred and ravaged earth, but no matter how she stared at it, all she could see was that bloated, tortured face. She knew that the youth was trying to ease the truth for her—she knew D'Arcy had died horribly, excruciatingly, and Errol would be torn apart when he learned of it—but still she couldn't feel anything. Not even a kind of righteous justification that the man who had hurt her so badly had been punished at last.

Errol appeared a few minutes later. Stacey did not hear him come, she was so absorbed in her own thoughts. She knew only that suddenly he was there, striding up behind her, turning her around with strong arms, searching her face for a long, penetrating moment, as if he, like her, had thought they would never be together again.

Then the tears came, and she reached out, desperate to touch him, hold him, feel at last that he was there and he was whole.

"Oh, Errol, I was so afraid. I heard that Mr. Cameron had been hurt, some man came riding up to the house—only he didn't know *which* Mr. Cameron! And I . . . I was afraid I was going to come here . . . and it would be you!"

He held her at arm's length one last second, taking

in the tears that were streaming down her face, the relief in her eyes.

"So I see, my darling," he said softly. Then she was in his arms, cheeks smudged with soot as she soaked the shoulder of his shirt. "It's all right now . . . it's over, sweet. It's all over. You don't have to be afraid anymore."

"But it was so awful," she sobbed. "I looked down, and for a minute . . . I didn't know. Then I saw his mustache, and I . . . I was glad! He was dead, he died horribly, and I was *glad* because it wasn't you."

"That's not unnatural, love." Callused fingers felt rough as he took her chin and tipped it up. "Wives are supposed to be glad when their husbands are safe. I'd be worried if it were otherwise. . . . And D'Arcy hasn't given you cause of late to be overfond of him."

"But I don't hate him," Stacey protested. "Truly I don't. And I'm not glad he's dead. Not exactly. Only . . ."

Only it *is* a relief, a little voice nagged at the back of her mind. A dreadful selfish thought, but she couldn't help it. Now that D'Arcy was gone, she wouldn't have to rack her brains to find a way to tell Errol about the past. Her guilty secret would remain a secret forever.

"Shhh, darling," he murmured gently, and she was back in his arms, her head against his chest. "You don't have to explain. It isn't your fault . . . anything that's happened. You mustn't take the blame. See, my shoulders are much stronger. Let me carry the burden instead."

They stood together for a long time, clasped in a healing embrace that went a long way toward easing the pain and horror of the last few days. Even when they separated, Errol's arm was still around her, and they walked over to the place where one of the men had hobbled their horses. He left her briefly, to speak to the others, who had moved discreetly to one side— about the disposal of his brother's body, she supposed— then came back again.

His eyes sparkled, just for a second, as he took in the two stocky grays standing side by side.

"Where did you find such a handsome mount, love?" he said, obviously amused.

"I borrowed her—and don't make fun, Errol. She may not look like much to you, but she got me here safely—and that was the worst ride I've ever had! I think she's absolutely gorgeous."

"She's looking better and better," he admitted as he removed the hobble and helped Stacey into the saddle. "As a matter of fact, she's got quite a chic look in her eye. We'll have to find a satin bow and a bit of lace for her forelock when we get back." He looked up, grinning. "Or maybe an old bird's wing. I seem to recall you have one around somewhere."

The mutilated landscape was as black and lifeless now as it had been when Stacey rode across it before, but somehow it did not look so desolate with Errol by her side. The cloudlike formations were even heavier in the sky, and she looked up once or twice, half-daring to hope that this time they were swollen with moisture. If only the rains would come, the earth would be drenched, deeply and finally, and the last threat of fire would be gone.

But the clouds had been dry for a long time—hope was such a futile thing—and she tried not to think that this was only a brief respite, and tomorrow Errol would ride out back down the hill and the fear would start all over again.

The terrible howling sound was still there when they reached the place she had heard it before. Still or again, she did not know. It might be the same animal, in the same unbearable pain . . . it might be another; it did not matter. The sound was shrill and agonizing. She could feel it penetrating deep into her bones, like the cries of some poor soul in hell, and she knew she would hear it in her nightmares for the rest of her life.

Errol stopped his horse, glancing around for a moment, as if to check the terrain. Then, with a brief warning to Stacey to stay where she was, he turned off the path, heading toward the place the noise was coming from. For the first time, she noticed he had a rifle slung across his saddle; he was tugging it loose with one hand as he rode. A minute later she heard a sharp report, and the wailing ended in mid-note. The silence that followed was eerie and all-encompassing.

Errol took her hand when he returned, and they rode on like that, slowly, unable to let go of each other. Embers still flared occasionally, trees cracked and thundered to the earth, but Stacey kept her eyes straight ahead. Nothing else was there, nothing existed but Errol, straight in the saddle beside her, and the knowledge that he was safe for one more day at least.

They were still holding hands when they reached Glenellen. Ashes dulled the wheat-gold grass, the beautiful limestone walls were gray with soot, but it was like a mirage in the desert, and they drank it in with thirsty eyes. The man who had lent her the horse was nowhere in sight. Probably in the kitchen with Dollie, Stacey thought, too weary even to chuckle. No doubt the little maid was in her element, regaling him with typical Irish extravagance—and telling him how she had single-handedly saved the house by climbing up on the roof!

Billy Two came running out of the stable, wide-eyed as before and jabbering all sorts of things Stacey did not have the strength to sort out. Errol turned the horses over to him, with strict orders to see that they were properly curried and given an extra portion of oats; then they walked together, still hand in hand, past the rear of the house, which Stacey suddenly realized did not look quite the same as it had when he left. She was a little nervous as she explained what she had done—why she thought the veranda had to be taken down—but she need not have worried. Errol approved, and even praised her for acting so sensibly.

"I always knew you were a beauty, love, and quite deliciously sexy. But sharp-witted too? Am I really so lucky?"

"Lucky . . . or cursed?" Stacey managed a weak smile. "Some men would be none too pleased to have a wife who thinks for herself. Especially if it means part of the house is going to be gone when they come home."

"How many times do I have to tell you, love"—his

hand was warm in hers, strong and comforting—"I am not 'some men'?"

They entered the broad central hall together. The light was subdued, as if night had already fallen, though dusk was nearly an hour away. The wind or the heat, or perhaps a combination of both, had shattered the glass in one of the panes under the dome, and a smoky draft blew through, giving a momentary illusion of coolness. Stacey could hear the grit crunching under her feet as she started up the curving staircase.

A sudden flash illuminated the room, bathing it for an instant in stark, unnatural white. The heat storms again, she thought, jumping nervously. She had hoped they were over—she had *prayed* they were over—but now it seemed they had come back, with jagged veins of lightning searing across the sky. Discouraged, she leaned against the rail.

Errol was beside her in a second, his arm around her shoulders.

"You're trying to do too much, love," he scolded gently. "You've worn yourself out. You should never have dared that madcap ride down the hill."

"I had to, Errol. When he told me—that man—when he said Mr. Cameron had been hurt . . ."

"You should have sent someone else. I'm sure the stranger would have gone, if you'd asked. Or you could have roused Billy Two wherever he was hiding. If you were determined not to think of yourself"—he lowered his hand, resting it lightly on the roundness that was her waist—"you should have remembered this little child of mine."

Stacey shook her head. Dark curls were damp and sticky as they bounced on her forehead. "I didn't know the stranger. He might have gotten distracted and never bothered to come back." She hesitated, half-smiling. "And I *did* know Billy Two! Besides, I was frantic with fear. I would have done more harm to myself—and the child—if I'd tried to stay, in the state I was in. You have no idea how terrified I was."

"Hush, darling." He brushed the side of her head with his lips. "You don't have to tell me—"

"But I do!" Now that she had started, it was almost

a compulsion, letting all the anguish out. "It was just so awful! I rode and rode . . . and then I saw the men, and there was that . . . that *thing* on the ground . . . and, oh, Errol, I was afraid it was you! I couldn't bear the thought that I had lost you."

"I know," he said quietly. "I saw it in your eyes when you turned and looked at me. The relief—and the joy." His lips twitched, just slightly, as if he were laughing at himself. "I was afraid too, you know."

"You? Afraid?" Stacey stared at him, puzzled. "But why?"

"For the same reason you were, my sweet little innocent. I thought I might have lost you. When I got there, when I saw you standing by yourself, so lonely and forlorn, I was afraid you were grieving . . . for him."

"But why would I grieve for D'Arcy? After what he did to me on the island? I didn't gloat at his death, I would never do that, but why on earth would you think I'd grieve?"

"Perhaps because I feared you still loved him."

"I . . . still . . . loved him?" Stacey caught her breath, too dazed for a moment to think, or even to feel.

"I *know*, darling." He chose the words carefully, not with any reproach in his voice, but a kind of softness, as one speaks to a child. "I have known all along. About you and D'Arcy."

"You . . . knew?" She felt like a parrot, echoing everything he said. "All along? But how?"

"I'm not a fool, Stacey. I know my brother well . . . too well. When you admitted you had been with someone else first, I remembered the way he had looked at you that afternoon, and some of the remarks he had made—and I guessed the truth. His behavior later confirmed it. And yours. You went to such lengths to avoid him . . . and you never looked in his eyes."

"Then . . . that was why you were determined not to keep me as your wife."

"That was part of it. I didn't want to set up an intolerable situation. A woman married to me and in love with my brother, who was living under the same roof? That's the stuff of which Greek tragedies are made."

Stacey caught the lightness in his tone and tried to smile. All that time she had been so afraid he would learn her guilty secret, so terrified D'Arcy would blurt it out in a burst of anger—and he had already known! "But you didn't offer to release me from my vows so I could marry him."

"D'Arcy would never have married you, dearest," he said gently. "Not while Maude was alive. He really did love her, as much as he was capable of loving. But that wouldn't have kept him from toying with you. As long as he held your heart, I knew he could make your life—and mine—a living hell."

"But surely you realized, after a while, that you were wrong. That he didn't have my heart any longer. That I did, truly, care for you."

"I knew you were learning to care." His hand was still on her waist; she could feel the powerful muscles in his chest as he pulled her closer. "I would not have come to you that night in the tent if I didn't think we had a chance. I was beginning to believe the worst was over and I had finally won you for myself when Maude died—and you ran away! You can imagine what went through my mind then."

"But I was only running because I was sure you were in love with her," she protested. "I needed time to get away, to work things out in my head."

"So you told me—later," he said wryly. "But at the time, all I could think was that Maude's death set D'Arcy free and you were agonizing over what you wanted to do about it."

"Oh, dear heaven . . ." Stacey shuddered visibly. "How it must have looked when you came to the island and saw D'Arcy there with me. You must have thought—"

"No," he broke in hastily. "I could see you were struggling. What I couldn't see was why. I didn't know if you were resisting because you didn't want him, or if you wanted him too much and were fighting your own feelings. I was never really sure until this afternoon, when I looked into your eyes and saw only relief . . . and no sadness for my brother."

And she had felt so guilty about that! Stacey leaned against him, drawing from his strength. She was glad now her feelings had been so selfish. "And you never said a word about it. All this time, you kept it to yourself."

"I was afraid to say anything," he admitted sheepishly. "Afraid you'd tell me what I didn't want to hear—and everything would be ruined. I am a proud man, love. Much too proud for my own good. I could not live with a woman who had openly acknowledged her passion for someone else."

Stacey started to laugh softly. It sounded so familiar, the same silly fears she had had herself. "And you accused me of being foolish. About Maude. You said I should have come to you and confessed my petty jealousy—and all the time you were doing the same thing yourself!"

"And I was wrong. But be fair, Stacey—your suspicions were cut out of whole cloth. Mine at least had some grounding in the past. You must promise, from now on, you'll never keep anything from me."

"*I* must promise? It seems to me, on that point, you are as guilty as I, my love."

"Well, then, we will promise each other. No more secrets, ever again."

No more secrets, Stacey started to say, but a clap of distant thunder rumbled through the hall, but rolling on and on, drowning out the words. *Thunder?* The whole house felt as if it were shaking. They stood for a moment, she and Errol, still touching, as the noise swelled, battering now, sharp and distinct on the roof. *No, not thunder at all.*

Once before she had heard that same sound, stood in the exact same place—only then she had been alone and bewildered, and Maude Quinn had beaten her outside. This time she recognized the welcome drumming at once. This time she was down the stairs without even pausing. This time she threw open the door herself and was out in the yard, Errol beside her, and water was streaming down her upturned face.

Rain. Thousands of things ran through her mind, all too jumbled to sort out. The drought was over . . . the rain was pouring down, and every last steaming ember would be extinguished . . . and like many a woman before and after, she realized suddenly what it was to belong to that hard, demanding land and to wed a man who had been nurtured on the soil. The station counted, the buildings and the crops and such live-stock as had been spared, but she was not thinking of them now, though she knew he was. She was thinking only that he was there and he would stay with her now.

The drought was over, and the terrible fires, and the man she loved with every throbbing beat of her heart would not be riding into danger tomorrow.

She looked up to see that he, too, seemed to be laughing and crying at the same time, as she and Maude had laughed and cried together that day so long ago. Water ran in rivulets down his face, follow-ing the craggy lines of his nose, his cheeks, his chin; all the soot had been washed away, and clean black hair was plastered like shiny satin to his brow. Stacey held out her arms, and suddenly his arms were around her, and she could feel his kisses mingling with the sweet cool kiss of the rain. Then he was lifting her strongly, forcefully, carrying her into the house.

Water trailed in a stream behind them, across the polished stone floor, up the graceful sweep of the stairs. The bed was drenched when he laid her down—moisture saturated the rumpled sheets and mattress—but they did not even notice. Their mouths were too busy with each other, their hands too eager as they tore off their clothes, ripping them in their hunger to lie naked next to each other once more. Gone were whatever last inhibitions they still possessed, gone all the concern and caution and overgentleness, and they made love completely and satisfyingly, again and again, with the healing passion that was a need in both their hearts.

It was only afterward, as they lay together, ex-hausted but still entwined in each other's arms, that Errol remembered her pregnancy. He smiled ruefully.

"A fine, considerate husband I've turned out to be." He had a slightly guilty look on his face, though not, Stacey was pleased to note, quite as guilty as she thought he wanted to feel. "I seem to have forgotten all about being careful with you and the little one."

"The little one is much bigger now." Stacey sat up, laughing as she ran a finger along the side of his face, still damp from the rain. "He'll be starting to kick his mama any day now. I think he's big enough to tolerate a 'madcap ride' on horseback. Or a bit of bouncing on the bed. Besides"—she tapped him lightly on the tip of his nose—"you've forgotten the most important thing."

"And what is that, love?" He caught her finger, nibbling it playfully.

"You've forgotten that this baby is an Australian." She leaned forward, touching his nose this time with her lips, only half-teasing now. "And from what I've seen, Australians are tough."

He seemed to agree, for when he drew her down beside him, he made no effort to be cautious.

38

The rains continued for a week and a half, drenching the soil until it could hold no more, and runoff rushed in raging torrents through streambeds that had been parched and powdery a short time before. Then at last it ended, the sun came out in a splash of gold, and, miraculously, the land began to renew itself. Steam rose from the charred earth, then tiny pinpoints of green began to show, and within days, a verdant mantle spread like velvet across paddocks that had looked as if they would never rise from the ashes again.

Like the people, the land was tough and resilient. Centuries of harshness, those long cycles of drought and fire and disastrous flooding, had weeded out the weakest of the species, and only those plants that were most resistant survived. Just as there were seeds with the ability to lie dormant for years beneath what appeared a lifeless desert, so there were seeds that had grown so accustomed to fire they could not germinate properly unless they had first been singed by flame. Now they burst forth, flooding the earth with color, as it had previously been flooded with water, and the long process of healing began. Wattles seemed to be everywhere, hundreds upon hundreds of seedlings springing up at once, and grass so thick even the sheep would have trouble mowing it back before it could grow, and carpets of wildflowers, blowing gently in sunlit breezes, hiding the dark crust of cinders beneath.

There were still scars, like the scars of the heart— the deepest healing would be a long time coming—but they were muted by the sudden softness of nature. Barren patches remained here and there, looking like outcrops of stone in the fields, and leafless trees clung to the hillsides, dead and black, but too stubborn to fall. There they would stand for many years, until they rotted from the inside out, a reminder of the terrible and awesome scourge that had swept across the land. But they would be fewer and fewer all the time, the blight on the landscape like the painful memories fading, until at last even they were gone.

The cost of the fire had been high, both in property and human life. Errol, as the largest landowner, had lost the most. Mirandola, which had become his on D'Arcy's death, was completely gone. Not a timber or wall or fencepost remained to show where sturdy buildings had once stood. Martin Quinn, mercifully, had died the night before the fire came through. He had not had to awaken, senses keen for one last moment, and realize that everything he had built was about to be destroyed. Or feel the smoke and flames close in . . . and be afraid.

Stacey had thought Errol might rebuild the place, if only as a tribute to Maude, but he had decided against it. The setting was beautiful, the perfect site for a house, and one day perhaps one of his sons would want to make his home there. But children had a way of going their own direction. Who knew whether that sunswept slope would appeal to a son of his . . . or even if the boy would make his life on the station, as his father had? There was no point looking ahead to things that might never be.

Rebuilding did go on, however, elsewhere in the area. Ned Harpur, who had not been too old after all to begin again, had been so eager to get started, he had gone back the first day after the rains ended, slogging in his boots through ankle-deep mud as he staked out new corners as near as he could reckon to where the old corners had been. He was too proud to accept charity, though he desperately needed it, and Errol, understanding, did not press his money. But in a land where survival was a day-to-day battle, help from neighbors which could later be repaid was not charity, and Errol was there with the other men, wielding saw and hatchet and hammer as the new house and barn went up, just as he knew Ned Harpur would be there when it was time for him to reerect the fences he had lost, and when additional sheds and stables were needed.

Most of the homestead buildings had been lost the last day of the fire, and like Mirandola, Errol had elected to let them go. The location was no longer convenient, the way the station had sprawled; all that was left were memories, and memories could not be reconstructed from wood and tin and stone. Only the stable remained intact, a quirk of nature, as sometimes happened in the fires. The winds had whipped the flames almost to the wide double doors—a black line still showed faintly on the earth—then changed abruptly, leaving only one side slightly singed. It would not be used again. Errol was moving the barns and sheds, together with bunkhouses for the men, to an area near the base of the hill from which Glenellen rose. The old stable would be utilized only for storage, if that, until eventually it decayed and was gone.

The shallow rise beside the creek, where Stacey had once stood and watched her husband say good-bye to the woman she thought he loved, was rich with color. Trees had burned and fallen, their blackened trunks were still visible even from the stream, but the grass was green, and tiny blossoms flecked the earth with purple and white. There were new graves among the others now. Errol had brought his brother's body there, and in the pouring rain dug the deep hole in the earth himself, not allowing any of the others to help. D'Arcy Cameron now lay—in peace at last, Stacey hoped—beside his wife and the infant son she had given her life to bear. He would be the last to be buried there, for the future Camerons would lie in a gentle hollow in the slopes behind Glenellen. He, and one of the men from town—the others who had perished had gone to their own people—and Fitz Blackburn.

It was funny, Stacey thought as she stood on the newly rebuilt veranda, sensibly roofed with metal this time, and looked out toward the mountains—it was Fitz she minded most of all the losses she had suffered. Errol had started over to the artist's studio the morning the rains let up, grim-faced and determined, but Ned Harpur and a man named Barstow, whom Stacey had never met, had gotten there before him. Both had lived through disastrous fires earlier in their lives. Both had gone to the houses of people they knew and sorted charred bodies out of the charred ruins, and they knew how it haunted a man sometimes, the things he had seen there. It was better, they told Errol when they ran into him on the way back and turned their blanket-wrapped burden over to him, that men who had experienced that horror be the ones to see it again. And because he knew they were right, and because the thing had already been done, he thanked them and agreed.

Of the paintings there had been no trace. Canvas stretched on taut wood frames burned with little ash. All that remained of the magnificent masterpieces that had so taken Stacey's breath away was the dome at Glenellen, with its enchanted forest of birds, and kangaroos and possums and koalas peeking out from blue-green gums. Even that had been severely damaged. The smoke that had blown in the windows had left dark smudges, so thick in places they obscured what lay beneath, and moisture had caused small cracks in the plaster. Errol had already sent for an expert from Sydney, a painter himself, but secure enough in his ego not to impose his own creativity on that other, more dazzling talent. He would paint over the damaged sections and touch up the plaster, and when he had finished, it would be almost—but not quite—the way Fitz had left it. As the years went by, and the sun and future restorations took their toll, it would become only a clever idea, with nothing left of the soul of the man who had created it.

All that remained was the painting on the dome— and the exquisite *Silver Swan*. No one had been more surprised than Stacey that afternoon early in the rains when Errol came home with the painting wrapped in old sacking and a bleating ewe in the back of his wagon. Rudolfina! She had been so involved in other things, she had completely forgotten the lamb she had bottle-fed the night of its birth. Now she learned that the sheep and the painting had been discovered at the same time. In fact, it was the former which had caused the rescue of the latter. If it hadn't been for Rudolfina, the painting might have lain in the stall for years, eaten away by mildew in the rainy seasons, or trampled underfoot when a cow came wandering in. One of the men had heard a pathetic *maaaaing* and, peeking in the door, had seen the ewe cowering, still terrified, in one of the stalls. If he hadn't recognized it as Mrs. Cameron's pet, he might have gone on—and never have found the *Swan*.

How it got there was a mystery—Stacey supposed they would never know—but she was moved to tears to think that something at least of that superb body of art had been saved. They debated giving it to a museum, and at first she was afraid Errol was going to insist. But to her surprise, he relented.

"It's only one painting," he said after a moment's thought. "It doesn't mean much by itself. Fitz's talent as a whole was what really counted. One painting, all alone, would only be a freak in some museum collection. It might as well hang where he would have chosen—or should I say second choice? The parlor that was never quite good enough for him."

His mouth was set in a hard line, and Stacey sensed he was angry. Angry at Fitz Blackburn for keeping his paintings carelessly stacked in a storeroom, even angrier at himself for having allowed him to do it. But, in an odd way, she almost understood. The paintings had been Fitz's personal obsession, guarded as tenaciously as a jealous man might guard a beautiful mistress. He had given them only twice. Once the *Swan*, out of gratitude to Errol, and perhaps respect. And once the dome at Glenellen, a gift to her—though she suspected it was less a reflection of her charm and persuasiveness than an appealing challenge. He would not have wanted strangers to have them after he was gone.

"Yes, thank you," she said softly. "Fitz would have approved. I think I can fix the parlor up adequately."

One last good thing was to come out of all that devastation. Errol brought it home one day in his saddlebag, a small, indiscriminately colored cat, yowl-

ing with indignation at the top of its lungs. He had
cornered it in a hollow log not far from the path that
once led to Fitz's studio, and the little creature had
put up a terrible fight. Errol's arms were a mass of
scratches by the time he got it out, but he had stuffed
it in the saddlebag anyway, sensing that his wife would
like to have it, and Stacey stretched out her hands,
delighted. It seemed to recognize her, for it came to
her right away, though it would have nothing to do
with anyone else. Its fur was mangy—bits were burned
away in places, just beginning to grow back—but its
eyes were green and willful, and Stacey fell in love at
once.

She had half-expected Errol to object, but beyond a
gruff "Good God, Stacey, you aren't bringing your
animals in the house now?" he had said nothing when
she carried it into the parlor "just for one night—until
it's less frightened." One night, naturally, had turned
into two, and two into three, and the cat and Errol
now maintained a subtly armed neutrality, eyeing each
other warily from their separate corners.

It was like an omen, Stacey thought contentedly one
lazy afternoon about a month after the rains had subsided. A sign that life was ready to go on. The earth
was bright with flowers again, and animals could be
glimpsed hopping across the paddocks; the little cat
was curled up on her feet as she sat in a chair by the
window, and the baby was practicing to be a ballet
dancer or marching soldier in her belly.

"You look so smug—it's hard to tell which of you
has just lapped up a platter of cream." Errol paused in
the doorway. It was a busy season—he should be out
in the paddocks—but he had taken to stopping by the
house more and more of late. The little cat opened
one eye, saw that it was just that man again, and went
back to purring in its sleep.

"*I* have, as a matter of fact." Stacey laughed. "Or
rather a huge slab of sweet butter on fresh sweet
bread—with a whole jar of wild-lime preserves. And I
don't feel the least bit guilty!"

"I should hope not." He bent over the arm of the
chair and kissed her. "You're supposed to be taking

care of that little one of mine. I expect you to present it to me fat and healthy."

"Not it, darling—he. You can't talk about your son as 'it.' You have to learn to say 'he.' "

"Or 'she' . . . if it's a daughter."

Stacey shook her head. She couldn't imagine a man as masculine as Errol Cameron accepting a daughter as his firstborn. "No, it's a son. Definitely and emphatically. I am the mother. I ought to know."

Errol smiled. "If determination counts for anything, love, you must know what you're talking about."

Stacey turned her head slightly, moving out of the glaring rays of the sun. Her eye lighted on the *Swan* above the mantel. They had hung it yesterday, and already it dominated everything else, a proud, timelessly graceful figure floating over the rest of the room. Fitz had been right. It belonged there, and not in that niche at the head of the stairs. The little cat moved, resting its paw, claws delicately retracted on her ankle.

"I wish she would come back too."

Errol looked startled for an instant. Then he saw where her eyes had gone, and caught the hint of sadness in her voice. The animals had returned weeks before, and flocks of birds forming dark patterns in the sky, but no matter how many times they went back to the pond by the old homestead, they never saw the swan again.

"That's just the way of nature, dearest. Nothing goes on forever. We were bound to miss her one season, sooner or later."

"I know—but she was so beautiful." Stacey couldn't help remembering the way the swan had looked that first time she saw her, gliding majestically across the pond, ebony black with a startlingly crimson beak. And the power of her wings when she spread them, a bold accent of white on the underside as she prepared to take flight. "Do you mind much—that she is gone?"

"Mind? What a strange way to put it. I miss her, of course—she was a lovely wild creature—but mind? No, why should I?"

"It seemed to me sometimes . . . she was a symbol to you."

Errol was thoughtful for a moment, looking back at the painted image, larger than life size, on the wall. Stacey could feel his hand resting absently on her hair.

"Yes, I suppose she was. A kind of dream, if you will . . . a symbol of all the beauty and passion I longed for in my life. . . . But have you forgotten, love?" His mouth was serious, but his eyes crinkled with amusement. "I told you once that you reminded me of her."

"So you did."

"Well, then . . ." He raised one brow, a lightly teasing challenge. "Why would I want a symbol . . . when I have the real thing?"

39

The baby was born two weeks early, on a blustery evening with rain beating on the window, in a wide double bed in the house that Stacey had for a long time now thought of as home. Errol, remembering what happened to Maude, had insisted that she go to a hospital, but she had been equally insistent that she was going to stay right there, and in the end, he had compromised by sending for a doctor from Sydney. It proved to be a good decision, for it was an easy birth, one that could have been handled by a midwife, and two hours after labor began, Stacey heard a loud, healthy wail—and was informed that she had a daughter.

If Errol was the least bit disappointed that his first-born was not a son, Stacey could see no trace of it as Pegeen wrapped the baby in a warm knit blanket and laid it for the first time gently in his arms. His face was a mirror of pride and wonder—he was so puffed up, anyone would think he had done all the work himself!—and he was actually making funny little clucking noises, as if he thought a newborn could possibly be interested.

"Look how blue her eyes are," he bragged. "And she has her mama's black hair. Anyone can see she's going to be a beauty!"

No one could see anything of the kind, that little face was so red and wrinkled—and rather annoyed, as if it had not wanted to come into the world.

"All babies have blue eyes, Errol." Stacey smiled groggily. "And her hair is going to fall out in a few days anyway. Who knows what color it will be when it grows back . . . if it grows back at all. Maybe she's going to be bald."

"My daughter would never be bald!" he said with

mock indignation, setting the little bundle back beside
her on the bed. "She's going to have thick black,
shimmering hair. And she *is* going to be beautiful . . .
just like her mother."

They named her Tasha, and by the time she began
to crawl, the last scars on the earth were nearly gone,
and it was hard to remember there had ever been a
fire. Only occasionally, when Stacey went for a ride
and saw tall black trees rising out of golden savannas,
did the memory come back, and even then it was
vague, gentled by time. Fear did not tighten around
her heart anymore, nor did she wake up in the night
sweating and trembling and calling her husband's name.
The wounds had closed and were nearly healed.

It was an enchanting world: the drought had shown
no signs of recurring, and Tasha's first awareness was
of vivid colors and warm sunlight and the fragrance of
honeysuckle and jessamine in the garden. Her eyes
remained blue, after all. Stacey would never forget
Errol's teasing triumph—"There, you see, I told you I
was right!"—when it became clear they were not going
to turn, and he asserted with equal determination that
except for her hair, about which he had also been
right, she was the image of his grandmother, the wildly
infamous Kate. Stacey, who knew better than to argue, said nothing, but secretly she knew the child was
a little miniature of her own beautiful grandmother
Natalia with the black-black hair and milky skin and
eyes the color of forest pools in the noonday sun.

Whoever she resembled, it was soon clear Tasha
was going to be her own person. At three weeks, she
already had a will of her own, and at three months,
her little jaw set as firmly as a bulldog's when she
didn't get her way, which was rarely if her doting papa
was around. Before she could walk, she screamed to
be set on a horse, and Errol and Stacey laughed themselves sick as they watched her stretch her legs, trying
to reach the stirrups.

"What a terror she's going to be," Errol said, chuckling one night after Pegeen had carried the child to
bed, howling with protest, though she was so tired she
could barely keep her eyes open. "Heaven help her

brothers when they come along. They're going to have all they can do, keeping up with her."

They were sitting on the veranda, enjoying the first evening breeze. The sun had gone down nearly an hour ago, but the air was just beginning to cool. Horse bells jingled nearby, and Stacey could hear voices drifting through the open kitchen window.

"Yes, I'm afraid little Harry is in for quite a time." She leaned against his shoulder, enjoying the feel of his hand as it lingered suggestively on her waist. She had just discovered she was pregnant again, but Errol, an old hand at being a father now, was not the least bit intimidated, thank heaven. She planned on having lots and lots of children, and the last thing she wanted was a husband spending all his time treating her like a china doll!

The smell of the garden drifted onto the veranda, a sweet scent of flowers and fresh-cut grass. The storage cisterns provided plenty of water, and Glenellen had blossomed like an oasis. Ribbons of pink and yellow and lavender edged the walks, and a profusion of roses tumbled up the rail, deep blue-red in the rising moon.

Like the roses of her childhood, Stacey thought, and for just an instant she could see Mara in the garden, with a basket filled with flowers . . . and Olga reminding her to act like a little lady, she was almost grown up now. And herself and Zee, rolling over and over in the dirt, trying sincerely and determinedly to kill each other.

She snuggled closer to her husband on the wide canvas chair he had had built especially for them. Somewhere in the distance, a wild dog wailed, a familiar sound now. Hard to imagine it had once seemed strange and frightening.

It had been such a long time since she had thought of her grandfather's home. It was like another world now, something she had read about in a half-forgotten story. The parlor where she had entertained suitors under the watchful eye of her proper oldest sister . . . her own room, with a faded quilt on the bed and Kolya curled up in the sun . . . Grandfather's study, dark-paneled and gloomy, thick velvet draperies half-obscuring the windows . . . the globe that had fascinated her so much in the corner . . .

The globe where she had first discovered Australia. The dingo was still now, the early-evening sounds had stopped, and the air was heavy with silence. It had seemed so exotic then, that land across the sea—she had been so sure she would be happy there. And all because of a man with a rakish mustache and even white teeth . . . and not an honorable thought in his heart.

She laughed softly.

Errol shifted his weight to look at her. "Keeping secrets from me again? After you promised not to?"

"I was just thinking . . . about a silly little girl I used to know."

"Were you?" The lamps were not yet on, but she could see him smiling in the moonlight. "And when was that?"

"A long time ago . . . in another life. I was thinking how very wrong she was, that little girl. And yet how very right."

"Right and wrong at the same time, love? That doesn't make sense."

"Oh . . ." she said softly, "it does to me." And she tilted her face for a kiss.

ABOUT THE AUTHOR

Susannah Leigh was born in Minneapolis and raised in St. Paul, Minnesota. After graduating from the University of Minnesota she moved on to New York City, where she worked at a variety of jobs and appeared in many off-Broadway productions. She stayed in New York for twelve years and then left for a year of traveling to such spots as Morocco, Nepal, and Afghanistan.

Ms. Leigh is currently living in the San Bernardino Mountains of Southern California, where she spends her nonwriting time indulging her interests in reading, travel, history, and hiking in the woods.